REFLECTION: REALM OF THE SOULWELL

BOOK 1

M.E. WYATT

ALSO BY

The Dragonrend Realms

Realm of the Soulwell:

Book 1: *Reflection*. September 5th, 2022
Book 2: *Resurrection*. TBA 2023 Pre-order available now

Realm of the Chaos Shards:

Book 1: *The Shards of Kestrius.* February 15th, 2022
Book 2: *Beyond the Shrouded Isles. TBA*

"Two roads diverged in a wood, and I – I took the one less traveled by, and that has made all the difference."
– Robert Frost.

CONTENTS

CHAPTER ONE
A STORY TO TELL

The army had been marching for weeks now. They were getting close. Through the frigid rains, perilous bogs, hostile forests and hazardous mountains, they had traveled; a single goal on everyone's mind.

Life.

Vi'eri called for a halt, and her Ri'sha carried her orders down the line. The army began its slow, inevitable halt for the night. As much as it would save time to continue traveling, utilizing the powers of the destroyers to light their way, the army was in their territory now.

The sun crested on the horizon, bringing darkness to the land. The dual moons gave off their eerie blue glow as fires in nearby camps lit small beacons of warmth and hope.

Small flames burst from the fingertips of the destroyers, dancing freely between each finger like a fae in flight before plunging into wood kindling.

Thousands of lights erupted into existence across the vast plain, banishing the ever-encroaching darkness in the hearts and minds of men and women.

After a time, Vi'eri heard sounds of merriment echoing throughout the camp. Humans and deminean sat around their fires, laughing and enjoying what brief lives they had left. She pushed a tear off her cheek with the back of her silver scaled hand, for it was a sight that filled her with untold joy. Never before could she have imagined a day where the two species could sit, laugh and eat together as equals.

Simply unthinkable.

Her joy was short-lived as a familiar melancholy washed over her. She struggled briefly against that deep loneliness and then, accepting the inevitable, plunged headlong into it.

This sight was just too much to bear. It was a constant reminder that she and she alone would always be separate from the others of this realm, never experiencing true comradery between those who shared so much with her.

A shared lineage

To press the issue, a nearby human pointed at her, whispering in the ear of his friend, who, in return, glared at her with a worried expression plastered on her youthful face.

The girl shook her head as if to ward off whatever her male friend had asked, turning back to face the fire, her face disappearing into flickering shadow.

Vi'eri looked at her own two hands. Distinctly human, lacking the long claw-like nails, a distinctly deminean trait, but also not human, as intricate and overlapping silver scales ran the length of her arms and onto her chest and back.

The blood of two unique species flowed through her, and yet, instead of being the beacon that united these two groups together, she was the lightning rod that the others focused their scorn on; their hate.

The culmination of generations of distrust, betrayal, and war between the two species was thrust upon her shoulders, and her shoulders alone. Truly, she belonged to no people, doomed from birth to be an outcast; misunderstood. And in her experience, the mortal way was to fear what they cannot understand.

Vulana suddenly appeared at her side, stepping out of shadow, as he had done many times before. He was a shade. Her shade. A being from the realm of celestials. Vulana's appearance was that of a dark purple fox, and a light red aura floated around him that wisped off his ethereal body like a dark cloud before a storm.

Why do we still sit alone? Vulana asked again for the countless time. We cannot give them the strength they will need to survive if we isolate ourselves from them. The shade addressed the words directly into her mind, as was his nature.

"I cannot be their savior," Vi'eri replied, a deepening sadness overwhelming the slightest bit of anger that hung at the edge of her words, like the blade on a hangman's galley. "They despise me—hate me!" She had long since let her hate go, but the anger...like a hot coal, still pestered her with its incessant heat.

They don't hate you, Eri, Vulana said, the words resonating in her mind with a push on her emotions toward contentment. We have seen humans hate. We have seen deminean hate many times. This is not hate, it is fear! Mixed with a bit of curiosity. They don't know you—don't know us! So show them who we are.

Vi'eri closed her mind. "Stop," she said, forcing Vulana to soften the shifting of her emotions; a pesky little ability of shades.

Vulana was her closest friend, but even that wasn't necessarily true. Shades, in essence, were their own beings, separate from their soulwardens, but also a part of them. To have a shade as a friend is to be friends with oneself. They shared a part of your soul. A part that no other could. Vi'eri chose Vulana as much as he had chosen her.

They sat together, taking in the revelry of jubilant soldiers. The sight of smoke tendrils and the smell of burning wood eased her frustrations, as did the sight of a thousand distant suns illuminating the night sky with their brilliant outpouring of colors. It brought upon a certain peace, the most one could hope for in these trying days.

She had lived a long life and during it, sights like this were one of the few comforts that had been afforded to her. It made her nostalgic for the past, for a time where peace was as easy as following another's command. Where the outcome of her choices didn't unravel the balance of the realm itself.

"How are you, Ri'sha sovereign?" a human boy asked, tipping his head slightly.

He looked around sixteen years in age, if she were to guess. Then, she realized that it was the same boy from before, the one who had pointed at her and had been subsequently rebuked by his female companion.

Casually, Vi'eri glanced toward the girl, still sitting next to the fire, staring daggers back toward her. But beneath the hostility, the look of worry was plain on her face. She was frightened...of her. Frightened for the wrath the hybrid would unleash upon her friend.

"Isn't your friend going to worry about you?" Vi'eri asked, seeking to deter the youngster from further discussion.

"Nah, Kasu is just scared of you. A lot of the humans are," the boy replied casually, as if the matter were of no consequence.

Vi'eri took a moment of reflection, assessing the boy. He was dark and tanned, with a medium build and unshaved stubble marking his face. The tiny growths of hair failed to make him look any older, patchy as it was. He had brown hair with brown eyes, and they held a weariness that had been all too common in the young these days. The weariness of loss. Most interestingly, a scar ran across his neck, as if someone had tried to slit his throat and missed the vital pieces to finish the job.

If she were younger, she may have considered him roguishly handsome

The boy, content to stand and wait, continued to stare at her, unbothered by the silence. She shook her head and sighed before asking, "What's your name?"

"Ax," he replied proudly.

She crossed her arms. "Ax? Is that a nickname of some sort?"

He shook his head. "It's the only name I got, I'm afraid."

"Well, Ax. Pleasure to meet you," she replied, and surprisingly, meant it. Daring to continue the conversation, she asked, "You said before that humans fear me. May I ask, why don't you?"

"Nothing scares me!" Ax replied, thumping his chest, a grin touching ear to ear. His smile revealed a few missing teeth. These, along with the scar, said he was more a man than she had previously given him credit for.

"Is that so? And what about them?" Vi'eri pointed out over the vast darkness spread out in the valley beneath them.

Ax's bravado broke under her question as he protested, "Well...maybe something does. But that's different!" She agreed with the boy's sentiment, their enemies certainly were of a different nature. Undeterred, he continued, adding, "I noticed you sit alone, night after night. Why is that?" His question struck straight to the heart of the issue. Such was the way of young ones.

We aren't alone, Vulana spoke in Vi'eri's mind.

"Vulana says we aren't alone," she reiterated for Ax's benefit.

"Of course! I meant to ask, why do you both sit alone? I'm sorry master fox, I didn't mean to offend."

How can we be alone if we are together? Vulana asked before adding, Master fox? I like this boy!

Vi'eri ignored the shade, focusing the discussion back toward the boy. "We enjoy solitude. It is...better this way."

"Then why do you always look so sad?"

She leveled her gaze at the boy, but Ax met her eyes as if nothing had crossed between them. Reluctantly, she had to smile. It was a harsh truth, but a truth nonetheless. She never had been good at hiding her emotions, but when someone was raised the way she had been, it was hardly a surprise. "Cruelty is the currency of this realm. Our minds, and our bodies, the payment." She touched her temple and chest to emphasize the point.

"You never answered my question."

Vi'eri sighed. "It is a long story, young one."

"Then why are the other humans afraid of you?"

"That's an even longer story still."

"I have time," Ax said enthusiastically, rolling his shoulders. "If you wouldn't mind telling it to me, that is. That's what we do, you know—the others. We share stories of better times. Times we hope to get back to. Times that, some believe, you will lead us to again."

"You make me sound like some sort of hero," Vi'eri said. Surprisingly, the boy nodded his head in agreement. She stood indignantly, adding, "I am not a hero! I am everything they say I am when they think I cannot hear. I don't merit your admiration, boy. The only thing I deserve is your scorn!"

"I don't believe that!" Ax replied, matching Vi'eri's outburst with his own.

This boy's abruptness and stubbornness took her aback—what a strange child this was. Ax appeared so confident and unafraid, and she had to wonder: Was he unaware of the battle that would soon come for them? Part of her wanted to send him away. To continue her solitude in relative peace. To prepare herself for the days ahead… She so desperately needed to prepare.

A gentle nudging of approval came from Vulana, but instead of resisting, she accepted the feelings her shade offered. It devoured the fears and doubts like dry sand soaks up water, leaving her in harmony, at least for a moment.

"Fine," Vi'eri said in agreement. "I'll tell you a story. But just a warning, it's not a joyful one."

"Look where we are," Ax replied, gesturing to the unnatural dark of the valley. "I kinda assumed it wasn't."

She laughed, despite herself. "Fair enough." She could see why the young woman looked at Ax so, even if he had yet to notice her affections toward him.

"I'll be back," he said abruptly, scurrying off toward his campfire without another word.

Soon, he returned, awkwardly carrying a bundle of kindling with a log balancing on top. The girl, the same whom had been staring balefully at her earlier, followed him with a certain weariness. "I'm back!" he announced, throwing the wood down in a heap in front of her. "Kasu, would you please?"

The girl, Kasu, ignited a small flame at the tip of her index finger. The flame flickered and danced around her hand before floating safely to the kindling, lighting it. Ax bent over and blew on the small fire, breathing life into it. It spread to the other kindling and, eventually, to the log itself.

He reached inside his pocket and withdrew a small quantity of bread eagerly, which he then handed to her. Vi'eri took it, not wishing to offend. The truth was, she could feed off the magic in the air—the magic that existed around all in the in-between. It was a trait she shared with her deminean brethren. The magic of self. She needed to eat, but it was so seldom that she would often neglect it for days at a time. Vulana, the pesky shade that he was, would admonish her for it. Often.

"Well, then," Vi'eri said with a touch of the dramatic. "Where should I begin?"

Ax shrugged. "The beginning of course."

She flourished her hands in front of her, and her two captive audience members took a seat on the cold ground near the fire. She smiled, remembering someone from her past as she said, "From the beginning it is. Know this, I have lived a long life. One that was often not worth living at all. I am a one-of-a-kind creature. Not unlike a human. Not unlike a deminean. I am what the people call a halfling, a freak, and, at times, a monster..."

"My name is Vi'eri Trueblade, the hybrid."

CHAPTER TWO

ALLGOOD THINGS

Be wary of the coming of the Hybrid, for when their presence is released upon this realm, it will signal the end of deminean sovereignty, and the coming of the age of humans.

Unknown, A Leger from The Destined Scrolls.

One of the earliest memories I have is from my ninth birthday. My mother, a seamstress by trade, had produced, for me, a gorgeous green dress to celebrate the milestone.

"Remember," my mother said, "you must still keep your hands hidden—even if you wish to be seen by all. Always keep them hidden."

We lived in a comparatively small human settlement named Elklan, under one-hundred in total. My mother, and by extension myself, were outcasts from the other humans of the settlement. As mentioned, my mother was a seamstress by craft, and a remarkable one at that. My new dress was a testament to her prowess. Those skills in her craft caused many of the deminean upper echelon to demand of her to make them the finest of clothing for many years before they eventually discarded her, like an old mule. This close work with the deminean caused much distrust between herself and the other humans of the settlement, who saw her as a potential deminean spy; someone willing to leak the secrets they thought to keep from their masters. Such worries as that were beyond my capabilities as a young girl, however.

My entire focus was on the dress my mother had created. It was long and flowing, with the color of deep green that somehow made the lushness of a forest in bloom seem pale in its shadow. Any girl—nay, any woman—would have given all to possess such an item. But this was mine, and mine alone.

She had sewn it in a modest style, one that provided ample coverings for the body. While the common onlooker may assume it was modest for modesty's sake, it held a deeper meaning. You see, shortly before my ninth birthday, I had begun to grow what appeared to be small silver scales on my hands. When I asked my mother about it, she told me that I shouldn't speak of them and warned me to keep them covered at all times; hidden from the world.

She said it would be, "Our secret."

Being the surly girl I was, I asked her in frustration and ignorance, "Why must I keep it a secret? They are beautiful and they shimmer in silver like a sword out of old stories."

"They are dangerous, my light," she replied in her ever-understanding way. "You are...unique. Special. Others will seek to harm you if they know just how special you truly are. You must keep them a secret...always."

Her words frightened me, but still, I protested. Despite my best efforts, in the end, she made me swear to this above all else: keep my malformations a secret from all. No matter what.

As the seasons changed and the summer's heat was defeated by the fall's chill, the brisk air brought down reddish-yellow leaves of the Bloodsoaked Forest, the outskirts of which our home lay. During that time, I had amassed some attention from a local boy. To this day, I still cannot remember the lad's face, but I remember the feeling of falling in my dreams, and he would always be there to catch me. In those dreams we would be older, and I would not have to hide my scales, which had grown to encompass my entire arm and my chest, glittering like silver sand under an ocean's tide. Gorgeous.

Now, of course, my mother had told me stories of young women who fall in love. That it had happened to her, and that I was the outcome of such love. "The shimmering light in her life," she would say.

The fall also brought about celebrations to mark the beginning of the end of the cycle, where the blue moons would align and bless the Soulwell, which would ensure that no soulless would be born to any woman expecting a child. Still, I do not know if that legend holds true or if it was just a fanciful thing to keep humans hoping for a better tomorrow. To keep them towing the line.

The deminean that ruled over Elklan were of a single bloodline: the Ironskin family. While the deminean despised the human culture of revering the rebirth, they knew that such resentment, and denying them the simple pleasure of celebration, would bring more trouble onto them than was worth the effort. Human disruptions and revolutions were always of the utmost concern for the deminean, whose numbers had always held under that of humans.

And so it was, the humans would celebrate and the deminean would fume silently. But on rare occasions, some deminean would take part in the revelry, usually at their own mother's consternation. Still, it was always an odd incident, and while I could never attend these festivities, I would hear secondhand stories being shared. Secrets that spread like a wildfire around town, speaking of which deminean had shown favor to which human or humans. If there is one thing that humans love more than revolting, it is rubbing superiority in each other's faces.

"But Bennan is ten, and he wants me to go to the moonlit dance with him!" I begged my mother for the hundredth time. She looked down at me, unamused by my antics.

Continuing with her sewing undeterred, she replied in her gentle but even tone, "*No!*"

I fumed, but knew the conversation was over. As young as I was, I had been getting quite full of myself. Before I turned to leave, I answered back with all the venom I could muster. "Just because you're an outcast doesn't mean *I* need to be!" I regretted the choice of words as soon as I spoke them, but my mother just kept sewing away at the gloves she regularly made for me. You see, I kept 'losing' them. Youthful defiance.

With a sigh, my mother paused for a moment, rubbing a small tear that welled from one of her eyes, and quickly wiped it on her pant leg.

I frowned. "Mother, I—"

"It's nothing, my light," she said, cutting off my words mid stride. Setting down her knitting so she could look at me properly, and added, "All is forgiven. I realize that what I ask of you is unfair. Don't think that I do not realize it. To be unable to play with other children. To be denied the right to foster friendships...to miss the experience of having loved and lost on your own. For your loss, I am so sorry."

I waited for a time before asking the question I desperately needed answered, despite already knowing the truth. "Does it always need to be this way?"

She frowned and nodded in affirmation. There could be no doubt, and my heart sank into despair.

My mother's fears ran as deep as the Soulwell itself. So deep, that I feared she would drown in it one day. I excused myself and went about my daily chores.

The only time I was alone was when I was sent out to perform errands. Sir Ladrey, a farmer, had ruined his shirt during a stumble while harvesting his crops. His shaking from some foreign ailment had made the task of restoring his clothing untenable. Thus, he sought the skills of the town recluse reluctantly. It grated on me, at the time, to help those who openly scorned us, but having the small influx of coins ensured that we could continue to live our modest lives, or so my mother had told me.

As I left the Ladrey farmhouse, I heard a voice call out. Assuming that whomever spoke did not speak to me, I hurried along to avoid whatever trouble was looming.

"You there, stop!" the voice called again, this time closer. Hesitantly, I turned to confront the owner of that voice. A girl, not much older than I, made a quick line toward me as if on a mission of high importance. Her light silver hair blew in the wind, setting off her dim golden eyes. Her long, pointed ears held a single jagged edge in the cartilage at the top, and silver tips covered the edges of six small horns on her head that came out in two distinct lines trailing up to her hairline.

When she finally arrived in front of me, my heart skipped a beat. It was the first time I had ever been face to face with a deminean, let alone had one address me, and the scowl she wore made me want to flee. Still, I remembered the manners my mother had managed to teach me, and I bowed low, crossing my right-arm in front of my chest before saying, "How may I serve you, Dem'i Ironskin?"

With that utterance, her face smoothed, and she replied, "Yes...that dress. It is quite fine for a human to possess. Let me see it." She did not await my permission as she moved toward me, pulling on the fabric roughly. "Yes, the stitching is excellent. As well as the cut. This color, did the seamstress dye it herself? Don't answer that. This looks to be about my size..." she continued to comment on the quality of the dress and the unsuitability of a human to possess it. This went on for a time as she poked and prodded at the dress. Suddenly, she stopped, proclaiming, "I would like this dress. Please strip and present it to me. Since I am being generous, I won't require that you wash it first."

I stared at her, dumbfounded. At my lack of proper acknowledgement, she rolled her eyes. I swallowed hard, forcing myself to say in a meek voice, "My apologies, but I cannot give you this dress. It was a gift from my mother and—"

"*And?*" the deminean girl mimicked crudely. "Do you disobey your betters, human?"

I had to say something, anything! So I replied with the first thing that came to my mind. "*Never!* I simply could not give such an item to you in such a ragged condition. Please, Dem'i Ironskin, allow me to wash it for you and deliver it by the end of day. If that pleases?"

The deminean girl seemed to consider for a moment, her golden eyes studying me as a horse breeder studies a colt. "Yes, I suppose that is the proper procedure. No need for you to go about in your undergarments. Fine, fine. Bring it to our home by the second moon's showing. It had better be washed and stain free. Best too if it does not smell of...human." The deminean girl strode off without another word and not a backward glance in my direction.

I took a deep breath, and then ran home like I had never run in my life, throwing the door to our home in a fit and babbling like a madman to my mother. She did her best to console me, to no avail.

"Easy, easy," she repeated over and over.

My words came breathlessly, and, ultimately, I had to let go of the panic lest I faint from exertion. "Dem...inean...girl," I forced the words. "She wants the dress. My dress! I need to take it to her tonight. She almost... She almost..."

"Hush now," my mother replied, smoothing back my hair. "Hush. It'll be fine. I'll make sure to clean the dress and deliver it tonight. Nobody will notice if I make the delivery myself."

"But...can't you just make her another?" I said, not wishing to let go of my possession. I knew it was a foolish thing to hope for such a thing. Dresses took time to create, and when I thought about it, I assumed my mother would just make me another one later.

I opened my mouth to ask but my mother shook her head, as if she knew exactly what I would say. "It isn't so much that she wants the dress. It's that she doesn't want *you* to have it."

A deep pit in my stomach opened like an ulcer, and I had to force out the question between sobs. "But why?"

"Because cruelty exists in this beautiful world, my light," she explained. "If they allow one human girl to have something beautiful, then others will wonder why they also cannot share in the finer things." And with no other explanation, my mother stood and beckoned me to undress.

I changed and handed her my prized possession, knowing that nobody, not even the deminean girl, would ever wear it again.

It was the first time I had experienced deminean cruelty, but it would not be the last.

CHAPTER THREE

A STROLL THROUGH TOWN

Tradesmen of Elklan, find your courage and rise against the tyranny of the deminean who seek to control our livelihoods and that of our children. Enough is enough! It is time to join the war and fight.

Unsigned, Hastily scribbled note found in Elklan tavard.

I waited patiently for my mother to return that night. Waited…until long past the second moon rose and crested on the other side of the realm. Then, as I had begun to worry, I heard the faint scuffling of feet outside.

I rushed to the door of our small cottage home and flung back the wooden door, exclaiming, "Mother I was so—"

My words died in my throat.

There my mother stood in the doorway, illuminated by the faintest of moonlight, covered in lacerations and dried blood. Something or someone had tattered her clothes to pieces, and I held my hands to my face to stop myself from gasping.

She dropped to one knee and retched off the side of the wooden steps. Wiping away the bile, she stood, swaying toward me as she said in a rasping voice, "Wa...ter." Slowly, she limped inside.

I slammed the door behind her and ran to my tasks, asking no other questions. I poured her water and handed it to her as I helped her into a seat. Then, I found some rags and a washbasin, which I filled with water and set in front of her. Placing some dried kindling in the hearth, I lit it with a candle. Speedily, I made up some tea and set it to the hearth to heat. Hot tea worked wonders for an achy body.

When the work was done, I noticed she had stripped down to her undergarments. Clearly, the task had taken a lot out of her. She appeared exhausted, even from the simple task; right on the precipice of feinting.

I remembered once being told not to let someone sleep after injury without checking for head wounds, lest they never wake again. For the first time, I recognized that my mother was mortal and thus was very capable of death.

The thought horrified me.

I squatted beside her and took up a rag, absently wiping away at the dried, crusted blood on her arms and face before finally finding the courage to ask, "What happened?"

"Nothing, my light," she said, her voice barely escaping her mouth.

I dropped the rag into the wash basin obstinately. *"Liar!"*

My mother smiled at me. Despite what had transpired, she still smiled with genuine kindness. "I never was able to get that temper of yours under control, was I?" She struggled to laugh. The sound was a haunted thing.

I felt ashamed. Guilty. But being hot headed and young, I could not admit it then. I sat in quiet contemplation and wiped her clean of blood, checking her head for injury. It was difficult searching through the matted mess of blond hair. When I was sure she was relatively fine, I helped her into clothes and put her to bed.

I remained up all night checking on her. Every rise and fall of her chest was a reminder of what I still had to lose. It was—and still is—one of the most daunting nights of my life. Suddenly, caring about an insignificant thing such as a dress felt like the whims of a little girl.

A foolish child.

In the morning, my mother rose as she always had and carried on like nothing at all had transpired the night before. She would not speak a word of what trouble befell her. I would regularly throw around ideas about what had happened. Had the deminean ordered her beaten? Had she been mugged, being out as late as she was?

Alas, whenever I would bring the topic up, she would shut it down just as swiftly. "My pain is my pain," she would say.

And that was that.

In the days after, I took a more dynamic role in helping my mother's modest seamstress business while she recovered. I was competent enough at repairing clothing, and I essentially carried all the deliveries to town myself.

During this time, I learned more about the conflict between the humans and deminean of the small town of Elklan. It was a ranching community, priding itself on the raising of good, healthy animals for both meat and trade goods. However, the steward of the town, Dem'i Ironskin himself, had seen fit to raise tariffs levied to the humans of Elklan to astronomical sums. The townsfolk protested about not being able to feed their families, but armed deminean put any talk of discontent down.

Harshly.

Tensions remained high, and the townsfolk would often direct their ire toward those who were seen less favorably. An elderly man named Jeneth, who had come on hard times, had been beaten for the simple mistake of standing in the way of another group of patrons leaving a tavern. Moods were reaching their boiling point and tension clung to the air like a pestilent disease.

Still, my mother remained in her typical high spirits and was recovering well as the days came and went, bringing winter's bite to its full breadth.

One night, she turned to me and asked, "Do you think we would be happier settling somewhere else?"

The question puzzled me. I had known no other home my entire life, so the thought of leaving was a foreign concept. Unthinkable.

Still, her question fueled my childish imagination, and I replied, "I don't know. But I do think I would like to see other places someday."

My answer put a smile on my mother's face, which I noticed for the first time, had more lines than usual, namely at the corner of her eyes and mouth. There was a certain weariness I felt looking at that face that I had not felt from her before. She was getting older. That, or the harshness of the realm was leaving its mark as the endless tide of an ocean breaks down the hardest of stone.

The entire winter went on with little more trouble. If the deminean were displeased with us in any way, they did not show or act upon it. Undoubtedly, humans like ourselves were not worth a second glance to them, and certainly not worth holding a grudge against.

The powerful do not hold grudges against the weak.

Seasons came and passed and it would not be until a fateful spring some time later that the full reality of our situation would come to fruition. Spring brings change, and that spring, my life was to be irrevocably altered.

The season was treating my mother and me well, for a time. With the warmer weather came patrons searching for changes in clothing or repair from the winter's damage.

My mother was fully recovered by this time. Despite that, I saw a fear in her eyes when a gust of wind would rattle awkwardly against our home or an animal would make a commotion in the night. The body had healed, but the scars left by that night still festered in her mind.

For her sake, I kept a cheery attitude toward the work and our way of life. While it troubled me, at times, that I was to be a recluse, perhaps for the rest of my life, I didn't want to show that to her. I treasured her far too much to cause more pain than I already had.

"I'll just pick up some bread in town when I drop off the deliveries," I said, pulling up my worn shoes, filled with holes. I pressed my finger through each of them and grinned. Townsfolk said that holey and patched clothing was the sign of a hard worker.

My mother rounded on me with a scowl on her face. "How can anyone take us seriously if your shoes are torn so?" I merely shrugged my shoulders and stood, moving around her to gather the deliveries for the day. "Wait a moment," she added, causing me to turn back to face her. "How about we both go out today? The weather is fine, and I think I would do well with a walk."

I nodded in agreement, smiling. It was the best news I had heard in some time. Certainly, some pleasant weather and a walk into town would restore the spring in her step.

She flung on a plain dress and, surprisingly, placed an intricate necklace with a small blue stone around her neck. I had seen it before, but this was the first time I had really observed it. The stone appeared to glow with an eerie light, and I could almost feel it tugging at me, begging me to reach for it. Abruptly, it disappeared under my mother's clothing, and she eyed me curiously.

"It's a beautiful necklace," I said.

My mother looked aside from me before replying, "It was your father's."

"Who is my father?" I asked, without considering the ramification of those words. "He doesn't live in Elklan, right? Does he live close?"

"No," my mother answered curtly. "And best we not speak of him, for now. Maybe someday…" She let her words trail off.

With that, my mother opened the door, and left our home, heading off toward town. She turned a few steps down the dirt path and waved for me to follow.

As we made it into Elklan, my mother turned to me and said, "Go on ahead and drop off the deliveries. I need to see old man Ritchet about something important."

"What about?"

My mother shooed me away without answering, and I was happy to run along to my next task. I loved her with all my soul, but she walked with the grace and patience of an aged person. I, being a child in both mind and body, wanted the wind rushing through my hair and the sun at my back.

I finished my daily tasks quickly, and went to Old Man Ritchet's. The man claimed that my mother had not come by that day and to bother someone else before slamming the door in my face. He was undoubtedly a grumpy old man.

Curiously, as I looked around town, I could not find her. What I found instead was the general discontent that had become all too common with the humans of Elklan as they moved around like apparitions, going about their days with little heart for their futures.

"The deminean are scum," I heard one man say, looking around paranoid, ensuring none other than his compatriots heard. Others in the group nodded their agreements, but when they noticed me, their faces twisted down in a scowl, and I got the feeling that I should move on quickly.

Suddenly, while walking down the main thoroughfare, I heard a shout.

A woman's shout.

Cautiously, I peered around the corner of a thatch-roofed building as if I were a burglar in the night. There, I saw a deminean girl. One that was very familiar to me. The one who had stolen my dress...

Kreza Ironback!

The girl stood above a human woman, shrieking at her with untold fury.

The woman was down on her knees, but my vantage was poor, and I was just able to hear the sounds of the deminean girl's regal voice over the whispering murmurs of the crowd of humans that had formed in a circle around the spectacle.

"I told you—why do you defy—humans are disgusting—" Kreza's words came in a flurry and I only caught a few before a deafening slap rang out.

The crowded humans collectively gasped and more than a few squeezed their hands into fists so tightly the veins in their forearms looked to burst. Anger and frustration clung to the air making it hard to breathe.

"What are you looking at?" Kreza suddenly blurted, directing this newfound anger toward the crowd. The humans slowly and silently began to disperse.

As Kreza went to speak on, the kneeling woman's voice called out, "*Wait!*" Kreza's eyes shot back toward the woman. "Please... forgive my insolence, Dem'i Ironback. I did not wish to offend you. I merely forgot my place. A lapse in judgment. I, of course, will perform any seamstress work required, free of charge for our esteemed rulers."

There could be no mistake, I recognized the voice perfectly.

"*Mother!*" I yelled, turning the corner and shoving through the startled onlookers. As I ran by Kreza in a mad dash to reach my mother, she casually reached out an arm, seizing me by my neck and lifted me up flailing into the air.

Kreza's grip was iron and her small stature hid the strength of a full-grown man, which she now displayed openly for all to witness.

I gasped, looking down at her, striving to breathe, and saw that her sleeves had fallen, showing off her glittering red and purple scales. Her eyes were now bright, and golden, compared to the dimness I remembered from before.

Kreza, likely sensing my prying eyes, scowled at me and threw me to the ground. I struck the ground with my back flat, and the air in my lungs fled forcefully. I gasped and pulled what little air I could, willing myself to remain calm.

"This simply will not do," Kreza said in a succulent, sweet voice, walking around me like a cat stalking a mouse. "You humans are getting far too full of yourselves. You fail to show the respect that I, heir to the line of Ironback, deserves. This insolence needs to be punished."

"No, please," my mother pleaded. "Punish me instead. Leave her out of it." Her words sounded far away as my head spun and darkness crept at the corners of my eyes.

"Silence," Kreza demanded. "Do not presume your words have any sway over me." She postured, placing her hand to her chin and strolling the dirt street back and forth as if putting on a show. "What to do, what to do..."

Suddenly, she snapped her fingers as the answer came to her. "I believe she called you mother, yes? So likely both of you are seamstresses by trade? Then, as punishment for this shameful showing, one of you must cut off a thumb and present it to me." She held one finger out and smiled.

Angry murmurings from the crowd of humans erupted in a hushed revolt. Even the two armed deminean guards looked uneasy by their petty lord's demand.

Kreza scowled at the frantic murmurings of the crowd. "What? You think this punishment is too harsh, humans? As if I have a care for what you think. Does the farmer care for the wishes of their pigs before a slaughter? I think not." She pushed back her silver hair and glanced casually out at the crowd, as if to challenge any to speak up.

None did.

"I'll do it," I heard myself say, to my despair. Our livelihood depended on my mother's hands. I could not let her do this for me.

"*No!*" my mother cried out in desperation. Pitifully. A man leaned down to hold her from rushing toward me, whispering assurances in her ear. She appeared deaf to his words as she fought his grip.

"*Excellent!*" Kreza replied, clapping her hands together. She twisted to one of her deminean guardsmen and pulled a small plain knife from a scabbard at the man's waist. Turning back to me, she threw it to the ground. The knife clattered to the floor just in front of me, kicking up dirt which stung my eyes. "Here you are, human. I consider this a kindness. The knife appears sharp, so this should be easy for you. Now, if you would kindly hurry, this show is making me bored."

Reluctantly, I reached for the knife. The sounds of my mother sobbing broke my heart, and when I turned to face her, a few others I did not recognize held her back as she squirmed against them like a trapped animal. She returned my gaze with tormented eyes.

Fearing what I held, I looked toward the knife and decided it would be prudent to take the left thumb. I placed my shaking hand on the ground and placed the blade in position, trying not to weep. As I pressed, I found the knife to be exactly as Kreza had described.

Sharp.

As I cut, the first few layers of skin broke and split like old leather, red blood leaking from the incision. A burning sensation cascaded from the cut and up my arm.

A prelude of the pain to come.

I gritted my teeth, and pushed harder when a voice from the crowd rang out, causing me to stop.

"*Wait!*" they yelled. "I won't let you do this." A man, no older than sixteen, came forth holding a blacksmith's hammer. His hands shook with fear, but determination was bright in his eyes and his stature showed he meant to fight.

"Neither will I," another voice added, and then another and another. Soon, the streets filled with human men and women holding makeshift weaponry, challenging Kreza and her guards directly. The guardsmen took a defensive stance around her and she merely yawned, as if this uprising were of little concern.

Not even worthy of her attention.

Seeing Kreza's casual demeanor filled me with a rage that I didn't know existed. Didn't know *could* exist. The rage in me broke free like a dam, cracking from the pressure of a season's rainfall and pouring through me like a flood that wipes away the land. I pulled the knife away from myself, and leveled it toward my enemy, charging Kreza Ironback, lost in a battle fever.

Kreza turned to face me and, for the first time, I saw a glint of fear in her eyes. But as I came closer, those golden eyes suddenly burst alight.

She caught my wrist, shoving the knife away from her. "Stupid pig," Kreza said, punching me firmly in the stomach. The blow made me want to retch; it felt as if a fully grown man had put all his weight into it. But my fury kept me upright, struggling to push the knife forward.

Time stood still, and I was briefly aware of how Kreza's guards were preoccupied with the rebelling humans to offer her any support. I pressed my second hand to the hilt and bit my lip so hard I tasted blood. I shoved the knife forward.

As if I had breathed my first real breath in all my life, power filled me to my very core. The burning sensation from the cut on my hand spread to my entire body. It fueled me. So powerful the feeling that it felt as if my body floated in an ocean that was mine and mine alone to command.

"What is this?" Kreza asked, struggling and in awe of my strength as the knife came closer and closer to her skin. She now stared into my eyes. In them, fear and bewilderment, as if what she was seeing was an impossibility.

Unthinkable.

With my newfound strength and the will to save myself, I pressed against the knife with everything I had left, and Kreza's grip waned.

The knife plunged into her upper shoulder, and a slicing sound, like the cutting of bone rang out. I fell forward, releasing the blade, which stayed fixed in her skin.

She gasped in surprise, and one of her guardsmen cried out to her, rushing to her aid. He dropped his halberd and picked her up, cradling her in his arms as the second guardsman swung in a wide horizontal motion to stave off any other attackers. They turned and fled with her toward their stone castle at the top of the hill overlooking all of Elklan.

I laid on the ground, smelling the soil which filled my senses as the power fled me. As I rose, I noticed light-blue sticky blood coated my hands, free of the gloves that once shielded them. Looking up at the crowd, I saw nothing but fear in their eyes as they regarded me.

CHAPTER FOUR

RUN, MY LIGHT

"*Vi'eri!*" my mother cried as she broke free of the humans who held her, sprinting to reach me.

"Mother, I—" My words died in my throat as she embraced me, wrapping me with all her strength, as if she alone could ward off the misery that threatened to consume me.

"Hush, hush. It's alright," she assured me, pushing a piece of hair out of my face. "Let's go home. Come."

I nodded my head in understanding and it was then that I realized I had collapsed to the ground in her arms. I rose, and the townsfolk, stark terror in their faces, moved cautiously away from us.

"What is she?" I heard a man ask in a hushed voice. "She looks so...human."

"Look at her hair," an elderly woman said, pointing a crooked finger at me. "I knew it was suspicious, ever since I first laid eyes on her. Only a deminean can grow ashen hair like that, right?" Others around her shrugged, but gave voice to her questions.

I heard another bear of a man spit on the ground as we walked by, uttering, "Deminean whore," under his breath. My mother glared at him, but he stared defiantly back at her with dark eyes that were edged with violence. He cracked his knuckles to emphasize his point, and we moved on quickly.

The town suddenly felt smaller and smaller as we walked through Elklan. Humans gathered, standing outside their shops and homes as they gawked. Apparently, the gossip had already spread like a wildfire through dry brush and they all wanted to see the deminean girl who passed as human.

My mother walked with a nasty limp. Not the limp that came naturally with old age and the turning of the years, but one from an injury taken. The deminean girl, Kreza, had hurt her. Still, she was determined not to slow us as she tenderly nudged me past the onlookers and toward our cottage at the edge of the Bloodforged Forest.

When we arrived, my mother opened the door hastily and slammed it shut behind us, breaking the hinge. Wordlessly, she grabbed a wool bag and began stuffing dried meats, water jugs, and clothing inside. She rushed out of the room and grabbed a second jug, filling it as well.

"What are you doing?" I said, standing dumbfounded in the middle of the room.

My mother never stopped packing, but simply muttered, "We need to leave immediately. They are coming for us—for you!"

The words struck me like a mallet. My heart raced and my chest tightened. "*Why?*" I said between soft sobs.

"Because you aren't human!" she replied, snapping to look at me with fury in her eyes. It was the first time I could remember her yelling at me that way. Her lips curled and her eyes shed tears. "It's because you aren't human, my light."

I didn't know how to even comprehend the words at the time. '*Not human.*' It sounded so foreign to my ears. Like a structure of words that you could recognize held substantial meaning, but meant utterly nothing to *you*. My mother ignored my bewilderment and continued shoving provisions into the woolen bags.

Quietly, I rummaged through my own belongings for something, anything I wished to keep. After a quick glance, I gave it up. It was meaningless. These objects I owned were mere possessions... I simply wished for everything to return to what it once was.

Before long, my mother put her arms around me, pulling me tightly. "Promise me, my light. Promise that you will run. No matter what happens to me. You will *run!*"

"I promise." I said the words as a scared child repeats a phrase spoken to them, without knowledge of what she was truly telling me. Still, a promise holds power...the power of a word given.

A vow to obey.

"That's good," she replied. "We go now. Quick, grab a bag. Hurry!" And with that, my mother frantically pushed me toward the broken door and I looked down to see that she had placed one of the bags in my hands to carry. I swung it over my shoulder as I left the cottage.

Outside, dusk had come and the blue moon was high in the sky, challenging the sun for dominion. On a grassy hillside that overlooked our home, where the path to town lay, silhouettes of...someone, stood overlooking. With a sickening knot in my stomach, I saw the glint of silver tipped weapons. Whoever they were, they were armed.

I looked at my mother, who stared at the silhouettes with terror plain on her face. "It's too late," she murmured.

In a flash, I felt my feet hit the ground beneath me.

We were running.

My mother had grabbed my hand and tugged me alongside her away from the path and toward the shadows of the nearby forest. The silhouettes on the hill doubled, then tripled, and then they descended, coming for us. The shadowed figures came with a swiftness that promised ill-deeds.

The lingering light from the sun disappeared completely as we entered the safety of the red trees. The flutter of birds fleeing the safety of the forest was cut-off by the sound of yelling guardsmen as they made it just outside the tree line.

My mother had slowed. She staggered as fast as her body was able, but she was tired.

Too tired.

Eventually, she faltered, which forced a stop as she heaved breath after ragged breath, desperately trying to suck in sufficient air to continue forward. It was useless. She leaned against a tree, as if it were the only thing keeping her upright.

She reached for me, grasping me behind the neck and pulling me close. "Run," she commanded, placing her forehead to mine. "You need to run. *Now!*"

"*No!*" I replied, disobediently. "You know I won't. We can explain—I didn't mean to hurt Dem'i Ironskin... it was an accident. *An accident!*"

My mother coughed and slid down the tree to rest at its base, breaking shards of bark along the way. Her sharp intakes of breath exhibited no signs of wavering. "They will kill you, just for what you are," she forced out with enormous effort.

"And what am I?" I asked, kneeling down beside her. "This doesn't make any sense... I'm just your daughter... I'm just—"

"You're so much more than that, my light," she replied, tightening her grip on me. "You're beautiful. Brilliant. You always have been. But you also know the truth. I can go no further, not in the condition I'm in." The intense rustling of feet echoed in the distance. "It's too late and there is so much to say. *Run!*" she pushed me and as I returned, she shoved me again with more force. "Run! Now! You need to run!"

Tired, confused and scared, I took one last look at my mother, who smiled back fondly at me. Tears clouded my vision, and, to my deepest shame, I turned from her and fled.

Stealth was of little concern in my mind, for I fled as an animal flees a hunter. I broke my body against wayward tree limbs, kicked through shrubbery and other foliage. At some point, I had even lost the wool sack my mother had packed in a tangle of vines.

I do not know how long I ran for, but by the time I was through, I saw the two moons in between a break in the trees. They were perfectly balanced between the two edges of the realm, giving the illusion that they were one single object.

Eventually, as I trudged further into the forest, I found a clearing and, as I continued on, found myself standing on a hillock. I basked in the openness of the realm before me. The Bloodsoaked Forest ran deep, but beyond, at the very edges of my sight, I saw flickering light. Not knowing where else to go, I made that my intended destination.

Slowly, I made my way down, and the darkness that greeted me was terrifying. The red trees seemed to ooze with evil intent, contrasting their lively and inviting counterparts of the day. The forest felt cold; empty. Despite what I knew, everything around me looked gnarled and twisted in an ugliness that was menacing to my sight. It was a trick of the eyes, I was sure, but rationality has no place in the mind of a panicking young girl. Despite telling myself that this was the same forest at night that it was during the day, my imagination got the better of me as I turned around to go back from where I had come.

"I found a clearing," a voice called out in the dark. It was close, and it startled me into action. Despite my trepidations, I ran headlong into that shadowy place of nightmares.

"Did you hear that?" another voice inquired. I felt a tree trunk at my back and I dared not move any further lest they detect me.

"Probably a squirrel, you dimwit."

"Or it's the girl!" the first protested. "Do you know what the Ironskins will do to us if we fail to bring her back?"

"Oh, *the Ironskins*, eh?" the other man mocked. "I, for one, am glad that someone stabbed that little tyrant, Kreza." They paused for a moment before adding, "Even if it was another deminean bitch. I was there ya' know, saw the girl's hands myself. Little silver scales. If I didn't see it, then I wouldn't have believed it."

"You think we head back then? Tell 'em she got lost in the forest? Likely is, she ends up a meal for wolves—or whatever other creature Arduinna sprouts from 'er womb."

The men laughed. Shortly after, I heard the rustling of footsteps getting quieter and quieter until only the soft sounds of the night creatures spoke to me. It was then I realized how cold I was. Freezing, tired and hungry—the three struggles that no traveler ever wants to experience.

Not any who wish to live, anyway.

Despite my fears of the dark, I lay down in the brush at the base of a tree. It felt soft. Softer, at least, than hard packed earth. It even offered a small amount of warmth against a chilled night breeze. I wrapped myself in the shrubbery, closing my eyes. Sleep, to my dismay, eluded me; each small noise sent a shiver of fear down my spine as I imagined the manner of creatures that hunted for little human girls in the night.

Still, I tried to sleep for a time. I tossed and turned and when I was about to lose hope, a small voice in my mind said, *Sleep, little one*. As I grasped for whoever it was in my mind, to ask what or who they were, a sudden feeling of serenity flooded me, blasting away any troublesome thoughts.

I drifted at the edge of consciousness, and the chill breeze that buffeted me suddenly felt like a warm zephyr of a mid-spring day.

Sleep swiftly claimed me.

CHAPTER FIVE

INCARNATION OF LIFE

To find oneself faced with the Life Incarnate is to stare into the eyes of death itself.

Finten Cretnoy, author of *The Collective.*

In my sleep, I wandered. Far and wide, my mind was cast from the very tips of the Harpy's Sky, to the depths of the Dweller's Court. The realm was majestic. From the simplicities of a bead of dew on a blade of grass to the intricate caverns that wormed beneath the ground, unseen by any except in dreams.

Beautiful.

Come back from that place, young one, the voice called from the unending void in my mind. I felt their consciousness tug on mine.

"But why?" I protested childishly. "It's so beautiful. I wish I could stay forever." I tried desperately to bind myself in that place and time.

You can... A second voice entered my mind like an avalanche, covering everything I knew in a sheet of pure white. I was powerless to stop it as it crashed against me.

Don't go there. Come back. Come ba— Gone was the voice, buried beneath a deluge of purity.

Child. Child, the unfamiliar voice beckoned. A woman's voice. *There is no need to fear me, for I am the creator of all the wonders you seek. The giver of life. Do you not seek me out? Do you not call for me?*

The voice overwhelmed me with its presence. It felt as if the weight of the entire realm collapsed against my senses. I felt joy, laughter, and every wonderful sense that existed from all beings in a moment of pure bliss. But it was too much, and it left me paralyzed. But there, at the very edge of that wall of ecstasy, wicked feelings laid in wait. Now that I was aware, the fear and doubt tainted the rest of the emotions and I tried wrenching myself free from it. I felt the pull of the creature and knew that they sought to convey the emotions they wanted me to feel, but they could not fully obscure their true nature.

With effort, I called myself back and realized that yes, I was still of flesh and blood. Asleep! I was still asleep. This was a dream, just a dream, and I answered the voice as the ruler of my own mind, replying, *No! I do not seek you. Phony! Liar!*

I blinked, and suddenly found myself in a meadow. The blossoms of spring were in their prime, blooming with reddish hues and in every shape and size. Each flower looked to be reaching for the yellow sun's life-providing heat.

I turned and noticed a figure that had not been there before. They loomed before me, easily double my height. It was a creature unlike any I had ever seen before. Green hair that was not quite hair, but vines, adorned with flowers and thorns, that made way to a woman's bare upper body. Curiouser still, the body of the woman gave way at the hip to some type of animal—a deer. The being's presence, even if shocking, made me glare in awe of its majesty.

I felt the need to bow. Surely a being such as this warranted only the most polite of manners.

To be revered.

I realized that I already had, and as I lifted my eyes to meet the creatures', I saw life in its purest form gazing back at me. Eyes glowing the purest green. She stood with her left side facing me, obfuscating the right, and as I tried to walk around, grasping at the full magnitude of her glory, she turned with me, keeping that one eye fixed.

"Child," she said, her voice sounding like honeysuckle to my ears. "Did I not say you came seeking me? You say you do not, but yet, you stand before me in *my* grove." She ran her pale, elegant hand through her weaved braid of vined hair. "What brings you to this place?"

"I don't know," I answered truthfully. It was getting very difficult to think, as if calm was being forced upon me. "But you are beautiful—if I may say so. What shall I call you?"

The creature laughed, smiling at me. A kind smile...a human smile. "I do not have a name as those of your kind do. I am known as many things to many creatures. Some, the mother of life and yet to others, the arbiter of souls—as if one such as I could force the impulses of a soul. Perhaps it is best if you call me by what the humans call me. Anduinna, the Life Incarnate."

The name brought sudden clarity to my mind, and I exclaimed, "*The forest!* The men chasing me. They said you would come, that you would send your creatures to kill me."

Anduinna laughed, placing her hand upon her chest to hold herself steady. "Human's say many things, child. It is their nature. They fear that which they do not understand. Those such as yourself."

I frowned at that, asking, "Me? What would they have to fear about me?"

"Yes, you," she replied with honey in her voice. "Why do you think you are here? Clearly, you seek my wisdom, and it is wisdom you shall have."

I thought about the situation for a moment and a slight wind blew a putrid scent over me. I smelled the stink, just for a moment, and when I locked gazes with Anduinna, she frowned at me.

Slowly, I found my tongue and said, "I think... I think I shouldn't be here. It's coming back to me, gradually. I remember being in a forest, hidden in some brush for warmth. Asleep. I think I should wake up now."

"There is no need to run, my light. I'll protect—"

"What did you call me?" Anger permeated from my words, but I could not figure out why.

"I called you 'my light.' Is that not your preferred name? The name that makes you most comfortable?"

"No," I replied. There was something wrong with the way the words sounded. Too...measured. Only my mother had called me her light, and when Anduinna spoke the words, they felt spoiled; rotten.

That lingering putrid smell washed over me again, more pungent this time. I held my breath against it and said, "I think I'll be going now."

"Wait, hybrid," Anduinna commanded. The soft, soothing tone of her voice now held irritation and loathing. She suddenly turned to face me head on. The left side of her body was full of life and the promise of bounty and fertility. Now visible was her right; a monstrous thing. Gone were the lush green vines that made up her hair. Instead, replaced by gnarled, gray creeper, speckled with barbed thorns of red. Split in half, the vibrant side of her gave way to that desolate, putrid side.

The stink of her decay filled the air completely now, choking me. But that was not the only change. A quick glance at the once sunny grove showed that it was now overcast and decaying; the flowers broken, starving for life. It looked to be a desolate bog.

A true place of horrors.

My words failed me as I tried to scream. As I turned to run, gnarled vines tangled my feet, thorns punctured my skin and drew blood.

"Here we are once again," Anduinna said as she took a step forward with her mangled, deformed body. Both her two right legs were tattered and the sinew of her muscle barely clung to bone. The skin that should cover said muscle was all but gone, exposing the innards to all the elements. "This is not the first time we have met, hybrid, or do you not remember?" She clicked her tongue as she came ever closer, like she had forgotten something important, adding, "That's right! Your souls are incapable of completing the journey without loss. It's just another reason why all should be a part of me. A part of the collective. I was hoping this incarnation would be wiser."

"Let me go!" I screamed and struggled against my bonds. "You are not of life, liar. You're a fraud. You reek of death and decay."

Where had I learned such brave words? Such brave, stupid words.

Anduinna snickered, and it did not ring pleasantly this time. There was no longer anything human recognizable in it. "What do you think life is, hybrid? To live is to experience bounty, fertility and lust. But there is an end. There is always an end. Every life must experience death, and that death is what you see before you. I am life in its completeness. How dare an abomination such as you think itself above me, the true incarnation of life!"

Anduinna was almost upon me now, and I struggled desperately to free myself, cold sweat pouring off my face. The scales of my hands itched, but fear clouded all other thoughts, and words eluded me completely. I feared what Anduinna would do to me. I felt as if a single touch from her left hand could provide regeneration and rebirth, while the other, decay and death.

I wondered which hand would reach for me.

Escape, young one, the voice called in my head. *Banish her! She makes you think this grove is hers, but it is not! She creates it from her memories, but this is still your dream!*

"Pesky interloper," Anduinna said, but she stopped, as if some unknown force caught at her feet. She struggled against the force and muscle tore from her decaying legs as she did. She screamed in frustration, like an animal caught in a trap.

I tried with all my might to drive her away and failed. This was my nightmare, but it no longer belonged to me.

Suddenly, a purple light kindled between Anduinna and myself. It was a weak thing at first, the small purple beacon. But, over time, it swelled in strength. It appeared to consume the decay that had begun to overtake the grove.

The flame spoke to me, telling me of its will, declaring, *I will lend you my strength this time, young one. But know this: when the time comes, the strength must come from you alone.*

Anduinna continued to struggle against her invisible bonds, turning her decaying side from the flame. "*Hybrid!*" she screamed. "When next we meet, I expect you to bend the knee or to return to the land. Consider that my only offer."

And in the blink of an eye, Anduinna was gone, and the grove stood clear and vibrant as ever. The putrid smell had vanished and the smell of fresh grass and the gentle breeze was uplifting.

Then, I awoke.

Chapter Six

TOMFOOLERY

My stomach gurgled fiercely as the bile burned up my stomach. The vile stuff plodded its way up my throat before I realized it had been the better part of a day since I had last eaten.

I was starving.

Looking around, I struggled to find my bearings. Lost, I was completely and utterly lost.

Trails of tears rolled down my face, and my cheeks flushed with heat. My eyes burned, and I rubbed at them irritably, pressing myself to calm. I assured myself that I only had to find the place where I had seen the lights from the night before.

It should be such a simple task, I lied, forcing my feet to move, marching forward through the forest.

Before long, my stomach lurched again, and I barely held back vomit. *Food...* I couldn't focus on anything else. I decided that finding something to eat was the most important of tasks. And, as luck would have, a small hike down a deer trail brought me to a downed tree which had been previously set ablaze. All that remained of it was a blackened husk, but beyond it, a small stream greeted me.

The water looked crisp and clean, and like a vagrant escaping a desert, I greedily scooped handful after handful of the cooling liquid into my mouth. It was the most delicious thing I had ever tasted.

A brown, bushy tailed squirrel sat perched on its wooden throne of branches on a nearby tree, eyeing me curiously with its small black eyes. Those beady eyes peered on judgingly as I stared back.

I won't lie, I considered eating the rodent.

Shaking my head, I decided that chasing the squirrel would be both a waste of time and energy. Reluctantly, I settled for scavenging through nearby foliage and I chanced upon some small red berries. They were tart to the taste, and made my body long for more water. But, in the end, my hunger won out, and I stuffed as many in my mouth as feasibly possible.

After, I went back to the stream and swallowed more water to force the sour things down my throat. I choked on them, despite my best effort. When I recovered, to my stomach's protest, I decided that one at a time would serve me best.

I turned to find the squirrel from before had gained friends who mutually inspected me as if I were some kind of anomaly. Thinking about it, I decided that I likely was. Feeling frustrated and lonely, I picked up a rock and flung it at the group. It clattered off the corner of the tree and they scattered away into their woodland homes. Seeing the squirrel with its companions made me jealous, and I longed for company of my own. The solitude of the forest was defeating. The only sounds that accompanied me were the rushing of water and that of my own breath.

Strangely, where the rock had struck the tree, a piece of bark was now missing. To my surprise, the tree appeared to bleed! A dark red liquid oozed down the trunk, and, to my horror, some of the squirrels came back, greedily taking small handfuls of it to eat. I decided it would be prudent to be wary of the woodland creatures...even the small ones.

Loneliness gripped me as I sat near the edge of the stream, aimlessly throwing rocks into it to hear something other than my own thoughts. Something had changed last night...something within me. My meeting with Anduinna had left me frightened, but there had been another there—something or someone else that had lent me aid.

Voice... I hailed in my mind, trying to force my thoughts far outward.

There was no reply.

I berated myself for being stupid. Likely, there never was a mysterious voice. Never a meeting with the Life Incarnate. Just my own mind playing tricks in the dark. Still, it hurt to learn that my solitude was so...absolute.

For a time, I looked around, trying to find any markers or signs of human presence. The only object I found was a stick about my height. It had a certain heft to it, and I used it as a walking cane as I followed the stream's flow. I once overheard a traveler say that if one were to find themselves lost, find a water source and follow the flow—for there will always be those who seek a permanent source of water waiting. Following the travelers' advice, I did just that.

As I walked the forest in the light of day, it no longer felt scary to me. On the contrary, the whistling of wind through branches, and the chirping of birds gave me a slight sense of tranquility, contrasting the torrent of ill-fate that had wrought me the previous day.

Perhaps things will get better? I thought. *Perhaps my luck is changing? Perhaps... Perhaps my mother will find me?*

I saw glimpses of various animals as I walked, but they all cowered away from me. The loneliness was a chain that weighed me down, and I longed fiercely for any companionship. Then, like an answer to all my wishes, I heard a snicker of laughter, and a nearby deer that was contently eating grass suddenly looked up toward the noise with startled eyes. After a brief moment, it ran, and I wondered if I should as well.

"Hello?" I said. "Is anyone there?"

Another laugh, then joined by another and another. Suddenly, I heard a voice echo from a nearby tree line. "Poor human," the voice said. "No one wants to play?"

I glanced around, seeing nothing. "Where are you?"

"*Here!*" the voice replied, so close that it felt as if they spoke the word from inside my own ear. I jumped back with a start to find a small floating ball of light before me. It buzzed around like a hummingbird in flight, flying so quickly that it would have been hard to follow if it weren't for the trail of rainbow dust it left in its wake.

The strange being laughed again, a high-pitched sound like the wail of a newborn child. More laughter joined in as a few more balls of light fluttered down, encircling me. They moved in synchronization—as if in a dance. Each stride was deliberate. Calculated.

Eventually, one landed on my shoulder, its light feet pressing into my skin through my clothes like little hooks. "Poor. Lost. Human. Girl." I could barely make out its figure through the glow. Guessing, it looked to me like a miniature human with wings, but I could not discern if male or female. The light continued on as if singing some type of melody. "Spin around, watch her twirl."

The creature jumped off my shoulder, taking flight. The others followed as they whirled around me, snagging my hair, tussling it around my face. Their dust buffeted my eyes as I tried swatting them away. Then, just as abruptly, they broke apart and laughed again.

A mischievous laughter that promised trouble.

"What are you doing?" I asked, continuing to swipe at the dust, to no avail. "I'm looking for a town. Can you help me? Just tell me which way to go."

"Human demands, care not we," one replied.

Another picked up the tune, adding, "Bad ones coming, why not flee?"

Off in the distance, the noise of broken branches echoed through the forest, sending all manner of wildlife scrambling for shelter.

I knew I should run, but I had one more query that I couldn't help but ask. "What are you?"

"Fairies," they said in unison.

"No song? No rhyme?"

One fairy landed on my shoulder again and whispered, "We do not hide what we are. Best you be going, it's not too far." It fluttered off to join the others, encircling me once more before heading off down the stream. Another breaking of branches in the distance sent me scrambling after them.

The trail of rainbow dust made it easy to distinguish where the fairies were leading me, even if I had no chance of holding their pace.

Through muck, water and shrubbery I ran, and over time, the rustling and breaking of branches behind me became quieter and quieter until only the natural sound of nature remained. But the fairies were gone, their dust trail fading into nothingness in the air around me.

I continued along the bank of the stream, lockstep with my walking stick, until I came upon a boulder diverting the stream around its massive body. I was tired and my feet sore. Glancing down at my shoes, I grimaced. The holes in the soles had grown to the point where I could put three fingers through; they scarcely clung to my feet now. Perhaps my mother had been right when she told me to get them mended.

I scaled the boulder, using other smaller rocks to launch myself off of to reach the top. I slid as I struck. Scrambling, I managed to hoist myself up. My hands bled small lines of red from the scrapes of sliding down the face of the boulder, and my walking stick fell into the stream below with a splash, cold water droplets striking my face. Shaking my head, I looked out upon the woodland. The fairies had been truthful.

Just off in the distance, I could see what looked like a modest village. Squinting, I could barely make out small thatched houses with chimneys that spewed trails of white smoke.

Finally!

As I slid down the rock face, I was extra cautious not to lose my balance and fall. The rocks below were jagged, and there would be no aid if I were to slip and hurt myself. The thought of being stranded out there alone another night sent a shiver through my body, but as my feet touched the earth safely, I calmed. I turned to my walking stick, which had been caught up between some rocks in the stream. With the town being so close, I abandoned it, deciding against getting wet as I walked away.

I walked and walked until my feet were bloody. I had disposed of my shoes, or what was left of them, earlier in the trek. The various clutter of sharp sticks and jagged rocks on the ground nipped at my heels relentlessly, leaving a multitude of scrapes and cuts on my feet and up my shins.

Felled remains of trees added up as I continued in the village's direction, a sure sign my path was true. I saw a trail and then a path that led to a gap in the trees. I hurried toward it, but just at the forest's edge, a soft melody caught my ear.

I spun and searched for the source of the tune. I knew I should continue on my way, ignoring any other distractions, but there was something about the sound that enticed me to find its origin.

A minor detour wouldn't hurt, would it?

My childish ways got the best of me as I followed after the melody, like a toddler attracted to the sound of their parents' voices. As it got louder, I realized what I heard was some sort of air instrument. A flute, perhaps? The song that played was beautiful and full, as if an entire ensemble performed for me alone. It filled me inexplicably with a sense of sadness to know that whomever played, played alone. But that feeling didn't last long as the music fully captivated my mind, drawing pleasant memories to the forefront, as if spoon-feeding a weary soul remembrances of fonder times.

I pressed on through a prickly bush, which cut a small red line across my cheek, but the music drove me onward and I ignored its biting sting. The music entranced me as I saw the clearing ahead. Leaning around a large tree, I glimpsed the musician who created such melodies.

Sat upon a rock, a creature with curved white horns and dark-red fur played on a pipe of purest white. It was glowing! As if the creature played a song of magic. They rested upon a log that sat above a small pond, staring down at their own reflection in the water while playing merrily, kicking their hooved feet back and forth to the beat of the tune.

Suddenly, the music stopped, and I hid myself behind the trunk of the tree in reply, pressing against it as hard as I could. My heart beat quickly, as if it too had kept pace with the suddenly quiet song.

"Come out, human. I can smell you," the creature hailed to me in a non-threatening way. Their voice was deep, and the words, almost spoken as if in a growl, but with no hint of malice in them. Cautiously, I rounded the corner to face the creature.

Without realizing it, the music had put me in a state of ease and I did not, could not, believe that this creature meant me any harm. I shuffled forward until I was just inside the clearing.

"Ah! A child," the creature said enthusiastically. "Children are the best at such things. Tell me, tell me... Did you enjoy my song?"

"Very much," I replied, smiling embarrassingly. "I think it was the most beautiful thing I've ever heard."

"Fantastic!" the creature said, slapping his hand against the log, the long nails of their hand tearing small pieces of rotted bark and throwing it down into the pond below. "It has been so long since I had a human perspective, and even longer from a child. Humans can be so...guarded when talking to one such as myself. Tell me, is there anything I can do for you? Having given such a wonderful compliment, it cannot go unrewarded."

"Your name," I heard myself ask, the effects of the music still addled my mind. My reluctance toward this creature had all but vanished and I fell back into my age, asking naïve questions. "For I wish to tell the story properly when I tell others of this moment."

The creature bared their pointy teeth in a grin. The teeth, normally something that would be frightful, instead complimented their face inexplicably. "My true name is unpronounceable in human speech," he replied, scratching the long tuft of red hair that grew at his chin. "But, the fairies call me Pipar the piper. I think that will do, yes? Now then, so that we are made whole in conversation, may I ask what yours is in return?"

"Vi'eri," I replied.

"*Vi'eri...*" the creature repeated back to me, as if saying the name allowed him some sort of power. "It's a beautiful name, that is certain. I think... Yes, I think it has inspired me further. You may pass freely in my land, child. A gift! As a friend of Pipar the piper."

With that, the creature turned from me, starting a new tune on their pipe and swaying their body to its rhythm. I turned to leave, but as I rounded the corner of the tree, a light caught my eye with a rainbow dust trail. A fairy. It appeared to dance along with the music, getting closer and closer to Pipar as it did. I smiled at the scene before continuing on my way, but, a moment later, the music halted.

The light from the fairy, so bright and vivid, suddenly winked out, but I did not see.

An ear-piercing shriek, followed by the cracking of bone, but I did not hear.

Entranced, I continued on without question, still mesmerized by the residual effect of the music, oblivious to what I knew I had just witnessed.

It was a short time before I reached the edge of the forest again, and outside, I learned a new appreciation for the bright sun of spring as I stood, basking in its warm glow. The foliage of the forest gave way to the grasslands of a well-kept grazing pasture. The ground was soft, and it took a bit of the sting out of the injuries that plagued both my feet.

It had been quite the adventure, but I was ready to return home with my mother. The events of the previous day seemed but a nightmare that the music had banished back into the night. Perhaps I would truly be ready to leave home behind someday, but for now, I was content with getting back to a tranquil, quiet life.

The whims of a naïve child.

CHAPTER SEVEN

CRUX THE TRUE BLADE

Not one but two human farmers, both elderly from what I could tell, yelled obscenities at me while crossing through their land. 'Vagrant' and 'Thief' were among some of the choice names they had called me. It didn't take a particularly sharp individual to sense that this town had issues with those they deemed *inferior*.

Ultimately, I made my way to the town proper. It was a lot like Elklan, with the simple houses and the farmland. As I stood in what I assumed was the city square, it dawned on me: I did not know what this town was named.

I looked around aimlessly as other humans milled around me, refusing to catch my eye. The deminean guards openly scowled at me, shouldering their halberds intimidatingly.

"Easthaven!" a voice suddenly said from behind me.

I spun and found myself face to face with a human man. He was around forty years of age by his peppered gray and black hair. He looked like a warrior...or a mercenary with his fitted leather armor that hugged his muscular body.

The man held in his hand an intricate knife that he used to carve small slices off an apple, placing each piece in his mouth delicately. Each time he did so, his face beamed, like it was the first time he had ever tasted something so wonderful.

"It's just an apple," I said with some hesitancy. "And I didn't ask. Why do you think I don't know where I am?"

"*Just an apple!*" he replied, as if I had struck him. Quickly, he wiped the shock off his face. "Nevermind that. Look around." He flourished his arms, stepping ever closer. I would have felt frightened, but the cluster of humans nearby gave me conviction. Surely they wouldn't let this stranger hurt me. As if he sensed my thoughts, he continued, adding, "You have that far off look that people get when they don't know where to go. Which means you're lost. Since the townsfolk won't meet your eye, it means you aren't from around here. And since you look the way you do..." he paused, gesturing toward my ragged clothing, "it means you're here alone. Did I get all that right?"

"No," I said with as much conviction as I could muster. To my deep shame, I tried to channel that deminean girl Kreza who commanded authority over Elklan so easily. "I am here with my mother. I simply went out into the forest and found...hardships, you could say."

"*Hardships...*" he repeated, taking another bite of an apple. "Indeed. And what, pray tell, was a girl such as yourself doing out in the forest alone?"

"I wasn't alone."

The man just stared for a moment, as if he struggled to find the right words to say. He stroked at his full-beard, pausing for a moment to scratch the deep cut that split his lip. The hair around the scar had turned stark white, and it gave him a certain rugged appearance that I had no doubt gave him an edge when dealing with others of his kind. A certain danger. That, combined with his natural height, made him a man that few would try to cheat.

"Well then, little lady, who is alone, but not alone," he said. "Can I get your name proper?"

The second person to ask for my name in such a short time. I considered lying, but decided against it.

"Vi'eri," I said.

"Well then, Vi'eri, allow me to introduce myself. My name is Crux. Some call me Crux Trueblade. But please, you refer to me simply as Crux."

I made a mental note of how vain he was. My mother would say that men who threw around titles were full of themselves and had concern only for themselves.

"Nice to meet you, Crux." I replied, putting on a fake smile.

Crux moved toward me, planting his arm around my shoulder carelessly. I remarked at how far he had to lean down to do this. He proffered me a piece of apple, and I refused with a wave of my hand.

"Listen," Crux said, taking the piece of apple for himself, and speaking through his chewing, "I'm looking for someone to show me the forest. I'm searching for something. Does that sound interesting to you?"

Curiosity got the better of me as I asked, "What are you searching for?"

Crux shook his head and pulled back, falling to one knee so we were face to face. "A mercenary never tells of his mark before an agreement is met. I see you're hesitant, and I respect that. You don't know me and you're cautious. That makes you smart. I'll have a private room made up for you at the tavern. It has no name, but it's the only tavern in this small town that the deminean allow. Ask about me there, and you'll see that I'm trustworthy." He rose and strode away, but turned just before rounding a corner to add, "I'll also have some new clothing for you as well. And some shoes... Where are your shoes? Nevermind. Come to the tavern. Even if you decide not to help me, consider it a gift from one weary traveler to a nother."

I turned and walked away from him without answering. I had no intention of taking him up on his offer.

As I wandered around the town, the numerous townsfolk became increasingly antagonistic toward me. Anytime I asked about my mother, they would scoff and mutter a curse under their breath. Then, as if I was the dirt beneath their feet, they would act as if I didn't exist at all.

It was a little past midday when I noticed a heightened attention from the deminean guards. They looked at me curiously with those dim golden eyes and I quickly made myself scarce, falling back into a nearby alley between what appeared to be two warehouses.

I leaned against an empty wooden box and tried to soothe my sour stomach. I had to eat soon. The mercenary's offer was sounding more enticing by the minute when I heard the soft clatter of footsteps enter the alleyway behind me.

Two skinny men entered the alley looking nearly as haggard as I was. Neither wore shoes, and one man was shirtless with ripped brown shorts. His long blond hair was matted and dirty, stuck to blood on his neck where he had sustained some type of wound. The other man's shirt was black, matching his short hair. It was as if he had never cleaned his clothes before, stained as they were. I noticed his right leggings were torn, revealing the leg up to the knee.

I purposefully looked away from the two, keeping my eyes low and to the side as they stepped in front of me. I exhaled a sigh of relief as they passed, which was shattered when the man with the long hair suddenly turned and asked, "Wadda' we have 'ere?"

"Don't know?" the other responded as they both stepped back to rest in front of me, blocking my only exit from the alley.

Steadily, I kept my eyes down as I replied, "It's nothing—I'm nothing. I have nothing for you, so I'll just be leaving."

As I tried to move past them, the black-haired man put his arm in front of me to block my way. "Wait," he said, using the back of his hand to brush my face. I recoiled at the touch. "Maybe we can come to some sorta' agreement, eh?" It was the slurred speech of heavy intoxication and I smelled it on his breath and sweat.

I tried again to move the other way when the first man stepped in front to block my escape. They had well and truly trapped me. The guards! Surely the guards would need to help.

"Help! I'm—" I yelled when the blond man shoved my head back into the building and covered my mouth with his hand.

I looked frantically for any sign of help, and I thanked the Well when I saw a deminean guard's stare down the alley to see what the commotion had been. I tried to call out again, but the man tightened his grip. It was getting difficult to breathe as his hand shoved against my nose.

To my dismay, the deminean guard merely scowled in discontent and walked away, not even offering a glance back. The black-haired man, who had been staring in their direction, turned his face back to me, giving me a yellow-toothed grin. "Where were we?"

I struggled and fought against my captors, and one man whooped in delight that I would not make it easy for them. They seemed to enjoy my distress, and it filled me with an anger that I didn't know I possessed. The feeling was comparable to when I had stabbed Kreza Ironskin. That felt so long ago now.

Seeing an opportunity, I bit down on my captor's hand and clenched my jaw as firmly as I could. The blond-haired man wailed as my teeth sunk in deep, a metallic taste washing across my tongue. In response, he pulled my head back and hurled me against the warehouse wall. I kept my jaw locked. Over and over, he slammed me until his friend reared back and struck the side of my head with a hooked blow.

My mind spun, and I felt as if I were floating beyond the confines of my body. Black dots danced in front of my eyes, much as the fairies had done before in the forest. I thought of them and of the mysterious piper Pipar and couldn't help but smile, stupidly. At least I had seen something truly magical before I was to die...or worse.

You will not die, a voice rang out in my head. *Riffraff of this sort are hardly worth your attention. Rise and fight, you know you can.*

There was a sudden push on my emotions. No, more like a shove! I could feel an outside force seek to alter me, and courage rose up in me from an unknown place. Like a bolt of lightning, my mind came back sharp and clear as I breathed in life, pure. The power of the realm swelled within me.

The man who had hit me reared back for another strike and I stepped into him, standing just up to his chest in height. I focused all my anger and despair and flung my fist into him with all the strength my tiny body could muster.

I struck true, hitting him directly in his sternum. To my surprise, I felt the cartilage and small bones in his chest snap from the pressure of my blow, and his body lifted from the ground and flew through the air, slamming into the wall on the other side of the alleyway. The sound of cracking wood accompanied the man's cry, which died as his body crumbled to the ground.

"What—" his friend started, his eyes going wide. But his words were cut off as he fell to his knees. I looked upon him with revulsion, my fury not yet quenched as I grabbed the front of his shirt and clenched my fist in anger, preparing another strike. It was then that I noticed a knife blade sticking out of his back. The blade's handle looked familiar.

"Got yourself in some trouble, I see," Crux said as he sauntered into the alley. "I leave you alone for such a short time and this is what happens? This town truly has gone to purgatory, I tell ya."

I heard Crux's words, but I gave him no mind. I focused all my attention on the one who would—no... Nobody would ever use me that way, not even in my imagination. My arm shook with rage as I battled my internal fury.

The man wheezed and coughed blood on the ground, which prompted me to step back. In a desperate voice, the man said, "We...had—" his words died in his throat as Crux pulled his dagger from the man's back.

"She's just a little girl," Crux whispered into his ear as he casually slid the knife across the man's throat.

The amount of blood that poured from the wound surprised me. How could one being possibly be filled with so much life-giving fluid? It seemed such a waste to spill something so essential to our existence on the floor, but the man it belonged to was not worthy of it.

I smiled in grim satisfaction.

"Are you okay?" Crux asked as he put his hand to my shoulder. I pulled away, eyes wide as I regarded him. He pulled his hands back in mock surrender. "Sorry. Sorry." He spared a glance for the man whose sternum I had crushed, his body lying in a broken heap, blood dripping from his mouth and his eyes stuck open with surprise. He was dead, and I had killed him.

I had killed.

Crux made a sound with his lips, a sucking sound, as if he pondered something of great importance. Eventually, coming to terms with the scene, he said, "Please let me take you to the inn. You've been through enough for one day, and we need to clean you up."

Just then, two deminean guards came into the alleyway. Wordlessly, Crux held his hand up to me to forestall the conversation and went to meet them. He seemed to explain the situation, and then he put his hands in his pockets and pulled something out. There was an exchange of some sort, and the guards turned and walked away, just as they had done when they had ignored my pleas for help.

"Sorry about that," Crux said. "No matter what happens, the guards expect their due—even when they deserve none. As I was saying, let's take you to the inn for some new clothes and some hot food." He paused, looking upon the corpses with a frown, adding, "And a change of scenery doesn't sound too bad now, does it?"

Stubbornly, I went to protest, but the sound of my stomach cut me off before I could. The growling it produced would have made any objections sound weak. I nodded my head in agreement, not trusting my voice to act.

I followed Crux silently to the inn, and he made sure to give me ample distance between us, which I appreciated. The thought of anyone touching me at that moment made my hair stand on end.

The tavern was a short walk, and when we entered, dreary-eyed men, sweaty and dirty from a hard day's work, turned to look at us. To me, they showed a disdainful glare, but when their eyes fell upon Crux, they turned back to their own drinks without hesitation.

"Merc!" the woman behind the bar yelled. "Think she's a bit young to be a mercenary, don't you? A girl that age should still be with her mother."

Crux grinned, the scar on his lip pulling awkwardly as he walked toward the bar. I followed wordlessly. "Jezza," he said, leaning his thick arms against the wood. "I just saved this poor lass from a couple of no good-doers. Did you get the room ready as I asked?"

Jezza frowned, her deep-red lips accenting her ebony face. She nodded affirmatively, adding, "I wouldn't have if I'd known you were bringing in a stray dog. How long has it been since you bathed, girl?" I looked up at the woman and glowered.

"She's had a rough day," Crux explained. He looked like he was going to lean his arm around me, but he apparently decided not to at the last moment. "She may have some information I want, and before you say anything, I'm being honest about it. While I won't force her to tell me anything, I'm hoping warm food and a warm bed will loosen her tongue."

Jezza shook her head, her short black curly hair rustling around her face. Suspiciously, she said, "Right... I think I'll let the girl speak for herself. Girl, tell me—no, don't look away, stay focused. Are you okay?"

Crux looked nervous, chewing on the part of his lip with the scar, but I met Jezza's eyes and replied, "Yes, it's as he says. He saved me from some men out there in the alley. I'm so...so tired. And hungry." My pride had eroded to the point of breaking.

Jezza clicked her tongue. "Of course you are, child. Of course. Come, your room and clothes are ready. I'll make sure hot water is sent as well. Some bandages too. Afterward, come down and eat. I'll prepare you a meal myself. *Crux!*" She turned to face the mercenary, and he went straight backed like a guard called out by a superior. "Do right by the girl and we won't have any trouble. Got it?"

"Got it."

Crux gently pushed on my back and aimed me toward the stairs to the second floor. I climbed, and he gestured to a specific door, opening it with a key and held it open for me as I walked inside. He stood outside the door, purposefully not coming in.

"Jezza and I are the only ones with a key, so no one will bother you. I will bring you the hot water myself, and I'll knock three times like this..." He knocked on the door as he instructed, adding, "That's how you'll know it's me. If you need to rest before you come down, that's fine. But if possible, I would come down as soon as you can. Jezza can be...troublesome, if made to wait after extending her hospitality. Which is quite rare, I must say. Consider yourself honored."

I nodded my agreement, and Crux spared me a final grin before shutting the door. I moved to sit on the bed, staring at the wall. So much had transpired in so little time. I had stabbed a deminean noble, and now I had killed a man with my bare hands. How was that even possible? My scales itched fiercely, and when I pulled my gloves off, they shimmered, reflecting the sun's rays of light that came from a small window above the bed.

I reflected on the incident and reached out with my mind. *Voice, are you there?* I thought I felt a reply back, but it was too weak to comprehend. I sighed and wondered if I was going insane.

How could my mother ever want me back, broken as I was?

Chapter Eight

BARGAIN

That night, I dreamed of death.

Back in an alleyway, I stood, two men laid out dead in front of me. No, it was a town center, a deminean girl bleeding from a stab wound. No, it was a battlefield, cluttered with the corpses of fallen soldiers. In each dream, they would stare at me with dead eyes and say the same thing.

"You did this to us."

Then, suddenly, like a guardian, the voice called to me. My dear mystical voice. It spoke but a single word, and that word drowned the world in purple fire as it consumed my despair, just as it had done before in the Grove of the Life Incarnate.

Wake!

I sprung awake covered in a cold sweat. The morning was still early and the bright sun of spring had yet to rise to thwart the night. I sat up in my bed and stared around in utter confusion.

"Where am I?" I said to the empty dark.

I rubbed the sleep from my eyes, pressing them with the back of my scaled hands.

My gloves!

I looked down to see them on the floor, but otherwise, I was fully dressed in clothes that I didn't remember putting on. For a moment, my mind was clouded in morning fog. I had forgotten all about the previous day's events.

A grave image crept into my mind like a plague; I slept only a short walk from the alleyway where those men had assailed me.

Those dead men.

I shook my head, sending my knotted hair flitting around my face. Stretching my legs, I stood and checked the room. A small bed sat under a small window, and there, in the corner, a used washbasin sat near a foul smelling chamberpot. On a small redwood counter, a mirror and a hairbrush had been set out. It is such a strange thing—the habits that tend to calm us. I took the hairbrush and ran it through my hair absently, just as my mother would do for me when I was home.

Home...

Three rapid knocks on the door startled me, and I dropped the hairbrush to the ground. I swore as it rolled under the bed and out of my sight. The knocks reawakened the headache I remembered feeling the past night, and I held my hands against my temples to try and ease it.

Memories fluttered back into my head. After washing up, I had frantically scrubbed sticky red blood from my gloves. Afterward, I went downstairs for a meal prepared by Jezza—as I promised I would. But a terrible migraine had sent me straight back upstairs with scarcely a bite eaten. I had never before had such terrible head pains, and I hoped to never again.

Already the day was turning out terribly.

I laid on the floor and reached under the bed, picking up the hairbrush, and placing it back in its proper place. I pulled on my gloves, hiding my scales, before I opened the thick wooden door.

Crux strode in with his usual swagger, as a man does who knows his business. "Mornin' to you, Vi'eri," he said, proffering a nod of his head at me. "And how are you feeling on this fine day?"

"Fine," I lied, closing my eyes against the light of the small candle he held. The flickering flame seemed to dance to the tune of my misery.

"Fine, yes," Crux replied. "That's good...great even, after the struggles you've had yesterday."

Recalling my manners, I reached and pulled over a small wooden chair, the only one in the room, offering it to him.

Crux shook his head. "Afraid I'm here on business. Remember when I spoke of requiring your aid with a certain task in the forest? I was wondering if it would be an appropriate time to ask again?"

I felt faint as the headache increased in pressure. "Okay...ask your questions," I said between the throbbing in my skull.

"That's excellent, Vi'eri. You'd really be helpin' me out." Crux walked over and leaned on the wall adjacent to the bed, absently staring out the small window at the lingering moon. "I'm looking for an item. A rare trinket... Do you know of Anduinna?"

I nodded reluctantly. It made me uncomfortable to hear that name spoken again, as if the mere mention of her name would summon her back to finish me off.

"Surprisingly well schooled for a girl of your age. Anyhow, Anduinna, the Life Incarnate, as some call her, spawns creatures not of human or deminean species. Did you know this?" I once again nodded, and he carried on, adding, "There is one such creature named a satyr. It is a being known for its curved horns and its capability to perform music. In your time in the forest, did you hear any such music? It would sound like an air instrument—a flute, perhaps. And there are rumors that it's...magical. Whatever that's supposed to mean."

A cold sweat broke out on my face, and my breath caught in my throat. My mind immediately ventured to Pipar. A satyr, Crux had called him.

Crux's face lit up. "See, I *knew* you knew something!" he announced emphatically, slapping his knee. "Come now, don't be shy. What did you hear? What did you see?"

"I..." My voice cut off, withdrawing completely. Pipar had never commanded me *not* to speak of him—on the contrary, he had given his name freely when asked on the promise that I would do just that. Still, something about Crux's demeanor made me fear to speak of the event that had befallen me in the forest.

Likely sensing my dilemma, he reached out a calming hand and placed it on my shoulder. "I mean the creature no harm, if that is your worry. I merely wish to ask for its mother's horn."

"Mother's horn?" I replied, thinking back to my conversation with Pipar. The satyr had made no mention of a horn.

"What's that?" I asked.

Crux raised his shoulders as if to say 'I don't know,' instead saying, "But a deminean merchant wishes for the mother horn of a satyr, so they called it. It's supposedly a keepsake that satyrs take from their mothers when they perish. Quite rare."

"And you think Pipar would want to give up such a token?"

"Pipar?" Crux said, and my heart sank. "You mean to tell me you *met* the creature itself? That it told *you* its name?" he finished, visibly excited now as he paced around the room.

"Yes," I admitted reluctantly. "He was...nice. I complimented him on his music and he said I'm free to come and go into his forest."

Crux stopped for a moment to consider. "*His* forest, eh? So this creature fancies itself as ruler of the woodland? This 'Bloodsoaked Forest'... Gruesome name, if you ask me." He paused, knuckling the scar on his chin for a time before adding, "That may be problematic. But this is why I need you, Vi'eri. See, I knew there was something special about you. This, along with what you did in the alley, confirms it."

The mention of the alleyway sent me into spiraling despair. I turned my eyes to the floor and, likely sensing my feelings, Crux kneeled to face me. "It's a good thing, Vi'eri. An excellent thing. I think... I think you have the power of an enchanter."

"An...enchanter?"

"Ay, same as me," Crux replied pridefully, holding up two fingers. "It's one of the two magics the Well bestowed upon humans in the times before written word. There are destroyers, with their fireballs and lightning from the sky. And then there are enchanters, who use their magic to augment other items. Look—" Crux pulled his knife from its sheath and for the first time, I noted the small white light that emanated from it. "I enchanted this myself—well, with the help of my former master. My will controls this knife. If I throw it, I need only to think of where it will strike and it will be so. If I lose it, I simply need to ask it to return and it will. That is the power of an enchanter."

"And why do you think I'm one?"

Crux grabbed me by both my shoulders, grinning. "Because of that man who you... The man who died, I mean. I believe you inadvertently enchanted your gloves in a way that increased your strength. I've never seen an enchantment work quite like that, but I noticed a small glow from your hands for a moment before we left the alley. The enchantment appears gone now, likely because of your inexperience. I can teach you, Vi'eri!" Crux let go and stood, moving to lean back on the wall.

"Teach me?" I repeated his words, not sure how to respond. "But what about my mother? What about my home?"

Crux frowned. "Well...if you wish to return home, that is your prerogative. You were lucky to have made it through the forest in one piece, alone as you were. To make the trip by road would put you at the mercy of highwaymen." Crux scratched at his chin, as if considering, adding, "How about a bargain? Help me with my task involving the satyr and consider my offer to join me. If, after we retrieve the mother's horn and you still want to return home, I will personally escort you. You may not know this, but I'm quite the mercenary, and I can promise you no harm will come to you if you travel at my side."

Crux's straightforwardness put me off guard. I don't believe that anyone had ever treated me in such a manner. Treated me as an adult. One with choices of how their life will continue.

I channeled my mother the best I could and replied, "I'll consider the offer to join you. As for the forest...I agree. I will help you as best I can."

"I expected nothing less," Crux concluded. "Then we have a deal. First, we deal with the satyr."

The sun had won its bid in claiming the realm against the dark by the time Crux was ready to leave the tavern. As I exited the building, the light glared in my sensitive eyes. Instinctually, I held my hands up to block out its rays.

"It's a fine day," Crux said, clapping me on the shoulder. "Would be finer if I knew anything more about this satyr."

"Sorry, but I have little to offer."

Crux shrugged his shoulders, but seemed to accept that he would not be getting his answers. At least, not from me.

We made our way down the lightly cobbled path, which ultimately gave way to an ordinary dirt trail. The new boots I wore were of sturdy leather, reinforced at that. They were comfortable, but my wounds rubbed irritably against the insides. The clothes Crux had provided were fine as well. A leather tunic and a plain brown hooded cloak to go with it. I felt as if I were a warrior going off to battle, and I chuckled to myself at how silly I must have looked in the getup.

"What's so funny?" Crux asked, casually using his knife to clean dirt from his fingernails.

"Just..." I tugged on my cloak for good measure, "yesterday, I had not a thing to my name, and now I have these fine clothes. Even if they are a bit rough for a seamstress like myself. The people of the town looked down on me. None offered any aid...except you. Then, in the alleyway..." I trailed off and Crux went to say something, but I waved him off, adding, "I still haven't decided whether finding you was a curse or a blessing. But, I think I am glad to have met you."

Crux grinned, his green eyes bright. "Ay, the feeling is mutual. Haven't had any kids of my own, was always so busy with my own life, you know?" He waited for a moment, but when it was apparent I wouldn't respond, he added, "Well, maybe you wouldn't. I forget how young you are. What I meant to say is, I imagine my daughter, if I had one, would have been a lot like you. You're strong, Vi'eri. Let nobody make you believe otherwise."

I smiled at him and he returned it cheerily. For the first time, I had developed a true kinship with someone unrelated to me.

I would cherish that friendship forever.

CHAPTER NINE

MOTHER'S HORN

Rays of warm sunlight penetrated through the red trees' lush foliage, cascading small shadows of leaves toward the earth below.

It was a curious thing—the way circumstances change an environment. Where once the fallen branches meant a painful walk. Now, it meant a well-lived woodland full of critters. No longer fearful, I truly appreciated the beauty of it all. To punctuate the thought, a squawking of birds from a nearby tree drew the eye to where a yellow feathered avian fought a squirrel who was scoping out a potential new home for itself in the roost.

Life was an ever-changing battle.

"What are you lookin' at?" Crux asked, pushing back a tree branch and allowing me to walk past unhindered, the leather of his greaves groaning against his taunt muscles.

"Nothing important," I replied, stopping and leaning heavily against the base of the tree.

He stepped in front of me with a curious look on his face. "Are you alright? You've got a distant look in your eye."

"Fine," I said and was genuinely surprised to find it so. The pain of the last few days flowed off me like the sweat on a hard day's work in the mid-spring heat. It fell to the ground and was eaten by the land. I somehow felt lighter; a small burden lifted.

"You may be fine," Crux said, his lips turning downward in a frown. "But I'm sweatin' like a roasting pig here. This would be quicker if you just pointed me in the right direction, eh?"

I shook my head in opposition. "I wouldn't even know where to point you. Pipar's music...it does something to the mind. One moment, I was struggling from the pain in my feet, and the next..." I mimicked a musical conductor with my arms, "the music carried me to him. After our talk, I found myself outside the forest. I barely remember a thing other than stepping out into the midday sun."

"So music that can alter a person's state of mind? Curious...and dangerous. I can see why satyrs are held in such high esteem. Well, for creatures of Anduinna's I mean. There are rumors, of course—"

"Pipar's not dangerous!" I protested.

Crux ignored my outburst and, instead, waved his arms to prompt us to continue onward.

The journey through the Bloodsoaked Forest was relaxing, albeit slow. Crux did not seem to do as well as I in navigating through the forest and its various obstacles. He stumbled on every other root or snagged various branches with his larger body. It had been funny...at first. But as time went on, his mood shifted from casual optimism to cold irritation.

Eventually, Crux signaled a halt and sat on the remains of a felled tree. He rubbed at his legs and complained, "Surely the satyr has to be around here somewhere."

I once again raised my shoulder to indicate that I did not know when suddenly, I saw a glitter out of the corner of my eye.

A rainbow trail.

"*Quick!*" I said, pulling on his arm. "Follow the fairy. *The fairy!*"

"What fairy?" Crux replied, but he stood with renewed vigor.

I pointed to the rainbow dust trail, but I failed to see a ball of light at its front. I rushed forward with Crux following close behind. As I pushed the branches aside, each snapped back with a thwack—hitting Crux on various parts of his body. With each strike, he grunted, and I laughed to myself as I pushed forward.

Eventually, we made it to a clearing. The same as the one that I met Pipar the previous day. The felled log the satyr had once sat was still half sunk into a small pond and little white-spotted frogs played upon it. Looking up, I spotted the rainbow trail as it went up into the trees. Slowly, it disappeared from view.

"This is it," I said, turning to Crux, who shoved through a nearby bush, entering the clearing. It was then that I realized just how much it cost the man in this environment to be so tall. While I had little trouble moving below the limbs of the trees, each step took him considerably more effort.

"Well," he paused to take a deep breath, "where is this 'Pipar?'"

Like his words held a summoning magic, a fairy fluttered into the clearing, burning brightly of yellow. The trail of rainbow dust followed its flight.

"Little girl, foolish spy," the fairy rhymed in a tune. "Satyr, traitor, now you die." It rounded me once and flew off in the opposite direction.

"That was...interesting," Crux said, wiping away the rainbow dust that a gust carried into his face.

"*It went this way!*" an unknown voice said from beyond the trees, the sounds of footsteps punctuating the words.

Crux looked uneasy, but I noticed the small glint of his knife, which he had unsheathed without a sound. "Get behind me!" he whispered.

I obeyed, tiptoeing behind him as he nudged me back slowly, never taking his eyes off the tree line where the source of the sound had come from.

We reached the base of a boulder and rounded it. He slid down and pulled me down with him, placing a single finger to his lips to bid me to be quiet.

"There is a clearing here," an unfamiliar voice said as the rustling of broken branches echoed out across the forest, sending all manner of animals dashing for cover. There must be at least ten others to make this much noise.

"We know you're out there," the first voice announced. "This is an order: reveal yourself immediately or face punishment for disobedience."

Crux looked at me with wide-eyes, and I stared back at him in astonishment. Were they still looking for me? My face must have told him everything that my mouth would not dare open to voice.

"It's just me," he said, stepping from around the boulder and re-entering the clearing. I looked downward, noticing his knife still on the ground next to me. "I surrender quietly. Although, I don't know what I've done wrong."

"Get down, human," a few commanded in unison.

Deminean! I thought dispiritedly. I dared to peer from around the corner and saw three clearly as they approached Crux. Deminean, as suspected, and armored for combat. Swords at the ready.

"As you command, Dem'i," Crux said, uttering the honorific, but he did not know to whom he addressed. Still, he went to his knees and placed his hands atop his head.

A deminean warrior stepped in front of Crux and kicked him straight in the abdomen. He coughed and fell forward, unmoving. Was he faking it? Or had the warriors' attack truly put him out in one blow?

As if he heard my questions, Crux coughed loudly, sending a stream of dirt across the boots of the tall deminean who stood in front of him, so armored I couldn't tell if they were male or female. The knife near me seemed to quiver in anticipation of the violence to come.

The presumed leader of the deminean, from the fanciful buttons that held his warriors' cloak tight, stood a bit taller than Crux himself. He pulled Crux's head up by his hair, saying, "You will refer to us as Dem'i Ironskin, human scum, for we represent the esteemed family in this matter." The leader let go of Crux's hair and his face hit the dirt roughly.

"Yes, Dem'i Ironskin. My apologies," Crux said through a mouthful of dirt.

The other two deminean warriors nearby pulled Crux to his knees by his arms and held him in that position, arms both out straight.

"Now tell me," the leader mused, his reddish scales glittering against his dark skin. "What are you doing out here? Wait, no... Have you seen a human girl? She would be around nine years in age." The leader's voice was cool and punctuated, but skin deep there was an edge that warned of danger for any who crossed him.

"No!" Crux replied emphatically. "No girl. I was looking for a satyr. Not exactly the type of quest you would bring a little girl on, eh?"

One of the deminean who held Crux gave him a knock on the back of the head. "Don't speak so casually, human," they warned.

Crux bowed his head again, lower this time. "Apologies."

"A satyr, you say. Quite a rare creature. And why do you seek them?"

"That is a private matter."

Another blow in the head, and this time Crux looked to have passed out. Quickly, the other deminean that held him pulled his head back by his hair and he awoke with a start.

Crux spit out blood. "Apologies, I seemed to have fallen asleep on you all. I really should go to bed earlier."

I ground my teeth in frustration and rage, but fear stilled me from action.

Another deminean gave Crux a gut shot as the leader said, "There are no private matters when your lords ask you, human. Speak."

"Ri'sha," Crux said. "It is a matter for the Ri'sha."

All three deminean stepped back in synchronization.

The leader was the first to recover, replying, "That's preposterous! I—"

"Would I dare lie about that?" Crux replied, and the leader went tight-lipped. He met his captor's gaze and did not flinch away from the scowl that crossed his face.

"If that is true, then I would not have this meeting between us spoken of to an honored Ri'sha," the leader said, as if they had come to an understanding. Crux nodded as if he agreed to the terms, but the leader added, "As for the girl—"

"What girl?" a different voice spoke out.

A familiar one.

The voice seemed to come from the other side of the pond. As fit as a spriggan in spring, Pipar the satyr launched himself atop the felled log, pipe in hand. "If you speak of Vi'eri, the human child, then she is permitted in my forest. None shall claim her here...and I mean none!"

"Creature of Anduinna!" the deminean leader spat. "Would you dare turn against your betters?"

"Betters?" Pipar glanced around toward them, and off beyond the tree line where I suspected more deminean stood just out of my sight. "I doubt one of you could best me in a contest of song, music or dance. Bah! Betters... The toads provide better songs for my ears than you lot."

"We do not play foolish games, creature. Come down from that log. If you answer some questions about the human girl named Vi'eri, then perhaps we will see fit to leave you to your hovel."

The insult did not appear lost on Pipar, who eyed the leader squarely. Then, to my horror, I noticed the gaze of a soldier who had snuck through the trees while monitoring the perimeter.

He glared right at me.

"Here she is!" the scout cried and the other deminean turned toward me, hands going for weapons.

Then, like some comedy troupe, Pipar pulled out his pipe and started playing a song. It was the same song Pipar had said was inspired by my name.

First, the music started slow, humming melodically as if there were an army of players surrounding the grove. Then faster and faster as the music divulged into pure chaos.

And chaos surely followed.

Pipar's music built in tempo, and I felt it in my head. It filled me with indescribable emotions as I felt myself slipping into the rhythm. Then the tempo increased yet again, and I felt rage. Pure, unbridled rage. A fury unlike any other. My consciousness fluttered, and I saw myself in that alleyway again, and the deminean who stared at me now with those hateful faces wore the same expression as those two men had back then.

They would die as well.

I turned and saw Crux's knife lift in the air on its own. Like a hummingbird in flight, it flitted in the space as if held by an invisible figure. Hovering as it was, it caught the light in such a way that made the white glow seem as bright as the sun.

Like a flash of lightning, the knife was suddenly gone, and I heard a deminean off in the distance scream in pain.

I shoved down my rage, which was now overflowing like a cup with too much liquid poured into it. The act of doing so threatened to send me to the floor as the pounding music compelled me to violence. I took one solid strike on the boulder next to me and felt the rock crack beneath my blow. With the rage slightly subsided, I forced myself to look for Crux.

I found him on his feet in the clearing, struggling with the deminean leader in mutual combat. The leader casually lifted Crux off the ground, throttling him in the air.

I saw the knife buried deep in the chest of one of the deminean warriors who had held Crux before. They looked dead with their wide-eyed stare, stuck motionless toward the sky. The leader spared a glance for his fallen comrade, screamed, and threw Crux against a tree. Small splinters of wood broke free as Crux's back slammed into it.

I roared my fury, finally giving into the music as I charged with nothing but my bare fists.

The soldiers themselves appeared to be frothing with rage, and, to my surprise, they fought blindly against each other. Two of them landed blow after blow on one of their unconscious comrades before ultimately turning on each other. Fighting littered the clearing, but it was deminean against deminean.

Ally against ally.

The leader held his head, trying to resist the anger the music prompted. I had trouble keeping it at bay myself, but the only thing that concerned me more than killing all in the clearing was saving Crux.

The man laid against a tree, holding his limp right wrist in his left hand. As his eyes fell upon me, he dropped his limp wrist and signaled for me to run with his good arm.

But I couldn't run.

To my horror, I realized my body was no longer my own. The music guided me to its will now.

I saw the leader shake his head and stare at me before turning to face Pipar. The satyr danced merrily upon his log, twirling around and around as his pipes burst forth with the all-consuming song. Pipar appeared happy as he spun, mindless of the destruction he brought with his tune.

The deminean leader attacked him.

Pipar, so enthralled in his playing, did not notice as the leader reached for his leg to drag him off the log.

I surged into action.

As the leader's hand seized the satyr's right hoof, I pulled life into me, just as I had done in the alleyway, and focused all my strength as I rammed the leader with my shoulder. He flew forward into the log, hitting it and sending a crack that splintered it completely in half.

This shift caused Pipar to look down, and he jumped from the leader's reach and out of my sight. My strength held as the leader tried to throw me from his back. Drawing more air into my lungs, I grabbed the leader's collar, and the man's body lifted off the ground as I threw him toward his companions. He came down, crashing and tumbling before one of the other deminean used their own body to catch him, taking the brunt of his weight for themselves.

The music had stopped, and the soldiers were slowly recovering from their blood rage. The infighting had significantly weakened them, but like experienced warriors, they formed up ranks, pulling out a multitude of small weaponry.

As they rearmed themselves, there was an uneasy look in their eyes, and they nervously glanced between their injured comrades. The comrades they themselves had harmed.

"Vi'eri is under my protection," Pipar announced. I turned and looked up to realize he had taken a seated position atop the log again. He looked majestic on his wooded throne. "You are to leave the woodlands. Tell your kind they are not welcome here. Know your place, deminean. Glory to Anduinna, and to the collective."

The leader seethed in anger, but after a moment, said, "Retreat, for now. And girl..." I turned to face him and his golden eyes were cold fury.

Dangerous, like a poison-tipped blade. But after a moment of staring, his mouth curled up, and a sinister grin creased his face. "I want you to know. Your mother is dead."

The deminean recovered their fallen, giving Crux, Pipar and myself a wide berth as they left the clearing, back where they had come before.

My body felt heavy and my legs shook before my knees gave out completely. I fell to the floor and put my hands to my face, barely holding the tears back. I wanted to scream—to wail my misery for all to hear. My mother was gone. Dead...

Because of me.

Then the sound of Pipar's pipe started again. This time, as he played my name's song, it was mellow. Soft...like the gentleness of a babbling brook or the light rustle of leaves on a spring day. It drowned my sorrow in its symphony.

I forced myself to stand and address Pipar, whispering, "Thank you."

Pipar stopped playing his music and faced me. "No," he replied. "Thank you, child. You risked yourself to save me."

"You saved me—us, first."

Pipar shook his head, and his red fur shook off condensation. Light beads of dew glinted through the air, dissipating into mist. "A good deed for a good deed, but it is I who still feels in your debt. For if these deminean would have found me alone, surely as you stand before me, they would have slain me. They can be...remarkably difficult to kill, you see. As you must already know."

"Then we are even?"

"We are not," Pipar replied with some agitation in his voice. "Name something I can give you, child, and it will be yours. Anything in my power, as my soul is bound to Anduinna, I will grant it to you."

I pondered the decision for a moment. This felt like a story from a fairy tale. I speculated if that made me the princess of said story, receiving a boon after a good deed? I looked to Crux, who still sat at the base of the tree, trying to splint his wrist with a broken branch and some cloth.

"Mother's horn," I said.

The satyr looked at me, and his gaze abruptly turned to fury and then to sadness. An eternal looking sadness.

"What did you say?" Pipar asked, the words coming breathlessly.

I hesitated, but knowing I could not recall the words, I repeated, "Mother's horn... That's why we're here. We heard you have a keepsake known as mother's horn and we were wondering if you could part with it. But if it's too much trouble..." I let my words trail off, not knowing what else to add.

Pipar wiped a tear from his black eyes. A single tear. With a look of regret, he looked down upon his pipe, white as the first snow of winter, and jumped down off the log. "Take it, child," he said, proffering the pipe to me.

"*This—*" A sharp intake of breath stopped my words, and I put my hands to my mouth to hide my shocked expression. Through my fingers I whispered, "This is the mother's horn? Your pipe?"

Pipar nodded, and he stared down at the mother's horn, looking at it as if it were the most valuable treasure in the world. "I would have you listen to a story first, if that pleases?"

I looked to Crux who was now leaning against the tree, stance casual, but the knife still in his good hand. He nodded in agreement.

"Please," I said and realized I was sobbing. Tears ran trails down both of my cheeks.

Pipar smiled at me. A genuine smile that pained me to my very soul. He reached out with his long black nail and let my tears roll upon it. He turned, leaning against the log, and said, "I was not always the keeper of this forest. Once, when I was but a child, such as yourself, my mother taught me the way of the song. The language of the satyr. Eventually, my mother passed, as Anduinna wills it for all beings, and with that, I received my mother's horn." Pipar presented it out in his hand and a gleam of light caught its edge, making it appear radiant. "When a satyr dies, their horn or horns detach, and the color bleeds from it. From that, we make the mother's horn, or, as you call it, a musical pipe."

Slowly, Pipar stepped forward and took my hand in his. His long black nails looked razor sharp, and he had to kneel low to face me.

"I do not blame you for what you do not know," Pipar said. "But this...the pain is just too great. Therefore, I banish you from this forest—for your sake. Let me see neither of you again, or I will surely use the opportunity to recover what I hold most dearly." He dropped the horn into my hand.

"No!" I protested. "Take it back—take it back—take it..." I reached forward and embraced the satyr in a hug. My arms barely reached his back.

"I cannot take it back. As my breath commands power in song, my word commands power in myself. I cannot break this promise, even if you would turn it away now." Pipar stood and casually climbed back on top of the log, staring longingly into the pond below.

I wanted to say something—anything. But the words...they would not come. I felt as if I had taken his mother away from him.

As if I had killed her myself.

I looked to Crux, who eyed Pipar with worry and sorrow. He also felt for the creature. I walked toward him and we wordlessly left the clearing together, having nothing more to add.

At first, the only sound was the soft rustling of the leaves beneath our feet. Then, after a small time of traveling, a voice rode the wind to our ears. It was low at first, but overtime, it grew and grew until the entire forest swelled with it.

It was pure agony.

My eyes poured tears so heavily I had to stop and, to my surprise, Crux put his head in his hands and wailed. Pipar shared his pain with us, and I could not decide if it was a gift or a curse. The strength of his emotions was akin to trying to catch a waterfall with a bucket.

Unable to move, we stayed that way for a time in shared misery.

Eventually, Crux recovered, reaching his hand over me to provide what little support he could. He prompted me and we both walked out of the forest together with heavier hearts.

In this telling of Pipar the piper, I would have it known that his final song was not my name song, but something else entirely. It was his mother's song, sung by a creature that had borne the burden of her death twice over. It was a song of seasons spent without the one you loved, lost to time.

I called the song:

Mother's Lament.

Chapter Ten
NEW PROMISES

As we left the forest, hearts still heavy, the power of the satyr's song slowly diminished, but it left me with no peace. The deminean leader's proclamation flayed me.

"Crux. My mother—"

"Not here. Not now," Crux shushed me, pressing his finger to his bearded lips. "We have much to discuss, Vi'eri, but now is not the place. Come, let's hurry back to the tavern, where it's safe. At least, I think it'll be safe for a time."

Reluctantly, I let him lead me back into town. We cut directly through the farmers' fields and Crux gave one man a rude gesture when he waved his rake at us threateningly.

Our pace quickened and quickened until we were nearly running into the town. Around every corner, Crux would look out carefully, searching for any deminean that may be waiting.

We found none.

We entered the tavern and Crux looked to put on a show of it, strutting along like the world belonged to him. Like nothing could spoil this perfect day.

He had mentioned we needed to keep up appearances, lest someone get the wrong idea and report us to a guard, but I was awkward about it. I held my head low, not having the stomach for the charade, and my feet shuffled like a child who had taken a whooping for being disobedient.

The townsfolk who sat and drank looked at us strangely. Not the attention we wished to acquire.

We strode to the bar as if nothing was wrong, and Jezza greeted us warmly. Upon seeing my face, she saw through the charade and shot Crux a glare that could kill a man. He raised his hands in a mock surrender, but she glared up into his eyes judgingly.

Jezza placed a small cup in front of me as Crux and I took two seats at the bar.

"Don't worry," she said in a sickly-sweet voice, almost masking her heavy country accent. "It's just some warm cider. My parents always told me warm cider makes everything a scant bit better. I even added a bit of cinnamon for you."

I didn't feel like drinking—I didn't even think I deserved to be happy. Still, the way Jezza stared at me expectantly made me feel guilty, so I raised the cup to my lips and drank deeply.

The warmness felt good in my body as it traveled downward. The cinnamon danced on my tongue, sending my tastebuds for a twirl. I exhaled audibly, setting the cup down.

Jezza smiled at me as she leaned her elbows on the bar. "Well?"

I nodded. "It's good."

"That's wonderful, sweet child," she replied, her smile widening. Suddenly, she turned to Crux, who sipped at a mug of sour smelling liquid, unwilling to meet Jezza's gaze. "You. The back. Now!"

Crux sighed, but offered no complaint as he stood and downed the rest of his drink. He set the mug down and his knife beside it, hilt facing me. "Just in case you need it," he whispered in my ear, casting his gaze around the room as he walked into the back through a swinging wooden door.

Jezza placed her hand on my shoulder reassuringly and followed right after him.

Immediately, I could hear them both yelling, which made me wonder why they had even bothered leaving the front of the tavern, seeing as at least a few of the patrons could hear the racket, muddled as it was.

I stepped off the stool and crept toward the door, leaning up against the wall, listening.

Jezza spoke first. "What happened, Crux? I've known you long enough to know when you are knee deep in shit. And I could smell it the second you both left that purgatory, forsaken forest."

"Not a very ladylike manner of speaking, Jezza," Crux replied.

"Shut it—this is serious! Now, I need you to tell me *exactly* what happened or I swear I'll go to the deminean and tell them all about your side dealings."

"Jezza..." Crux tried to speak in a soothing voice, but a sudden crash indicated that she had thrown something at him. "You're right. You're right," he relented.

He proceeded to tell Jezza of our mishaps through the Bloodsoaked Forest, omitting quite a few missteps by himself. He did, however, speak of the deminean who had attacked us and of Pipar the satyr.

"By the Well, Crux," Jezza said, her voice wavering. "What a mess this is. Are you sure they were after Vi'eri? What possible reason could there be for them to go to such lengths for one little human girl? Have you spoken to her about it yet?"

"No," Crux admitted. "And there is something else. The girl is some sort of enchanter, like me. Her power is unharnessed, of course—having had no training." He paused, as if considering if he should say more. Eventually, he added, "She manhandled a deminean warrior like he was but a little doll. It was incredible, Jezza, you should have seen it!"

There was a pause for a moment before Jezza responded, "And you shouldn't have! *Shit!* Piss and shit. Damn your soul to purgatory, Crux!" There was a loud crash of flung pots and pans. "You really stepped in it this time. I made a life here—one away from your gambling and schemes. Why did you drop this shit on me? Have you learned nothing from your past?"

"Jezza I—"

"Save it," she interrupted. "It's done. Obviously, the deminean know of the girl's power and they either want it or fear it enough to come after her. What will you do?"

"I don't know," Crux replied. "But there is one more thing."

"Something else? Great, what is it?"

"The girl's mother. I promised I would take her back to find her in Elklan. But that was before. The leader said that her mother is dead. The situation seemed so…personal. Like he enjoyed the thought of telling such a young girl the heartbreaking news. Damn heartless. Either way, there is no life to be had there. Not for her."

Hearing him acknowledge my mother's death was like an arrow in the heart. I turned away and slid down the edge of the wall with my back to sit propped on the floor. I put my face in my hands as if I could hide from the truth.

I couldn't.

I teetered on the edge of calamity, rocking back and forth and lightly tapping the back of my head off the wall. I wanted to cry…

I wanted to scream.

"Oh, Vi'eri." Jezza's voice roused me as I looked up to see her horrified face.

"What's wrong—" Crux's words cut off as he looked at me, his face twisting into horror. "Why did you do this, Vi'eri?"

I looked down at my hands and realized they were red with blood. Deep under my nails, small bits of my own skin clung lifelessly. But I didn't care—no amount of physical pain could ever compare to what I felt inside.

"Crux?" I asked, forcing him to meet my gaze. "Is she really dead?"

"Is who really dead?" he replied. I stared at him as if my eyes could pierce his very soul. He disassociated. Eventually, he gave way to me and replied, "I don't know, Vi'eri. Truly I don't. But what I do know is this: alive or dead, you cannot go back to Elklan. The deminean bastards do not waste their time on one little girl. You're special, as I told you before. And special people wind up used or dead."

"Special," I said the words musingly. "My mother told me that before, but I don't want to be special."

"We don't get that choice," Jezza chimed in. "And I agree with Crux. You cannot return home—perhaps ever. This will sound cruel, child, but the sooner you accept that as fact, the better your life will go, looking forward."

I felt anger boil in me.

Jezza likely sensed my aggressive attitude and suggested, "Perhaps you can get some rest. It is getting late and your room is still available to you."

"Crux," I said, drawing his attention back to me. "You promised me, right? Come with you and you would bring me home. Do you still hold on to that promise?"

"Eri—"

"*Answer me!* Do you keep your promises? Are you a man?" Crux's silence told me everything I needed to hear. I stood, adding, "Jezza, I'll be gone in the morning. Thank you for your hospitality."

My words were rude, and I knew it, but I couldn't bring myself to care. I shoved past them and stalked to my room, slamming the door shut.

I laid in bed for a time when three knocks rang out from my door. Over and over, the knocks came.

I ignored them until they finally ceased.

In the morning, I climbed out the small window of my second-floor room. Following the gutter on the roof, I found a small patch of grass below. I jumped and rolled onto the landing, green streaks covering my new clothing.

I felt bad for saying nothing as I left, and it was an unfair thing to do, but Crux wasn't willing to help me, so...I would need to help myself.

I knew if I followed the path south-east, it would eventually split off. Then west would bring me to Elklan. I repeated the directions to myself a few more times to commit them to memory. When the townsfolk of

Easthaven considered you more than a vagrant, they could be surprisingly helpful.

I was just on the outskirts of town when I heard a familiar voice call out to me. I turned to look and saw Crux leaning against a tree with his knife out, eating an apple, just as he had been when I first met him.

"You can't do this, Vi'eri," he said. "I've been treating you like a child, but no more. Your mother is likely dead, or, at the very least, fled. Either way, there is nothing for you in Elklan except slavery, death, or worse." He did not mention what the worst could be, adding, "I offer you another choice in replace of my broken promise. You are special, no matter how you wish it otherwise. Let me teach you. Become my ward!"

Crux's words took me aback. I felt a gentle nudging on my emotions that bade me to accept this offer.

I ignored it.

"No," I replied, turning from Crux to continue down the path.

He ran to block me. "Don't be stupid!"

"Move," I warned in as menacing a tone as I could muster.

"Or what?" Crux crossed his arms, standing to his full height. "Don't make me stop you."

With those words, I lost all rational thought. Anger propelled me forward as I breathed in life and blindly charged him like a rabid wolf.

His eyes lifted in surprise as I reached him. I had no idea what I was doing, but I knew that my only way home was through him.

I threw a punch at him, aimed at his gut. It was a pathetic thing that he easily side-stepped, shoving me to the ground as casually as shooing a fly.

"Again," he said.

Does he think this is some sort of game? I thought, driving me to more anger.

I picked up sand and threw it into his eyes. He cursed, raising his hands to block it, and I kicked him in the groin with all my might.

Crux let out an audible grunt, falling to his knees, hands clutching at the front of his pants.

"You. Little. Bitch," he said through stiff breaths.

As I tried to run past him, his arm reached out, seizing me by the wrist. He pulled me back, lifting me off the ground and the next thing I knew, my body hit the solid earth. Air drove from my body in an instant, leaving me breathless and writhing on the ground.

Then, Crux's hand wrapped around my throat and he whispered through clenched teeth, "You think me strong? You've seen nothing. Deminean have magic beyond us humans and as much as it pains me, they are stronger by far." His grip seemed to get tighter to emphasize his point. "So, do you think you have a chance if you can't even beat me?"

Crux stood, holding me straight out by my neck, as if I were a kitten held in its mother's mouth. I flailed against it, scratching at his muscular arms, but my feeble attacks did nothing. I felt life draining out of me and as it did, a peace threatened to take its place.

I rejected that peace.

With one final bit of effort, I grabbed both his hands with mine. Light shone from underneath my gloves as his fingers slowly gave way to me. I breathed, pulled my legs up to my chest, and kicked forward, catching him squarely in the chest.

Crux's body flew away from me and he landed on his back, sliding a few steps away.

I fell to the earth, landing flat on my back. I was so tired that I dared not move.

After a time, I slowly lifted my head, and the world spun. I turned to the side and wretched in the dirt, then I rolled the other way, putting my back to the mess and closed my eyes against a pounding headache.

I heard Crux groan in pain first; it sounded like a beast more than a man. Then, a soft rustling of the shifting of earth and I opened my eyes to see him standing over me.

He opened his mouth to speak, but instead, sat in the dirt beside me. Slowly, he reached into his pocket and pulled out the mother's horn.

My eyes went wide as he put the pipe to his lips and blew.

He played terribly. The notes foreign and wrong, especially compared to the pipe's true owner. Still, hearing the soft off-key music eased some of my frustration.

I forced myself to sit up, and Crux lowered the pipe. He just smiled at me before saying, "Let me teach you, Eri. Don't be like me. Don't throw your life away for nothing."

The tears fell down my cheek, and I couldn't make them stop. I pictured my mother's face, fixing it in a small box of precious memories in my mind, and agreed with a nod of my head.

THE MARCH TOWARDS OBLIVION

For the power of the hybrid will be two-fold. They will take from the deminean the magic of self and, in turn, degrade its power. From the human's, the hybrid shall receive one of their lesser magics and, in turn, elevate it as it melds freely in blood with its greater counterpart.

Unknown Seer, a leger from The Destined Scrolls.

As the hybrid grows, so shall their power. If the hybrid rises to challenge the Ri'sha for the title of Sovereign, they must be eliminated.

Ri'sha Sovereign Krottik of clan Drekhide, declaration addendum to Seer foretelling in The Destined Scrolls.

A frigid wind blew, sending a chill down Vi'eri's spine. "Perhaps that's enough for tonight," she said, focusing her gaze on Ax.

The young man looked as if he would protest, but yawned instead, casually stretching his arms above his head. Reluctantly, he nodded in agreement. "I suppose we should get some rest, eh Kasu?"

Surprisingly, Kasu looked to be dismayed by the situation.

"Are you alright, Kasu?" Vi'eri asked.

"It was just gettin' good, is all," she replied in a voice fit for a mouse. "But I could use some sleep."

"Mind putting that out?" Ax said as he stood, stretching his legs. His knees made a small pop in response, and he let out an audible sigh.

Kasu looked up at Ax with admiration plain in her eyes. She cared deeply for him—perhaps even loved him. From his stark indifference, she guessed he hadn't even noticed.

You purposefully left some of the story out, Vulana spoke into her mind. *I rescued you far more times than you gave me credit.*

Vi'eri scoffed. *I'm sure you did, but it was I who did all the heavy lifting while you rode in the back of my mind.*

I saved you from the Life Incarnate.

And I gave you credit for that! Vi'eri countered. Just then, she recognized the shade pushing agitation into her and she forced it back.

Careful with that, Vulana. Remember the last time we shared too much emotion?

Her shade looked oddly hurt by the comment. *Perhaps rest would be best for all*, Vulana replied sullenly. *I suppose I'll 'ride the back of your mind,' for a time.*

Vulana— And just like that, he was gone. *I'm sorry.* She pushed the thought far, but received no answer of acknowledgement.

"Ri'sha Sovereign?" Kasu said.

Vi'eri was brought back suddenly and realized the girl had been standing over her. The girl looked concerned. "Yes, what is it?" she asked.

"I wanted to thank you for the story, and I hoped that I would be welcomed back tomorrow as well?"

She scratched at the scales on her back. "I... That would be fine, Kasu. But what changed your mind? You didn't appear too eager before."

Kasu stood still for a moment, as if pondering whether to reveal an important piece of information. Eventually, she relented, saying, "It's my mother... I lost her as well. So when you spoke of yours and what you went through. Well, I realized that maybe you aren't so different from us." Kasu flushed, adding, "Are you?"

"I am," Vi'eri replied. The girl frowned at her words, and she added, "But not in the way you mean. I breathe, I eat...I piss. But most importantly, I love. So in the manner in which you speak, no, I'm not so different."

Kasu grinned, and she noticed that she too was missing a front tooth. She tucked that piece of information away for later and then chastised herself for it.

Why am I bothering with trying to make these humans like me? she thought. *It hasn't bothered me in such a long time. Why does it now?*

Because you're getting old, Vulana replied. She sent discontent back to him and found nothing.

Pesky shade.

She felt the slight pull of magic as Kasu doused the fire with a splash of water that formed as a small ball above the embers. She stood and stretched, feeling old battle wounds pull uncomfortably.

"Can I march with you tomorrow?" Ax asked, moving to stand in front of her.

She looked down at the young man, much shorter than she was. He was just so...human; the way he spoke, his abrupt honesty. Ax rekindled a light that had long died in her. Hope for a brighter tomorrow.

"Yes..." she whispered, trying not to choke on her words. "Let us march toward oblivion...together."

The lad's face broke out in a grin. "Great! I'll see you tomorrow." He turned abruptly, and then spun back around to add, "Ri'sha Sovereign."

"Eri," she replied. "You can call me Eri."

Ax smiled wider and ran off. Kasu muttered a wordless apology as she followed shortly on his heel. Seeing them go reminded her of what she was fighting for. It was the reason that she still existed in a realm that was far too small for someone such as her.

The lights of the camps dwindled and the stars burst alight in full glory. Makeshift tents littered the grounds, and all found their way inside.

But not her.

She found a soft patch of grass and laid, staring upward at the unending glory of a sky full of stars. Each twinkle of a light spoke of a different realm with a unique set of rules. Perhaps, up there, she wouldn't be so special.

Perhaps there, she could be at peace.

The chill wind once again blew, and she pulled the free-flowing magic from the in-between, using it to increase her body temperature. The chill wind now felt as tame as if it were in the middle of spring.

She let the wind drift around her, remembering simpler times as she slept.

Vi'eri awoke the next morning well rested—more rested than she had felt in a long time. For once, the nightmares did not hound her.

She stood and bent her knees, working the joints of her aging body. It was still early, and the dim sun of winter sent its rays cascading down the mouth of a valley sprawled out in front of her.

"Mornin'," a familiar voice said, catching her by surprise. She turned to find Ax as plucky as ever, running a hand through his wet brown hair. "Figured I could do with a small bath if I'm going to travel side by side with the *Sovereign*."

Vi'eri snorted. "I've had my sense of smell dimmed for weeks now."

"You can do that?"

"All deminean can. To varying degrees, of course," she replied. "Deminean have the power of self. An internal magic. Using the magic that exists between all things, they can alter their bodies in minor ways, and sometimes, in not so minor ways."

Ax looked on with amazement on his face, asking, "So I could make myself more handsome if I were a deminean?"

"Nobody could fix that face," Kasu replied, balancing three bowls in her hands. Ax snorted, but Kasu added, "Aren't you going to help me?"

He moved to her side, grabbing a bowl just before it slid out of the girl's hand. He turned, handing her a bowl of 'soup,' and she tried not to think about what was actually in it.

They all ate in relative silence, but every once in a while, she would catch Kasu staring at Ax. Kasu's eyes wandered on her, and she gave her a sidelong glance that said that she knew exactly how the girl felt. Kasu flushed, but could not keep her eyes from the boy she loved.

Ax tore through his food with ease, hardly taking the time to chew. The young man really was blind to Kasu's advances, and she suspected Kasu would move to more promising pastures if Ax didn't catch the hint soon.

"Ri'sha Sovereign," a deminean woman said, saluting in the traditional deminean honor address of placing both forearms together, blocking the face with the palm-side of the hands. "If it pleases, I've already relayed the order that we will march soon."

"That's fine, Akkora," she replied.

"So," Ax preempted, "if that's taken care of, can you continue on with the story? It was just gettin' good."

Kasu nodded her approval, and Akkora looked at her questioningly, her golden deminean eyes going bright with wonder.

"Story?" Akkora asked.

"It's nothing," Vi'eri replied, heat touching her cheeks. Even at her age, she was still able to feel embarrassed.

Ax thumped his chest with his right arm. "Eri is telling us a tale!" he said emphatically.

"Eri?" Akkora laughed. "Is that so? Well, I think I too would like to hear it as well. If that pleases...*Eri?*"

Vi'eri shot her second a warning glance and Akkora turned from her, but she could still see the outline of a smirk at the corner of the woman's lips.

"If you insist," she said. Standing and looking out over the valley, she added, "As I left off yesterday, I had agreed to allow Crux to train me…"

Chapter Twelve

PORT WHITELINE

Whiteline has become the most prominent port of the north. Just south of the Soaring Isles, it provides a safe haven for all travelers looking to unload their wares from the more frigid north. Ri'sha Isodros, despite her waning popularity in high deminean society, has the love of not only her deminean brethren of Whiteline, but of the humans who serve under her as well.

Atlura Exl, from a letter to Ri'sha Sovereign Dem'i Krottik of Clan Drekhide.

I set my feet to the dirt, hands on my hips. "We have been traveling for three days now. Are we there yet?"

Crux rolled his eyes at me. "If I knew you'd gripe so much, I would have let you go back to Elklan. Besides," he took a quick huff of his pipe, "you're the young one! Try being thirty years old and then complain to me about traveling."

"Forty, you mean?"

"Watch it," Crux replied, pointing the stem of his pipe at me. "If you're going to join my mercenary band, then you're going to have to be a lot tougher than this."

I stared at Crux, not hiding my shocked expression. "Mercenary band?" I asked.

"Ay, Mercenary company: Crux's Crew. Has a nice ring to it, eh?" I shrugged my shoulders, and he waved his hand at me dismissively, adding, "Eh, what would you know?"

He turned and continued to walk down the dirt strewn road.

My feet were sore, and I was tired. I didn't want to admit it to Crux, but our fight on the outskirts of Easthaven had left me exhausted. Far more than I would have thought.

The scales on the edges of my hands itched terribly and when I checked, hiding them from Crux's view, there was a noticeable amount more than before. Worse, they almost crested the top of the gloves. I made a mental note that I would need to get a larger pair when we got to our location...

Wherever that was.

As mentioned, we had walked for three days to meet his handler. According to Crux, he was a greasy, portly man who dressed far above his actual station. And for some reason, this man had connections with some well-to-do deminean citizens.

"Our destination is the port town of Whiteline," he announced. "You should be excited. A young girl like you should love it! It's known for the almost translucent shells that wash upon its pure white sand. It really is a sight to see, Eri. Maybe you can make yourself a necklace, or whatever little girls like you do." He turned and gave me a sickening grin.

I shook my head at him and felt like I could hear a small laugh off in the distance of my mind.

After a time, the midday sun blazed down on us with an unrelenting intensity. The mellow spring sun gave way to the heat of summer.

"Let's rest a moment," Crux said as he moved off the side of the road to take shelter in the shade of a rather large tree.

"Finally!" I complained, dragging myself to the other side of the tree and dropping to the earth. "By the Well, my feet are covered in blisters. How do you walk in these leather boots all the time?"

"You get used to them," Crux replied, standing over me. "Not so fast. You don't get to rest yet. Let's continue your training."

"Again? It's clear to me that I am not one of those so-called 'enchanters' you keep speaking of."

Crux rubbed at his facial scar irritably. "We've gone through this, Eri. What else could it be? I've seen you twice now perform feats well out of the reach of some of your...stature."

I eyed him curiously. "A woman?"

"A girl," Crux amended. "A small built girl at that. Some of the strongest fighters I've ever known have been women. Always remember, Eri, raw physical strength can only get you so far, and that's before contending with destroyers and enchanters."

"What about the deminean?"

"That's another tale entirely. They have the strength of the beasts in them. Why do you think this realm is the way it is?" He nodded at his own words and added, "But the Well blesses us humans above the deminean and they know it. Soon, our numbers will trivialize theirs and then... Well, enough for now."

"No, wait," I protested. "How soon will this happen? Do you know?"

Crux crouched over me, leaning his arm against the tree. "Not in my lifetime, and likely not in yours, either. But soon. As the souls return, the Well seems less and less inclined to grant the deminean new souls and their women have trouble conceiving. Do you know that a deminean woman cannot conceive without the Well granting a soul first? Not sure how they manage that. Has something to do with them requiring magic to live."

"And humans can?"

"Yes," Crux said with a scowl. "But it is more of a curse, really. While the Well has given humans more souls than deminean, any human born without a soul is...wrong. I've heard they do things to the surrounding space—something unnatural. A draining, if you will. Every soulless born dulls the realm's light."

"And what happens to them?"

Crux scowled. "Enough! I know what you're doing, Eri. Come, stand. And take off your gloves this time."

He reached out to grab my hand to pull me up. I pulled my hands to my chest as if to shield them. "No!"

"Why must you be... Ugh, fine—have it your way! Remember, it's always easier to enchant an item with the touch of bare skin. So you're hindering yourself with this nonsense."

"That's fine," I replied. In truth, I cared little for these lessons, but I had enjoyed learning everything else Crux had to teach. So, reluctantly, I continued to put up with them.

"For this test, I just want you to try learn the enchantment," Crux said as he pulled his knife from its sheath. The magic glided off it, like a soft white wave of power surrounding the entire weapon.

I took it in my hands and looked at Crux with anticipation.

"Try to draw in its magic while leaving out everything else," he explained.

I did so, pulling a full breath of air as I tried. It was like attempting to breathe underwater, and I was only able to pull small bits of magic from the white mist that fell from the knife. In other words, impossible. Still, I pulled and pulled until I could not draw anymore. I choked and exhaled in a raspy cough.

"Again!" Crux demanded.

I rolled my eyes at him defiantly, but tried again to the same effect.

He frowned at me as I wiped the sweat from my forehead. "I don't understand what the problem is. I've seen you do this before. Dredging an enchantment is the first skill we learn to do. The actual enchantment is the hard part. Are you sure you can't just take your gloves—"

"No!" I snapped, finally having enough.

"Ugh!" he said, shaking his head at me. "Well, I'm feeling less confident in my abilities to teach you. Usually children start at a younger age, so maybe you are stunted? It could be your…" Crux paused for a moment, looking as if he internally chastised himself, adding, "predicament."

"Maybe I'm just not cut out for it?" I offered.

"It's in your soul—you cannot simply shut it down. If the magic exists, then it will edge you toward using it. If you're not trained properly, well, let's say that bad things can happen when you let those with untapped magic use their powers untamed. Not to mention the deminean who will find cause to exterminate a human who poses even a miniscule threat."

Crux seemed to ponder his own words for a time, and a cool wind blew refreshing gusts against us. I sat and leaned my head back against the base of the tree and let myself be lost in the wind's gentle kiss. My ashen hair blew carelessly around me, tickling the nape of my neck.

He boorishly continued on with the conversation. "I think you can only use your powers when your blood is running fierce."

"Can we talk about something else?" I kept my eyes closed.

"I suppose—for now. But I don't want you to think you've gotten out of training. I will break this damnable wall you put in front of your powers. Well bless me, I will."

I let the wind drown out the rest of Crux's words, now actively trying to lose myself in it. It would be so easy to let go. Like this, suspended in the nothingness at the edge of sleep, everything felt so much…easier.

"Let's go!"

Crux's words jolted me awake, and the shadows of the leaves were in a different place than before.

"How long did I sleep?" I asked, rubbing my eyes.

"Not too long," Crux replied, "but I figured you deserved some rest. Remember this when you think I am cruel for pushing you so. I only have your best interests at heart."

I stared into his earnest green eyes and replied, "I know."

I stood and faced our destination. North-east to the Port town of Whiteline. It couldn't come fast enough.

As we moved closer to the Port of Whiteline, the crowds of humans became larger and larger until the road we traveled on was completely full of horses, cattle, and both human and deminean. The humans gave their deminean overlords an ample amount of leeway, as most shied away from standing too close or obstructing their path.

I ground my teeth at the sight of it.

"Here it is!" Crux said, breaking me from my anger. I noticed a certain weariness had drained from his normal tenor. "The port town of Whiteline and the new home of Crux's Crew."

"Are you still on that?" I asked. "Crux's Crew. Your new mercenary group. What exactly does a mercenary group do?"

"Jobs, of course." He turned his gaze on me as if I had just asked the dumbest question he had ever heard. "Jobs typically go easier with more people, which is why mercenaries start such groups. It also allows them to take bigger and more dangerous jobs... At a premium, of course."

"Premium? So you do this solely for coin?" I replied, judgingly. He merely smiled at me in response and I added, "Well, what kind of jobs then?"

"Any, I suppose. Nothing illegal, of course. Well, nothing *too* illegal." I shot him a sidelong glance, and he smirked. "Don't worry your pretty head. I won't put *you* in any danger. Besides, if you can master your enchanting, then I fear for any who get in your way."

"And what about you?" I asked. When Crux's face changed to a look of confusion, I added, "You're an enchanter too, isn't that right? What about your powers? Aren't you powerful as well? To make a knife do your bidding by thought alone seems like a powerful enchantment to me."

He looked uneasy for a moment, and a few humans grumbled curses as they parted around us. "Yes, I made the trueblade. More helped, really. It's a really long story, Eri. Perhaps another time—"

"It's always 'another time' when I ask about your past," I replied. "You know my secrets. Maybe try sharing some of yours." I knew my words were a lie, but I was indignant that he still kept so much from me. I felt like we had gotten closer in the few days we had traveled together, but there was still a wall between us, and I knew he sensed it, too.

Crux smiled and placed his arm around me, pulling me into an embrace. "That's why I like you, Eri. Always ready to call me out on my shit. You remind me a lot of Jezza, you know. Well help me. Come now, let's go meet my broker."

I noted that he avoided my question as he continued on, ignoring my protests.

We moved quickly through the city, and I had little time to garner my bearings as we sifted from alleyway to alleyway, crossing primary thoroughfares, dodging around the crowds of deminean and humans alike.

Setting itself apart from Elklan, Port Whiteline hosted far more patrons than I had ever seen in one place before. And yes, while humans gave preference to the roads to the deminean, the fact that they shared the space was something I was wholly unused to.

I could see the ocean in the distance. It was the first time I had ever seen it. The vastness of it filled me with a new sense of wonder, and I couldn't help but think of how grand it would be to set sail to new and unexplored lands, like in old stories my mother would read to me.

Crux, during my wanderlust, had made his way across a particularly busy street, turning back toward me to wave irritably.

I looked from left to right, judged my path, and moved. Dodging a horse-drawn cart, I slid between two humans holding hands, narrowly dodged an elderly woman with a cane and ran headlong into someone, knocking me to the ground.

The sun's glare caught my eye as I looked up, and I squinted, placing my hand in front of my face to block it. As my eyes focused, I saw a figure...

A tall figure.

A deminean woman with a single long horn in the middle of her head stood in front of me looming, a look of utter disgrace upon her face.

Two deminean men stood beside her side. Both held a shocked expression.

One spoke, saying, "Human! How dare you touch a Ri'sha with your filthy human body!" The disgust in the man's voice was evident, and he wiped at his clothes as if I were a diseased leper.

I turned away and noticed others in the busy street had ceased in their constant movement, shying away from the incident before them.

"Apologies Dem'i Ri'sha," I said awkwardly, placing myself on my hands and knees. With a sickening realization, I remembered a time where I had seen my mother in this exact same position—begging for mercy in front of that deminean tyrant, Kreza. I forced my head lower until it touched the ground and grated my teeth in frustration.

"Leave it," the woman replied, her thick clothes obfuscating her entire body. Her voice carried the tone of command as she added, "The girl is not worth the effort. Not when such a disaster has befallen me."

"Yes, Ri'sha," the two deminean attendees said in unison. Both spared me a quick glare of distrust before moving on. Not a soul on the street moved to help me. Not even Crux. When I looked up to see him, he was at the edge of an alleyway with a look of dismay.

I ran toward him.

"Thanks for the help," I said, not hiding my annoyance as we both continued at a slower pace.

"And what would you have me do? Out of all the people you can run into, you run into the only damnable Ri'sha in Whiteline? You have the worst luck. Do you know that?"

I nodded in agreement. "I do," I mumbled, more to myself than as a response to his question.

As we moved closer to the ocean, we quickly found ourselves at some type of warehouse. Outside the white painted building, gulls squealed and fought over various foodstuffs from a fallen box that a dock worker must have dropped from the morning load. Quite the rare treasure for a bird.

Crux performed an intricate knock on an entrance to the warehouse, paying little mind to anything else.

As we waited, the potent smell of the sea brushed against me. It made me feel ill. All thoughts of taking a voyage in the vast blue fled me as I pushed back the bile that burned my stomach. The glistening waves of the ocean made me feel queasy as I watched them roll endlessly onto shore, only to be swallowed back by the ocean again.

The slow churning of time.

"Are you alright?" Crux asked, likely noticing my sickly appearance.

I didn't trust myself to answer as I swallowed a mouthful of vomit. I gave the lightest of head nods and, to my relief, the warehouse door swung open. I didn't even see who had opened it before I ran inside, pushing past a round man to escape that disgusting smell.

The air in the warehouse was stale, but at least it didn't have that...scent. There was something about the freshness of the rank water outside that made me want to gag. Even thinking about it threatened to turn my stomach into knots. Slowly, it settled and returned to normal as I breathed a sigh of relief.

"Ain't you a firecracker?" an unknown voice said from behind me, causing me to almost jump out of my skin.

I turned to find myself face to face with a portly-looking fellow. He dressed fancily, if fancily was being dressed in clothes that obviously belonged to someone else. The burgundy overcoat he wore near tore at the seams of his bulbous stomach, and the man's pinstriped pants looked like they belonged to a man half his size. The man appeared as if someone had put the topside of a heavyset man on top of a skinny man's legs.

He looked utterly ridiculous.

The man took his hat off, a rather large black top hat that completed his strange costume, and bowed deeply with a swing of his arm. "Allow me to introduce myself," he said. "My name is Bezur Pesh. At your service, miss..."

I stared at him for a moment and he remained low in the bow, looking at me and gesturing with his hand. Realizing my mistake, I said, "Oh! Vi'eri. Nice to meet you!"

"Just Vi'eri?"

I shrugged my shoulders at him, and Bezur turned to Crux.

"Long story," he said, scratching at his scar.

"Sounds like it. Well, I know you are a busy man, so should we get to it?"

"Gladly," Crux replied with a renewed vigor.

"To my office then."

We followed Bezur through the warehouse and to his office at the building's rear. It was like a maze built with wooden shipping boxes. The boxes had handwritten messages that were scribbled so poorly I couldn't make out even a single letter.

The portly man led us effortlessly through the labyrinth, clearly skilled in its navigation, until we met a small office fit for two at most. We packed in and Bezur sat behind a small desk in the corner.

"So. The mother's horn, if I am not mistaken. That was the job?"

"Aye," Crux answered.

"And you have it?"

Crux produced the white horn hidden in his coat with a flourish, unwrapping the cloth that bound it slowly as if revealing a grand treasure. Bezur's eyes lit up at the sight.

"You actually did it! You're insane, Crux Trueblade. Truly mad."

"Insanely rich is what I hoped you were going to say," he replied with a sly grin.

I suddenly became very angry. *Had this really been what it was all about? The coin?* I had hoped that there was more purpose to the adventure than pure profit. A greater purpose to Pipar's sorrow. But I was to learn, most humans and deminean share a common affliction...

Greed.

Bezur cut off my thoughts as he said, "You would have been, if not for your creditors. This really puts my mind at ease, Crux. I vouched for you! How do you think they would treat me if you had come back empty-handed? I've been so stressed, I could not sleep, except in the arms of—" turning to look at me, he froze, adding, "Perhaps not in the company of such a young girl."

Crux turned to address me. "Could you wait outside, Eri?"

"Why?"

"Because," he explained, "this is a personal matter for me."

I threw my hands up in frustration, shaking my head at him. I opened my mouth to reply, but his stern look gave me pause. I relented, walking outside.

The wooden door closed behind me as soon as I stepped out. I peered around the warehouse and quickly decided that I deserved to know who I was taking lessons from. Who I was trusting. Sneakily, I put my ear to the door and listened in.

The wooden door muffled the sounds far more than I would have thought. I had not considered its thickness, and I felt a slight sensation of urging from deep in my mind. With the next breath I took, I could hear the voices more clearly.

"Don't spend my coin on your whoring—I'm warning you. As for Lithre, you tell the wench that we're even now."

"I hope you don't want me to use those exact words?" Bezur replied.

"Do as you will. As long as you get the promised amount from our buyer."

Just then, the echo of a door sounded throughout the warehouse. I could hear the punctuated, even steps of fighters.

A lot of them.

"Shit," Crux said. "What is this, Bezur?"

I opened the door, saying, "Crux, people are coming!"

"I know, Eri. *Bezur!*" Crux grabbed the man by the front of his coat and shook him.

"I don't know!" the pudgy man replied, sweat beading on his face. "They must be here for you two."

"Crux Trueblade!" a voice boomed out clearly throughout the warehouse. "I am to bring you to Ri'sha Isodros! None shall offer him any shelter!"

All three of us remained as quiet as possible, but then I heard Bezur let out a guttural sneeze.

"Sorry," he whispered.

Crux sighed. "I'm here!" he called back, matching the man's tempo. Slowly, he stepped out of the small room.

We waited until four deminean guardsmen appeared before us. They were armed with swords and wearing heavy looking chainmail.

"Crux, and is there a last name?" one guardsman asked.

"Crux and the title Trueblade are all I have, unfortunately."

"And you?" The deminean guardsman looked toward me. "A little young to be with a gentleman of his years, are you not?"

"It's not like that!" I blurted out indignantly.

"It is as she says," Crux explained. "She is an abandoned human girl who gave me some information I needed, so I took her under my wing. I know what it's like to be an orphan, and I wanted to give back a little, so to speak."

"A mercenary with a heart of gold," the guardsman mused. His compatriots laughed and jostled each other. "Interesting. I suspect Ri'sha Isodros will find you such as well. We are to escort you immediately to her. If you please...not that you have a choice in the matter."

"I figured not," Crux replied, raising his hands in a show of defeat.

The guardsman gestured with his hands to indicate that we should move ahead of them. They closed ranks around us as we did and I spared a glance at Bezur, who stood in the doorway of his office patting the sweat off his brow with a shaking hand.

Crux turned to him. "I'll be back, Bezur. Remember, no whoring."

Chapter Thirteen

RI'SHA

The deminean guardsmen led us through the city proper, and I gaped openly at the large structures that lined the streets. They were built of white marble and the blue of the sea sent light bouncing off the structures, cascading a glittering array of colors across the sky.

Humans and deminean alike stared as our entourage led us down the main thoroughfare toward the largest building at the top of the hill overlooking the rest of Port Whiteline. Horses, carts, humans and deminean all were shoved against the edges of the street as we were led. None would meet our eyes, turning away as if they would be cursed if they but glanced in our direction.

This indifference to our plight from the humans was a stark reminder that they were still just as fearful of their deminean rulers as any other human I had known before.

Is this just the way of things everywhere? I thought to myself sullenly, dragging my feet until one guardsman prompted me to haste with a quick shove.

Out of the corner of my eye, I saw a bread shop with fresh loaves sitting atop a wooden table and I turned toward it, my stomach letting out a sound of protest. Crux looked at me with surprise at first, but then a small smile crept on his face and he stifled a laugh.

The deminean guardsman was not amused by the childish scene, and he quickly shoved me forward. I tripped, hitting the ground hard.

"Don't dawdle, human," he said as I pushed myself upright.

Crux turned toward them, standing nearly as tall with fury in his eyes, but I reached for him, pulling his attention back. I shook my head warningly, and he bit his lip. We kept moving.

This was proving to be a long day.

Dark wooden doors, near black to my eyes, held sketches of past battles carved into it as we approached the largest building in Port Whiteline. Two deminean guards stepped forward to bar our path. With a quick nod from our 'guide,' the guards pulled open the doors to allow us entry. They shoved us through impatiently.

The inside matched the outside in terms of vastness, and it starkly reminded me of olden human fairy tales. Stories of kings and queens that were said to live in lavish buildings overlooking their lands and subjects. A castle, I believe the name was called.

"Are the Ri'sha royalty?" I whispered to Crux.

He looked down at me and seemed to consider my question, scratching at his scar before replying, "I suppose you could say that." When I returned a still curious gaze, he elaborated. "It's more like they are powerful warriors—but that doesn't quite cut it either. They are the most powerful of the deminean. I've heard that—"

Crux's words died as a sword scabbard struck him in the back of the head. The blow was not hard enough to render him unconscious, but rough enough to rattle him and send him to his knees. I moved to help him, but a deminean guard held me back. He held out a hand to me and forced himself up with some effort.

"That is quite unnecessary," a voice rang throughout the enormous chamber, echoing against the various walls with their numerous paintings of great deminean deeds of old. A deminean man in cloth garb with a hood of dark-gray stepped around a swirling white pillar that looked as if it had grown from the ground as opposed to being built by mortal hands. "These two are our guests. Do you wish to upset the Ri'sha with your cruel treatment of her privileged visitors?"

"Apologies, advisor," the guard replied, giving the traditional deminean two-armed salute. "I will remember your words well. Please, I beg your mercy."

"Indeed," the advisor said, casting a sidelong gaze at the guardsmen. They visibly gulped at the advisor's piercing stare; the man's golden eyes drilling into each guard sent a chill down my spine. The advisor broke the glare as he turned back to the guardsman, adding, "Bring them to the conference room. The Ri'sha wishes to meet with them—" Suddenly, the advisor's gaze turned to rest on me and his face flushed with surprise. "Personally."

His words sounded like a threat to my ears—a whisper from the hangman before they pulled the lever.

The guardsmen wasted no time, demanding us to move with a quick-step up the stairs toward our destination.

They placed us in yet another ornate room with a long wooden table at its center. Much like the doors, the wood had been blackened and etched with pictures that were so faded from a time long gone that it was hard for me to tell what they once depicted.

Upon the table, there was finery like which I had never seen. Elaborate spoons, forks and knives shone from the light of a diamond-shaped glass that floated over the table. There were multitudes of these magical light glasses, each with its own intensity and colors.

Crux looked struck with awe at the display of wealth. I could practically see the lust he held to possess such items for himself, and noted the temptation. Such greed was a dangerous trait to possess.

Despite that, I had to admit that the finery here awakened in me a greed that I had never known before—but it differed from Crux's. My greed came from the privilege of the mighty. I longed to be so powerful that I could own items such as these and never worry about thieves coming for what was rightfully mine.

The freedom of living fearlessly.

A door swung open and dragged my attention away from my musings. Two deminean men with scales of deep-green strode in, as if they floated on air. They stood a head taller than Crux, who was already tall for human standards. Their sleek bodies were muscular, and each wore an open chested garb that highlighted the trait, their scales giving way to a very human core.

Shortly behind them, a deminean woman walked in, and her presence near floored me. Unlike most deminean, this woman's scales were in a multitude of colors, but that wasn't the only difference. Her scales covered nearly her entire body, only the face and center of her body remained human-like. Most surprising of all, however, was that she was completely and utterly naked.

Crux's eyes were fixated on her and he looked near to passing out from holding his breath. I nudged him with my elbow.

"Do they not teach you proper etiquette, humans?" one of the deminean men said, coming to stand in front of Crux, looming over him. "Do you not know to bow to your betters?"

"Dem'i," Crux said immediately, bowing deep, but never taking his eyes from the woman. Her gaze turned to meet him, and she smiled, her pointed white-teeth making her appear both beautiful and deadly. Suddenly, Crux reached over and pushed my head down as well. "Apologies for my ward here—do not mind her. She is a simple country girl."

"No need to apologize, Crux Trueblade," the woman spoke in a soothingly eloquent voice that seemed to drift in the air like a sweet perfume.

"Ri'sha, please," one of the deminean men pleaded. "Do not speak to them, it is not—"

The Ri'sha silenced the man with a raised finger. Her black nail was long and sharp. It looked like the nail of a beast rather than that of a human.

"Do you presume to command me, advisor?" she asked, turning her dangerous gaze upon him.

At the rebuke, the deminean man placed both his arms in the proper salute and went to both knees. "Your pardon, Ri'sha."

"Good," she replied, running her finger down the length of her stomach. "Now, where was I? Ah yes, Crux Trueblade. And you, young one...who are you?"

"Nobody of concern," Crux replied. "As I said, just my—"

"I would have the child answer for herself," she demanded, silencing Crux with a sidelong scowl. Slowly, her eyes came to rest upon me and the force of that stare turned my stomach, but I forced myself to meet her gaze. Once again, the Ri'sha smiled, adding, "A child with spirit, I see. I would have your name...please."

"Ri'sha—"

"Vi'eri," I replied, cutting off her advisor's complaint.

"Vi'eri... Yes, that is a fine name," she repeated as if tasting a fine wine. "Yes, I like this arrangement very much. Come sit." The Ri'sha walked to the largest chair at the head of the table and sat without ceremony. It was built to be higher than the other chairs, but I suspected she would have loomed over us even if it had not been. "Sit," she demanded.

Crux and I both sat at the edges of the table furthest away from her. Neither of us could take our eyes off of her. Her scales shimmered with the magical light of the floating glasses, and it appeared as if her mere presence warped the surrounding air in the room. I noted that the colors of those scales shifted slightly between different hues near constantly.

I'd seen nothing before as beautiful as the woman who sat in front of me.

The deminean men chose not to sit, instead, standing just behind the Ri'sha, as if to guard her from some unknown threat. Perhaps they thought Crux and I dangerous.

"Pardon my asking," Crux dared, breaking the silence. "But what could we do for one as glorious as yourself, Ri'sha?"

"Isodros," she replied. "Call me Isodros."

"Ri'sha please, this has gone too far—"

"You are dismissed," Isodros said with the wave of her hand.

The advisor looked as if he would protest, but instead grumbled something under his breath, stalking out of the room. The other advisor seemed to grin in satisfaction, watching his counterpart go. I sensed a tension in the deminean ranks.

"I apologize for the rudeness of my advisor," Isodros said. "He is young and inexperienced, unlike me." She pulled back her long silver hair to reveal a pointed ear which looked to have eight distinctly carved cuts, scars from the wound long since healed.

"What's that?" I asked before I could reign in my words.

Crux's gaze rushed toward me. "Vi'eri! I'm so sorry, Ri'sha, I—"

"It's quite alright, Trueblade. It's just a curious child. How could I chastise a human for wanting to know more of my people?" Isodros paused, turning to reveal the marks on her ear more clearly. The deep grooves in the ear looked cut clean, as if done with delicate precision. "This is a deminean tradition, Vi'eri. Each cut marks ten full cycles of the seasons that we have lived in this realm. It is a point of pride for our people and it allows us to identify to whom has authority. Generally, authority goes to the eldest. But, as I assume you have already determined, I as a Ri'sha am granted authority even above my many years. None have authority over me except the Ri'sha Sovereign." She let her silver hair fall back to its natural s tate.

I felt...intrigued by what I had learned. Not just at the knowledge I had gained, but that a deminean, and a Ri'sha for that matter, would even explain it to someone as lowly as myself. I found myself drawn to Isodros in a profound way that I did not yet understand.

"You honor us with an explanation, Ri'sha," Crux said on my behalf. At the baleful glare she sent him, he added, "Isodros, I meant to say."

"Then shall we get on to the business at hand, Trueblade?" she asked. "I'm sure you're dying to know." Crux nodded and she added, "Simply put, I have a job I wish to hire you for."

"A job?"

"Yes, a job. That is what mercenaries do, correct? Take on jobs for monetary gain?" She looked disgusted at the thought of what they were discussing, but she quickly masked it.

"And what is this job you have in mind?"

Isodros held up her finger once again. "First, a question. And I would ask it of young Vi'eri. How did you come to be in the company of Trueblade, and did you really acquire a mother's horn?"

Crux looked shocked at the question, but dared not speak.

"That's two questions," I replied without thinking. Crux slapped his palm to his forehead, but Isodros merely grinned at my inappropriate joke. Sensing I may have pushed too far, I added more seriously, "Crux found me in Easthaven and agreed to help me if I helped him find the mother's horn."

"Help you?" she asked. "With what?"

"To become a mercenary," I lied. No need to mention my troubles from Elklan.

Isodros laughed, and even in that, she sounded more eloquent than any other I had ever encountered. "You, a mercenary? Why would a small child want such a life?" I glared at Isodros, on the edge of anger. I forced myself to swallow it. When it became plain that I would not answer the question, she added, "And the mother's horn?"

"I had found the satyr in the woods the previous day. He played me a song and sent me out of the forest. I didn't know at the time that the pipe the satyr played on was the mother's horn." I said the words as if I were making an excuse and the more I considered it, I realized that I was. Her gaze never shifted from me and she appeared to prompt me to continue with the wave of her hand. "I asked the satyr for the item and he granted it to me."

"And the cost?"

"I am never to return to the Bloodsoaked Forest at the edge of Easthaven."

"A small price to pay for such an item," she replied, but still looked at me piteously. She tapped the table with her long finger, adding, "I admit,

I believe you. When my ears spoke to me of a mercenary named Trueblade who came to town with an item as rare as a mother's horn…well, I was skeptical. But hearing your story now, I choose to believe it." She turned to whisper something in her advisor's ear and the man turned, leaving the room. "Now then, the job."

"The job," Crux repeated. "What would you have me do?"

"You?" Isodros replied. "I expect you both to go together. I sense this one is special, Trueblade, and I expect you to keep her alive and raise her for a time as I see fit."

"Is that the job?" he asked in disbelief. "To raise Vi'eri?"

Isodros laughed. "Hardly. The job is much more simple than that. Simply put, thieves stole an item on its way here to Whiteline. I would have you be my intermediary to retrieve it."

Crux seemed to consider a moment, scratching at his scar, asking, "And how would I go about retrieving your stolen item? I would imagine the thieves will not part willingly with it."

"The universal language of the realm…coin. Buy it back. The item…is of great importance to me." She scowled. "I would rather not see any harm come to it."

"Then why not send one of your own kind to perform the task?" Crux asked, but realized his words sounded harsher than he meant. "Apologies, Ri'sha."

Isodros seemed to consider Crux's words for a moment. "It is a valid question," she said. "This theft is of a personal matter for me. One that I would rather not have come to light. I will provide you with the necessary coin to pay off these thieves. If you can retrieve my item discreetly, then I will see that your time in Whiteline is a pleasant one. And if you would continue to do business here, well, I can assure you, having a Ri'sha to lend weight to your…proclivities will be useful to you. Besides, I may have future use for you two." Her eyes locked with mine and she held them, as if she knew a secret about me that even I did not know.

Isodros appeared satisfied with the explanation and I held my breath, waiting for Crux's answer.

I didn't need to wait long as I saw the glint of greed flash over Crux's face as he replied, "We'll do the job, Ri'sha."

She brimmed with delight at his answer, raising her glass to us to mark the start of a mutually beneficial partnership.

We both took them up in response.

Chapter Fourteen

EYES TO THE SKY

When I awoke the next morning, I felt as rested as I'd ever had. The Ri'sha had treated Crux and I to the top inn that Whiteline offered, aptly named the High Tide Inn.

It was early and the sun just peeked through the blinds of my rather large room. I dragged on my new clothing, also a gift of the Ri'sha, sturdy pants with a blue-studded vest that was made specifically for someone with a slim body. It made me feel as if my mother were still with me and tailoring my clothing to a perfect fit.

I frowned at the thought.

Looking over at the wardrobe in the corner of the room, I saw my white gloves. I looked down at my scaled hand sullenly. The scales were silver and seemed to hum with energy. Grimacing, I thought, *what is happening to me?* Rising panic rushed through me. I had never encountered another human with scales such as I, and the fact terrified me. *Am I sick? What will others do to me if they find out?* Determined to hold on to my mother's promise, letting no one find out, I dragged the white gloves on to my hands.

I left my room and knocked at Crux's door. There was no response. Either the man was already awake and in town, or he had had a late night and was determined to sleep in. Either way, I left him to his designs.

As I was leaving the inn, patrons that had risen early to partake of the morning servings: fresh bread, butter and what looked to be little sausages gazed at me with an intensity that most would consider rude.

Their hard stares made me feel naked. In my vulnerable state of mind, I felt as if my secrets were laid bare for all to see. To punctuate the issue, a nervous-looking older woman actually pointed toward me, holding a hand to her mouth to speak to her white-bearded husband in a hushed tone. He visibly scowled at me as I left the inn.

Such was the attention a meeting with Ri'sha brought, and I didn't care much for it.

Port Whiteline was by far the largest town I'd ever been in. If I were to put both Easthaven and Elklan together, it would still be less than half the size of this place.

I took the better part of the morning just looking around, and decided that I didn't care much for the cramped lifestyle a large city brings. The streets were filthy with the mess of animals. A putrid stink assaulted the senses and brought tears to my eyes. Worse still, when I got too close to the sea, the rankness of the ocean made my gut wrench with pain.

Still, I urged myself closer and closer, and off in the distance I saw a sight that I never would have believed real if not for my own eyes. At the very far-edge of my vision, I could just make out what appeared to be floating islands. I'd been told of them before, from boastful men in Elklan, of islands that floated where the realm's magic ran its deepest. The call of adventure stirred in me and I longed to journey to those islands in the sky.

As I pressed closer to the sea, the gut-wrenching pain became too much to bear, and I reluctantly turned back inland, heading toward the inn to seek my room for a time.

On the way, I saw a familiar sight. A male human kneeled before a deminean man. Apparently, the human had asked the deminean to pay for produce they had taken. For this, the deminean had dragged the human into the street, throwing him into the piss and shit to bow and beg for forgiveness. They even went as far as to make the human kiss his dirty shoes.

The murmur of discontented humans broke out among the crowd, and it reminded me of a time that was still too fresh in my mind to dwell upon. Unlike the situation with the deminean Kreza and my mother, where I had blindly charged in without any type of plan to fall back on. This time, I turned and left without a backward glance. I was determined not to get caught up in any more deminean machinations.

It's not my business, I told myself. *This is just the way of the realm. It always has been, and it always will be.* It was all lies, of course. The truth was, I was just a coward, like all the rest who stared on but did nothing. *Crux said I was special—that I had real power! Maybe someday I could—*

Something suddenly struck me, breaking my internal monologue and sending me reeling to the floor. I fell into a small puddle of water and wished with all my heart it was just that. Looking up, I saw a fiery red-haired girl with freckles littering her lightly tanned face staring back at me, stunned. She appeared about my age and looked ragged in worn-down clothing that were more like potato sacks than actual clothing. I brushed off my sudden judgment by reminding myself that I, too, had looked very similar less than a week before. As I stood, the girl recovered first, shooting me a grimace, revealing her slightly crooked teeth. I heard a voice call out in anger, and she sprinted down a nearby alley without a word.

I reached out for her, but a portly brown-haired woman near trampled me as she rounded the same corner. This time, I managed to stay upright, and the woman asked breathlessly, "Did...you...see a...girl?" She looked like she was about to faint.

I pointed to the alleyway. "But she's long gone. Are you okay?"

The woman leaned on the nearby building and continued to wheeze, clutching a single hand to her chest. I just stared, unable to comprehend what to do, when the woman's mouth down-turned into a frown, and she looked up accusingly. "You're in leagues with her, ain't ya?"

"No!" I exclaimed, taking an involuntary step back. The woman approached me quickly, as if she were about to strike me right then and there. I raised my hands defensively, adding, "I swear, I don't know who she is."

"Wait..." the woman said, her look of disapproval turning to horror. "You're the girl everyone's been talkin' bout. The Ri'sha spy!"

"Ri'sha...spy?"

"I'm terribly sorry, miss," the woman replied suddenly, her voice turning from anger to meekness in an instant. "Sorry to have bother'd ya. Please forgive an old woman—my eyes haven't worked so well of late. My regards to your master and praise to the Dem'i who rule us lowly humans." She sputtered the words near incoherently as she got on both knees, pressing herself against the street floor. Her white apron fell into a puddle, soaking up the filth, but she paid it little mind.

"That's alright," I replied for lack of anything better to say. "Please, you can get up now. There is nothing to forgive, I promise."

The woman stood back up with a haste, bowing and muttering additional apologies as she backed away from me. Eventually, she melded into the flowing streets of people.

Gone and out of sight.

Afterward, I was determined to find my way back to the inn without further conflict. I was distinctly more aware of the people who stared at me. Some ignored me, and some uttered curses under their breath. Just as they had once done when I sought to escape Elklan. I hadn't done anything to anyone, yet every human here seemed to have a distrust for me, if not an outright loathing. I was an oddity to them, and I felt alone despite the crowded streets before me.

As I entered the inn, I made my way directly for the stairs to the second floor when a voice caught my attention.

I turned to see Crux wearing similar clothing to myself, light cotton attire, likely provided by the Ri'sha as well. He was sitting with someone I did not recognize.

I didn't feel like engaging in discussion, but Crux looked insistent that I join him, so, reluctantly, I walked toward him, giving up the dream of a midday rest and a change of my dirty clothing.

"Vi'eri, where were you? I've been loo—" Crux suddenly held his hand to his nose. "Why do you smell like piss?"

I sighed. "It's been a rough morning. I'm just going to head upstairs—"

"Nevermind. Sit down. Sit down. We've had little time to talk since yesterday." He pulled out a chair and beckoned me to sit. I complied begrudgingly, scraping the wooden floor as I shifted my seat toward the table. "By the way, where were you?"

I told Crux of my morning, leaving out the part about the girl and the woman. I didn't want him to think I got us involved in any more trouble. Crux's friend was a darkly tanned man who wore a silver embroidered black cloak with short black hair and a scar that ran the length of his eye, which had been replaced with glass lookalike. He nodded silently at my retelling, gazing at me with his good eye as if committing my words to memory.

Crux suddenly turned toward his friend, as if he had just remembered something of great importance. "Oh yes, Eri. This is my new friend, Vrakenti. He—"

"Please," the man said in as deep a voice as I have ever heard. "You can call me Vrak."

Vrak held out his hand to me and I reached over to shake it, replying, "Pleased to meet you."

"Well-mannered girl for being a country lass, as Crux here would have me believe."

"Well now," he replied with a jovial smile, "I never said she was bereft of manners. Only that we met under...precarious circumstances."

"Precarious indeed..." Vrak said, letting the conversation trail off.

It was an awkward silence, and they both seemed to stare at me as if expecting something. Nervously, I asked, "Vrak, where do you hail from? I've never heard someone speak with such an accent before."

"Oh, that's a long story, little miss. But if you're asking where I was born, it was far to the south. As south as your mind can take you, and then south of that." He smiled, as if he were remembering better days from his past. "But pleasantries are not why we are here, I'm afraid. I must admit, I thought Crux here was trying to pull one over on me when he said that a Ri'sha took a special interest in you. But now, having met you, I do sense...something." He mockingly tapped at his glass eye, adding, "I've an eye for this sort of thing."

"That's what everyone keeps telling me," I replied with some bitterness. "Special... But I don't see what makes me so. I just want everything to go back to normal. Well, the new normal, that is."

Crux frowned at my honesty. I believe he thought I had already gotten over the turmoil of my near past.

I hadn't.

"I can see your pain, child," Vrak said in his long southern accent. "I've once shared it as well. These deminean play with our lives as if we were..." he trailed off when the mention of deminean caused other patrons to turn and stare at us. "Well...no need to discuss such unpleasantries here. The past is the past—let's talk future."

Crux's eyes lit back up. "Here's to that." He raised a mug and the smell of alcohol wafted toward me. Shooting me a grin, he tipped the mug down into his mouth. Small lines of liquid trailed down his peppered beard, and he slammed the cup down on the table. A young barmaid nearby glared him down and he averted his eyes from her like a chastised child, chuckling softly to himself.

"About the job," Crux said as if nothing had happened. "The Ri'sha made it out to be simple, but in my experience, nothing is ever as simple as it seems. Take our latest mishap with the mother's horn as proof of that. Then, there is the matter of the item itself. This Isodros was none too keen on actually revealing what it was. Which means, potentially, it's a powerful artifact. Perhaps a new type of enchantment? Maybe, instead of handing it to the Ri'sha, we could—"

"No," Vrak replied flatly, setting his cup gracefully down on the table and wiping liquid off his clean-shaven face with the back of his hand. "That is not a battle you wish to start, Crux. Nor one I want to be a part of. You would find that even the great Trueblade is easily outmatched. No, I think for the safety of all involved, we cooperate with the Ri'sha. From what you've told me, she offers fair coin and future business. Business begets more business, my friend. Do not be so keen on betraying your clients. That is, if you want *Crux's Crew* to survive."

Crux seemed to consider Vrak's words as he scratched at his scar. Most of the meaning went well above my head, so I simply waited for the response. Still, I didn't understand why the Ri'sha had chosen us, but I could see no reason why we would betray her. From what little I knew about the woman from the citizens of Whiteline, I judged her someone not to be trifled with.

"You're right, Vrak. Sorry. Old habits die hard, it seems. I really am trying to keep on the straight and narrow, my friend."

"We all have our struggles," Vrak replied, smiling. I felt a sort of kinship between them, one that I felt apart from. "But moving on. This job interests me, and I am very willing to lend my aid to it...for a price."

The mention of price set the two off in a wild scramble of bartering and trying to one-up each other. I listened, but only just as I drifted off into wild imaginations of traveling to the floating islands. Suddenly, the mention of my name brought me back to reality.

"Huh?" I said in confusion.

"I asked if you were okay with Vrak joining us," Crux replied. "Are you okay?"

I couldn't figure out why he was even asking my opinion. But, with sudden realization, I determined that he was treating me as an equal of the group. This brought my attention back to the conversation at hand, and I nodded enthusiastically at his question.

"Great," he replied. "Then it's settled—"

"Not so fast," Vrak interrupted. "You forgot to mention my ward to her as well. She, unfortunately, couldn't be here at this time, but I would have her accompany us when we set off on the job."

"I don't see why not, as long as Vi'eri agrees as well."

I nodded my head in agreement once again.

Vrak suddenly reached out to shake my hand again, saying, "Then we have a deal."

After a time, I excused myself and made my way to my room on the second floor, where I threw off my still soaked clothes. I dared to smell them and nearly gagged—they smelled as bad as Crux had indicated. Hastily, I washed myself with the small amount of water I had left from the previous night, scrubbing my skin so thoroughly that a red rash formed from the pressure of my cleaning.

The tiredness that had once threatened me was all but gone when I finally laid down in bed, the sun still bright, shining light through the shudders. For once, I contemplated my future and where this new life was to take me. Crux was a mercenary and intended to start his own mercenary company. I thought, *is that something I really want for myself?* He had treated me as an equal—well, maybe not quite an equal, but not as a helpless child. Now that I could never return home, what did I want to do with my life?

"My life…" I whispered to the empty room as I shut my eyes and dreamed of floating islands in the sky.

Chapter Fifteen

TREASURE

A few days passed before we were to set out on our journey.

Crux, ever diligent, gathered provisions for us to take, and I was doing my best to shy away from any trouble. The Well knows I'd had my share of trouble of late.

One morning, just before the sun crested the horizon, Crux knocked on my door with his typical three knock rhythm. I opened it to reveal a fully travel-dressed Crux, complete in a sturdy brown coat with silver buttons up the seam. A wide-brimmed hat adorned his head, matching his polished boots. He appeared more like a wealthy merchant than a mercenary.

"Here, Eri. Take these," he said as he shoved some clothing into my hands. "You'll match my attire, more or less. Congratulations, we're merchants now. Well, in spirit at least."

I smiled, feeling the quality of my new traveling attire. Before he could turn to leave, I caught his attention, asking, "So are we leaving soon?"

"Sooner than you think," he replied. "Gather what you will need for a few days' trip. We leave today."

"Today!" I exclaimed, but Crux had already turned, walking down the hallway, his boots throwing dust into the air with every step. He spared me a glance and waved over his shoulder. I understood the message.

What's done is done.

I closed the door and eyed the clothing; he was right. The deep browns of my new vest matched his set very well, and he had even provided me with a matching pair of studded gloves. They were longer than my previous pair and I thanked the Well for my good luck. Recently, my scales crested my gloves, and I had taken to tucking my long-sleeved shirts to hide them.

Packing my things, I found that it wasn't much. Like the time I had fled Elklan, all of my worldly possessions could fit into a single armful. Thinking of the Ri'sha's lavish meeting room, I frowned. I knew it was improper to lust over simple possessions, but I couldn't help it at the time. Having glimpsed the other side—the side of lavish beauty, wealth, and power—I longed to have a place I could call my own. Where I could live in safety. Free of the uncertainties of life.

To be deminean.

I gripped my hands tight around the gloves, squeezing until the muscles of my arm were sore. Suddenly, my arm shot out and I slammed my fist into the door. A crack of wood sounded just above the handle, and a small piece of wood splintered away.

I will never be like them! I thought to myself, and I'd never felt more sure of anything in my life.

I made my way downstairs and discovered that Crux was nowhere to be found. I longed to go outside and look around the city again, but my last excursion had brought me too close to calamity. I resigned myself to sitting alone at a table in the dining hall, alone.

I waited, and eventually, an elderly man who ran the inn—Old Man Grath, people would call him—spoke to me for a time.

The innkeeper set a cup of hot tea in front of me. Long wisps of heat wafted from the top, bringing a pleasant scent as I raised the cup to my lips and took a sip. It was good, tasting of ginger and nutmeg, and with more than a splash of honey and cream.

The skin on his skinny arms barely seemed to hold the tautness of his muscles as he wrung his hands. "How is Crux treating you, little one?" he asked in a grandfatherly tone.

It was not the first time Grath had approached this subject. The constant asking of the same question irritated me, but I knew he only asked from a place of kindness. And kindness is what this realm needed more of, not less. I swallowed my bitterness and replied, "Fine, just fine. Crux bought me some new clothes. We are to travel soon, or so I hear."

"Are you now?" Grath said in genuine surprise, crossing his arms on the table as he took a seat in front of me. "And where might you both be heading?"

I shrugged and thought of the island in the sky, longing for that to be our true destination. Quickly, I shoved the thought away.

Childish fantasies are not becoming of a mercenary, I told myself.

"Well, if you are sure everything is alright, then do be careful. There are all manner of bandits on the roads these days; a shameful thing. Not to mention Anduinna's creatures stalk the nights and inhabit the greater parts of the forests. Strange sightings, I hear. Men driven mad—like animals who've been cut off from the collective of the Life Incarnate." The man paused for a moment before adding, "Apologies, miss. Just the ramblings of an old man. Don't let me frighten you. I'm sure you'll have a safe trip. When you come back to town—even if you lodge elsewhere—come and say hello to me. If you do, I'll serve you another cup of tea. On the house."

I thanked Grath absently, and he left me to my drink, which had grown considerably colder during his questioning. The man had a weariness in the way he walked. Was it old age? Or perhaps he was truly discouraged by the happenings of the realm which had left him behind. Older, wiser, and yet powerless to change anything. I put Grath from my thoughts. I had to worry about myself before all others.

I looked absently at my tea, swirling the cup, and watching the small tendrils of heat escape, breathing in the vapor. If traveling was anything like it had been before, then I'd best savor the small pleasures while I still could.

Crux entered the inn a short time later with Vrak in tow. Behind him, a considerably shorter person followed. I twisted my head to get a glance at her face and gasped when she turned to look at me. It was the lightly tanned redhead girl with freckles.

"You!" I said, pointing a finger accusingly. They all turned to stare at me silently, and I realized how rude my gesture must have seemed. Quickly, I amended it, adding, "I meant, it's nice to see you again. I never got your name in the alleyway."

The girl, about my age, was dressed considerably better than the first time I had seen her. After a moment, I realized she wore very similar clothing to my own traveling attire. Deep brown with silver trimmings.

"You two know each other?" Vrak asked in surprise. Crux nodded at Vrak's question, obviously curious himself.

"Well, sorta," the girl replied sheepishly. "We just kinda...bumped into one another."

"Is that so..." Vrak replied, his tone indicating that he didn't believe a word of what the girl said. After a time, he shook his head, adding, "Well, no better time than the present for proper introductions. This is Tesro Aline. Tesro, this is Vi'eri... I never caught your last name."

"Vi'eri," I replied. "Just Vi'eri."

"Vi'eri," Tesro said, her face suddenly wrinkling as if she smelled something rotten. "What a weird name."

Vrak's punishment was swift as his hand clapped her on the back of the head. She yelped at the blow, but appeared unharmed by his open-handed slap. "Play nice, *Tessy*." A smile creased the man's face.

Tesro's temperament shifted to match her fiery red-hair as her face scrunched up in fury. She leveled a glare at Vrak that would send the heartiest of men running. "Don't call me that!"

"When you cease acting like a child, I'll cease giving you a child's nickname. Deal?"

She huffed in frustration, crossing her arms and turning from him. He shot me a stare and winked with his glass eye.

Crux shrugged his shoulders. "This isn't going to be a problem, is it? Vi'eri is part of this—the Ri'sha demanded it. Your ward, however..." he let the thought trail off.

"It's not a problem," Vrak replied, unbothered. "Isn't that right, Tesro?"

She nodded sullenly, her eyes fixated on the door that led outside, her feet shifting uncomfortably.

"Good," Crux replied, moving to sit next to me. Vrak followed, and shortly after Tesro, who opted not to sit, but instead, stood behind Vrak, leaning her arms on the back of his chair.

"Now then," Crux said with some flair. "Let's get on with it."

We traveled west for a few days on the Silver Sea road. Crux set an easy pace, and we each carried our own weight in provisions and tools.

My new clothing chaffed irritably against my skin, but the weather was mild. It was the tail end of spring, and the relentless glow of the upcoming summer sun threatened us in the midday. The upside to this was that we spent the nights in cool air, rather than a freezing chill.

On one such night, under the gleaming shine of a thousand distant stars, the four of us sat huddled around a fire. Crux had chopped a few limbs off a nearby tree to make the flame, and Vrak, to my surprise, had a pan of iron with him that looked like it had seen a fair amount of usage.

A bit earlier, when we had come across a small stream, Vrak had made a pointed effort to have us stop for the night. The man was quite the angler and managed to catch not one, but two greenside trout, known by that name for the greenish hue of their scales.

As he cut into the fish with a long knife that looked as if its primary use was for this exact task, he spoke to Tesro and I about what he was doing. "Cut the head off first, no use in making the creature suffer. Anduinna's wrath is said to come down upon those who make her creatures suffer needlessly." As he explained, two distinct *thuds* rang out, separating the heads of each fish with a single masterful stroke for each. He then ran the blade across the fish's body, removing scales. I watched in awe as his deft hands performed the task. The man had a clear talent for this, and I got a distinct satisfaction from watching a master display their craft.

Tesro appeared less interested as she kneeled on the ground, carelessly running her hands through the dirt, leaving little trails with her fingertips.

"Tesro," Vrak said, his tone adopting a more parental tone. "If you aren't busy, why don't you get us some hardtack out of the provisions?" As she went to leave, he added, "And when Crux returns, help him light the fire."

She glared at him defiantly, but eventually relinquished to his demand, moving wordlessly to the task he had given. I followed her, curiously. I've heard of those who could make fire by creating a spark with the clashing of two stones and I wished to see it done myself.

As Crux returned, he built the small sticks in stacks and added dried brush underneath. He tiptoed back and nodded to Tesro. She put her hands out in front of her face and concentrated. After a brief moment, a small tendril of a flame ignited at the tip of her index finger. She pulled in air, held it, and then exhaled. As she did, it was as if she breathed life into the flame and it rose from her finger, growing larger as it gently drifted down to ignite the brush.

The fire lingered, almost dying out before she leaned close into it. Holding her palm up to the sky, she blew across her hand, aiming the air toward the fire. As the air came into contact with the fire, it burst into brilliant light, going white for just a moment before dying back down to a milder red.

"*Tesro!*" Vrak yelled, drawing my attention. "Control, Tesro. How many times must I say it? *Control!*"

She winced at the words, but solemnly nodded, replying, "I'm sorry. I'll be more careful." Tears formed at the edges of her eyes.

Vrak's stern face became soft again as he replied, "Oh, Tesro."

I was distinctly aware of the bond between them. A bond, I feared, was born from tragedy and despair. They had a type of understanding that Crux and I had yet to become accustomed too as we both looked on curiously at the pair.

Tesro's green eyes seemed brighter with the light of the fire bouncing off of them. Her red hair and red freckles seemed all the more punctuated in that light, and I felt drawn to her. The power she wielded was incredible! I had heard stories of humans who had the skill to alter the magic that existed around us, floating in the space between this realm and the next.

The *in-between*, they called it.

Tesro snorted, and it brought me out of my trance. I found I had been staring at her, and her look of anger turned my head away faster than any words of rebuke could have.

I sat near the fire in silence, minding to myself when Vrak set his iron-pan to it. A small bit of butter popped from the heat before he added the two filets of fish.

By the time the food was done, I was ravenous. I ate every bite of what was offered in a heartbeat. Tesro looked to do much the same, while Crux ate casually and Vrak seemed to pause in delight with every bite, truly taking the time to savor the meal.

And so we sat, the four of us. We sat under the sky of a thousand stars that seemed to exist for our pleasure alone.

This fire. These stars. This food. These people. This time...it all belonged to me. Nothing, save my death, could take it. Smiling, I fixed the moment safely in my mind.

It became one of my most valued treasures.

CHAPTER SIXTEEN

ETERNITY

"The plan is simple," Crux said, using a stick to draw in a dirt patch off the side of the road. "From what I've been told, the bandits make camp in a place called Fae Rock. We will approach and initiate contact to make the exchange. I've done some of the legwork already and spoken to a middleman that sells these bandits' pilfered goods. They'll be expecting us soon."

"And what if they don't want to trade? What if they want to take?" I asked, not trusting the plan as much as he apparently did.

He scratched at his scar in agitation. "That's why we have backup in Vrak and Tesro."

Vrak turned to look at me, adding, "I assure you that you're in safe hands, Vi'eri. No need to be fearful."

"I'm not scared," I replied flatly. "But you don't even have a weapon. Your knife looks to be good for killing fish, not people."

He frowned at my blase attitude. "What's happened to you, child? Someone as youthful as you shouldn't confide in death so carelessly. You're just—"

"And why not?" Crux asked, rising to move between Vrak and me. "Vi'eri's right. We should be weary and ready to defend ourselves. By any means necessary." He pulled his knife, picking at his fingernails as if to emphasize his point.

"Crux..." Vrak replied in a tone of disapproval. "We need to be more subtle than that. Defending yourself is well and proper, and I would never berate a man for preserving themselves when needed. But if we leave behind bodies everywhere we go, people will learn to fear us. People don't hire those they fear."

I clicked my tongue, drawing their attention back to me. "They also don't hire the dead."

I hesitated for a moment and speculated as to where those words came from. I felt a gentle pushing on my emotions and I whispered in my head, *Voice?*

Crux and Vrak stared defiantly at each other for a while before I broke the silence. "If someone attacks me, then I'll kill them. I've done it before!" I said the words to make myself sound tough, but they made me sound a braggart instead.

Vrak frowned, weighing my words for a time before asking, "Have you really killed, child?" I nodded to him and he glanced at Crux, anger flashing wildly. "Did you know about this?"

"Yes," he replied, almost with pride in his voice. "The girl knows what needs to be done to survive. By the Well, she damn near killed me when we quarreled. She's been through a lot, Vrak—you couldn't understand."

"Crux says you're an enchanter? You must be a particularly powerful one at that. Therefore, it's even more imperative that you remain in control of your emotions." Vrak glanced at Tesro for a moment before turning back to me. He kneeled to be at my eye level, heedless of the dirt that now muddied his pants. "Tesro and I are destroyers, as much as I hate the word. While you can imbue objects with magic, we can control the magic freely in the air." He stood again, as if to address both Crux and me simultaneously. "This is a warning to you both. We will only apply our magic to kill if it is absolutely necessary for our survival. Otherwise, if things go poorly, we will use our powers to make an escape route. Is that acceptable?"

Crux looked uneasy listening to Vrak's words, but he silently nodded at them.

I did the same, despite my reservations.

When we reached Fae Rock, it was midday, and it was a short walk off the road to a canyon that went on and on, past the point of vision. It was as if the ground had sunken in and in its place, thousands of jagged rocks of red, pink and white reached out toward the sky.

The columns of rocks looked foreign to me, as if it was not of this world with their spiraling formations. Looking from above the valley, it appeared to have plenty of crevasses in which to hide, and I immediately understood why bandits would choose to set up refuge here.

"This is it," Crux said, scanning the immense canyon that spanned out before us as if searching for an indicator of some type.

"There," Vrak said, pointing to a red flag in the middle of the maze of rock and dirt. "But why do they want to meet so far in?"

"So we can't ambush them, most likely," Crux replied.

"So they can ambush us," I muttered in response.

He threw me a baneful glare, and I turned away from it, shamed. I decided that I should try to be more supportive of Crux's methods. All of his plans had worked out so far, no reason to start doubting him now.

Crux stood and slung on his pack, ignoring my comment. "Alright, let's get going. We are wasting daylight resting here. Let me do the talking and everything will work out fine."

We walked slowly into the jungle of pointed rocks, and it was truly a maze of stone and dirt.

We silently followed a man-made path down and down until we were at the base of the spikes. Here, the color of the rocks had shifted to red. The further up the rocks climbed, the lighter and lighter their colors became, until they became stark white at their very tips, like fingertips of bone.

There were so many passages to choose from that I almost immediately lost my way. The paths winded up and down, left and right, under arches between two more rock formations and through caverns that appeared to be a mixture of naturally occurring and man-made.

Tesro ran her hand across the stone and halted, staring at a carving in the rock. "What is it?" she asked, tracing the craving with the tip of her finger.

"A remnant of an old people," Vrak replied, setting his hand to the stone. "If circumstances were different, perhaps we could learn more...but we don't have the luxury. Come, come."

We kept moving, and the carved drawings came more frequently, but with less detail, as if we traveled reverse through time to a more primitive era. Eventually, we found the flag and its carrier.

A shirtless young man rested upon one of the stone pillars—the tip just wide enough for one person to perch. Upon spotting us, he drove the flag into solid rock with extraordinary strength and, to my terror, slid down the edge at a near vertical angle.

He struck the ground hard, but, surprisingly, appeared fine. Now that he was closer, I noticed how tight his muscles appeared. They looked distinctly...inhuman to my eyes. It was the unnatural way that some of his body remained slender while other parts brimmed with muscular mass.

"You the merchant I was told 'bout?" the boy asked, shaking dirt out of his unkempt curly black hair with one hand. His other rested on the hilt of a knife tucked into his waistband.

"Dannet," Crux replied. "Names Dannet, and I am supposed to be meeting with Roese."

"Aye, Dannet, that was the name." The boy smirked, his deep brown eyes lighting up from the rays of sunlight. Tesro appeared drawn by his roguish manners, attempting to hide a smile. "Come on then, follow me." He turned and continued down the path.

From the boy's steady gate, it was clear he did not fear an attack from behind. The thought made me nervous.

What does this boy know that we do not? I thought. A quick glance at Crux told me he had similar feelings.

I followed and anxiously eyed every nook and cranny of the canyon, waiting for the dagger in the dark. To my surprise, it never came.

We walked in total silence, and the others appeared as nervous as I was, their eyes darting around as they wiped sweat off their faces, leaving trails of dirt. The young man who led us appeared unperturbed by the rising heat, even though he sweat furiously, his shirtless back glistening with it. His darkly tanned body spoke of how much time he spent outdoors.

"Through here," the young man said as he turned to point at a slight break in the rock that led under a stone slit. "Roese will meet you inside."

"Thank you," Crux replied, but when we turned back, the young man had already sauntered off down another pathway. He shook his head at the boy's back.

Crux walked into the cave, and the others followed. I spared one last glance around and saw nothing except the colorful rocks. They truly were beautiful things, and I committed them to memory as I turned to the crevice. I swallowed hard and walked inside.

Torches lined the hallway, mantled in little holes carved into the cave walls. A myriad of dark spiraling paths webbed their way away from the entrance, but only one of the paths had torches that guided the way. We followed them like moths drawn to a flame.

Eventually, we strode into a rather extensive corridor. Unlike the rest of the pathways, this larger space appeared to be shaped with human hands. In this space, hammocks staked into the wall swung in rows and small tents littered the areas in-between. There were brief bits of movement from some of the tents, but the space looked largely deserted for the time being. Half-eaten food and drinks that still had some unknown liquid in them littered the place, and I wanted to hold my nose to the smell of it as the mixture of unwashed body odor, liquor and rotting food scraps assaulted my nose.

The corridor led into another smaller walkway, which then led to another larger corridor. Not as large as the first, but still substantial compared to the rest. It was there we saw a few humans gathered around a stout woman with black hair.

Upon seeing us, the woman stood, revealing her off-white shirt, cut off half-way at her stomach. Surprisingly, her muscles bulged from every visible space on her overly exposed body. We stepped forward cautiously, drawing the eye of everyone there until we stood in front of her. The people at her side stepped away hurriedly, but remained close enough to intervene if unavoidable.

"Dannet, I presume?" the woman asked.

Crux put on his best smile, replying, "Aye, and you must be Roese. Pleasure."

"Pleasure indeed." A coy smile parted Roese's luscious red lips, revealing a neat set of perfectly white teeth. "I always like to dine before discussing business. I feel it...loosens the tensions of both parties." She gestured for us to follow her. "Follow me. Let's make ourselves more comfortable, yes?"

"Yes, please," he replied, a stupid grin taking over his face. I nudged him in the side with my elbow and he coughed, adding, "I hope you don't mind if my bodyguard and our daughters join us?"

"Not at all. In fact, it gives me joy to see men taking such care of their young. Kinship and family! That is what makes humans strong in the face of deminean oppression. But we will get to that soon enough. For now, let's eat and drink!"

I liked this Roese, despite my weariness of her machinations. My mother said that you could never trust a cutpurse, and a bandit is even worse than that. Crux, his eyes scanning her lustfully, seemed to like her a bit too much for his own good. She put on a display of confidence that I found uncommon among other humans I'd met recently. Especially humans living under deminean rule.

Roese twirled her long, curly black hair as she brought us down yet another corridor that led to what I assumed to be a private audience chamber. There, a wooden table greeted us and, oddly enough, five seats.

We sat and others of Roese's people came bearing plates of cheeses, bread and what smelled like wine. One woman lit the candles on the table while another poured a dark liquid into brass cups, placing one in front of me without a word. I eyed Crux, who returned the stare with a smile that implied, 'Go ahead.'

The sun was relentless that day and despite the coolness of the cave, my thirst got the better of me as I lifted the liquid to my mouth, drinking a nice hearty gulp. It burned, and I choked on it, sputtering. Small lines of red-wine rushed down my chin as I forced myself to hold it in, swallowing roughly.

Roese laughed. "You aren't supposed to drink that much at once—especially if it's your first time."

Tesro seemed to take this as a challenge as she picked up her own cup.

"Tesro!" Vrak exclaimed as he reached to take it from her. Too late. She had already guzzled an amount at least matching my own.

Her face turned down in a frown as she also struggled to hold it in. Eventually, she swallowed with great effort, saying, "It's, uh...good." She turned a baleful eye on me, and a smile of satisfaction lifted her sun-kissed face.

Roese brimmed at this, her brown eyes lighting up in amusement. "Such spirited young girls you both have. It fills my heart to know the next generation will have strong-willed women after I pass. My son is strong as well, but it's women... Bah, look at me! It just fills me with pride is all I'm trying to say."

Crux raised his own glass at that, giving her a sort of salute before he tipped it back. Vrak frowned and swirled his own glass, staring down into the liquid.

"Oh come now, bodyguard. Don't stare like that. All doom and gloom. I assure you, it's not poisoned," she said. "But I wouldn't allow them to drink too much. I heard this wine was specifically created for the Ri'sha who have a near legendary tolerance for drink." She rolled her eyes as she finished off her own glass.

A serving woman came and filled it back to the top. The thought of a bandit leader having a servant gave me some pause.

This woman Roese shattered my expectation of who I thought we were dealing with. All stories I had previously heard had bandits pegged as bloodthirsty killers, thieves and rapists. This woman just looked like someone who struggled to survive away from deminean rule.

I envied her that.

The food came and wiped all other thoughts from my mind. Roasted pork on a skewer with root-vegetables cooked in rendered pork fat. It was delicious, and I devoured it, even licking the grease off my fingers.

I felt the weariness of travel driven out, and my strength returned tenfold. There was nothing better for the pains of travel than a hot, hearty meal.

From the looks of it, everyone agreed with my sentiment as they easily finished their fill with little concern. I knew it wasn't the wisest of choices—to eat the food of a potential enemy—but one did not shy away from whatever food was offered on the road. Besides, if Roese wanted us dead, then she had the manpower to see it done without resorting to poison.

After the meal, Crux turned toward Roese, saying, "Always grateful for a full meal. Now then, as I discussed with your middleman, I'm looking for a recently stolen item that I've been told is in your possession."

She smiled, cheeks flushed red. I suspected the drink addled her a bit as she replied, "I was hoping to indulge in more pleasure." She said the words seductively, eyeing Crux like a piece of meat. To my surprise, he looked her down coolly, not giving anything away. She smirked, leaning back in her chair and topped off the rest of her drink. "Ah, but I see we are in the midst of a true professional. Very well."

She leaned forward and pulled a small box out of her pocket. It was ornate in a blackened wood with gold inlay, and I suspected the box itself was worth plenty of coin. It popped open and something inside shone brightly. I squinted against the light for a moment as I adjusted. Wiping a wayward tear from my eye, the item inside became clear. It looked like a small blue gem...almost like a tear itself.

"It's beautiful," I whispered to no one in particular.

Tesro leaned against the table to get a better look before bringing her eyes to meet Roese's, asking, "What is it?"

She smiled, a parental smile that one would give to a daughter. "Tesro, was it? This is what the deminean call the tear of eternity."

"'The tear of eternity,'" I repeated. I felt my face flush as I gazed.

I longed for it—craved it more than life itself, and it baffled me how anyone could hold it so close to them and not clasp it in their own hand. It consumed my thoughts—my entire being—and I knew that I would have done anything to possess it. I felt as if I was drifting outside my own body, my soul leaving an empty husk behind to find safety in that eternity.

Roese closed the case, and I was thrust back into my own mortal shell.

It hurt.

I shook my head and found it was painful to even think. A presence pushed a warning into me that chilled my soul.

Crux noticed my odd behavior and glared at me. Roese merely looked at me with curiosity.

"So as you can see, merchant, this is no simple trinket." Her hand stroked the fine black box with the gentleness one showed a lover. "No, this is an opportunity that I cannot simply give up for just coin."

Crux stood, shoving his chair back. "But we had a deal—"

"What deal? Like the one you made with the Ri'sha?" Roese slammed a fist into the table, knocking a few cups over and, surprisingly, splitting a piece of the thick wood away. Ignoring our shocked faces, she added, "Yes, I know you met with her. And at first, I was content to accept your coin and be gone by the time you could report our location to the Ri'sha. The war has many battlefields, you see. Or, with this much coin, we could disappear—find our ways into the free human colonies of the world. But I've had a change of heart, as it were. A better idea...an idea that involves you, merchant Dennet."

Roese stood, the chair scraping the floor as she slid it away from her. Her muscles looked larger than before as she flexed them, revealing deep veins lining the skin. I peered around and found the servants were not servants at all, but fighters, each and every one. None brandished weapons, but each appeared well-muscled, far more than should be feasible for an average human.

Everyone was standing now and Tesro and I shared a nervous stare toward one another.

"What are you?" Vrak asked, his hand heading toward his skinny curved knife.

"Human," Roese replied, but her voice was unmistakably deeper than before. "Or what humans could be. What they *should* be!"

There was a flash in the air, and then a crash of wood on wood as the black box that held the tear of eternity hit the table—a knife sticking out of it.

Crux leaped across the table, seizing the box and sliding off the other end, landing directly beside me. He pushed himself off the ground and yelled, "Run!"

Chaos struck the room as at least five of the servants lunged for us. I turned to my left to see Crux's knife fly through the air and take a servant at the knee, dropping him to the floor with a yelp. In a heartbeat, all four of us were in the narrow corridor between the attendee room and the larger room.

I turned toward Vrak and Tesro. They stood directly behind us just inside the narrow passage with their hands palm out, facing our assailants.

The air appeared to shimmer in front of them, and then a large burst of air sent the table, chairs, silverware and uneaten food flying. I saw broken pieces of wood smack against our attackers as their cries of fear and rage broke through the large rushing of air that blew my hair back in a wild frenzy.

Suddenly, before I could comprehend what was happening, we were running again. As we entered each corridor, more assailants attacked. A woman grabbed at Crux's arm and, to my surprise, lifted him off the ground with ease. She threw him against a wall, and he bounced off, letting out a grunt of pain.

Vrak lifted his palm, and another gust of air hit the woman squarely, throwing her to the ground.

Tesro looked scared and didn't appear to notice a big man that crept from behind her. I rushed and tackled her out of the way as the man's hand narrowly missed seizing her.

We landed in another passageway, one that we had not traveled before, bereft of light. I heard Vrak's voice call out amidst the fighting, *"Keep running!"*

I didn't think, I just reacted. I grabbed Tesro's wrist and hauled her up to her feet and ran down the dark corridor, pulling her along with me.

Chapter Seventeen

FIRE IN THE HOLE

"What are you doing?" Tesro hissed at me in disgust, wrenching her wrist from my grip, and stopping in the middle of the dark, narrow passageway.

I shoved her into a narrow gap in the wall and not a moment too soon as two of our assailants passed, muttering threats as if they were in a crazed fury.

They didn't notice us.

She pushed me back. "Don't touch me!" The words came harshly, but at least she had the good sense to dampen her voice.

"I just saved you!" I replied incredulously. "And you're welcome for it."

"I could've handled them."

I stared directly at her and forced her to meet my eyes. "Could you? How about when they had their hands around your throat? What then? Did you see how strong they were? Or were you so busy gawking that you couldn't even use any of that magic?" Surprisingly, my words silenced her, and she looked away from me like a whipped animal. A pang of regret filled me, but I shoved it aside, adding, "We need to find Crux and Vrak. We can't fight between ourselves—not right now. So..." I reached out my hand in rapprochement, "Truce?"

Tesro scanned me up and down, as if she sized up a potential suitor and eventually took my hand in hers, shaking it. "Truce."

"Good. First, despite what Vrak warned before, can your magic be used to kill? Or at least hurt badly enough so they can't fight?"

"Yes," she replied, looking at the ground. "But…" Trailing off, she let the thought die on her shut lips.

"Okay," I said, ignoring her hesitation. "We need to find them first, and we should be careful not to be caught. Let's go, quietly." And with that, I took the leadership position between the two of us without either realizing it.

Distantly, I heard the calls of men and women signaling to each other as to which passages had already been checked.

They were determined to catch us.

I wondered if maybe Crux and Vrak had managed to escape—perhaps they were even outside devising a way to come and find us? *Maybe it would be best if we find a secret hiding place to wait.* A sudden shout caught my attention.

It was Crux.

He screamed obscenities at his captors, and his voice resounded through the passages like the wail of a dying animal.

He must be hurt, I thought in horror. *He has to be!*

Panic rose in my chest and I didn't realize how hard I was breathing until Tesro put her warm hand on my shoulder to steady me. Her hand felt good, and I felt calm take hold as I refocused on the task.

Traveling through the passages turned out to be a tiring affair as we stayed low and moved at a snail's pace. The darkness worked well in our favor. Whenever we heard anyone coming our way, we shoved our small bodies into the gaps in the rock formations to allow them to pass, unbeknownst to our location.

"How much further?" Tesro asked me as we advanced.

"How should I know?"

She stopped, as if she heard something I could not, and then I heard it too. There was another passage in front of us and we rushed toward it. Quickly, we both pressed our backs against the rock and listened as soft steps echoed around us.

"Interesting," a woman said, and I recognized it as the voice of Roese. "This blade is enchanted. It goes wherever the owner wills it. Even now, I can feel it being pulled. Dangerous—"

"Exciting!" a young man's voice said in return.

"I wonder what it'll take to pass the enchantment on to another?" Roese halted close to where we hid, so close that I could hear her soft breathing. We held our breath. "Find the girls and bring them to me uninjured…if possible."

"Aye," the young man replied, and I heard them both walk away toward another passage, silence following after them.

"Too close," Tesro said as she sucked in a deep gulp of air. "Why are they doing this?"

"I don't know," I admitted. *Roese had the opportunity to take more coin than she was ever likely to see in her life*, I thought, trying to piece it all together. *Why had she turned it down? Why?*

"Let's keep going," she insisted, and I went along with her, my questions left unanswered.

We continued to wander for a long time. Lost, we were truly and utterly lost.

The dark passages splintered in the cave, and more than a few times, Tesro had to lead us with a little spark of fire that she kept lit at the tip of her finger.

She had leaned more heavily on me the longer we walked. Tiredness dragged on her, and her eyelids sagged. Using the magic of the destroyers must have been far more taxing on her than I realized.

"Let's rest," I suggested, leading her toward the passage's edge.

"No!" Tesro forced herself to stand straight, moving away from me. "I'm fine."

Suddenly, she appeared to become lightheaded and almost tripped, catching herself against the wall. The light of the fire on her finger winked out of existence.

"You're not fine, you're tired. I am too! We don't know what happened to them, but if we need to save them, then *you*, at least, need to be ready."

"And what about you?" she asked. "They said you're special, but I've not seen nothin' special about you. Vrak said you're an enchanter, but I've seen no proof of such magic. So what are you? A liar?"

I knew Tesro's question came from a place of frustration and fear, but young as I was, I had a hard time letting the slight go unanswered. I grit my teeth and replied, "I'm not a liar! I've even killed a man before...even if I didn't mean to. That's still more than I can say about you!"

"I've killed four," Tesro replied solemnly, opposing my false bravado. She stood with her eyes closed for a while before she opened them to meet mine, adding, "By accident."

That took me aback. But in that moment, we seemed to build a small bond between us. The bond of those who have killed and lived with a guilt that gnaws at the soul.

"What happened?"

Tesro slid down the wall and I sat beside her. I could faintly see her outline as she held her knees to her chest. A small fire suddenly burst alight on her finger once more, bringing light to her face that ran with tears.

"My family," she said, her voice so low it was barely a whisper. "I killed them."

"Your family?" I gasped in surprise. She shuddered at my remarks. I amended my words, adding, "I'm sorry—it's surprising is all. I'm sure that whatever happened wasn't your fault."

"But it was!" she replied angrily. "I'm a destroyer, and when the deminean found out, they came for me. I was so scared. I... I—"

I placed my hand on her shoulder and finished her sentence for her. "You fought back."

"I lost control!" Tesro's voice echoed down the passage, and I held my breath.

Nothing stirred in the dark.

She sounded as if she were done speaking, her head lulling and her eyes fluttered between wakefulness and slumber.

"Two men came for me in a dark alley," I said, and she forced her attention back to me. As she looked at me, I knew it cost her. "They wanted...*something* from me."

"What?"

"I... I—" Realizing my body was shuddering all over, my words failed me.

Tesro returned the support and placed her hand on my shoulder. It lifted a small bit of the anguish that I did not know I harbored deep inside. "I understand."

I wiped tears from my eyes and pushed on. "When Crux found me, I had already killed one man, although I didn't know it at the time. That's when he named me an enchanter. Said it was the only way I would have had the strength to do...*that* to a fully grown man—given my size."

We both went quiet, sitting next to each other huddled around the small flame. I saw Tesro nod off and the flame flickered and died.

"Rest," I prompted her, and she offered no protest as she leaned against me.

She felt warm...very warm. The slow rising and falling of her chest gave me a certain peace, and I leaned against her, despite my nerves, closing my eyes.

I'll watch over you, young one. Rest now. Rest...for soon your strength will be needed once again, the voice spoke directly in my head, and I felt a small push of relaxation and comfort.

Sleep took me.

Wake up! the voice called in my dreams.

"What is it? I'm already awake."

You must wake, now!

I opened my eyes and was immediately drawn to an outline across the passage from me. I squinted and could just make out a male figure. He just stared at us, unmoving.

"Tesro!" I said and shook her from her slumber. She awoke with a start, as if I had doused her in cold water. Her face looked frightened, like a bad dream had plagued her relentlessly.

The figure moved toward us like a snake striking at its prey, silent and deadly.

Tesro came to her senses and anticipated the figure. Placing her palm out in front of her, she tore a ripple through the space in front of her hand as a blast of air burst out. It ripped pieces of rock off the wall, and the burst sent me tumbling away from her. She remained at its epicenter.

I could no longer see the figure and Tesro had the good sense to light the tip of her finger once again, banishing a small bit of the perpetual darkness.

"What...was...that?" she asked, her words coming breathlessly.

"I don't know, but it was definitely—" Suddenly I was on the floor. I heard Tesro scream and another blast of wind swept over my body—it didn't phase me. The sound seemed a distant thing to my ringing ears, and I knew I needed to stand; that everything depended on me standing and fighting.

Get up! the voice demanded. *Vi'eri. Get. Up.*

Sound returned and Tesro frantically cried for me as the figure bore down on her, grappling her limbs to the cold floor.

I launched off the ground and felt much of my strength return. I felt the voice's power swell in me once again, somehow feeding my body with energy. I turned to face our attacker as he turned to face me.

It was the young man who had led us to the entrance of the bandits' hideaway—it felt so long ago now. Despite only being a head taller than either of us, he held Tesro's limbs down with the ease of a cat bearing down on a mouse.

I felt my body move on its own as I lunged at him. He casually lifted one hand to bat me away with a single swipe. The blow hit me in the ribs and it sent me sprawling sideways. Despite having no weapon, the attack felt as if a club had struck me. The force of it made me wheeze, and I feared to touch my side to find that I had broken ribs. The only thing that stopped my outright panic was that my breath still came in full and deep.

Once again, I stood, and I knew Tesro could not fight this boy off—not with the unwieldy strength he possessed. This time, I came more slowly, deliberate, reaching out for him. He eyed me curiously as he raised his arm again, swinging at me. I dodged under it and his fist slammed into the wall. I heard a crack and small pieces of rock fell to the ground, clattering off the cold ground.

I took my chance and tackled him by the waist, shoving all my weight into him and willing him to give way.

He did not even budge.

I felt his hands grasp around the collar of my shirt and then, before I knew it, he sent me flying through the air. I hit the wall on the other side of the passage and felt my breath leave my lungs in a ragged gasp.

My assailant stared at me to make sure I was truly down, and I dared not move. I knew that I still could...but I was scared. Scared of this young man. Scared of what he would do to me...and to Tesro.

He picked her up by her neck, and she squirmed in his grip. Her shadowed face was hidden from me, but I knew that he was choking her.

She was dying.

I screamed and lunged once more at him. Gracefully, he caught me by the front of my shirt and, in my mad fury, I drove my finger into the bottom of his eye with a wild flail. He grunted, pulling back, and while he was distracted, I bit his hand. Hard enough to draw blood.

The young man screamed as he let Tesro go, turning to face me outright. He put one foot behind him and then kicked forward. I tried to dodge, but I was too slow as the kick hit me squarely in the chest. The power of it sent me skidding on my back, my head hitting the wall.

My eyes swam in misty black as I tried desperately to focus them. I saw double—triple of the young man standing in front of me with a wild look in his eyes, one puffy and red, with a grin fit for a monster.

He reached down with both his hands and I felt his fingers drive into the flesh around my neck, latching into my skin like little hooks. I felt life pour out of me as I desperately tried to breathe. Hopelessly, I reached forward to scratch at him, but my hands fell uselessly to my side. With a sinking realization, I knew.

I would not cheat fate this time.

Just then, like the first glimpse of sun on the horizon, a flash of light illuminated the entire passage. A heat, unlike any I'd ever felt, wafted over me, blocked by the body of the young man who fell on top of me, wailing in pain.

Another flash of light; another wave of heat.

I tucked my body under him and held him close to me as he writhed in agony, screaming a guttural noise that was only fit for nightmares. His breath was hot against me, but I just held him tighter.

A third wave.

The young man slumped on top of me now, completely silent from his previous screams of agony. He made no other sounds, not even those of breathing. A sickening relief washed over me, and I knew that he never would again.

I shoved the body off of me and the smell of his burned flesh near sent the contents of my stomach spewing onto the ground. I forced myself to hold it in, turning away from the ruined mass of flesh and bone.

Piles of lingering fire spread out across the passageway and I could clearly see Tesro bending over with her head to her knees. The soft sounds of her whimpering just carried over the soft burning of the fires.

I went to her.

"Tesro," I said, being extra cautious as I touched her. Her face shot up toward me, her palm facing out. Horror mingled with the expressions of pain in her face. She did not recognize me for a moment, so far was her mind from the here and now. I dared to press forward, cupping her hand in mine. She relaxed as she regained her wit.

"Oh, Vi'eri. What happened?"

"Nothing, Tesro," I lied. "You scared our attacker away when he found out you were a destroyer. He simply ran. Let's keep going. We still need to find Vrak and Crux, remember?"

Tesro seemed to accept my explanation as logical and I helped her to her feet. I faced her away from the mangled body and we continued down the passage, leaving the burned corpse behind.

Chapter Eighteen

Blood of My Enemy

We traveled slowly through the narrow passageways of rock and stone. Tesro walked next to me like a ghoul, still in a daze about what had just ensued.

She had killed again, although she did not yet know it.

We kept quiet, and I wasn't sure if it was that neither of us had much to say about our situation or the hopelessness of it all. We didn't want to admit it to ourselves at the time, but if we found Crux or Vrak, they would likely be dead.

A fork suddenly split our path, forcing us to choose. To the left, a wider passage that looked to have been expanded by human hands, complete with lit lanterns guiding the way. On the right, darkness. Narrow, jagged rocks lined the roof and dread seemed to waft from it.

Tesro looked frozen in place as she looked down that dark passage. A grimace plagued her face. Clearly, going back to that oppressive dark petrified her to stillness.

"We've been wandering in the dark for hours," I said. "If they're here, then I don't think they are being kept down one of these narrow passages. I think... I think we need to risk it and go left."

She nodded, as if she were just a child, absently agreeing with what her parents had ordered. I suddenly realized that she *was* a child—we both were!

How am I here? I thought, trying to push back the despair that threatened to overwhelm me. *How did it come to this?*

I forced those thoughts aside and prompted her to follow me into the lit passage. Now was not the time to despair.

It was but a moment of travel before I heard a low whining grunt. It sounded like a wounded beast and I heard the faint rattling of metal chains as they scraped a hard surface. I rounded the corner and could not believe what I saw.

An enormous creature with a long, thin nose and a flat face sat shackled by both wrists and ankles to pegs nailed to the floor. A small ceremonial bowl had been placed on top of a pulpit that stood just out of the creature's reach.

The beast was skinny. Too skinny, and I could see the remnants of a once muscular being that now appeared starved, all flesh and bones. Its ribs were clearly visible, and the creature's skin had a sickly gray hue to it. Warts littered its body and face, making it appear one of the ugliest things I had ever seen.

I wanted to turn from it in disgust.

"Troll," Tesro said in amazement. She swiftly regained the strength to stand on her own, stepping away from me, and her eyes lit up at the sight of it. Her jaw went slack, and she just stared onward, awestruck.

I regarded her curiously, asking, "Troll? How do you know?"

"Vrak," she replied, keeping her gaze firm on the creature. "He teaches me things like this. It looks too skinny to me, but it is definitely a troll. Look at the warts! Like little pieces of rock grown from the skin. They grant the creature protection. They say a troll's skin is very thin on its own."

Tesro was surprisingly insightful in this, and I saw her in a new light. She was so confrontational before, so difficult to deal with or speak to with any friendliness. It was nice to see that she also enjoyed other things besides torturing me.

I looked back at the creature, and it pathetically pulled on the chains, as if it meant to frighten us, but it didn't appear to have the heart for it. I turned back to her, asking, "Should we help it?"

Tesro seemed to consider this a moment before she shook her head disapprovingly. "It'll attack and eat us, I think. Vrak told me that while they don't actively search for human prey, in desperation, they will kill us. Worse, we won't be able to communicate with it. They speak in their own trollish language."

"But what is it doing here?"

She shrugged and ventured forward slowly. I followed closely behind.

As we got closer, the troll took more notice of us and stood with haste. It was tall, and the chains connected to its wrists stopped the troll from standing at its full height.

I noticed numerous incisions on the creature; hundreds of them, but I could not guess the precise amount. The creature looked as if the realm's smallest knife had been used to torture it, and the torturer seemed keen on making the death by bloodletting as aggravatingly slow as possible.

Tesro looked horrified as she saw what I had already noticed. She held her hand to her mouth to stop herself from gasping out, and I wondered why she showed this creature—a creature that would kill us if it had the chance—so much concern.

I was close enough to the bowl now to glance inside. The outside of it gleamed from the light of the torches beset on the walls. It appeared made of copper, but inside, it was stained a deep red—deeper than any human can bleed. Whoever these bandits really were, they collected this creature's blood for some demented reason that I could not even fathom.

"Why do they want the troll's blood?" I asked, grimacing at the situation, but not daring to turn away from the troll, who continued to eye down at us. With a heaviness of breath, I wanted to retreat from this place. Something just felt...wrong.

She considered my question for a moment, absently scratching at a bruise the young man had left her. "I think trolls are supposed to have healing blood. Maybe if they...drank it?" As soon as the words left her mouth, she looked like she would be ill.

"That's...useful," I replied, not wishing to pull the conversation further in that direction. Tesro shot me a baneful glare, and I amended, "But this is wrong! No creature should be made to suffer like that."

Her gaze softened.

"Wrong, you say?" a voice asked from the passage we had previously come from.

I turned to look at who had spoken and my heart sank into my stomach. I rubbed my eyes as I thought they must be playing a trick on me. There, standing shirtless with burned clothing, stood the young man whom Tesro had incinerated before. To my shock, I observed no other discernible wounds on his body.

"H—How?" I stammered the words out. I couldn't think straight. When I looked at Tesro, she stared as if someone dangled a corpse in front of her.

"How?" the young man repeated, leaning casually against the wall. "Why, magic, of course. Enchanter magic. The troll's blood provides some healing effects—albeit mild on its own. But when an enchanter enhances the magic that exists in the blood, well..." Suddenly, he slammed his fist into the wall and it sent a splintering crack through it, splitting from the ground up to the ceiling. He looked at his handiwork and smiled wickedly at his grim achievement.

Tesro and I had backed up to stand next to the bowl of troll blood. The troll itself was close to us, far too close for comfort, but I didn't know which fate sounded worse: the troll killing and eating us...or this boy capturing us.

There can be worse things than a quick death.

I stared around for an escape, but there was none to be found. The young man blocked the only way in and out of this section. I was so enamored with the troll that I had neglected to look for our next course of action. With a sickening certainty, I knew that I had killed us both.

Some leader I turned out to be.

"So you can see, there is no way out for you," he said in a mocking tone. "Now be good girls and come with me. Roese is looking for you."

"No!" I replied, trying to make my voice sound fierce. "Don't force us to kill you...again."

Tesro looked at me, confusion by my comment clear on her face. She had not regained her memory of the event, and I didn't think I could rely on her to end things the same way as before.

Voice, I need your help. I need your strength! I shouted in my mind, hoping they had heard.

I felt...something. The voice had received my message, that much I knew, and whoever they were, it seemed as if they tried to will me...something. But in the end, no strength came to me, and I felt no nudging on my emotions.

I was alone.

"I've run out of patience," he said as he stomped toward us with a single-minded ferocity.

Tesro screamed and started back, knocking the copper bowl to the floor. As it hit, it rang out, sending painful spikes of pressure into my head. Dark blood splattered from the bowl onto the right side of my body.

The young man was coming quicker now. He ran—no, sprinted. He was coming toward me and my panic rose. In desperation, with no other options, I remembered what he told me, and licked the blood off of the back of my hand.

He stopped his furious run to stare at me with astonishment. Then, after a moment, he laughed. "Are you stupid?" he asked. "That isn't nearly enough, and even if it was, I've had some as well. So what if it increased your puny strength a paltry bit? Shame, really. I would have liked to have some real fun."

My stomach lurched, and it drove me to my knees. My heart beat faster. Faster and faster until it hurt, each beat sending a rippling shock through my muscles. My blood boiled in my veins, as if something had lit my insides on fire. The pain of it faded quickly, and what remained was power. Pure, unfiltered power.

I had never felt stronger in my entire life.

I stood back up, and the young man stepped to me, unphased by my inward transformation. He reached forward, setting his hand to my shoulder, and then pressed down. I knew he tried to force me back to the ground, and I could see the veins bulging in his arm as he strained to do so. But I did not budge against him, despite his gloating of his supposed power.

Frustration marred his face, and he placed a second hand on me, shoving downward with everything he had.

I resisted still.

"What...is...this?" he managed to say through gritted teeth. Blood trickled from the sides of his mouth and he wheezed. Sweat poured down his face.

I drew in a deep breath and let it fill me near to bursting. My body moved on its own as I reached up and grabbed his wrist. He struggled to pull back, but with one quick twist, his wrist snapped, the bone breaking through skin, and sending a torrent of blood rushing to the ground.

He screamed in agony, stepping back from me, and gripping his limp wrist pathetically. I felt nothing for him; no anger, no rage, just the quiet desire to do what the situation demanded of me. This lad was in my way, and so he needed to die. Logic told me the reason was adequate, emotion had no say in the matter.

With a disgusting snap, the young man thrust the bone in his wrist back into its proper place. The regenerative process was quick, and his wound closed in but a moment. He rolled his wrist around to test it. When he was satisfied with the healing, he prepared to attack me again.

His attack came quickly, and it had the ferocity of a trapped animal. It was not the trained attack of a skilled fighter, but more a brawler who sought to end a fight as quickly as possible, no matter the damage to their own body.

His first strike hit me square in the lower jaw, snapping my head to the side. I caught a glance of Tesro's horrified face before his knee caught me in the stomach, dropping me to the floor.

I spit blood from my mouth as he dragged me to my feet, hitting me.

Smack!

Smack!

Smack!

Each blow that struck was weaker than the one that came before. I felt the pain as a distant thing, as if I was witnessing someone else taking the beating, only experiencing it third hand. I knew that it was doing damage to my body, but it mattered little to me at that moment.

I shoved him back, and he took a handful of my hair with him as he twisted away, ripping it from my scalp. We circled each other as if we were two predators fighting over a kill. He attacked again, but this time, I was ready.

I saw his stance and judged where he would swing. Instinctually, I dodged and kicked forward, hitting him on the side of the knee. I felt the bone break and the kneecap dislocate as the power of my strike hurled him sideways. He laid on the ground wailing, holding his leg, and writhing on the floor.

I paid his pleas little mind as I kicked at his head, and he narrowly dodged my attack, rolling to the side and kicking up dirt. He shoved his kneecap back into place and the rest of his leg healed instantly. In a moment, he was standing again, taking his brawler's stance. Sweat drenched him from the sheer effort, and he panted wildly.

I smiled, and it seemed to unnerve him. The young man struggled so much, and yet, my body still felt as light as a feather.

Suddenly, I felt a shaking of earth. Tendrils of stone burst forth from under the young man, wrapping him as he attempted to swat them away.

He failed.

The rock hardened, and a crevice formed underneath him. He sank down and down until only his head remained above the rock.

I looked at Tesro, who stood with her hands planted forward. She nearly fainted as she lowered her arms uselessly to her sides.

He screamed and wailed, cursing and babbling in an incomprehensible jargon. In the end, he could not break his prison of stone.

"Let's go," I heard Tesro say, and she grabbed my arm.

Something deep and dark compelled me to break her neck.

It would be so easy, I thought. *So simple. If she were dead, I could escape easier. I could—* I gasped, and shame flooded me as my mind cleared. I felt as if I had held my breath for hours. *What am I thinking? Why would I hurt Tesro?*

I looked down at the smeared blood on my skin and vowed to never resort to taking it again. Silently, I thanked the Well that I only had such a negligible amount. I shuddered at the thought of taking a full dose.

She pulled on my arm, unaware of what I had almost done to her, but she could not force me to move forward. I still had some lingering strength from the troll's blood. Reluctantly, I gave in to her will, forcing myself onward.

The troll behind us howled and twisted against its chains, matching the struggling of the young man who now laughed hysterically.

As we left, neither of us spared a glance backward as the mingled sounds of the creature and the young man followed us as we fled.

We didn't make it far as we nearly ran headlong into three bandits immediately upon passing the split in the cave. They seemed to have followed the sounds of fighting and they now shouted at us, giving chase.

We ran down the other passageway with its oppressing darkness and jagged rock formations. Panicking, we didn't bother to check where we were going as we foolishly sprinted headlong through the total black.

Then there was a drop.

The ground under us was loose, and I heard Tesro gasp for just a moment before it gave way. Suddenly, we both fell as if nothing had ever been there to hold us at all. I heard the screams and turned to see the terror in our pursuers' eyes, lit by the torches they carried, just before they vanished from my sight.

Instinctually, I reached out and grabbed her mid fall. As I did, we struck the ground, and all went black.

Chapter Nineteen

A Deal in Blood

Eri... Eri! Get up! Get up! a voice called to me.

"Ugh..." I replied from the depths of sleep.

Wake up! the voice called again.

I awoke suddenly with a splitting headache, and the light that surrounded me pierced my skull.

My head felt as if it were on fire.

Oh thank the Well, a voice echoed at the edge of my senses. I groaned at the sound, the pain nearly toppling me again.

"Who... Where am I?" I asked, dragging myself up blindly.

I felt a sudden kick hit me in the stomach and I retched, falling back to the ground, and into my own spit-up. I wanted to stay down, but my chest felt heavy and I was having trouble breathing. Reluctantly, I pushed myself up again and forced myself to open my eyes against the pain.

At first, the light blinded me, but as my vision adjusted, I made out a woman's form standing just in front of me. I met her eyes—it was Roese.

"You piece of shit!" Crux said, the rattle of chains punctuating his words. "I'll kill you! I swear on the reincarnation of my soul I will."

"You can try," Roese replied mutely. "Something tells me you aren't up to the task, my impotent friend."

With great strain, I sat all the way up and as I tried once again to stand, I felt, for the first time, the shackles that bound my wrist preventing it. They were tight, and the skin they clung to chaffed, leaving a slight itching sensation. The metal, dark with rust, cut shallow lines into my skin that bled down the length of the chain.

I kicked my legs forward and sat, not breaking the glare I leveled at Roese. I forced all my hatred into the stare.

She merely smiled back at me before saying patronizingly, "That's quite the glare, girl." She turned toward Crux, adding, "I think she gets it from you."

"Leave. Her. Alone," Crux growled, like a caged dog.

"And what will you give me in return? I wonder…"

Shackles held Crux down, much like the troll had been. Much like I was now. They bound his hands and feet to chains tethered to the floor, and his clothes were ripped to shambles. Such a shame to ruin such fine clothing. His face appeared swollen and purple.

They had beaten him in my absence.

Roese went to speak, but I interrupted, asking, "Where's Tesro?"

She scowled at me and tugged at her black hair. "Not here." A look of disgust overtook her face. "My son told me how the girl incinerated him and then buried him in a tomb of rock. She is dangerous… Perhaps too dangerous to be allowed to live, as much as that pains me to say."

"No!" I screamed and pulled against my shackles. I nearly ripped my arm out of the socket. Silently, I wished I still had the strength of the troll blood, but something in me was relieved that I did not. I was not myself under its influence, and if I was going to die, I would rather die as myself than someone or something else.

Roese seemed to delight in my pain, a cruel smile cracking the edges of her lips. "You see, this is why we need to change. Look at the despair that comes to you at the thought of one simple death. It's what makes us humans weak…our inability to sacrifice. My own son was the first I administered my troll blood concoction to. He was a sickly boy in his youth, and I was always so worried, dripping with despair for the day I would wake and he would be gone; his soul returned to the Well. That was a weakness. I was weak."

"That's not weakness," I replied, so tired that I let my head sink to the ground where I rested it. "It's what makes us human."

"Exactly!" Roese spat on the floor near me. I couldn't tell if she had wished to spit on me, or if she did so just to prove she could. "With the beast's blood, we will create a new human ideal. A better one. There is just one thing we need to do first...sow chaos in the eyes of our deminean oppressors. And what better way than killing a Ri'sha."

"Useless. Utterly useless trite," Crux said, putting as much disdain as he could in his words. "A new human ideal? Making the deminean fear us?" He spat on the floor near her feet. "Nonsense, all of it. You're a two-bit enchanter that is corrupting your own son with the blood of Anduinna's bastard creations. Do you not think the Life Incarnate will come for you? Do you not think the deminean will come for you? You've already killed everyone here and you don't have the good sense to realize it yet." He took a deep breath and calmed himself, adding, "But it's not too late. Give us the tear of eternity, take the coin and leave this place. Give up your foolish pursuits and content yourself that you caused a certain Ri'sha a bit of discomfort, for that is the *only* comfort you will get to live with."

Roese seemed to consider his words for a moment. To really consider them. Eventually, she shook her head and walked toward him. Leaned down in his ear, she said something. Her voice was so low that I couldn't make out her words, but from Crux's expression, it wasn't good news.

"I won't... You're mad!"

Roese laughed. "You will!" She kicked him in the ribs and he doubled over onto the ground, groaning.

After a moment, he lifted his head, and his peppered beard was covered with dust. He spat out dirt and said, "I won't kill a Ri'sha. It's suicide."

"It is." Roese pursed her deep red lips, adding, "Why do you think I'm sending you to do it?"

"I won't," Crux repeated. "Even if you threaten my life..." he paused for a moment to glance at me, "or hers." He made his words clear—not even the threat of my death would convince him of this path. He shook his head weakly. "If you don't kill Vi'eri out of spite, the deminean will hunt you down. All of you. They won't discriminate. They will only see human, and only the death of *all* will sate their bloodlust."

"Enough useless ramblings. You will do this, because I can make you." She turned to two others who stood by. "Bring the blood."

"Why?" Crux asked, his head lulling for a moment.

"Because I will make you powerful...like us."

"And you think I will help you then?"

"Not by choice..." she admitted. "Which is why I won't give you any choice in the matter." Pausing for a moment, she seemed to consider whether to speak on. Twirling her curly black hair, she walked back and forth in front of Crux before adding, "You're an enchanter too, are you not? Well, there is a link between all of Anduinna's creatures. The collective soul of the Life Incarnate and the magic that flows in the blood of beasts that bind them to her. I can enhance that connection—change it. Use it to bind another's will to mine...to take power over them. You *will* kill the Ri'sha, because I command you to do it."

Crux looked at her with horror on his face. "They're your slaves? Your own son?"

Roese turned away from him. This seemed to be a particularly sore spot for her, but when she turned back, her face had hardened and she stepped close to Crux to give him another kick. "My son," she said, her mouth near foaming with rage, "is *not* a slave."

He coughed—a ragged thing. Exhaustion was clear in his expression, and it was a miracle he could sustain the conversation. Was he trying to change her mind? To find some sort of weakness? Or was this the simple desperation of a man without an option?

"But the others?" Crux asked. "Are they bound to your will?"

The conversation was interrupted when the bandit returned carrying a large cup. Roese took it from him and turned toward Crux. "Enough conversation—it will do you little good. Don't worry, once you drink, all will be clear. I will take your fears and doubts and change them into a single-minded focus. You will be a weapon for the human race. The kindling of war."

"The sacrificial lamb," he replied.

Roese smiled. "Yes, but what glorious purpose you will have, little lamb. Come, sit and drink. It is time for action."

Crux laid still, defiant to the last. He kept his eyes focused on her, but made no movement to show he would obey her command.

Roese shook her head as if she were dealing with a petulant child. "I considered this might happen. To declare you will sacrifice another is just words, but to do so is an entirely different story." Roese grabbed my hair and wrenched me up. "For every time you refuse me, I will take a finger. After that, an ear. Then her nose...and eyes...and—"

"Enough!" Crux said. His tone was unmistakable; defeat and misery. "Enough. I know when I've lost. Roese, I throw myself at your mercy... If I do this, will you let Eri go?"

She seemed to consider this for a moment before replying, "I have no reason to keep her. Once you drink and leave, I will release her in a day's time. It is a fair bargain; her life for yours."

"And Vrak...Tesro?"

"Don't get greedy, merchant. This girl is the best bargain you'll get. The others...well, we may have uses for a pair of destroyers. Especially the girl... so powerful! After she has been properly persuaded to my way of thinking, that is."

"Fine," he said, wasting no time as he sat up. "Then let it be done."

Crux turned toward me with a genuine smile on his dirt strewn face. I realized it was the smile of a man who knew he was about to die. He wanted me to remember him this way—not what Roese would soon make of him. Tears welled in my eyes and I forced myself to seal that smile to my memory.

To carry him with me after he was gone.

"I failed you, Eri," he said, masking his pain. "When they release you, *run*. Go south and never come to the north again. Perhaps our souls are fated to meet again, in another life. There is so much I have to tell you, but what's most important is that I'm so—"

"Enough!" Roese cut him off with a wicked laugh. "Such fond words—it's like she really is your daughter. Here," Roese handed Crux the cup, and he took it as one willingly partakes of poisoned food, "now drink and change the path of this realm. We will remember you as a legend to humankind. Take pride in that."

"Pride is for the weak," he replied. "I don't need to be a legend, I've had my fill of them. No, if one person remembers me fondly, that will be enough."

I felt a rage build up inside of me. Panting, ragged breaths filled my lungs with as much air as they would hold, and I pulled against my bindings. The muscles of my arms screamed in agony and the tightness of my clenched jaw drew blood from my gums. I focused every bit of strength I had and willed those bindings to break.

He just stared at me as he slowly rose the cup to his face, regret spilling out from his bloodshot eyes.

He did not believe I could save him.

That lack of belief shamed me and fueled my rage even hotter. The muscles in my arm tore as my shoulder pulled from the socket. I howled in pain and still these bindings would not break.

The cup was on his lips now, and Roese stared at me with amusement.

He tipped the cup up.

"No!" I screamed, and was submerged in an almost primal sensation. Time itself paused, and for the first time, I could see the small speckles of magic that floated in the air. Hundreds? No, thousands of little strands connected between each other, each giving off a small flicker of light before blinking out. Ever moving, ever blinking. I reached forward, as much as my bound arms would allow, and pushed on one strand close to me. I wanted Crux to stop.

I needed him to stop.

A turbulent wind exploded from the palm of my hand, throwing everyone and everything in the room crashing against the walls and roof of the cave. The pressure was so intense that I could not move my body against it as the gale twirled around the room like the heart of a tornado. Eventually, the air sought its freedom and went shrieking down the halls of the various passageways, leaving the screams of others affected by the force in its wake.

My shackles fell to the floor and the dust the wind had kicked up stagnated in the air, blinding me and making it difficult to breathe, dirt filling my mouth.

"Crux!" I hacked the words out. "Where...are...you?"

"Here!" he said, and then I heard him coughing as well. I crawled on the floor toward where I had heard his coughing fit. It was painful and slow, but I eventually touched the chain, running my good arm up to find his wrist shackles. He was still down on the floor and his restraints felt painfully tight against his flesh. "Your shackles... How?" he asked, but I ignored his question. We could talk when we were safe.

I found a nearby rock and began hitting the pin that fastened the chains.

Strike!

The chain didn't budge.

Strike!

A spark flared, but it did not break. I channeled my frustration and swung again.

Strike!

The pin broke, but the rock crumbed in my hand. I noticed the blood covering the broken pin. My blood. Something had cut my hand to shreds, but I thanked the Well that I couldn't feel any pain. Not yet, at least.

Crux pulled on his chains enthusiastically, like a man who sensed freedom was a real possibility. Now that the pin was released, the entire chain could be pulled through, releasing him. The shackles still cut into his flesh, but that was a small price to pay until we could find greener pastures.

He leaned in toward me and whispered, "Let's go. Let's just get out. Screw the tear of eternity. Screw the Ri'sha."

"What about Tesro? Vrak?"

Crux looked away from me. "I don't know where they are... Likely dead, or worse."

I stopped in front of him. "Then I'm not leaving!"

"We can look on the way out, but—"

"Don't bother," Roese's voice boomed from beyond the cloud of dust. First, I saw her silhouette, then she walked through the sandy mist. "My child, you have some power. I am surprised that you too are a destroyer. Three destroyers and an enchanter. Quite the group."

Then, with no other warning, Roese charged us both. She kicked at Crux, who blocked with the metal of the shackles. Her blow struck and Crux screamed as the metal shackles bent and dug further into his skin. She continued with a punch to the gut that sent him slouching back.

Like a flash of light, Roese was on me. Her knee connected with my stomach, and it felt like a blacksmith's hammer, and I the anvil. Her attack staggered me, but I forced myself to stand against her onslaught of attacks.

Crux suddenly grabbed her waist from behind, pulling her away from me. "Run, Eri," he said as Roese elbowed at him to break his grip.

I ignored Crux's command and attacked Roese as best I could. I must have looked like a fly attacking a horse for all the good it did. She battered me away and then threw Crux across the floor with ease.

Plainly, Roese was still trying to preserve him to use for her machinations, and she now had a greedy look in her eye as she studied me.

"It will be such a waste to damage a destroyer," Roese said in an even tone. "But I will do what I must." She walked to where the cup had landed in the corner of the room. Finding it tipped on its side, blood spilled out from its edges, she looked inside and smiled, pleased with the remaining content of blood. "I know your intentions now, girl. If you even try to fling magic at me, I will kill you. But worse, I will make Tesro suffer for it."

Roese smiled and knew she had won. It was over, and I had no more will to fight. Even if I did, my body refused to listen to me any longer as I held my injured arm meekly to my side. I had tapped into my potential for just a moment...and it was still not enough.

"You'll make me suffer?" I heard a voice call from the passage entry. Tesro stepped through with a look of pure hatred on her face, a wounded Vrak close behind her.

"You!" Roese said before a ball of condensed water surrounded her entire head. The woman dropped the cup and the remaining blood splattered across her and the floor. Desperately, she tried to fend off the water, striking continually at her face, but her hand simply passed through it.

I looked at Vrak, who looked to draw strength from Tesro. Both of her hands rested on him to provide support to his one working arm. His palm faced out, and he looked to be continually tapping the air in front of him as he followed Roese, who fell to the floor, rolling and writhing as she slowly ran out of oxygen to breathe.

The quietness of the deed was unsettling.

Her flails became less and less as the pockets of air that drifted toward the top of the orb ceased. Her body stilled, but her eyes remained open. Piercing, lifeless eyes. Vrak kept tapping at the air, his dark eyes holding as he glared at her lifeless body with absolute intensity.

"Vrak..." Tesro looked frightened by Vrak's mad tapping, getting more frequent by the moment. She shook him, adding, "Vrak...enough!"

He held the spell longer, even stepping closer to Roese as he *tap, tap, tapped.*

"Stop!" she yelled, grabbing at him pleadingly.

He held the spell still.

Then, like dew coats a blade of grass in the morning, a thin layer of ice formed around the globe of water. Thicker and thicker it grew until it encased Roese's head entirely. With one sickening crash, Vrak kicked the woman's head, causing it to separate from her body entirely as it rolled to shatter on a nearby wall.

"Recover from that," he muttered disdainfully, collapsing into Tesro as she strained to ease him to the ground.

Crux, undeterred by the gruesome display, went to Roese's body and scavenged through her clothes. I stared at him in disbelief and he met my judging glare, saying, "If we don't recover the tear of eternity, we're as good as dead anyway. Don't criticize me for this." His face lit up suddenly as he pulled out the blackened box, adorned with a new knife mark carved into the side. He opened it and closed it just as quickly, grinning.

Vrak wheezed. "Good news, I presume?"

"Very good, friend. Now let's move, if you can."

He sighed and forced himself to stand, slowly. "I'll manage. Tesro?"

She nodded, and I stood as well. I was tired, but now that the fight was over and the chance of living seemed hopeful, it filled me with renewed vigor.

"Does anyone know where we are?" Crux asked.

Not one of us responded.

CHAPTER TWENTY

FOR A BRIGHTER FUTURE

We traversed the inky black of the tunnels for what felt like days.

My left arm hung limply at my side, each step sending an agonizing shock through my body

A painful reminder of my failures.

We found the bodies of bandits broken by fallen debris laid out among the ruin of the caves. Some looked far worse than others, like a beast had savaged them, large pieces of their flesh missing—ripped from their bodies. The surprise in their dead set eyes was haunting.

We did not encounter a single living soul other than ourselves as we passed through the tunnels, searching for an escape. My summoning of air had caused multiple cave-ins which blocked many pathways. We were losing hope by the minute that an escape was even possible.

Is this place to be my tomb? I thought. *Have I damned us all?*

Crux suddenly stopped; an excited look plastered on his dust covered face. "Over here!" he said enthusiastically. "My knife, I feel it. Just around here, I think."

We followed his directions, and were led to a caved-in passage with a single bandit that an enormous rock had flattened. The rank smell of spilled intestines assaulted my nose, but Crux insisted we press on.

Crawling over the boulder, I did my best to avoid the smears of blood that covered the walls and floor. I muttered an apology, but I wasn't sure why. Somehow, the thought of dying alone and forgotten in a cave filled me with a new type of dread.

Such eternal loneliness.

Crux vaulted over first, whooping in delight on the other side as he found his knife on the floor at the end of the passage. I was close behind and found the passage sealed by a massive cave-in of rocks, blocking us from venturing forward. I frowned; despair as palpable as the blood that hung in the air. It pestered me, making it hard to breathe.

"What's that?" Tesro asked as she landed next to me. Slowly, her finger lifted to point at a small gleam of light at the edge of the pile of rocks. Frantically, I moved to dig, but Crux held me back.

"Just watch," he said, pointing.

Vrak landed near Tesro and let out an audible grunt. She reached for him, but he merely pushed her hand away. They shared a nod, and both faced their palms forward.

The floor shook as two pillars of rock formed to hold the unstable passage open. Then, in an instant, the rocks that blocked the path exploded outward, revealing an exit to the outside.

Fresh air rushed in and I took the first breath of clean air in what felt like an eternity. Looking around, the others seem to share my enjoyment of the life-restoring breath.

Between Tesro and Vrak, I could almost see the same shimmering of magic I had during the confrontation with Roese, but the sudden pouring in of light from the twin moons near blinded me. It had been too long since I had seen natural light.

I felt the sticky sweat cling to my body and, with the light, I saw how filthy my clothes really were. I didn't even want to know what I smelled like. My own nose had long ignored our collective odor.

Tesro ran outside first, yipping in glee. I moved to Vrak's side to help him. He shot a contemptuous look at Tesro, but surrendered it just as fast as the cool air cleansed him of negative thoughts.

As we exited, the cooling night wind hit my skin, and it felt as refreshing as a drink of water from a fresh spring after days of dehydration. The wind brought in the natural, clean smells of nature, which quickly supplanted the smell of blood and death. I thanked the Well for the blessing.

We made it out. We were finally free.

"Thank the Well," Crux said, relief plain on his blood-smeared face.

"You mean thank Vi'eri and Tesro." Vrak coughed a bitter laugh. "Some mentors we turned out to be. Our pupils already outmatch us both."

"Ain't it the truth?" Crux struggled to wipe sweat from his face, but it only made the dirt smear more. He looked like a beggar boy on the streets. "I really need a bath."

"We all do," I said, and we all shared a laugh.

We moved to sit under the light of the stars and the twin moons in their full glory. I was tired, I ached, and I was hungry...but also, I was alive.

"So, Vi'eri," Crux said, grinning. The light of the moon shone in his wide eyes as he continued to stare toward the heavens. "I thought I was a poor teacher, but you turned out to be a destroyer this entire time. You were never an enchanter! My eyes must have been playing tricks on me that day in the alley."

Vrak looked at both of us. "Day in the alley?"

Neither of us answered him, but I stared back at Crux. "I don't know what I did in our fight with Roese. I just knew I didn't want you to drink the blood. I had felt its effects on me before."

He turned toward me in shock. "You drank the blood?"

His tone made me feel insecure. Judged. Like that was information I should have kept to myself.

Crux stared at me, aghast, as I said, "Only a little. I had to!"

I don't know why I felt the need to defend myself, but his discerning eyes made me feel embarrassed and weak.

Crux's face suddenly downturned, like a burden had fallen upon his shoulders. "Well, there's nothing to do for it now. We have a long way back—best we get moving. And Vi'eri...keep it a secret. All of it. The blood, your magic. It will only bring you pain, I promise you that."

More secrets, I thought to myself, longing for the day I could live my life free of them.

"Tesro," Vrak said, drawing her attention away from the stars. "Can you guide us? I'm afraid I'm quite useless at the moment." She nodded, and with a tap, a small flame kindled at the tip of her finger.

We all stood, and she stepped out in front of the group. Crux and I assisted Vrak, who appeared drained, barely able to stand on his own. We traveled slowly out of the valley, up to the road, and made our lethargic and painful way toward Whiteline.

Within the day, on our trek to Whiteline, we found a group of traveling merchants who called themselves the White-Raven Caravan. They had come from the frigid north, aptly named the lands of Frostwyern. Their carts, led by a pack of mules and a beast called a grayhorn, were loaded with hides and thick furs.

They told Tesro and I stories of the lands of Frostwyern. Stories about its near constant snowy terrain and the abundance of wolves, bears and yetis—all of which yielded magnificent furs. A fact the merchants seemed particularly proud of.

Crux traded some of the coins the Ri'sha had provided to buy some of these coats for us. The nights were getting colder, and I welcomed the large gray yeti coat blanket gladly.

He bought himself a pristine gray wolf cloak that hung to his knees. Silently, I wondered at who would willingly choose to hunt a wolf of that size. It had to have been taller than a full-grown man, even on all fours.

The leader of this merchant group called himself Botolf Adkin. He was an elderly man who complained near constantly of his age and what trips like this now cost him. His frame was slight and his skin looked like thin paper. His son, Botulk Adkin, bore a fleeting resemblance to his father. He was stouter than his father. Shorter, with light-brown hair—but muscular in the way a man gets from constantly lifting heavy loads.

Crux had spent most of the journey to Whiteline speaking with the two, and by the time we reached our destination, he had made some strong connections with them. I suspected that if he was granted his request to start a mercenary company from Ri'sha Isodros, that these two, and the White-Ravens, would be excellent business partners.

"Looks like we will have some more jobs lined up to the north," Crux whispered to me in passing. "I hope you don't mind the cold."

I nodded, not sure if I should be excited or terrified considering how well our first job had gone. Still, he appeared happy and Vrak looked content as well, mostly recovered from whatever had ailed him in the caves. As for myself, Botulk had been kind enough to relocate my shoulder, relieving the pain a great deal, but leaving me with a dull ache in the muscle.

I spent most of my time with Tesro. Our bond was not as strong as I had perceived from the time we spent together in the tunnels, but it was still there, just out of reach. She seemed distant from me in a way she hadn't been when we were completely alone. I suspected that she did not think we would make it out alive and now that we had, thinks it a mistake to have been so open with me. Any mention of the personal topics we discussed in the caves was met with a scowl and a change of subject.

I forced myself to let it all go.

The merchants had been very generous with the shelter and food they provided us for the journey. It seemed as if another group had spread the news of our dealings with the Ri'sha to Botolf. He had made the connection to us quickly. Likely any hospitality made to us was to garner favor from someone they perceived as close to a Ri'sha. I could not blame the man. It was just good business.

The journey to Whiteline went faster than expected, and as we entered the town, Vrak and Tesro went to reserve us a room at The High Tide Inn, just as before. I suspected it would please the owner when I showed up relatively intact.

I made a mental note to do just that.

It is rare that someone offers kindness for kindnesses' sake, and I would not forsake him my tale of woe.

Offhandedly, Crux mentioned that Tesro and I would need to share a room, for the time being at least. Now that the coin would come from our pockets, it just made sense.

Crux and I had the more arduous task. We were to present the tear of eternity to the Ri'sha personally.

Both of us.

Her previous instructions had been very clear on that point.

We went straight to the Ri'sha's estate at the top of the ridge overlooking the town. Whiteline was much the same as it had been when we left. The passersby gave us a wide berth, and I was thankful they did. My skin prickled whenever a stranger came to close...as if my body sensed their ill-intent and alerted me to the dagger they all hid in the dark. That way of thinking exhausted me in a way that is hard to explain.

The last time we were here, everything around me inspired a sense of awe. This time, however, I made calculated notes of the things I witnessed...as if I expected that one day I would need to escape this place while being pursued.

Such is the way trauma presented itself to me.

Well-groomed and well-dressed humans littered the grounds of the Ri'sha's estates. They appeared as servants and maintained the land of their lords. They kept their heads low and focused on their tasks with a single-minded certainty. The deminean in leather and chainmail that held weapons, I assumed, were guards. I still didn't know what to think of the deminean clad in robes of varying colors and shapes. Best to assume they were some type of royalty and do my best to avoid drawing their attention.

A guard stopped us at the entrance, but we recognized him as the deminean who had led the small entourage to bring us here the first time. He admitted us with a suspicious look, saying, "Wait inside and someone will guide you, human."

Crux scoffed at the guard as we entered and the man stared at Crux's back as if he had just leveled the most insulting comment they had ever heard. The deminean guard slammed the door hard, as if trying to make a point.

Like the guard said, a human servant quickly found us and ushered us back into the meeting room where we had previously met with Ri'sha Isodros. Upon entering the room, it was...different. Gone were the fineries of silverware and the glass decanters of light. Instead, the simple blackened table was bare, with only a few lit candles adorning it.

We waited in silence, but not for long. Ri'sha Isodros entered and slammed the door in the face of her advisor as he let out a hiss of frustration at having been denied entry. Isodros, dressed in a simple gown of light blue, practically ran toward us, hand outstretched. "Did you retrieve it?"

Crux took a step back before unceremoniously pulling the box from his pocket and handing it to her.

Her eyes lit up as sharp teeth poked out of her wide grin. She examined the box, spinning it around in her hand like a treasure unlike any other in the realm. When she came up the single knife mark, her golden eyes turned toward Crux and a frown creased her otherwise elegant face.

Crux wordlessly raised his hands as if to say, 'What did you expect?' Isodros took the hint, nodding to herself.

She fumbled with the small latch and opened the box to reveal the blue gleam of the tear of eternity. She used one long fingernail to nudge the object, as if reassuring herself that it was real before promptly closing the box again.

Isodros pointed to some chairs at the table. "Sit," she said. We both obeyed, taking the same seats we had before. Seeing us, Isodros also assumed her previous seat, adding, "I haven't decided if I am pleased or angry with you yet, Trueblade. I ordered you to retrieve the box for me with the item intact...and you did. But I also expressed the item was *not* to be endangered. In this, you disobeyed me. So before I pass judgment, I would have you explain," she tapped her nail irritably on the table, "why?"

Crux admitted everything that had happened freely... Well, most things. He spoke of Roese and her bandits. Of their hideout in the caves and of their plan to have him kill Isodros. She appeared amused at that. Pointedly, he omitted the troll's blood and my newly found destroyer magic.

I had no intention of contradicting him.

Isodros nodded along to his words and when he finished, she clapped slowly. "Bravo, Trueblade. Bravo." She picked the small black box back off the table, turning it in her hand as if she still did not believe she possessed it.

"No applause needed, Ri'sha. I simply did what you asked to the best of my limited ability." I noted the humility that he showed Isodros. It was something I hadn't seen him do for any other. Did he do so out of fear or respect?

"Too modest," she replied. "It doesn't befit one such as you, Trueblade." She once again assumed her *tap, tap, tapping* with her long fingernail, considering for a time. Her eyes rose to meet Crux's face. "Very well. I believe your mission to be completed in satisfactory terms. You have earned my boon...and my trust. Not something I give out lightly, I might add. However, I wonder as to what this 'Roese' offered you to kill me?"

Crux met Isodros' eyes as if they had a battle of wills. He replied, "Nothing I could afford to live with."

She smiled. Lucky for us both that she did not press the issue.

Isodros turned to me. "And are you okay, child? From what Trueblade has stated, you were in the fighting's thick as well. I do wonder how you made it out unscathed." Her golden eyes stared at me as if she could piece out all my secrets with just a glance.

I forced myself to meet those piercing golden eyes. "I did little." Holding up my limp arm to her, as if to emphasize my point, I added, "And I didn't come out unscathed." I let it drop unceremoniously to my side.

"Is that so?" She stood from her chair, her brilliant multi-colored scales catching the light from the candles. Slowly, she walked toward me, running her long black nail, sharpened to a point, across the table as she came. She stopped directly in front of me and I held my breath as she reached out her hand, as if to shake mine. "This is how humans seal a deal, correct?"

"It is..." Crux replied suspiciously. "But what deal?"

Isodros held her hand in the air, unperturbed that I did not reach for it. "The deal I offer to you both now. Stay in the city and do the rare odd job for me. In return, I will see you are able to do your business as you see fit—so long as it doesn't interfere with my own dealings."

Not knowing what was proper, I went to shake, but Crux interrupted me, asking, "I can make that deal Ri'sha, but not her. She's not old enough to know of what she promises to you. Do not force this—please."

Isodros let her hand drop as she frowned at him. "I was hoping to avoid this...unpleasantness. But I suppose some things are fated to pass." She grasped a nearby chair, pulling it out, and sat in front of me. Even sitting, she loomed over me in a way that made me feel as if I were an insect about to be squashed by a superior being. "Vi'eri of Elklan, I presume?"

I swallowed hard, and Crux almost gasped.

"Yes..." I replied, my eyes no longer able to meet hers. My chest felt heavy as I held my breath for what was to come.

"I read a curious report from a missive sent from Elklan. Can you guess what it was about?"

I shook my head, not trusting my voice to hold.

"I think you do," she replied, leaning ever closer to me, as if her words were for my ears only. "It read of an ashen-haired human who not only attacked a deminean girl, but actually managed to injure her. High house Dem'i Ironback's daughter, to be precise. She suffered a stab wound to the shoulder. You wouldn't happen to know anything about this?"

Isodros played with my emotions...and it worked. I panicked, a primal panic of a desperate animal that knew its death was near. I glanced at Crux, but he avoided my gaze as if acknowledging me would bring about his death as well. With a sickening realization, I remembered that the townsfolk had seen my scales. *They knew!* Isodros would certainly know and if my mother was correct...she would kill me for it.

Crux found his courage. "Wait, Ri'sha. Please—"

"Not another word, Trueblade," she replied, not bothering to turn toward him. "You are in my favor, but you will not interrupt again. Do we have an understanding?"

Crux nodded, even if she couldn't see, and turned away to stare at the floor, defeated. I saw the muscles of his arm flex as he squeezed the arm of the chair he sat in, his knuckles white with the effort.

"It was me," I said. There was no use denying the truth they already knew. "But I did it to save my mother. I..." Frustration boiled over in me. *Why did I need to fear that deminean girl? Why is she better than me, or any other human for that matter?* I ground my teeth. "I attacked her because she tried to hurt my mother. Because she tried to hurt me! And for that, we had to run...and they killed her for it." I stood, throwing my chair back. "They killed my mother!"

Isodros leaned back from me, as if she were afraid I would attack her as well. This reignited a fire in my chest and I kept my gaze firm upon her, unrelenting. If I was to die, I would die defiantly.

She matched my gaze, as if trying to break me. Eventually, she relented. "Then it sounds like the debt is paid." My glare focused and the fire in my chest burned hotter at her words. Sensing this, she amended her words, "More than paid is what I meant to say. You have suffered for this, Vi'eri. Believe it or not, I can understand." She stood and paced the room, still holding her black box in one hand and tapping at her own scales with the other. "You see, this is why I want you both to stay. No, I *need* you to stay. This...relationship between the deminean and humans—it's unsustainable. It breeds hate and war...such as the war in the south. I believe—no, I *know*—our species can work together and forge a peaceful society where there is equality between us. I believe we could accomplish it in our lifetime, Vi'eri."

The words spoken so plainly astonished me, and as I went to reply, Crux interrupted. "I doubt it." Shocked at his own words, he added, "No disrespect intended, Ri'sha."

"I take no disrespect from words spoken honestly, Trueblade. But this attitude of yours is defeatist. You already assume the outcome before we have even started. You... *You* will be my example of what union between our two species looks like. An example of what the deminean have to gain if they give humans independence rather than servitude."

Crux seemed to consider her words, asking, "And if I choose...not?"

"Then I will be disheartened," she replied. "But I would respect your wishes and see you paid for a duty well performed. If you wish, we will go our separate ways."

"So I truly have a choice?"

"You do."

The words hung in the air like a pendulum, ever-swinging between the two choices that would change the course of all humans. No, change the course of the entire realm.

A choice... Ours and ours alone to make.

"And what about me?" I said, steering the conversation back to my time in Elklan. "What will become of me?"

Isodros turned back to me with a smile. "Why, nothing. As I said, your debt has been paid. I will see a missive sent to Elklan declaring such. I can assure you that while I may not be most prominent among my Ri'sha brethren, none shall dismiss my orders. You can breathe easy Vi'eri, none will come seeking retribution."

And for the first time in so long, I breathed. I truly breathed. Tensed muscles I had not even known existed eased, and I felt relief...and guilt, knowing that my mother's death bought such peace.

I turned to Crux, and he smiled genuinely at me. He appeared happy at the outcome, but a small tear crept into the corner of his eye. He turned from me and wiped it away.

"So what say you, Trueblade?" she asked. "Will you change the realm with me?"

The irony was not lost on me. Isodros sounded much as Roese had, but instead of offering death, she offered life. A new life. Instead of offering slavery, she offered choice. A true choice.

Does this woman really stand at the peak of deminean society? I thought. *Could she really force this change?*

Crux didn't take long to answer. He stood and walked toward her, who now sat at the head of the table. He stood in front of her, his head barely taller than hers, and proffered her his hand.

Isodros looked down at his hand, and then up at him. She stood, and he had to crane his neck to meet her eyes. She took his hand and shook.

Grinning, she said, "Deal."

Chapter Twenty-One

THE TRUE BLADES

Crux avoided me over the course of the next few days. After our conversation with Ri'sha Isodros, I assumed he had a lot on his mind.

I placated myself by speaking to the various humans who came into the High Tide Inn. I even started helping old man Grath, the owner, for a small allowance of coins. This attention I was receiving seemed to make Tesro jealous in a way I did not understand, as she often took to sitting alone in quiet contemplation.

During this time, Tesro and my relationship waxed and waned. At times, she would be genial; considerate. We would speak of simpler times and of our adventure, both recently and from before we were both forced from our homes. Other times, she seemed spiteful, as if I were to blame for all the trouble she had ever come across.

Vrak pulled me aside one day and said, "Don't mind her. She's been like this since I met her. She has a good heart, but she lets her own head impede showing it at times."

I accepted his words for what they were.

Tesro would be Tesro.

She was who she was and neither of us was going to change that.

I managed to corner Crux one day to have him explain what was in store for us. He tried to wiggle out of the conversation, but after some choice words, he agreed to have a sit-down with the four of us to discuss our respective futures.

Strangely, he could not meet my eye as he made this promise and kept muttering excuse after excuse until I allowed him to leave in peace.

The night of the aforementioned meeting had come. Vrak, Tesro and I found ourselves at the corner booth of the inn's bar on the first floor. The candlelight was kept dim here and the place would have had a gloomy air about it if we had not already claimed it so often as our own.

I spent a great deal of time at that booth, speaking with travelers and other townsfolk. Tesro and Vrak as well.

"Do you know what has been troubling Crux lately?" I asked, turning to Vrak, who loaded a small dark red pipe.

He held the pipe out to Tesro and smiled. She rolled her eyes, casually lighting the tip of her finger with a small flame, and transferring that fire to the tip of his pipe.

Vrak dragged a large lungful of smoke, turning to blow it away from the table. It smelled of vanilla. Before I could comment on it, he said, "I was wondering the same myself, Vi'eri. Ever since you both spoke to Ri'sha Isodros, he has been...distracted. Any attempt to ask what was spoken of is met with silence or excuse. By the Well, I would have already left this place if he had not dropped such a large bag of coins with the promise of more to come. Despite that, a man can only wait so long before his blood grows cold and adventure calls him away."

Tesro glared at him. "Only men?" she asked in a dark tone.

She seemed to be in a mood tonight.

"It's just an expression, Tesro. Don't worry, I'm not planning on leaving you behind." He smiled, and she nodded contently. "Now then, Vi'eri," he turned his attention toward me, "you were there when Crux spoke to the Ri'sha. What did they say?"

"Vrak..."

"I know. I know. 'It's not your place to say.' It's the only thing you've said to me about it in days. Which is more than Crux has said. It seems like there is a lot happening and a lot of silence about it. I won't lie, it puts me on edge."

I weighed my next words carefully. I didn't want to betray Crux's trust, and he advised me to not speak of anything until he was ready. But I felt I had to say something—needed to say something. We... *I* owed Vrak my life, and I hated keeping him in the dark.

"I was there, yes," I said, and Vrak leaned in close to listen to my words, "but the entire conversation, it was...different. The realm is different now—I feel it. Vrak, I think Crux and Isodros changed something, they—"

"We did," Crux interrupted as he strode up, casually taking a seat next to Tesro and I. "It seems you didn't want to wait for me. I suppose that's fair. I've kept quiet the past few days about my comings and goings, but that changes now. We have some things to discuss, the four of us." All were silent, waiting patiently for his words. Like a tavern bard, he looked at each one of us individually, meeting our eyes as if forming some type of connection before he spun his tale. When he was satisfied we were giving him the proper acknowledgment, he nodded, adding, "We've done it. We've actually done it!" His voice rose in jubilance, and it drew the attention of the other patrons in the tavern, who gave him a range of rude gestures. He ignored them. "I wanted to make sure Isodros was telling the truth. The long and short of it, she was."

"The truth?" Vrak asked.

"So...?" I said, asking the obvious question. "Crux's Crew, she granted you the permission you needed?"

Crux frowned. "No...that was a terrible name, Eri. Never should have let you pick it."

"But—"

"No! Our mercenary company's name was right in front of us the whole time. The 'True Blades.' Has a nice ring, doesn't it?"

I looked at Vrak, who took a draw of smoke from his pipe and as he smiled, small tendrils whisked out between his teeth. "Just like you to name it after yourself," he said. "If you can promise us coins like the last job, and perhaps a little less danger, I'm in." He looked at Tesro, adding, "If she is too, of course."

Tesro stared at him, and then turned to Crux, candidly ignoring me before giving him a nod in agreement.

Then all eyes turned to me. Nervously, I looked toward the door and pondered if escaping was an option. The truth was, I never even considered what to do with myself after this was all over.

Before I could make my grand escape, Crux pulled my attention back, asking, "So, Eri. What do you think?"

"What do you mean?" I replied, faking ignorance. "I'm happy for you, Crux. You got what you wished for."

"No." Crux frowned, scratching at his scarred lip. I noticed he had a hard time meeting my eyes now as he quickly turned to ask Grath for a round. The old man nodded, hobbling away. "Eri, you heard the Ri'sha. She pardoned you. You could go home, if you wanted."

He opened the wound that I desperately wanted to stay closed. I could feel Vrak and Tesro's eyes drilling a hole in me, their attention firm and relentless. They waited for my answer with bated breath.

"No," I replied, shaking my head. "I don't have a home—not anymore." I frowned and tried to push the negative feelings away, but they were as persistent as a gnat.

"Why not?" Tesro asked as she stood, placing both hands on the table.

"Sit down, Tesro," Vrak demanded in a harsh tone. He motioned for her to sit, and she obeyed, crossing her arms defiantly. "Don't bother, Vi'eri. Can't you see this is painful for her?"

She slammed the table. "But in the caves... I told you what happened to me—the whole truth. And you held back. Why? What really happened to you?"

Crux looked shamed by the way the conversation had turned as he pulled out his knife and awkwardly carved small bits into the table. Grath quickly slapped him on the back of the head as he returned with the drinks. He didn't respond, instead picking up his glass and sipping silently.

I drew on my courage and said, "You're right, Tesro. The truth is, I attacked a deminean girl. Dem'i Ironback's daughter."

Vrak coughed on his pipe smoke and Tesro's mouth hung open.

"How do you still live, child?" Vrak asked as he recovered from his choking fit, sending small bits of spit cascading across the wooden table.

"I ran... We ran. My mother and I. She didn't make it, and it was my fault. I should have let them do it. I should have..." To say the words of truth would have left me hollow. The pain was still too real. It was too soon to speak of those things.

"Do what?" Tesro asked. "Should have let them do what?"

"Cut off my finger."

Vrak looked downtrodden upon hearing my words, and Tesro had a grim look on her face. She didn't aim to seek her anger toward me, but toward the deminean who had not only caused the death of her parents, but mine as well. I saw a new hatred bloom in her. Perhaps it had always been there, dormant, waiting to be released.

My words were the catalyst that made such pain possible.

"So, if not in Elklan, where will you go?" Crux asked, pulling the conversation back. He set his drink down and wiped small bits of liquid from his beard.

"I don't know," I replied truthfully.

It was Vrak's turn to slam the table, and when he did, he tipped Crux's drink over, spilling the remaining liquid onto his trousers. He puffed out his chest and said, "Just ask her Crux!"

Crux leveled him a dirty look, but he eventually sighed out the words, "Eri... I mean, Vi'eri. I would like you to join The True Bla—no, sorry...it's not that." He paused, clearly frustrated with himself. Then, as if he opened his soul up to us, words spilled from his lips. "Eri, I want you to join *me*. I know I can never take the place of your mother, and you've never spoken to me of your father, but I know what it's like to be alone." He breathed out the onslaught of words, and I didn't know how to respond. Before I could answer, he continued in a calmer voice, "While I cannot teach you to hone your powers like I originally promised, you will still need someone to help. Vrak, I'm sure, would not mind taking on your training. Truth be told, it's not about that either. Eri, I would miss you if you were to leave. That's all I wanted to say."

His words were like a spear through the chest. Like a hammer to the heart. Tears burst from my eyes and ran down my cheeks. I tried to breathe, but the breath came in pathetic sobs between my heaving chest. I put my head in my hands and wept.

I felt Crux's warm arm around me, and he held me. His chest rattled as much as mine did, and I embraced him, refusing to pull away.

He said nothing. Offered no soothing words and no promises of better times. He understood.

Truly understood.

When my flowing tears dried, he let go, and I wiped my red, stinging eyes on the back of my gloved hand. He sat back in his seat and Vrak leaned in another direction to give me some privacy. Tesro appeared in another realm entirely, staring off into nothingness and occasionally cracking her knuckles as if she prepared to fight invisible enemies.

"You don't need to give me your answer now. I knew I shouldn't have sprung this up on you—"

"No, wait!" I said. "I want to join, Crux. I want to learn about this magic I have. To become strong. Isodros spoke of a unity between humans and deminean. What better way to honor my mother than to help bring about this peace?" I waited, and his expression turned to pure delight. Before he could speak, I added, "Crux Trueblade... I would like to join the True Blades, if that's okay with everyone?"

Vrak nodded and, to my surprise, so did Tesro.

"Then it's settled," Crux said, raising his glass. "To the True Blades, and to its newest member...Vi'eri Trueblade."

I raised my glass in celebration of my new life.

A life that I had chosen for myself.

Chapter Twenty-Two

A Name

For I believe the hybrid will serve as the bond that will bring our two species together. For too long, the deminean have struggled to control the Well—to control the humans that our ancestors have oppressed, unjustly. Cruelty only induces more bloodshed.
When the hybrid is born into this realm, we should exult in their coming! For they shall usher in an era of unprecedented peace. It is my wish that all deminean will follow in the path that I shape to foster a new unity between all human and deminean kind.

Ri'sha Dem'i Isodros Zhesko, condemnation of Ri'sha Sovereign Dem'i Krottik of Clan Drekhide.

"And...?" Ax asked, leaning closer as if he expected Vi'eri's answer would come as but a whisper.

"And?" she replied. "And I became a mercenary for many years."

Kasu nodded at that, but Ax looked agitated by the answer as he chewed his lip sulkily. "That's it? You became a mercenary, and what?"

She eyed him up and down and frowned at his remarks. "Did you expect something else?"

He scoffed and slipped behind the group a bit.

They had been marching for roughly the entire day, stopping only to refill water and eat on the move.

The first moon had just appeared in the sky and she turned to Akkora. "Send the order down the line. Prepare to halt for the night." Akkora looked away from her, cheeks flushing red. She leveled a questioning glare at her deminean general. "What is it?"

"I already relayed the order," Akkora replied, refusing to meet her eyes. "You seemed...distracted."

"Distracted..." Vi'eri shook her head at the woman. She was a superb right hand, but, at times, she overplayed her position.

Looking around, she felt far more eyes on her than usual. Typically, deminean and humans were more than content to give her a wide berth, lest her ill-luck spread to them. *Or I kill them.*

Give it up, Vulana said, appearing next to her, emerging from her shadow. At a push on her emotions, Vi'eri bent down and stroked his dark fur. Small tendrils of purple flame wisped around her hand, but it did not burn. *You've changed. They all must know that.*

Have I? she replied in thought. *You realize what I set out to do? What we set out to do?*

Vulana was subdued by the comment. It grated on her endlessly that even her trusted shade didn't know how best to proceed.

Well, no use berating yourself for past mistakes, Vulana said. *It won't help now, and it won't help what's to come.*

"Let's stop!" she announced suddenly, drawing in a small bit of magic that lit the limbal ring of her eyes bright golden. Everyone took a step back from her, their attention firmly in hand.

All came to rest atop a grassy hill, and she looked out across the vastness of the realm. The Everplains were beautiful, and the backdrop of white-peaked mountains that surrounded them made it even more so. The air smelled crisp and vibrant. Alive! It almost hid the scent of an army of unwashed bodies.

Almost.

"Are you going to continue your tale?" Kasu asked, daring to take a step forward to stand at the head of the small entourage. She turned and noticed the unwanted attention, nervously running her hand through her sleek black hair. "I'd like to hear more."

"More," Vi'eri repeated, tasting the word on her lips and letting it slip into the air like tendrils of smoke. "Child, I do not know if I can say more. Those times were some of the best in my life...and the worst."

Kasu opened her mouth to speak, but Ax cut in. "Then that's more reason to speak of them. We still don't know why we're here—"

"You're here," Vi'eri said, letting an edge of anger taint her words, "because a fate worse than death waits for you if we fail. You are here for yourself—never forget that."

Ax walked toward her and reached out, gripping the front of her leather armor. He looked ridiculous as he had to stare up to meet her eyes, and her ashen hair whipped his face as the breeze rolled by. The light of the moon glittered off her scales, cascading brilliant silver into his eyes, but this did not deter him. He kept his eyes locked with intent.

"Ax!" Kasu said, moving to grab his shoulder. "What are you doing?"

"I need to know," Ax replied in a low voice only meant for her ears. "I *need* to."

He surrendered his grip and turned away from her, staring at the ground for a moment before slinking away, kicking up dirt as he walked with a defeated gait. She stood still, glancing around. Other humans and deminean turned their gazes away from her, afraid to draw her ire away from the delinquent Ax. All except Akkora, who met her eyes and grinned a wicked little smile.

"Does this amuse you?" she asked, but chastised herself for how childish the remark sounded.

"Not at all," Akkora replied. "I'm just thinking that if all had Ax's spirit, maybe we would stand a chance in this war after all."

Indeed, Vulana said in her mind. Then the shade had the audacity to walk toward Ax, who had taken to lying in the grass, staring absently up at the sky. The shade let his tail whip the boy's hand playfully, and Ax accepted the prompting, petting him.

Traitor, she sent Vulana in thought. Despite that, she smiled to herself. Perhaps Akkora was right—we needed Ax's spirit. By the Well, we needed all the strength we could get. Had her words truly inspired a reaction like this? Perhaps...

"Sorry about Ax," Kasu said, drawing her attention back. "He has lost so much, is all."

"Haven't we all?" Akkora replied, rustling Kasu's hair as if she were a child. She gave the deminean woman a shocked look, and then her cheeks glowed bright red.

"I don't hold it against him, Kasu." Vi'eri kneeled to meet Kasu's eyes directly. "I deserve far worse, if we're being honest. Worse for what I put you all through now. Worse, for what I've already put so many through."

This drew the attention back from the few onlookers, who still kept their distance, but waited patiently for her next words.

She straightened herself and projected her voice outward. "Do you all wish me to continue?" There was a murmuring, and, eventually, a collective agreement between the few human and deminean littered around. "Then set up camp, make a fire, and return after *all* have eaten."

Her words inspired as every man and woman practically ran to their duties with a renewed vigor.

Hours passed and an even larger group of both deminean and humans now accompanied them by the fire. Most stood outside the fire's light, but still close enough to hear her every word; around ten or so, and Akkora now joined them as well.

Vi'eri held her arms out for all to see. "Now then, where was I?"

The night was upon them and the light of the twin moons cast the shadows of mountains that looked to be monsters in the dark, trying to flood the army. Only their fire, made large to encapsulate the increase in listeners, battled the encroaching shadow.

"You became a mercenary, I think?" Kasu replied.

"Ay, that I did. A True Blade mercenary."

"I've heard of them," Ax said eagerly. "It was said that the leader, Crux Trueblade, was one of the greatest human warriors to have ever lived. He mastered the art of the blade without even carrying a true bladed weapon. Just a single knife, that, they say, acted with a will of its own."

Vi'eri nodded to the words, adding, "Crux would have loved to hear himself spoken of. It was always his weakness...the seeking of glory for glory's sake."

Not a true bladed weapon? she thought. *Oh, how wrong he is.*

She frowned at the return of unpleasant memories long past. Crux was no longer of this realm, but his memory and legacy lived on in the stories others told of him. Truly a fitting end to the man she once called father.

"I won't bore you now with the details of every job I took as a mercenary. I could sum most jobs up as a merchant from the north needing an entourage to protect them from banditry, or worse. No, that's not important. I can sum up my time as a mercenary with the utterance of a single name."

Humans and deminean alike held their breath, waiting for her to speak that one name. One could hear the drop of a pin at the silence and Vulana nudged approval at her skill of showmanship.

Like Crux had in the past, she turned her head to gaze across the fire and into the eyes of all who listened, meeting each individually, as if sharing a secret between each of them. She let this tensity hang in the air for a time before she spoke the name in a loud, clear voice.

"Tesro."

Chapter Twenty-Three
WELCOME HOME

"Can you believe we've been stuck doing this for over five years?" Tesro said as we walked lockstep with one another. A rather large pack beast called a grayhorn suddenly sneezed, sending Tesro's hair whipping around her face.

"Stop complaining," I replied, laughing at her misfortune. "At least it's better than the time we were helping wrangle the wild horses of the north. Remember? You slipped and fell in horse manure. You reeked for days."

She sneered in disgust as she pulled long tendrils of snot from her hair, wiping it to the lightly snowy ground. She turned and wiped her hands on my coat. "You promised not to say anything." I laughed again, and she returned it, with merchant Rhas joining in.

Rhas was a relatively new merchant for the White-Raven Caravan; the first deminean merchant in their ranks. She was a young deminean, or so she claimed. Four slits on the top of her right ear indicated that ten years had passed for each. It would make her forty years old, yet she looked no older than twenty by human standard.

Still, it was an oddity to see a deminean work under a human; a thought that still bothered me. Such a notion was unimaginable in the not-so-distant past. I wondered if it was a sign that the realm truly was changing.

Tesro petted the horned beast, leaning heavily against its thick furred body as she raised her eyes toward the deminean merchant. "So, Rhas..."

Rhas looked down at Tesro with those golden deminean eyes, her blue scales gleaming in the midday sun. With a note of curiosity, she replied, "Yes?"

"If you had to choose one of us—between Vi'eri and myself—who would you choose to protect you?"

"Vi'eri," she replied promptly.

Tesro frowned. "Wait, why?"

"Because she knows how to keep a low profile." Rhas shot her a genial smile. "Unlike another fiery redhead I know who sends balls of fire the moment something goes awry. I've lost more than a few patches of hair because of you."

"It was one time," Tesro replied. "Besides, the bandits were trying to capture you. Couldn't let that happen, could I?"

Rhas scoffed. "Better than being burned alive."

"To each their own." Tesro shrugged her shoulders exaggeratingly. "You know Rhas, I was just beginning to think you were alright for a deminean. I'm just too quick to judge, I suppose."

"And here I was beginning to think the same...human."

An awkward silence came between us, as palpable as morning mist. When Tesro had heard a deminean would join the ranks of the White-Raven Caravan, she took her complaint straight to Botulk Adkin. When her complaints fell on his deaf ears, she went to Vrak. After that failed, she finally went to Crux, who offered her no recourse. There was no living with her for some time, and for months following, she was an absolute nightmare.

Still, I understood Tesro's feelings—I really did. The deminean had taken as much from us. She could never bring herself to trust the deminean or Ri'sha Isodros, whom she felt made a show of wanting to work with humans only for her own ends. No, she could never fully trust them, not after the deminean had stolen her family from her. "She'll betray us someday," Tesro would whisper to me when no one else was around. I would nod in agreement at her words, not wanting to spark trouble.

But truthfully, I had secretly hoped for the unity between human and deminean that Isodros promised.

"What are you two arguing about now?" Vrak asked, walking to the front of the caravan and petting the grayhorn.

"Oh, nothing," Tesro replied in a tone that betrayed her lie.

"Is that so? Well, I was hoping the two of you would want to do some training. But if you're busy, I could—"

"Let's go!" Tesro replied, cutting him off. He shook his head at her, but she paid him little mind. I smiled at the exchange as I, too, shared in her enthusiasm.

We stepped away from the caravan, which halted to allow the grayhorn to rest a bit. They were fantastic beasts for the cold and snow, but when introduced to a little heat, they wore out quickly. Donkeys were the primary pack animal for most of the world, or so Crux had told me. Although, down in the heat to the south, I heard rumors of large salamander-like creatures named sandelard's who glide along the desert sand like fish glide through water. It was something I hoped to see one day.

The midday sun of winter was overhead, and with it a chilly wind buffeted the front of my body. However, the large gray fur wolf's cloak kept me warm. During my travels, a merchant in Frostwyrm told me the cloak was actually from a creature known as a varg, which explained its unusually large size. Crux had passed it down to me and it now hung to my ankles. The years had seen me grow. So much, that the cloak no longer dragged on the ground behind me. I pulled it close to me—my protective barrier from the chilly bite of the wind.

"What are you doing, Graywolf?" Tesro asked mockingly.

"Why don't you ask yourself, Firethorn?"

"Ugh," she replied in frustration. "I hate that nickname. If I find the ones who started it—"

"Would you prefer Tessy?" Vrak asked, taking a puff from his red pipe, the light of the embers shining in his brown eyes.

When had he packed and lit that thing?

She ground her teeth in frustration. "You always do that—team up against me. One day, I'll make my own nickname."

"You can have mine," I replied. "I don't care much for it. It doesn't even make sense. I'm called this nickname because I occasionally wear a gray fur cloak? Why don't we use the names 'Leatherarmor,' or 'Rippedpants,' while we're at it?"

Tesro laughed, adding, "Or 'Tornsoles.' Still, those are better than Tessy."

"Enough!" Vrak said, cutting into our mindless chatter. "Are you both ready to train, or should I come back after you're done?"

"We're done," we replied in unison. Stealthily, we shared a grin between each other.

Tesro and I, over the course of the years we spent together, had become the best of friends. The only genuine friend I'd ever had. We shared everything; a room, clothing, training—we even shared the same magic. She had been as tall as I when we first met, but now, I stood at least a head taller than she. I knew this fact irked her, although she would never outright concede to it.

Still, I envied her stature. She was lean and small, and the freckles on her face had only multiplied with time. As for myself, I was lean, but tall. Too tall for a girl. At least that's what others in Whiteline would say.

Vrak coughed and brought me back from my wild daydreams. "Today we will work on control."

"Again?" Tesro complained.

"Again and again, until I can trust you not to blow up the entire caravan. Or me, for that matter." He pulled a large drag of smoke and I knew a lecture was imminent. "Tesro, you're powerful," he blew the smoke out his nose and continued, "perhaps the most powerful destroyer I've ever known. You're at least twice as strong as myself and I consider myself of adequate strength. What you lack is control, not strength. Just because your own magic won't harm you, doesn't mean it won't harm others *near* you. I don't say this to stroke your ego, it is merely a fact. Now come, let's train." He tapped his pipe on the bottom of his shoe and pushed his long graying hair out of his eyes. "Now assume your stances."

With his order, I squared my posture, facing Tesro. She mimicked my movement.

I breathed life into my body slowly, letting the air fill my lungs and then focused on the power that exists in the in-between. Just like that, small flashes of light, like little fireflies, appeared all around me. Thousands of them clustered, sparking in and out of life. I held my right palm forward and waited.

"Good," Vrak said, assuming a similar position to us. "We destroyers deal with the magic that exists freely in the realm. It reacts to our will. The stronger our will and natural talent, the stronger reaction the magic has to us."

"We know, Vrak," Tesro replied, but she did not break her stance. I could see the strain it took for her to stay in control. Magic amassed around her, as mosquitos are drawn to light. It was almost as if the magic pleaded for her to use it. She fought that impulse, small drops of sweat forming on her freckled face.

"We will go over all the steps of control each time we train," he said, glancing at Tesro. "Now, do something easy. Create a small cyclone of air around your finger. Focus on what you want and find an appropriate amount of magic near you and tap it, forcing it to bend to your will."

I held my breath and found a small cluster of magic near me. I turned my hand toward it and, with my index finger, lightly tapped it, willing my desire. Light flashed in front of my eyes as the particles of magic burst, connecting with other strands near them. I held firm and, with my left hand, controlled the bursts until a small ring of wind circled my right index finger. Other particles of magic buzzed nearby, wanting to join, but I held them apart easily.

I smiled, looking at Tesro, who appeared to struggle with the relatively simple task. Sweat trailed down her face as if she had dipped her head in a river. Her wild red hair matted to the sides of her head in a tangled mess.

Desperately, she fought the magic near her. It looked to have a mind of its own. I could feel the pressure of that magic—it wanted so desperately to unite—to create a larger cluster.

For a moment, it succeeded. The entire mass of magic particles hummed with anticipation of a command that would allow it to expend the gathered energy that now reverberated with power.

Then, surprisingly, Tesro forced the magic apart, thrusting the larger mass away and stabilizing the smaller amount before touching it gently. A small ring of air surrounded her finger, and the magical particles that surrounded her stabilized, drifting aimlessly away.

"Good!" Vrak exclaimed, a grin creasing his cleanshaven face. "And this is why we demand control. Magic is useless if you cannot anticipate its outcome. Just because we are called destroyers doesn't mean we need to destroy."

"It wasn't too bad this time," she said breathlessly. Her exhaustion made for a poor mask in which to hide her lie.

"Well then," Vrak replied, "I'm sure you wouldn't mind doing it again?"

She looked shocked for a moment, but quickly hid it, assuming the standard casting stance once again. I followed her lead this time, and saw determination hidden behind her hard-set eyes.

We, and the White-Raven Caravan, finally made it back to Whiteline after some time away.

Whiteline looked more or less the same as I remembered. Gulls flew in unison, encircling the town with their noisy calls, and the people hawked their wares on narrow streets meant for half the population.

Deminean guards moved around with purpose, and the smartest of the humans stayed away, while the less fortunate took elbows and the occasional scabbard strike that forced them to move.

Some things never change.

"Home again," Tesro said, and she stretched her slender arms until I heard a crack. She let out an audible groan. I rolled my eyes at her, and she returned my look. "What?"

"Oh, nothing," I replied, rolling my neck to work out a kink. "Should we check in with Crux first?"

"No way! We're back in the city...a proper city! And proper cities call for proper food—not that fat, gelatinous stuff they eat up north. It stinks, and it's oily." She made a noise of disgust as she stuck her tongue out.

"It's not that bad," I lied. "But I could go for some 'proper' food, as you so elegantly put it."

"Meat!" she said with a lust in her eyes. "Beef, preferably."

"Steak? I think I would prefer something greener," I replied. She stared at me with shock in her eyes. Before she could object, I amended, "I'm sure we can find something that accommodates us both." I turned to address Vrak. "If you're heading back, can you tell Crux we'll be there soon?"

He nodded, taking another drag from his pipe. The man really did smoke entirely too much.

I turned and wordlessly waved goodbye to Rhas, who genially returned the gesture as Tesro grabbed my arm and hurried me along.

When we made it to the primary thoroughfare of Whiteline, we slowed our pace, walking down the streets of the city toward a favorite restaurant of ours. The roads seemed to get more and more crowded every time we came down to the seaside.

Humans littered the streets. Far more than I remembered, and I hardly recognized anyone in the mass of people. At the rumor that the Ri'sha of Whiteline was treating humans as equals to deminean, humans flooded to the northern port town in droves. It was a patently untrue statement; the deminean did *not* consider humans equal to themselves here or anywhere else I knew of. Nonetheless, thousands of them poured into the city.

With Whiteline expanding so rapidly, it created what they referred to as slums on the outskirts of the town. Because of the limited amount of work, crime had been steadily on the rise as well. Which, to my dismay, was actually good business for the True Blades.

Tesro and I dodged around the mass of vagrants that lined the streets with proffering hands and unwashed clothing. Their stench assaulted my nose. As I turned from them, I felt a pang of guilt. *Hadn't I once been just like them?* I thought. *But what can I do about their situation? I can't help them all.* I was forced to let the thought go as we reached our destination.

We ate quickly, and after our meal, we walked back toward what was formerly the High Tide Inn. Now, after the death of the previous owner, old man Grath, Crux had saved enough coin to buy the inn outright. He'd expanded it, creating the official headquarters of the True Blades. He liked the name, so he kept it, but dropped the 'Inn.'

I hadn't been paying attention, thinking of all the conversations I'd had with the old man. Haphazardly, I ran headlong into a veiled deminean. They hissed a swear at me and I backed away, palms forward, to show I was not a threat. A circular embroidery of a reptilian-like creature with wings sewn into the chest caught my eye.

I'd seen it before.

The vestment declared they were a member of the Dragon's Court, a relatively new religious sect of the deminean population who believe they were descendants of beings known as dragons. It seemed made up of younger deminean men and women who seemed at odds with Ri'sha Isodros' declaration of human independence in the north. Their beliefs can be summed up as thus: restoration of deminean superiority over humans.

Tesro pulled me to the side and the veiled deminean stalked past me, muttering something under their breath.

I'm sure it was unpleasant.

The members of the Court would always take an opportunity to show cruelty toward a human, whom they decreed less than cattle.

"You don't wanna get on their bad side," Tesro warned. "Make an enemy of one member of the Court and make an enemy of them all. With how many members they've gained recently, I don't even know if Isodros could protect you from that lot."

"What are they going to do? Pray us to death?"

She shot me a sidelong glare. "And here I thought I was supposed to be the reckless one?"

I smirked at her. "What can I say? I like to vary my preferences from time to time."

She laughed, which prompted me as well. Like two giggling girls, we dashed through the crowds toward High Tide.

The city was more dreary than I had remembered it. Besides the issues with population control, sanitation had also become the forefront of everyone's mind. Where once, the raw smell of the sea only lingered closer to the actual ocean, the rank smell of waste coated the streets, making them slick. I grimaced at the thought of slipping and falling into that filth.

They had erected new buildings in the city, but only those with plenty of coin to spare could afford to own anything now.

Reluctantly, I faced a thought that I had been holding back from. In our wild pursuit of a peace between humans and deminean, we seem to have accidentally created a different type of society that functioned similarly to the one it proceeded. Instead of status coming from whether you were a deminean or human, status now belonged to those who had the coin to pay for it.

Had we really made any significant change at all?

Perhaps that is just the nature of the world. There will always be the *haves* and the *have-nots.*

"Come on!" Tesro said as she pulled at my arm. I moved, narrowly avoiding a horse-drawn cart that galloped past my way. The horse snorted in my direction, hitting me with snotty mist, as if annoyed by my reckless abandon. "You're going to be trampled. Where's your head been lately?"

"Huh? Oh, nowhere," I replied, itching my hand through the leather gloves I wore. "Just have a lot to think about."

"Can you not 'think' in the middle of the street?" She pulled me under a thatched building. "Come on, you need rest. Truth be told, I could use some myself. And a bath. Definitely a bath."

"Not yet," I replied. "Crux first."

"Vi'eri, come on. Crux will want to hear everything that happened on the job. Nitpicking bastard. We'll be there for hours! He'll say, 'It's bad luck to not celebrate a job well done.'" She mimicked Crux's speech while scratching at her distinctly scar free lip.

"Rules are rules, Tesro. Best to stop complaining and just get it over with."

Soon, we found ourselves at High Tide, avoiding any other distractions as we entered. It looked much as it had before, burly men and women drank and drank to their heart's content and vied with each other over jobs that Crux managed. The True Blades had taken to hiring freelancers on recommendation, the best of which were offered a more permanent position in our ranks. We'd grown from the pitiful four that we started with to over ten strong.

Our primary client had always been the White-Raven Caravan, and its trades of exported furs. They'd even expanded southward themselves, which offered our 'little' mercenary company even more opportunities. We were growing, and my knowledge of the world was getting larger by the day. Funny, the more you think you understand about life, the tougher life becomes as a way of reminding you of how little you actually know.

"Eri, Tesro!" Crux called from the bar, a drink in his hand. It'd become an all too familiar occurrence with him of late. Without ceremony, he strode up and hugged me, squeezing me as if to let me go would condemn me to death. The first thing I noticed was his belly—a little rounder than when I had left. Likely feeling self-conscious, he added, "I need to lose a few, I think." He pulled back and slapped at his stomach.

The second was that he reeked of spilled beer, it covered his clothing.

"That isn't helping," I said, pointing to his mug, which slouched drops on the floor as he pulled away from my extended hand.

Unlike some men, Crux was not an angry drunk. He didn't belittle or berate, but his habits were not without worry. He could become irritable, and had sharp downturns in mood if the drink hit wrong.

"You just got back, Eri. Let's not rehash old conversations. Not today."

"Conversations..." I replied. But, relenting, I shrugged it off and reached forward to hug him again. "I missed you too, Crux."

As I pulled back, he had a genial smile on his face. A grin rose from ear to ear and the corners of his eyes welled with pride. The smile pulled my attention to his face, which showed he was a bit grayer than I remembered. His peppered beard became less and less peppered every day, and even his hairline grew thinner edges. It hurt me to realize that Crux was getting older; that he had already been middle-aged, even when we met for the first time.

His mortality terrified me.

Tesro coughed, and Crux turned to face her. "Ah, yes. Tesro. Sorry, come here, come here." He walked forward and embraced her in a hug as well. "Would never forget about my little firethorn here. Hope you had a good time?"

She pointed at the mug. "I will, if you know where a girl could get one of those?"

"Of course. Jezza!"

"Crux," Jezza replied with a scowl from behind the bar. She was busy wiping the bottom of a glass mug, her dark hands showing through the clouded glass. "You can't be lettin' the girls drink. If you have to pass something on, don't pass on that vice."

He glowered at her. Ignoring the comment, he moved to the bar and poured two mugs of beer. She continued to stare daggers at him the entire time, not breaking her judging gaze from him. He met her eyes as if they participated in a contest of wills. Slowly, he came back and set the mugs in front of us on a nearby table before Jezza finally relented, going back to sorting out the glassware.

He turned with satisfaction at his perceived victory. "Here's to another job completed," he said, lifting his glass.

I caught Jezza's eye that warned me off of the drink, but I ignored her. It had become somewhat of a tradition to drink the first night back from a job. And at the acceptance of a new job. And during the job…

There seemed to be a lot of drinking involved in mercenary work.

I lifted my mug with him and drank a single gulp, setting the mug back down on the table, mostly full. Crux and Tesro seemed to have a small contest between them of who could down their mug faster. Surprisingly, Tesro won as she spun to whip Crux in the face with her curly red hair. The small distraction gave her the advantage needed to beat the man at his own game.

Crux gasped, catching his breath before he leveled a finger at Tesro. "Cheater!"

"Finally got you, old man," she said in delight. "Vrak told me you were an easily distracted drinker. Said you 'lacked the discipline' to put all else aside while you focused on your task."

Crux developed a slight frown at the jest. "Well," he replied, forcing a false smile back to his face, "Vrak would know something about the drink, I suppose. Although these days, he seems more interested in that mind-altering smoke."

"Isn't that the truth?" she replied with a sigh. "Some role models you both are."

"That we are. And perhaps, one day, that will be a regret of mine. I'll sit alone in my room awaiting my return to the Soulwell and think about what I could've done better." He suddenly laughed, hitting the table with the palm of his hand. "But that day is not today. Today we celebrate both of you returning safely. Welcome home."

CHAPTER TWENTY-FOUR

SOULREND

Bright sun rays shone through the small slits of my bedroom window.

Spring had come once again.

I lay on my bed, letting the small particles of shining, glittering light dance elegantly on the scales of my extended hand. The heat felt good as it banished the night's chill from my bones.

Tesro yawned noisily from the other side of the room, and I quickly slipped on my pair of gloves, looking toward her. She laid sprawled on her narrow bed, shifting irritably. Her red hair—naturally curly—lay in a tangled heap, like a bird's straw nest around her head.

"Mornin'," she said, sleep still ingrained in her words.

"Good morning," I replied. "It amazes me that after all this time, each new morning still treats you so roughly."

She yawned again, exaggeratingly, and rose slowly. Without a modicum of grace, she slipped her legs off the side of her bed and dropped to the floor. Her flat feet patted the ground loudly as she walked to a small dresser with all the poise of a duckling.

A drunk one.

I told her as much and she turned to glare at me before smiling and laughing my comment off with a wave of her hand.

Tesro and I, after all this time, still shared this modestly sized room at High Tide. At one point, after Crux had bought the inn, he offered us each our own private quarters, but Tesro suffered from strong nightmares.

Especially when left alone.

She complained that in the pure silence of the night, she could still hear her family screaming as they burned. Still smell their flesh as it popped and boiled. I felt for her, and agreed to stay by her side until the night belonged to her once more.

That time had never come.

The truth was, it scared me to be alone as well. Tesro provided me with a certain…comfort. One that I didn't quite know how to describe.

She raked at her hair with a bone brush, now lengthened to the mid of her back. The brush had been a gift from Vrak, but he had never said where he'd purchased it from, despite our persistent prodding. Either way, its elegantly carved beauty made a fine piece for that of a beautiful young lady.

"It's not fair," Tesro complained and yelped when the brush hit a knot in her hair. She pushed and pulled the brush through the thick tangles while holding the base of her hairline to keep it from tugging on her scalp. Eventually, the hair gave way, straightening, but only just. She sighed a breath of relief, adding, "Your hair is straight and silky—it's not fair. You don't need to deal with," she gestured at her hair emphatically, "this!"

"You could always cut it short," I replied. "Many women keep their hair short. Look at Jezza."

"I hate short hair. And your hair is so cursedly smooth. It's enough to get the blood burning, I tell ya."

"Tesro…" I said, forcing all the sympathy I could muster in my words. "You know how you get after you drink too much the night before. It always leaves you in a dispirited mood the following morning. Give it up. I'm sure all the young men appreciate the efforts you take in maintaining your beauty."

She frowned at that, turning to look at me. "I don't do it for them," she said with disdain. "I do it for— Wait, why am I explaining this to you?"

I nodded at her words and replied, "I'm glad you do this for yourself, then. My mother always said to do the things, even if inconvenient to others, that make you joyful."

"Did she now...?"

We let the conversation die. Tesro could slip into deep depressions when speaking about her family, and I, while better at hiding it, was much the same when speaking of my mother.

"We've got to find something else besides drinking to do today—" A loud banging from downstairs cut me off.

"What was that?" Tesro asked with excitement as she dressed quickly, forgoing boots entirely. I followed her example, pulling on an unwashed shirt and straightening my pants. I also left my boots and went to the door, where she and I ran into each other. We pushed and shoved at each other playfully, but she tapped at the air and a small wind buffeted me away, throwing my hair around in circles. Laughing, she slipped out the door. I ground my teeth. She always was quick to solve her troubles with magic.

I ran into her a moment later at the bottom of the stairs. Instinctually, I reached forward to grab her, steadying myself. She paid me no mind, too mesmerized as she looked on at both the horror and amazement of the scene that laid before us.

Ri'sha Isodros, dressed in blue garments with gold inlays that paled compared to her natural scaly body, shouted frantically at Crux. He bravely backed into the corner of the room and away from her fury.

"When I summon you, Trueblade. You come immediately!" she said, throwing a chair out of her way so she could stand directly in front of the man.

Crux stood straight, and I knew it took all his grit and determination, as well as some liquid courage, to do so in front of the angry Ri'sha. Isodros stood half a man taller than Crux, but, nevertheless, he held his ground, pondering his words carefully before saying, "Ri'sha Isodros, pleasure. May I ask why you've come to visit? And so early?"

She looked to be grinding her pointed teeth, her neck muscles taut with fury. The muscles on her arm visibly flexed underneath her glittering scales. "Trueblade, we had a deal, and I am not one to be trifled with. I summoned you, and you deliberately disobeyed my summons."

"Apologies," he replied, bowing his head. As it came up, he looked around Isodros and caught my eye. He smirked at me, adding, "I was just spending some time with Eri."

Isodros turned to face me and her tense face of stress lines eased at the sight of me. She strode toward Tesro and me and said, "Oh girls, you're back!" Her anger had calmed, and she gave us both a smile before turning back toward Crux, adding with an edge, "It is still not a good enough reason to ignore my summons. Already, some of my own people think I am too lax with you humans. And the Court! They would have my head on a spike, if they could manage it."

Isodros said the words with such disdain, but, after a moment, she smiled. "Fine. We will ignore this mishap...for now. I am here with a purpose, and I do not wish to have it darkened by a petty quarrel with you."

"A job, then?" Crux asked, motioning for Jezza to bring them two mugs of beer.

She looked struck at the casual way Crux handled Isodros's anger, but with his motion, she snapped out of her stupor and filled two glasses, bringing them out and placing them on the table. She bowed wordlessly toward Isodros and slowly backed away, as if she backed away from a rabid animal, never breaking eye contact until she was firmly out of reach.

"Now there's someone with proper manners," Isodros said, bringing the mug to her lips.

"Jezza? Manners?" Crux replied, and then he burst out laughing. A towel suddenly hit him squarely in the side of the head, and when he turned to face Jezza, she gave him a grin and a small wave of her hand. She had made it behind the back of the bar quicker than I had ever seen before.

I shook my head at both of them. *Children.*

Isodros looked at Jezza and smirked. "She has spirit too. I do wonder, what attracts these humans to you? Is it something about you? Something special? Your mannerisms, perhaps? The way you speak?"

"My dashing good looks?" He raised his eyebrow at her, but she kept her gaze firm, as if the joke passed unnoticed. Finally, he shrugged his shoulders, adding, "I dunno. Lucky, I guess."

"Luck it is then."

Jezza laughed before covering her mouth, and I found myself grinning stupidly.

Crux coughed. "So, a job, then?" He took a long swig from the mug.

"This, Trueblade, is more than just 'a job.'" At Isodros's words, Crux sat forward, his piqued interest plain on his face. "This is—" she stopped. There was a type of battle going on in her head, the lines on her face deepening with worry. After a time, she sighed and shook her head. "No, this is too important to keep the details from you. Simply put, I need you to recover an item for me."

Crux crossed his arms and I could see the wheels turning in his head. "And what is special about this item? I can't help but think back to the last time we helped retrieve an item for you."

"That's none of—" Isodros said, but Crux's cool glare killed the words in her mouth. "Trueblade, send your barkeep from here."

"Tesro and Eri?"

"They can stay."

Crux raised his hand in the air, looking at Jezza. She took the hint and walked to exit the front of the building, giving them a wide berth as she went. Before she exited, she shot Crux a crude gesture and walked out the door, which slammed closed, rattling the glassware behind the bar.

I looked around, and the place was now empty, save us four. If there were any patrons here before, they must have quickly left when Isodros arrived in all her fury.

Smart of them.

"The item?" Crux asked, scratching at his scar.

"An amulet," she replied, "by the name of soulrend. I'm sure you'll recognize the name, being an enchanter."

Crux's eyes went wide, and he visibly shuddered.

"Soulrend?" I asked, and everyone turned to face me. "What's that?" I said the words nervously, not sure if I had just stepped into a viper's nest.

Crux stood and his shaking hand fingered at the base of his knife. "It's…" His voice broke, and he swallowed heavily. "It's from the story *Battle of Lost Souls.* Cei Tain, one of the greatest enchanters to have ever lived, created an item of immense power; an amulet named soulrend."

Tesro and I exchanged a glance. She smiled at me, as if she expected this was some sort of game, and they were playing a great trick on us.

I wasn't so sure.

"Why did she create it?" I asked. "And the amulet, what does it do?"

Isodros stood now, stretching her fingers out, revealing her long dark nails. "It's an abominable thing. It has the capability to bring a fate worse than any death you or I can imagine." She ran her nail across the scales of her chest, which let out a soft scraping like metal on metal. "Like the name suggests, it tears the soul from any the bearer touches. This rending fills the amulet and merges with its master's soul. It allows humans to use the magic of self reserved for us deminean. It extends a human's life far beyond the natural order. It is—"

"What a load of trite," Tesro said with the wave of her hand. "Is this some sort of jest, Crux? We aren't children anymore, we won't fall for cheap—"

"Tesro! Shut your mouth!" Crux slammed his knife into the table, causing her to jump back and let loose an audible gasp. I felt her trembling body nudge against mine, as if she willed my strength into her by the physical contact. Her body shook again under my tremulous touch.

Crux, looking older, appeared stunned by his own outburst. "Tesro. I'm so sorry—"

Isodros held a hand to him to steady his tongue. "It's alright, Trueblade, they're still young. They do not know what we had to endure. Although, you wouldn't have been born as of yet. Did your father tell you of the amulet?"

"Something like that," Crux replied.

I swallowed hard and forced myself to courage. "This amulet—you wanted us to hear this for a reason. So I will hear it all."

Isodros pulled out a small vial and popped open the top, opening her mouth, and revealing a full row of sharp white teeth. She dropped a single drop into the back of her throat and placed the top back on. When she leveled her gaze back at us, her golden eyes were huge saucers, and as bright as the sun.

"That's better," she said. "Now then, you wish to know all? Very well. After a long and bloody battle in which many deminean, including Ri'sha, lost their lives, Cei Tain fell—but not before passing the amulet on. Season upon season, year after year, the amulet was passed, until one day, word came that its bearer lost their life, and the amulet was lost with them. It has remained lost...until now."

"And us?"

"And you two," she replied, glancing over at Tesro and I. "I need you both to retrieve it for me."

"No!" Crux said, pulling Isodros's attention back to him. "I will not allow this."

"By the will of our agreement, you shall," she replied, leveling a finger at him. "I do not trust many with this task, but I trust in the skills of these two destroyers you have raised."

Crux went silent at that.

I was shocked, but my mouth reacted before my mind. "How do you know—"

"You won't take me!" Tesro said suddenly, moving away from me and toward the door. She looked like she would run. "I won't go with you! I won't be a deminean slave!"

Isodros put her hands forward in a calming gesture. "I don't want to send you anywhere, child. Think, if I wanted you serving the Sovereign at the Well, then I would have sent you long ago. As I haven't means you can trust me."

Tesro scoffed at that, but relented in her frantic flight, calming her tense muscles and offering no additional resistance.

"Now then," she continued, as if uninterrupted. "I trust these two, and you will not disobey me in this. They will go, and you, Trueblade, will not."

Crux threw a wooden chair back, which crashed against a nearby table, the leg splintering and falling to the floor with a crash. "To purgatory I won't."

"I have too many enemies around me now. I need you close in case any dare rise against me."

"Those are deminean problems, not our—"

"My problems *are* your problems," Isodros said flatly. Her words were unmistakable; it was her influence that protected all of us. "You need not worry, Trueblade. I will not send them alone. Two of my most trusted wards will accompany them. Both are excellent fighters and adept at the inner magic."

"Wait," I said. "I still don't know why this amulet is so important? How do you even know where this lost treasure is?"

"I have my ways," she replied with a coy smile. "As for importance, can you not see what this entails? For a human to steal the soul of a deminean, all of our work to unite our species would be for naught. Every deminean, even those sympathetic to our cause, would turn on humans the moment the amulet was revealed. Sovereign Krottik Drekhide would come down on the humans with a fury that none of this age could comprehend. I'll put this bluntly: he would wipe out humanity before he allowed the amulet to be used against the deminean again."

I felt as if time stood still, my hands trembling as if I stood in a labyrinth of ice. Lightheadedness threatened to overtake me, but I forced myself to calm, breathing deep breaths. *Tesro and I are to take a job of this magnitude on?* I thought. *With strangers we've never met?* It was preposterous. Ridiculous. Surely this couldn't be right.

"Ri'sha," I said, bowing my head respectfully. "I must politely decline. I don't think we are the right people for the job at hand."

"Vi'eri—"

"I'm scared!" My words rang out clear for all to hear—the frantic shrill of a terrified girl. I moved Tesro to the side as I stepped close to her and gazed up into those bright, golden eyes. "I'm not ready for this burden. Why don't you just go yourself!" Regretfully, tears streamed down my face.

Isodros leveled her gaze at me, and the shadow of anger crossed her regal face. But just as quickly, the anger faded and what was left looked of pity and sadness. The look of a mother who was sending her child out into the dangerous world.

A necessary evil.

She reached out to me and, to my surprise, pulled me into an embrace. I had spoken many times to Isodros over the years—she had been like a mentor to me, teaching me the ways of the deminean. But I never suspected she held this kind of regard for me.

Quietly, she said, "You've done me a great service in the past. And now, I choose to tell you what you've gained for me. The tear of eternity…it was not just a beautiful gem. It is from the Soulwell itself. A single small tree stands on an island in the middle of a pond in the Soulwell. Every once in a great while, what we call a tear forms like a dew of nectar. It is made of liquid, but eventually, when it falls, it crystallizes mid-air. This tear, when consumed, links one's soul more firmly to the Well. It draws from it—" She paused as her words broke. Holding the embrace, she seemed to force the words across her tongue. "Vi'eri, with the tear, the Well has blessed me with a child! I can feel it inside me. I can feel the pouring in of the Well's power, giving my child life!"

Isodros wiped a tear from her eyes. It was the first I had ever seen a deminean cry, and I had not realized up to that point that they even could.

Sympathetically, I wiped a tear from my eye as well. "But—"

"You gave me something far greater than you could ever understand," she said. "It's no secret that deminean have a far lower birth rate than your kind. It is almost as if the Well rejects us in favor of humans, as much as my kind denies that theory. This is the reason so many of my kind despise yours."

Isodros paused, releasing me from her grip. Carefully, she composed herself, straightening her garb and standing straighter. Proud.

"But I will give you the choice," she continued. "I shall not force either you or Tesro into this task, but I would have the two whom I credit for giving my child life take on this duty for me. It is even more important than my life...or my child's. Oh how I wish I could go myself, but to leave the city and nearby territories undefended from the Court's bigoted actions would be a disservice to both you and Tesro. To all humans. So I ask...will you see this job through?"

"Yes," Tesro answered immediately, stepping forward.

"Tesro!" Crux and I replied simultaneously.

She merely shrugged at each of us and faced Isodros with a grin. "Vi'eri can speak for herself, as can I. I'm willing to take on the job, with or without Vi'eri at my side."

"Vrak would have my hide!" Crux replied, shaking his head. "No! no, no, no—I cannot let you go."

She crossed her arms. "Vrak doesn't control me, and neither do you." She tapped at her chest. "I'm old enough to make my own choices, Crux. Or would you use your authority as the leader of the True Blades to forbid me this? I am ready, and you know I am. You cannot protect me forever." She pointed a finger at me. "Or her."

Crux looked struck. His face went stark white and his hands shook in a rage that I had never seen in him before. Thankfully, he forced himself to calm before saying, "Fine, do what you will. You have my permission to go, but as soon as Vrak returns, I'm sending him after you." He turned toward me. "Vi'eri, I would have you stay."

I stepped away from Isodros and walked toward him. He turned his eyes from me as I came. I reached out to touch his face, moving his head to face me, forcing him to match my stare. "Crux, I'm going. I cannot let Tesro do this alone, and you know that."

He stared at me stubbornly for a time before his face relaxed. "I know you can't," he replied, wiping tears from his eyes. "It's just not who you are."

I hugged him, and he returned it. I heard his raspy breaths come and go until he eventually sighed out, like a man who had come to terms with a choice he made out of necessity.

Crux eased me to the side, looking to Isodros. "These two deminean you have in mind, do you trust them? Truly trust them?"

She nodded. "I will allow you this bit of insolence, due to the nature of my asking. But when I give my word of trust, I am not to be questioned in it."

Crux nodded. "Understood." He grabbed his mug and emptied the contents into his mouth. "When should they depart?"

Isodros looked to me and then Tesro, who returned her stare with a pensive look about her face. She replied in almost a whisper.

"Immediately."

CHAPTER TWENTY-FIVE

CROSSROADS

"Thank you for going out of your way. We really appreciate it."

Rhas looked at me and smirked. "It's not a problem, Vi'eri. After all you and Tesro have done for me and the Caravan, it's the least we could do to repay you. Now stop mentioning it every few minutes. It's getting on my nerves."

Our group had traveled for a few days into the frigid climate of the Frostwyrm. The near perpetual snow still clung to the waning winter as spring battered the land for dominion.

Soft crunches of snow sounded as we trudged through, leaving small signs of our existence in the otherwise perfect white coat that covered the land. Ice covered the road we traveled on yet again, leaving it slick and covering all signs of previous travel. But Rhas, ever the traveler, knew the way by memory, using the signs of the realm that no other in our group understood.

"This is it!" Rhas announced as the grayhorn stopped at the pull of the reins. I walked around it to see a wooden post at a fork in the road, clearly marking two splintering paths.

Walking toward the sign, I saw icicles still clung to it, frozen in place as they reached for the ground. I balled my hand into a fist and smacked the sign. The ice fell, and I wiped the frost off the face, breaking chunks of lingering ice.

The sign, now bereft of clouded mist, showed two arrows pointing in different directions. The name Cloudrest was etched under the arrow pointing west. From my previous visits to the Frostwyrm, I knew it to be the impromptu capital of the land. The ruler, Goxir Stoutclaw, was not a Ri'sha—although rumors say how that fact irked him so. Reluctantly, the deminean ruler accepted the lax rules Ri'sha Isodros commanded regarding human and deminean coexistence. On top of that, he expressed no ill will to the White-Raven Caravan that I was aware of. As far as deminean rulers went, I'd seen worse.

On the other side of the sign, pointing to the east, barely legible, the name Sleetward sat carved into the wood.

"Looks like we're splitting up here," Tesro said as she silently arrived behind me, putting her hand on my shoulder. It radiated warmth. Somehow, she always emitted such a heat that I wondered how well she would fare in hotter climates. If I had to guess, I would say poorly.

"East it is then," a woman's voice replied. I turned to find Sho'ti, nicknamed Sho, with her arms crossed against her chest. The deminean woman's scales caught light that bounced off the snow, revealing an unnaturally deep red tint to them.

A deminean man appeared next to her, standing a head shorter than she. Hask, the other of Isodros' favored wards, looked toward Rhas, shaking his head. "I suppose this is where we will depart. Sho, a word." He turned without sparing either Tesro or I a single glance.

Rhas eyed us from atop her grayhorn and then glanced toward the other deminean, shaking her head. Tesro and I approached her, giving our deminean companions space.

Rhas leaned off the side of the grayhorn. "Deminean like those two are the reason I hate working with my own kind. So stuck up and full of themselves. Be careful, you two. I know Ri'sha Isodros gave you her word, but—"

They returned and Rhas bit her lip to silence her words. She sat up straight and strong, fixing her green cloak that ran so lengthy it trailed off the edge of the grayhorn's back.

She masked her conspiratorial tone, saying jovially, "You all be careful. The people of Cloudrest keep the roads clear of Anduinna's minions, but the further away you travel, the less protection you will have. Still, stick to the roads and you should be fine...maybe."

"Get going." Hask dismissed her with the wave of his hand. "And remember, merchant. Speak not a word of this to anyone. That includes your...human employers."

She let out a long breath, as if she wished to convey something in return. Hask stared her down with those golden deminean eyes and she turned from that gaze, replying, "I'll keep that in mind."

With a quick kick of Rhas' heels, the grayhorn moved, and with a pull on the reins, it started off west, toward Cloudrest.

"Is that really necessary?" Sho asked, leveling a judgemental stare at her accomplice.

Hask spit on the ground. "Makes me sick to see. I know Ri'sha Isodros has plans, I just..." he trailed off for a moment, shaking his head at no one in particular. "I just cannot see how any proud deminean could live with the shame of serving a human."

Tesro cleared her throat as if she would respond. Instantly, I recognized the look she had on her face, and I reacted swiftly, throwing my arm around her and whispering, "It's not worth it, let it go." Reluctantly, she relaxed, and I let my arms slide off her.

Sho looked at us curiously, her golden eyes as piercing as all demineans' seemed to be. She turned back toward Hask and her words took on a lecturing tone. "Perhaps she doesn't see it as shameful? I suspect the opposite is true. Think, Isodros has lofty plans for these humans that involve some level of cohabitation and acceptance between us. Perhaps Dem'i Rhas White-Raven does the Ri'sha a great honor by taking the nature of her comments to heart and applying them in reality?"

Hask's mouth stood open disbelievingly at her. "Sho! You can't be serious? You'd become subservient to a human?"

"If Ri'sha Isodros ordered it, yes. I suspect I would," she replied. She waved her arms around, as if she addressed a crowd. "Take our current situation, for example. While we may not be subservient to our human companions, they stand on equal footing as us—now don't look at me like that, Hask. You heard Ri'sha Isodros' words: 'Treat them as you would any of your own kind.'"

Hask scoffed at that. "And yet she keeps herself above them...and us."

Sho eyed him, her mouth going very flat. "Be very careful what you say, friend. Words like that may be...misinterpreted. And not just with the humans in our midst."

He took her meaning and turned away wordlessly, stalking down the road west, toward Sleetward, alone.

Sho moved closer to us and Tesro took an overt step behind me, as if the mere presence of the deminean woman disgusted her. "I'm sorry for my companion's behavior. He is in a bit of a...transitional phase, with the way the realm is now. It's nothing personal. I assure you, we both have nothing but the utmost respect for you both. In fact, as a commitment of goodwill, I will tell you this: Ri'sha Isodros has expressed nothing but extraordinary words regarding the two of you. Speaking for myself, I hope I get to see you both in action before this is through!"

Tesro coughed uncomfortably, as if she choked back a witty retort.

The deminean woman stood far taller than me, almost reaching the height of Isodros herself. I craned my head to meet her eyes, and I saw genuine kindness there, as well as something deeper just below the surface. "We don't take offense," I replied, nudging Tesro with my elbow.

She rubbed her side. "What Vi'eri said. No offense taken."

"Good!" Sho said, turning to where Hask had set off. The man was almost cresting a hill in the distance, his footprints making a nice track straight toward him. "We'd better hurry or he'll take all the glory for himself."

Tesro smiled at that, and I returned it. We followed after Hask toward Sleetward.

We caught up with him a short time later. He had stopped and had, at some point, lit a pipe which he now smoked the contents of. He breathed out, and I couldn't tell if I saw smoke leave his lips, or if it was the heat of his breath that gave misty life as it touched the chill air.

Sho crouched beside him and seemed to wave her hand over the snow before her. The gleam of her rust-colored scales cast a shine atop the white canvas and made it seem a gruesome scene. As I approached, the tracks in the snow became clear.

Wolf tracks.

"Animals have taken to the trail," Hask said, sucking in a large breath of smoke. He held it for a moment before releasing it out his nose, adding, "This is why humans need deminean leadership. Left to their own devices, they are greedy and reckless. And this," he swept his hand over the tracks, "this is the result of human coexistence."

Tesro balled her fist up and her face was a contortion of rage and imminent violence. She looked as if she would sling a spell at the man right then and there—anything to stop his constant onslaught of insults.

Sho coughed. "Enough, Hask!" she paused until Hask turned to face her, still leaning over the wolf tracks. She met his eyes and added in her naturally silky tone, "Honestly, if I need to endure this the entire time, then I'll...well, let's not make this any more unpleasant than it already is, eh?"

"Whatever you say, Sho. Whatever you say."

We trampled our way through the tracks and continued onward.

It would not be the last tracks we would see that day.

Deer tracks were aplenty, with wolf tracks almost always following after, like a dance painted in snow. A deadly dance indeed. There were a few bear tracks as well, along with some others I didn't recognize. At that, our 'friends' shared a glance of nervousness between each other, and I noted they proceeded far more scrupulously than they had before.

Eventually, we came upon even more tracks. These looked like wolves, but somehow different. Larger by far, these tracks somehow appeared more...menacing.

Perhaps it's just my eyes playing tricks on me, I thought, pushing my reservations to the side.

"Look at that," Tesro said breathlessly. A sudden gust of wind sent a strand of hair cascading into her mouth and she coughed, pulling it out.

"Quiet, human!" Hask spat. "Are you trying to attract Anduinna's creatures that wander out here—"

A sudden howl killed the words in his mouth. Tesro shifted her body tightly to mine, and I stared into the thicket of brush and trees that littered the path on all sides.

Another howl, then another. Howl after howl resounded, reverberating off the branches of the trees and causing small pockets of snow to cascade to the ground, pattering it like the soft footsteps of rabbits. It sounded as if the howling creatures beset us on all sides.

I forced myself to calm and focused on my destroyer magic. Small sparks of light appeared before me, shimmering in and out of existence as the strands of magic tended to do. It was the magic that existed in the in-between; the space between this realm and the next.

I lifted my arms in a casting motion, determined not to be taken by surprise. I would be ready for anything that was to come.

Tesro eyed me, matching my posture. She held her left hand back and her right hand forward, palm facing the tree line. A cold sweat broke on her forehead as she did so, and I knew she saw the shining fragments of magic floating in the air all around us. The magic here was dense; it would be of little trouble to cast the most potent of spells. However, looking at her, it worried me if she would manage to maintain control.

Sho and Hask rushed to our sides, which was a surprise. They encircled us both, as if they sought to protect us.

Tesro's mouth hung open in astonishment, and I focused my mind back on the task at hand. There would be time to contemplate the puzzle of our deminean companions after we survived.

If we survived.

A rustling drew my attention as I saw a figure stalk out of the woods. As large as a bear in diameter, but a wolf in body and shape. What appeared before me was a creature straight out of a volume of myths and tales.

"Vargs," Sho said, never taking her eyes off the tree line, as if she'd seen something we had not.

Not a moment after the words left her lips, another of the beasts trampled out of the trees, their dark gray body contrasting the pure white snow.

The lumbering form of the creature broke branches with a sickening snap, and the piles of snow that fell atop it from the branches above did little to slow them.

Two, three, four...the creatures kept coming, each as menacing as the last. From various shades of gray to white, at least eight vargs surrounded us on all sides.

"Let's see the True Blade destroyers in action then, shall we?" Hask said, as if in taunt. But when I spared a glance at the man, he was smiling ear to ear, his mouth open, bearing his sharp teeth to the foes that stood before us in a type of snarl.

The creatures advanced a step in unison.

"Come now, Hask. They're terrified! Try not to make the situation any worse for them," Sho replied in a lighthearted condemnation. Then, she laughed, she actually laughed. It was at this moment I decided that our deminean companions were completely and utterly...

Insane.

As if sensing the challenge, the vargs all lifted their heads in synchronization, as if they stood upon a stage, and howled their acceptance of said confrontation to the world. The sound sent ringing vibrations through my body, rattling my ears as my mind tried frantically to separate the sounds and where they had come from.

I felt woozy and sick, and I thought the contents of my stomach would empty at the gut-wrenching noise. Tesro looked little better than I, clutching at her head, her knees wobbling frantically. Neither of our deminean companions shifted a step, taking the sound attack with little bother.

What I presumed to be the alpha of this pack stepped forward. They were not the biggest of the bunch, but they bore the most scars. A gash across the eye left it pure white in the socket, and another across the creature's mouth pulled the skin back further than intended as they bared their teeth at us, showing plaque filled yellow cavities with what I presumed was meat stuck in the crevices between.

The creature's muzzle was deep red of the otherwise white coat near the mouth. This creature had killed recently. I hoped that it was from another of Anduinna's creations and not...human. Suddenly, the creature's eyes turned from a brown to a deep red, almost glowing, and there was a shift in the creature's stance. It stood straighter, and I could almost sense a sort of pride pouring from them.

One after another, the vargs eyes changed from browns, greens and blues to that of pure red, their stances shifting from hesitant to outright aggressive. Their haunches rose toward the sky, adding to their already immense size.

And then, without ceremony, they attacked.

All at once.

Chapter Twenty-Six

THE CHILL OF DEATH

Heat struck me as a varg screamed in a way that only a suffering animal can.

Tesro, down on one knee but head still raised high, looked on furiously at the enemy that wailed before her. It writhed pitifully in the snow, twisting and turning as its fur and flesh melted into one gelatinous mess.

Again, a wave of heat touched my skin—like the opening of a clay oven as the heat rushed out to escape its prison. The blackened varg screeched once more before its voice died in its throat.

I stared in horror as the creature, its red eyes still piercing in fury at us, found the fortitude to stand. Flesh hung loose off blackened bone, and it whined softly with each excruciating step it took.

Tesro looked dazed, her stance swaying as she tried to keep herself upright. I focused, forcing myself to look past the suffering and do what the situation demanded of me. I reached for fragments of magic near my hand and tapped them, forcing my will into reality.

The ground shook as a thin pillar of earth formed under the varg's feet. It appeared not to notice as it continued its arduous journey. It took a step, then another, and as it did, I twisted my left hand, palm up, as I willed the earthen spike toward the sky.

A cry, and then silence. The varg stood still, impaled on the spike of rock, its eyes finally returning to their natural brown, and then white as red life spilled from the creature to the snowbound ground. The creature looked peaceful, as if it welcomed death. With a sickening assuredness, gazing upon the creature, I knew that it had.

"Tesro, Vi'eri, recover!" Hask shouted as he lifted a varg in the air, slamming it to the ground a moment later. The creature squirmed, but the deminean's grip was far too strong. He closed his fist and jabbed downward.

Strike after bloodcurdling strike, he pummeled into the creature's soft body. He showered it in attacks as it twisted helplessly in his grip, desperate to free itself. As the blows struck, I heard the sounds of bones cracking under the pressure, like the screeching of a bad axle wheel.

"Why are you just staring?" Hask's words drew my attention away from the brutality. "Use your magic!"

I needed no more prompting. I put my hand on Tesro and helped her recover. She did so after a moment's respite and I resumed the standard casting formation. Palms out, fingers separated, right hand forward.

She matched my stance as two more varg appeared silhouetted behind a wall of sleet. I breathed out and tapped the fragments of magic that appeared before me. Suddenly, the branch on a tree above the varg fell. Where before the branch had been a solid object, it now hung like a vine that moved as if it had a mind of its own. I poured my will into the magic that flew into the vine, moving it as it wrapped around the neck of the varg. Connected through magic to the vine, I could feel the strain of it as the varg thrashed against its noose.

Quickly, I tapped more fragments of magic, and more branches changed, falling upon the varg and wrapping around the neck and body of the creature until it was near motionless against the onslaught. With one more tap, the vines retreated, lifting the varg off the ground and into the air, where it continued to thrash wildly, its body bouncing aimlessly off the tree it hung from. With a final tap of magic, a strong and focused gust of wind twisted the varg's body violently. Its red eyes winked out as the vines released, dropping a corpse to the snowy floor.

Tesro, with her wild magic, had turned the sleet of drifting snow into little icicles that hung like crystalized daggers in the air. The second varg kicked off the ground and charged straight into a hail of sharp ice. The magic punctured the poor creature under an uncountable number of ice daggers. One landed in the creature's neck—the killing blow. It dropped to the ground, where its red blood ran like spilled ink from a fallen decanter.

I turned to find our deminean companions all but vanished—lost in the deluge of slurry that buffeted at my eyes. It felt as if we had been fighting for a long time, my body tired from use. The little light the sun now provided through the dark clouds was going under the mountains in the distance, leaving us in complete darkness.

"Hask! Sho!" I called out.

Neither responded to my cries.

Tesro collapsed suddenly, and I went to her, dropping to my knees in the snow. "Are you okay?" I asked, although I already suspected she was just tired with the continued effort of casting. She had done far more than I had in the previous battle.

She groaned, craning her head to look at me. "Yeah, I'm alright. Where are our deminean friends?"

I shrugged. "I'm not sure. I think I heard Hask's voice not too long ago, but now he's gone. They both are."

"Do you think... Do you think they're dead?"

"I don't know."

"How about the creatures? Are they gone too?" I shook my head again. The wind was picking up and the adrenaline from battle was deserting me. It left me fatigued and freezing. She sighed. "We really don't know anything. Why, oh why, did I let you talk me into this?"

I stared down at her, aghast, and she returned a playful smile. It surprised me she could accept the situation we found ourselves in with such stride.

To be completely honest, it astounded me.

Then, the wind picked up again; a frigid chill. I felt my very bones go cold with its icy touch. Instinctually, I nuzzled myself closer to her, and she accepted my shared warmth in return.

"We need to find somewhere to stay for the night," I said. "A cave. Something, anything!" I couldn't help the bit of panic that spilled from my lips.

"I think... I think I can make a small fire," she said. "We can try to walk with it and—" As she tried to stand, her fatigue sent her immediately back down to one knee.

"I don't think you can cast anything at the moment," I replied, helping her back to her feet. She leaned heavily on me and I was glad to allow her to do so, her warmth fighting the encroaching frost. "Come under my cloak."

Tesro complied without hesitation. Her warmth radiated against me more fiercely than before. But, with a pang of guilt, I realized it was less than usual.

It worried me.

And her face, which had gone completely white, did nothing to ease that worry. I wrapped an arm around her and we began the slow trek through the blizzard.

We walked on in complete silence. The wind blowing over our shared cloak was the only sound other than our chattering teeth and soft crunch of boots against fresh snow.

The lessons of Botolf Adkin, before his retirement, came into the forefront of my mind. In the past, he had taught us the ways to survive the harsh cold of the north—something every youth of the north knew, but was less common knowledge to those from fairer climates.

I heard the old man's voice in my head as I recalled those lessons. *The wind will get you as quickly as any blizzard or animal. If you find yourself out in the blackness of night, find a shelter. And if you cannot find one, make one for yourself.*

"Tesro..." I whispered, drawing her attention to me. The white of her face had traveled down her neck and, I suspected, the rest of her body. "I don't think we can survive in this blizzard much longer." She looked at me with hard-set eyes and nodded. "We need to dig a shelter in the snow to protect us from this cursed wind."

"I've got a better idea," she replied, taking a casting position. She struggled to remain straight, but the hard look in her eyes told me she would manage. I lifted the cloak to give her space and to do my best to block the wind from her as she concentrated.

I focused and saw the fragments of magic she tapped, forcing her will into it. As her finger darted out toward a cluster, her eyes rolled in the back of her head and she collapsed into me. I caught her and eased her to the ground.

She panted, and when she opened her eyes, she had a prideful look in them. Turning her eyes away from me, she muttered, "You do it, Vi'eri. I'm still too weak at the moment." I knew what it cost her to admit those words. The shame, and the youthful pride she had to deny for the sake of survival.

I didn't press the issue or jest at her expense. After sparing her a glance that bordered on pity, I tapped at the fragments she had reached out to before, being careful to control the reaction as a small jet of fire burst from my hands.

She shied back, dropping the cloak to the floor, and I quickly aimed the stream at the snowy ground, drilling a hole into it. When the stream of flame died out, I felt drained. The cold was really weighing on me now, and the numbness of my hands and feet told me we had little time left. I pulled the cloak back up and she nudged back against me.

The hole was small, but with a few quick scoops, I reached a small crevice between some overgrown roots from a nearby tree.

A lucky break.

Despite that, the hole barely allowed the both of us to squeeze our slender bodies into it. As we did so uncomfortably, I wrapped the gray wolf cloak around us completely, closing us in from the outside chill.

Our breath and body heat quickly fogged our makeshift shelter, and it smelled of battle-sweat. Musty and heavy.

The dark was so complete—too dark to even see my own hands in front of my face.

Then I felt her arms wrap around me. Not the grasp of a child reaching for their mother, but a defensive grasp. One of protection. It was then that I realized the cold still crept in through the cloak and that she shielded me with her body. I tried to shift, but she held me tight, as if she could read my thoughts and knew my intentions.

She would bear it...for my sake.

I wanted to move, I truly did. But I was tired; so exhausted that I couldn't think straight. Her rhythmic breathing slowed, and the beating of her heart thumped relaxingly into my back.

"I love you..." I heard her whisper into my ear.

The impact of those words nearly woke me entirely. But a moment later, I heard the soft snore escape her mouth.

She was sleeping.

I chuckled to myself and wondered to whom she meant those words for. Either way, they etched upon my heart. Even if she did not mean them for me, I would treasure them all the same.

I let her rhythmic breathing lull me to sleep.

CHAPTER TWENTY-SEVEN

THE WARMTH OF LIFE

Drifting through the darkness of sleep, I heard a voice.

Eri... it called, but I ignored it.

Vi'eri... it called again, and this time, I reached for it, but the source narrowly slipped from my fingers.

Vi'eri!

My heart leaped into my throat as I awoke in total darkness. Panic blossomed inside my mind for just a moment before I eased, remembering the events of the previous day.

How long had I slept?

"Tesro," I said to a silent response. "*Tesro!*" I tried again. Nothing; not even a hesitant mumbling. A rising terror filled my senses, making my chest tight, and I turned toward her.

Light! I needed light!

Light is a tricky magic to control. The fragments of magic become unstable being used in such a pure way.

I pushed past my hesitations and focused, finding the smallest particle of magic that I dared to touch. The small flickering of lights floated near me, and I tapped at them delicately. At the tip of my finger, a small bead of what looked like luminescent water appeared. I craned my head, and what I saw horrified me.

Tesro looked unwell. The color in her face was all but gone, her skin tone now matching that of the snow that had somehow crept its way into the back of the cloak shelter. Using the light, I could see something had ripped the cloak, and that she had sealed this hole with her own body.

"Tesro!" I shouted, using my left hand to nudge her. I put my hand to her mouth and felt the slightest measure of warm breath escape her blue lips. My stomach turned in knots as I realized the truth:

She was dying.

I wished to cast a fire right then and there. Anything to warm her up—to give her a chance to live! But weak... I just felt so weak. I doubted I had slept enough to recover myself in any substantial way.

Quickly, I shifted, moving her in front of me and placing my own body to seal the rip in the cloak. The chill as the snow touched my clothes felt like daggers dragging across my back.

How had she borne the pain? I thought, tears blurring my already limited vision.

It won't be enough... I heard a voice say clearly in my mind.

Voice! I replied. *Help me, I know you can. Save Tesro and I'll do anything for you. Anything at all.* I knew my words were desperate, but I didn't care. I cared only about saving her life.

There was silence for a time. Then, almost as if I could feel the disappointment myself, the voice replied, *I cannot.* A terrible sadness menaced me, but before I could express anything in reply, the voice added, *The girl is dying, and I fear there is little you or I can do for her. At least, not as you are now.*

"No!" I screamed, and I didn't know if I used my actual tongue or had screamed internally. Possibly both. "Show me the way. Find somewhere safe and I will get us there."

Vi'eri...

Do it! I commanded. *I've felt your strength in the past. Felt it flow through me. Lend me that strength again and show me the way.* The voice said nothing more, but I felt approval push against my emotions.

There was no time to waste as I moved forward, pulling Tesro with me.

The blizzard had buried us as we slept, and I shoved through the packed snow that sealed us under the hole we had created. The chill assaulted me as soon as I broke through, but at that very moment I felt an increase in strength, and with it, new conviction.

I stood, sending small patches of snow falling off my shoulders. Breathing in the icy night air, I somehow felt warmth thaw my frozen bones and muscles. The cold did not slow me, instead, it fueled my efforts.

When I was outside the hole, the realm was black as pitch. Using the small light of the dew that still clung to the tip of my finger, I found Tesro and wrapped her in the cloak. I felt fine...warm even, despite only wearing the traveling clothes Rhas had provided me. I lifted her in my arms, pulling her close so that I could feel the smallness of her breath brush my face. She felt light as a feather.

Voice, where do I go?

Follow the tracks, the voice replied.

How? I can't see.

Yes, you can.

And with the voice's words, I found that I could. Blinking, my perception of the world changed. The small waves of moonlight that crept through the opening of clouds looked like the brightest of beacons to me. It hurt and left me reeling as I adjusted to this new power.

When I regained my balance, the landscape looked brand new, as if I saw for the first time in my life.

Truly saw.

But there was no time to delay, and I easily found tracks leading away from our previous cover. The tracks were small and oval-shaped, and they reminded me of a little fox trail.

My body, light and full of energy, made quick work of trudging through the snow. Even carrying Tesro in this lifeless state was not enough to deter my newfound power. I kept a fast pace, and found an entrance to a cave where the tracks abruptly stopped at the mouth.

With my heightened senses, I gazed for predators or any manner of enemies hiding in the night.

I found none.

With reckless abandon, I raced into the cave. Immediately, its dankness wrinkled my nose. It smelled of feces and wild, unwashed animals. I pushed all of that aside, readjusted Tesro in my arms, and stepped further inside, leaving the chill behind me.

A short way in and I could no longer feel the wind pressing against my back. The air, while stale, was certainly warmer than outside, even if it smelled worse than the dirtiest of taverns. Still, the wind continued to howl its fury at the cave of the mouth, almost as if it cursed us for escaping its icy embrace. I set Tesro to lean against the wall.

A fire is what she needed, and quickly.

I first thought of the trees outside the cave, then dismissed the idea just as quickly. They would be worthless, drenched from the weather as they were. Instead, I sought deeper into the cavern, sparing a final glance toward Tesro, who looked surprisingly peaceful wrapped in my gray wolf cloak, leaning against the cave, drawing in shallow breath after shallow breath.

Slick and jagged gray rocks were what greeted me as I continued inward, and the weariness I felt in my body was but a distant thing at the back of my mind. As if something sealed my pain away. And, as with every other unexplained happening that night, I suspected it was the mysterious voice's doing.

Eventually, I came upon signs of mortal inhabitants, others whom had used this cavern for shelter in the past. Remnants of their existence littered the area, including a fire that had long been extinguished. Luckily, an untouched log laid propped against the drab wall of the cave and I prayed to the Well it kept dry. Picking it up, I was pleased that it had.

Turning to head back, I stopped when I found some small kindling. Truly, this cave was a blessing from the Well itself. But, as I picked up the last of it, I heard a faint scratching from further down. My inquisitive nature almost got the better of me, but I forced myself to turn from the sound and head back toward Tesro, turning to look over my shoulder more than once as I walked away.

It was good that I did, for when I arrived, I found her sprawled on the floor. The cloak I had placed over her now laid on the floor, only a small bit still covered her lower half.

She looked so frail and weak, her body shivering violently and the wind's howls seemed to laugh in delight at her peril.

The scene sickened me.

As quickly as I could, I set the log and kindling, and with a tap of magic, a small fire burst alight in my hand. Using my left hand, I guided it toward the wood. Light flared as it caught, and I leaned down, blowing life into those flames. Slowly, it spread to the log, and I breathed a sigh of relief when it lit. I had done it. Silently, I prayed to the Well that it would be enough.

It will, I heard the voice say in my head. *You saved her, Eri. You really did it.* It felt so far away, much further than it had before. I could sense a weakness in the words, and the usual pressing on my emotions never came. I suspected that whomever they were, they did not have the strength to do so. This mysterious being had saved me more times than I could remember and yet, I still did not know their name. It just never seemed important at the time.

That ends now, I thought. *What's your name? I'm tired of calling you Voice, as if that is all you have ever been; a nameless, bodiless apparition in my head. I wish to know who you are.*

The voice was quiet for a time. Eventually, I felt...happiness press on my emotions and I knew it cost them to do so. The feeling grew and grew until I was elated. Overwhelmed. Perhaps the liveliest I had ever felt. With great reluctance, I forced myself back from it. I could be happy when Tesro survived the night.

If Tesro survived the night.

Your name! I recalled to the voice, knowing they were fading.

You know my name, you always have.

And suddenly, I realized I did. As if the saying of the name would make this being real, I spoke loudly in my mind, *Vulana!*

Vulana was silent, and I felt the slightest brush of contentment, and then they were gone, and with them, my enhanced senses.

A chill engulfed me, and darkness consumed the cave. I focused my attention back to Tesro. I re-wrapped the gray wolf cloak around us, leaving a small opening for the heat of the fire to trickle in. This time, I held her tightly in my arms, letting her body be closest to the fire. I monitored her for a time, and her color returned slowly.

The light of the fire cast dancing shadows off her face. My heart raced, and I felt myself gravitate toward her in a way I couldn't explain. I pulled her tangled hair behind her ear and it brushed across her nose, causing her to sneeze in her sleep. I smiled and held her tighter—as if some unknown enemy would take her if I released my grip the slightest bit.

I would never let her go.

I stayed vigilant, feeling as if I could not sleep or her heart would just stop in the night. If my vigil kept her from that fate, I would bear it heartily.

My heart sank in my chest as I once again heard a distant scratch coming from the back of the cavern. I wanted to ignore it, and I hoped that whatever manner of creature this was would just leave us alone. But, as if some unknown force was always present in my life to throw me off course, I heard it again. Whatever lived at the back of the cave, I couldn't let it get to her.

I *wouldn't* let it get her.

Carefully, I laid Tesro down in front of the fire, making sure the cloak completely covered her, and tucking it under her back. I looked down at the rip in the fabric, but there was nothing I could do for it now. The fire would keep her warm. It had to.

Without my link to Vulana, it was now freezing. My breath came steadily, misting in front of me as it did. I walked slowly and carefully toward where I had discovered the noise before, using the dew of light at the tip of my finger to guide the way.

First, I heard a scratch, and then a wheeze as I turned the corner of the cave. There, I found a gray varg, but not just any varg. The scar on its face confessed all—it was the alpha!

The creature laid on its side and scratched absently at the wall with an extended paw. Its wheezing breaths made me shudder. Despite my reluctance, I glanced upon the pitiful creature, and the red glow of the eyes that had previously stood out like rubies were now absent. Only misery remained. Instead of hate and savagery, I saw only fear there now.

The creature noticed me, and its blood soaked and scarred mouth pulled back in a snarl, but it quickly let out a yip of pain, its face returning to a pained look. The creature's unnaturally large chest appeared broken as it lay sunken into its body. I suspected the varg's ribs had been broken during the battle and its lung collapsed. It would soon be dead, no matter what I did here.

I moved to turn away, knowing the creature was of no threat anymore, but that pitiful look just drew me back.

I had to do something.

Reluctantly, I stepped toward the creatures with a timid caution. At first, it recoiled at my presence, but, being so close to death, it just breathed out, accepting my company. I reached out slowly and brushed the creature's head. Surprisingly, its ears flicked in pleasure at my little scratches. Then it whined again, loudly.

"Hush..." I said soothingly. "Shh."

I continued to scratch softly behind the varg's ears with my left hand. With my right, I tapped at a small fragment of magic, and a small spike of rock formed under the creature's neck. I continued to shush the creature, guiding the rock to the place where I felt it needed to be. Tears welled in my eyes and I choked back sobs. Every moment of hesitation would only serve to hurt more.

"Let the seeds of your soul return to where they were once sown. You are part of the collective. Anduinna's collective. With this, I willingly return you to her. May your next life be less painful than this."

I pressed my will into the magic. With a clash of stone, the sharp spike of rock impaled the creature's neck.

The varg did not cry out, it simply shuddered and then all was still. It almost seemed peaceful to me at that moment, or perhaps, that's just how my mind chose to remember the event. As a way to protect myself from what I'd done. Regardless, I never relished the suffering of any creature.

Enemy or otherwise. This was no exception. I contend that I did the creature a mercy, but it still hurt me to do it all the same.

The cold now bit at me and I knew that if I didn't get back to the fire soon, I would share the varg's grave.

Searching for my way back using the dew of light at the tip of my index finger, I saw the light of the fire from around a corner. I hadn't been gone long, but to my surprise, as I came closer, the fire revealed to me that Tesro had woken at some point while I was away. She held her hands toward the fire and lines of worry marred her face.

As I stepped out of the darkness, she screamed, putting her hand to her mouth to block the outburst. Then, when her eyes focused on me, tears welled in them and she said in a joyous voice, "Vi'eri! You're alright."

To my surprise, she leaped to her feet and rushed toward me. It enamored me—the strength she still possessed as she hurled herself into me, wrapping me up in an embrace and lifting me into the air with a twirl. As she set me down, she asked a thousand questions at once, stopping momentarily for breath and then asked a thousand more.

I put both my hands up to quiet her insistence. "Easy," I said, pressing my hand to her shoulder, as if I could physically force calm onto her. "Breathe—I beg you. Just breathe."

Tesro acquiesced, calming her frantic blitz of questions and forcing herself to relax. When she regained composure, she looked around the cave curiously, asking, "Where are we?"

"I'm not sure. A cave?"

"Obviously!" She rolled her eyes at me, but grinned coyly. "How did we get here? The last thing I remember is...something to do with an enormous wolf?"

"A varg," I explained. "They besieged us—the beasts known as vargs. We won, but during the fighting, we found ourselves separated from the other two. You were...reckless, and you taxed yourself far too much! Were you ever listening to Vrak's lessons?"

Tesro frowned. "I listen...sometimes. Clearly that particular lesson didn't stick though." It surprised me that she didn't argue. It was a testament to how tired she must have felt. "I don't remember a thing, just waking up here, alone. Vi'eri, I've never been so scared before in my life."

I rubbed my gloved hands against my upper arms to ward off the cold. "I'm not surprised. It must have been terrifying waking alone and not knowing where you were."

"Not that!" she replied, her lip quivering. "It's you! I was scared for you!"

"For me? Why?"

She threw up her arms. "Never mind." Her tone told me I had missed something crucial. "It's freezing, and I'm still so tired. Let's go back to the fire."

I nodded my head, and we did just that. Once again, we shared the gray wolf cloak, and this time, we sat side by side, staring into the lively flame.

I wanted to say something, but as if reading my mind, she asked, "You never explained how we got here. So?" She stared at me expectantly.

"I carried you," I replied. A sidelong glance told me she expected more, and I found myself telling her everything since the varg attack. Of sheltering under the tree branches, to my wrapping her in the cloak and finding this place, to killing the injured varg deeper in the cave.

She winced at that and her eyes told me she shared in my woe. I was thankful for it. Finally, I added in jest, "You were so delusional that you said you loved me! I imagine you dreamed of your family when you did. I'm just glad you had pleasant dreams while you slept." Her expression never changed, and that was what set off signals in my head. Her eyes gazed into those flames, the red gleam in them matched her wild hair. "Tesro, I—"

"No, don't." She turned her head from me, showing me the tight muscles that stood out on her neck. I breathed her in, and the small glistening of her sweat hung sweetly in the air. "I expect nothing more than what we already have. But if we are being truthful, for once, I had terrible nightmares—it's what awoke me. What I said, under the roots of the tree...that is how I feel."

We sat in silence for a time, and before I could fathom a response, she added, "It's a stupid fancy. Vrak says it'll pass." She turned back to face me, and I knew how much bravery it took for her to do so.

My voice quivered as I asked, "Vrak knows?" She shook her head approvingly. I swallowed hard and mustered my courage. "And does he approve?" I said the words so quietly that I didn't know if she had heard.

Her eyes went wide and the light from the flames illuminated in them. She was beautiful beyond words...beyond expression. I could not hope to explain what I felt at that moment. I saw a tear well in her eyes, but I threw caution to the wind as I leaned forward, pressing my lips to hers.

She tasted...of Tesro.

No words can describe it. No lofty remarks, no proclamations of greatness, not even if spoken in a bard's tale. I felt her hands wrap around my back and my body moved on its own, doing the same. We maintained this position for an awkwardly long time, but neither of us cared. I held her—truly held her. Not as a friend, but as something much deeper. It felt more right than anything I had ever experienced before in my life.

Perfect.

With reluctance, our lips parted.

We spoke no more that night. We simply enjoyed the intimacy of our contact as we embraced each other next to the warmth of the fire.

And of each other.

Chapter Twenty-Eight

SLEETWARD

I woke to see gleaming light illuminating the once dark corridor that led to the cave's entrance.

The fire had long since died in the night, the log all but reduced to a gray ash that still gave off small bouts of smoke that twirled in the air like two intertwining serpents.

I looked at Tesro, who still lay next to me, her mouth slightly open as she continued to snore lightly. I stifled a laugh and shifted. At my slight movement, her eyes opened, and upon seeing me, she smiled—a smile I had never seen from her before. A warmness blossomed in my chest.

As I stood, she snatched at me and pulled me back down into a kiss. I embraced her for a moment before I pulled back.

"Mornin'," she said, stretching her arms exorbitantly. "Did you sleep well?"

I gave her a coy smirk. "You know I did."

She shrugged, as if she had no clue what I was talking about. I shook my head at her playfully and finally stood, shaking dirt from my hair. Suddenly, I realized there was no need to get ready—we both had slept wholly clothed in our traveling attire.

I reached out a hand out toward her, and she pulled me back down again into the cloak we had shared the previous night. She was silent as she set her bare hand on my gloved one. I pulled back instinctually.

She frowned. "It can't be that bad? Can it? Even after last night, can I still not see them? Can I still not feel your ungloved touch? The warmth of your hand?"

"No!" I replied, perhaps too abruptly, as her frown deepened, looking far more hurt than I imagined she would. "I mean, it's just…" I let my words trail off, not trusting myself to form the correct sentences to explain without giving away my secret.

"It's okay," she replied, and I could see she forced a smile. "It's too fast, I know. So much changed so quickly. You hold on to this one thing, even if I don't understand it. I've given you my all, Vi'eri. I hope—" She choked on her words.

I wanted so fiercely to tell her everything about myself. About my scales. About my promise. But my mother… I couldn't shake her words of warning. If anyone in the realm would understand, surely it would be Tesro. But a dark pain I didn't recognize kept me from revealing more.

"Turn around," I said simply, surprising even myself. She looked at me curiously and when she didn't move, I added, "Amuse me."

Tesro gave me a sidelong gaze, then reluctantly, she nodded to my request, putting her back toward me and holding her hair to the side.

Removing my leather glove was one of the hardest things I've ever done. My heart raced and the fear of discovery plagued my mind as I saw the gleaming silver scales that lined the back of my hand and arm. I shoved my fears aside as I reached out and placed my hand on the back of her neck. She flinched at my touch, but as I pressed harder, she slowly eased into the pressure of my fingers.

"Oh, enough," she said as she struggled to turn to face me, but with my other hand, I held her steady.

"I'm not ready," I explained. "But please, this is all I can offer you."

Tesro eased as my hand massaged the back of her neck. Her muscles were taut, but I suspected it was more from exhilaration than stress. Slowly, I moved my hand down her spine, tapping deeply with the tips of my fingers as I went. When I got to the swell of her lower back, I shifted, rubbing the muscles that lined each side of it as I worked my way back up. I did this for a time, and she lay there, quiet—her subtle movements speaking louder than words ever could.

She reveled in it.

Finally, I kissed the back of her neck and slipped my glove back on unceremoniously.

Tesro respected my wishes and turned slowly to face me after it was apparent I had finished re-gloving. She leaned up and gave me a last kiss, saying, "We should probably go now. Don't ya' think?"

I felt breathless, but I managed to reply, "I think that would be best."

Tesro looked exasperated as she said, "So you executed a varg in the cave last night? The alpha? I can't believe I can't remember any of this. Only small bits and pieces come back to me like a fleeting dream."

I shook my head at her. "Could we not say 'executed?' The creature was dying already, I just put it out of its misery."

She rubbed at her forehead. "Sorry, slip of the tongue."

We exited the cave side-by-side and looked out on the wonder that laid before us. Crisp, new snow littered the ground and trees. From this vantage, we could see all the way into the valley under the path. The blanket of snow before us was largely undisturbed, except the small prints of various woodland creatures that looked like natural artwork.

I spun to see a squirrel scurry up a tree, and my heart leaped in my chest. It turned to stare at us curiously, and the memory of the mocking squirrels from the Bloodsoaked Forest put me in a sour mood.

So many years ago now.

I frowned at the woodland critter and, likely sensing my hostility, it turned and bolted into its wooded home.

Tesro stared at where the squirrel had been, then at me, asking, "Anything I should know about?"

I sighed. "Squirrels and I don't get along."

She stifled a laugh. "I seem to learn something new about you every day."

"And I, you."

We smiled at each other—a smile that only two young people in love can show each other.

"We should head back to the trail," I suggested. "It may be dangerous, but I think traipsing out here completely lost would be more so."

She nodded in support as we stomped our way back toward the trail, leaving little stamps of our existence in the purity of fresh snow.

We reached the road soon after with relative ease. As we did, I insisted, to Tesro's dismay, that we check the site of the battle. Perhaps our companions would be there, looking for us. The small shake of her head told me she was not hopeful.

When we arrived, we found the few varg that Tesro and I had slain. She looked grimly upon that scene, and I wrapped my arm around her comfortingly. A short way from there, we found a few more dead varg. These we had not slain by us. I was uncertain of the exact number that had attacked our group, but the lack of Hask or Sho's body was a comfort.

Perhaps they had survived.

"Hask!" Tesro said suddenly, and I turned my gaze to follow the line of her distant stare. A short ways away, the deminean man sat propped on the base of a tree.

We both rushed to him, but slowed as we noticed the blue blood trail, just visible through the snow that had nearly concealed it last night. We approached cautiously to face the carnage that laid before us.

Hask's body was in pieces. One arm was completely missing, and a leg ended in a splintered bone where a foot should have been. Tesro held her hand to her mouth to stop from gasping at the grisly sight, and I could see ancient memories flooded her mind.

Painful ones.

The temperature had frozen Hask's body solidly to the tree. Clearly, he had died either during the fighting or shortly after. There was little we could do for him now. Any attempt at removing him would damage the body further and would drain us of precious stamina that may be needed before the day was through. I dared not even incinerate the body using magic, weak as I felt. Despite that, curiosity got the better of me, and I stepped closer.

She grabbed me by the shoulder. "There's nothing we can do for him." Her words echoed my own thoughts perfectly.

"I know," I replied, letting my distaste for the situation radiate through me. "But I want to know what the killing blow was, if I can, so I can explain later to Ri'sha Isodros. So she can tell his family and friends."

Tesro spared a quick glance at the dead man. "Friends?" she scoffed and then guilt plagued her features. Finally, she nodded, letting me go, but she herself dared not venture forward.

I crept closer and when I stood in front of him, I leaned down to his level. His eyes were open and the look of shock still stuck frozen on his face. I suspected it would be for all time.

Shockingly, his eyes looked very...human. Gone was the golden limbal ring that all deminean were known for, leaving the lightest amount of green in those clouded eyes. I reached and pulled his clothing to the side. It stuck, at first, but with some prying, I pulled it away. Looking down, I found what had killed him.

A puncture wound straight through the heart.

I shook my head and stood. There was truly nothing we could do for Hask now. I walked back toward Tesro, who shared my look of sorrow.

"The man was a brute, and I didn't like him," she said, turning to face Hask one more time, "but he died fighting with us, and that puts him ahead of other deminean in my book."

"He was a brash man," I replied agreeingly, "but he was our companion. He likely saved our lives as well. In that, I thank him for his sacrifice, and I'll make sure Isodros knows it."

We both nodded our agreement at each other and walked back toward the road, each saying a silent prayer to the Well.

As we reached it, I faced a tree close to the path and concentrated. I found a small fragment of magic. Tapping it, I willed concentrated air in my palm.

I stepped closer to the tree and struck it. The wind spun and dissipated, sending small bits of bark flying all around. A clean spot, free of bark, now showed plainly on the tree. I took my knife out and carved the word 'Hask' in the bald spot.

"There," I said, "now we can easily locate him." She placed a comforting hand on my shoulder, and I turned to face her. "And I think we best be off now. I don't relish spending another night in a cave."

"I don't know," she replied, giving me a nudge, "I didn't think it was so bad."

We traveled for the better part of the day, taking few breaks. My stomach growled in protest at our arduous pace. Our deminean companions had our provisions, so we were stuck scooping snow into our mouths and letting it melt for hydration. As for food, we hadn't had any luck capturing any woodland creatures as they darted away from our every attempt, to the great frustration of Tesro.

"I need meat!" she said, holding her stomach and leaning over as if she would vomit on the ground.

Then, as if the Well answered our prayers, we saw gray smoke in the distance, just over snow covered treetops. At the sight of it, propelled by our stomachs, we hastened, making considerable speed. We dug in our heels and forced ourselves through the thick layers of snow, ignoring the constant protest of our tired bodies.

At one point, I slipped and fell into a snow pile. As I recovered, a loosened patch of snow that hung in the tree above me promptly fell on my head. Tesro laughed hysterically, wheezing and begging herself to stop lest she pass out. Hunched over with this laughing fit, the sight of her made me join in.

Eventually, once we claimed our senses back, we crested a ridge and finally found it.

The town of Sleetward.

A wooden sign just outside the cozy town of brick houses and thatched roofs confirmed it. We had made it. The hard ground was a welcome change from the laboring walking that one does through tall, soft snow.

Someone had meticulously swept the snow off the cobblestones, leaving a path that led to the town center. The small gleams of sunlight that had broken through the clouds completed the task, leaving a thin layer of water on the stone which made walking quite hazardous. I proceeded cautiously. Nevertheless, more than once, I slipped. Tesro and I resorted to holding onto each other for balance. I chuckled to myself at how ridiculous we must have looked to the other townsfolk.

"We better find an inn," I said, and she nodded her head in agreement.

"Are you two looking for an inn?" a middle-aged woman said from behind us, as if reading my mind. The woman's brown hair and brown eyes gave way to her pale face. She had a rounded middle section, and I suspected that she was...expecting.

"Yes, ma'am," I replied, bowing my head in deference.

She frowned. "None of that, ya' hear? We're a bit more simple than all that. My name's Elenda, but folks around here call me Mother."

"Why?" Tesro asked.

The woman looked down and rubbed her stomach. "This'll be my eighth."

Tesro's eyes lit up and she nodded joyously.

"And you said you can point us in the direction of the inn?" I said, pulling the conversation back.

"Ah, yes." She pointed to a building a little larger than the rest with no discernable signage. "It's that building there. Be careful, a cursed deminean woman is in there scaring all us good folk."

"Deminean woman?" I replied.

Tesro caught my glance and muttered curiously, "Sho?"

I raised my shoulders in response, but turned back toward the woman, who eyed us both considerably. "Sorry to be rude, but we best be going. Nice to meet you, and may the Well bless your child."

She smiled at my words. "Seven children so far and none born soulless. The Well truly blesses us humans. Go in peace." She turned, hiked up her skirt, and walked away.

We made our way to the building the woman had indicated and as I stepped up the wood stairs, I kicked the snow off my boots and pushed open the swinging double doors. I let them slowly swing back, and they struck Tesro's extended hand. She gave me a baleful glance, and I returned it with a bashful smile.

The first thing I noticed was the heat. The intense warmth of the inn stunned me, and I immediately wanted to discard my cloak and drink the coldest liquid they had handy. Tesro looked much the same as I, perspiration already appearing in small droplets on her forehead. She wiped them away with the back of her hand in an unladylike fashion, shrugging her shoulders at me as I cast her a judgmental stare.

Not two steps inside, and I heard a woman arguing with a man. I stepped from beside a support pillar to see a tall, slender cloaked woman yelling at a much shorter, stockier man. The sound of that voice, combined with that height, could leave no mistake.

"Sho!" I called out and hurried toward her. I spared a look at Tesro and she appeared...disappointed. Ignoring it, I turned back to the deminean woman and was surprised to find that my arms were wrapped around her. I had only come up to her abdomen, and my cheeks flushed red.

Quickly, I let go, taking an enormous step back. "I'm so glad you're here. A townswoman said a deminean had taken refuge. You're alive. You're—"

"I'm okay..." she replied in her slow melodic voice. "Calm yourself, Vi'eri." She stared at me for a moment, and then a grin split her face. "You're a sight for sore eyes yourself." When she saw Tesro, she added, "Both of you."

"Nice to see you as well," she replied, but her tone and posture said otherwise.

Sho let the comment slide past as she gestured for us to join her at a nearby table. She shot what I assumed to be the innkeeper a disdainful look before we found our way there. As I sat, the sounds of other humans talking excitedly all around us filled me with a rush. Their brash callousness and disregard for any other than themselves reminded me of home.

Just what I needed.

The realm could be such a quiet place outside of dwellings such as these. Far too quiet for my tastes. I had missed the smells of old beer, and the sounds men make when they lose a card game. It was the general chaotic ruckus that humans and deminean made for themselves that was the spark of life. Some would call it civilization. A quick glance at Tesro's far-off look told me everything I needed to know about how she felt.

"So..." Sho said, tapping her long fingernails on the wooden table, her golden eyes piercing through us, as if she sensed the secret Tesro and I shared with each other. I swallowed hard, and she turned her gaze to me, asking, "Aren't you going to tell me what happened to you two? One moment, there was fighting...oh, I don't remember how many of those vile beasts. And the next, you both are gone."

I grasped for my courage and addressed the hard news first. "We found Hask... He's dead. There wasn't much we could do for him."

Her facial expression didn't change. She looked toward the barkeeper and held up three fingers. He quickly grabbed three mugs and began filling them. She turned back to face us. "I know, I was hoping you wouldn't see that. Truth be told, I have no idea as to what happened to him. During the snowstorm, I found myself blinded by sleet. I heard him cry out, but when I made it to him, the beasts had already set upon him. I battered them away, but I had to fend for myself first. By the time I had finished the last of the beasts, I found him torn and broken, sitting on that tree. He was long dead. I assume that's how you found him as well?"

"Why didn't you bury him?" Tesro asked accusatively, banging the table with her fist. "You just left him there!"

She looked at Tesro curiously before shaking her head. "I was looking for you two. Why waste time on the dead? Besides, did you two take the time to bury him yourselves? Or did reaching Sleetward and completing our mission take a higher priority?"

She had us dead to rights and as Tesro's anger built for some type of retort, the innkeeper dropped a mug of cheap smelling beer in front of each of us. My drink slouched, and some dripped onto my cloak. It was already filthy with dirt, blood and ash. What was a little beer going to do?

Sho drank her entire mug before the innkeeper could even step away. She reached and grabbed his arm, causing his whole body to seize up. He pulled on the end of his thick mustache, and she handed him the mug. Reluctantly, he took it and as he stepped away, she shouted, "And this time, use a real mug! Not something made for children."

Her mannerisms shocked me into silence. Her cool sensibilities and soft-spoken, almost musical tone did not match up with this hard drinking, varg slayer I now knew her to be. I made a note to not judge people with such a broad brush in the future.

"Poor Hask," she said suddenly, her head turned down, almost shamefully. Regret burned in those golden eyes. "I wish we had the time to bury him properly—I truly do. But my duty comes first, and I suspect yours does as well."

I nodded at her words as the innkeeper returned with a mug double the size of the previous. She casually flipped him a coin, which spun shining in the air. He reached for it, snagging it before it hit the floor. His frown instantaneously turned into a grin as he bowed graciously, his mustache-pulling becoming more exhilarating. Still, the man left quickly, as if Sho would snatch back the coin without a moment's hesitation.

"To Hask," Tesro said with a sudden earnestness as she raised her mug in the air. I looked at her curiously, but said nothing as I raised my glass in imitation. Sho followed soon after with her comically large drink. We tapped them together as we each tipped the liquid into our mouths and drank deeply at our fallen comrade.

I spent the next few hours of time explaining to Sho about all that had befallen us. Blatantly leaving out the part about the mysterious voice in my head, Vulana, and what had happened between Tesro and me. I decided it really was none of her business what happened between the two humans who accompanied her.

Sho nodded absently at my words, and I suspected she speculated more than what she let on. This explanation went on until the light that came in the shuttered windows dwindled to nothing at all, indicating night had crept up on us.

I hadn't noticed before, but patrons filled the room like a hive of bees. The place was close to bursting now.

Sleetward was a human town, allowed to exist at the behest of their ruler, Goxir Stoutclaw. Rhas had mentioned that the people of Sleetward mined for rare goods, and fished the glacial lake to which the city lay adjacent too. From the look of the humans who stared at Sho, I suspected few deminean made their way out here. And they didn't seem particularly pleased with our company.

"I'm heading to bed," Sho said, finishing her draught and sliding the mug away from her. "I suggest you two do the same. I've already procured a room for myself, but I suspect if you hurry, there may be one left over. If not, then I'm afraid you may have another night of sleep under a cloak outside...perhaps in a barn?"

Tesro shot her a disdainful look and she shrugged, grinning at her before turning to head upstairs.

"Deminean..." Tesro whispered, wringing her hands around her drink. "Always so full of themselves."

"She's not so bad, as far as most deminean go."

"You have more patience for them than I, but I cannot see the reason. Ah well, it's not my business who you decide to trust, as long as I'm the one you trust most."

I turned to her and smirked. "You are."

I found the innkeeper who wore stained white overalls, his face dripping with sweat. His sensibilities toward Tesro and I were much harsher than when Sho was in company, but when I flashed a coin, he perked right back up.

"I'm looking for a room," I said, making sure the coin stayed firmly within sight.

The man licked his lips greedily and gave his mustache another pull. He stepped closer as if he would snatch the coin and I saw Tesro's nose shrink up at the stench of the man as she took an awkward step backward.

He eyed her and then looked back toward me. "I think something can be arranged." He stood straighter, with a bit of a leer in his eyes. "Tell me, what are you doing with that deminean bitch—I mean, woman?"

"We'll take the room," I said, ignoring his rude comment and placing a single coin in his hand. With deft fingers, I quickly pulled a second coin, adding, "And our business is our own, understood?" I reached over and dropped it in his hand.

"Of course," he replied, greedily shoving the coins into his pocket as if I were a thief hiding a score. Slowly, he fished in his pocket, stitched on the breast of his shirt, and eventually pulled a small gray key from it. "Here you are, honored guest. I hope you and your...companion have a pleasant stay."

I gave him a glare. It was difficult to ignore his rudeness, and I wished to flatten him right where he stood. Tesro looked of similar mind. But instead, we turned from the man, leaving him standing awkwardly in the common room muttering to himself.

She was quick at my heel as we went upstairs and retired to our private room, each of us taking one of the two small beds. Despite the closeness we had shared the previous night, neither of us went to the other, and instead resumed our respective roles as we always had. I told myself we would have time to explore our newfound feelings later.

We had time.

CHAPTER TWENTY-NINE

FROZEN MAN

I entered the first floor of the tavern to the smell of warm bread, butter, and some type of smoked meat that sizzled as the server brought it out on a large glass plate. My stomach growled at the sight of the feast, the juices of the meat slopping off its container as the boy set it down. I pulled a coin out of my pocket, dropping it into their hand.

"Much obliged," the boy said, tipping his hat to me as I snatched at the items like a starving beggar receiving their first meal in an age.

I noticed a disdainful look from the innkeeper who was tidying up near the back exit. I hurriedly grabbed a few more pieces of food, bowed my head to him, and retreated as quickly as my feet would carry me. As I went to head upstairs, I heard a familiar voice call my name.

"Vi'eri!" they said and I turned to find Sho sitting in a corner booth at the opposite side of the inn's common room. She held a steaming cup in both hands and looked to have already partaken of breakfast, indicated by the crumbs of bread that littered the worn wooden table she sat at. I walked toward her, taking the seat opposite as she asked, "Where's Tesro?"

"Sleeping," I replied, a smile tugging at my lips as I turned my head to hide my flushing cheeks. "She isn't what you'd call a morning person."

"Is that so..." she let the thought drift off as she raised her mug to her mouth, the steam drifting in small tendrils around her face and parting as they reached the tips of her small horns atop her forehead. She sipped and seemed to enjoy it as she hummed a tune to herself.

I moved to stand and she reached out, grasping my arm. I pulled back, saying, "Actually, if you don't mind, I was going to—"

"I hope you don't mind me asking," she cut in, setting her glass down and leveling her golden gaze at me. I settled back down in the uncomfortable wooden chair. "Did something happen between the two of you? I can't quite put a finger on it, but something seems...different."

"No!" I replied, perhaps too hastily as a smile broke through her curious expression; her eyes lighting up.

"Well, if it has, it's alright. Traveling can make us do things we wouldn't ordinarily do." She paused to take another sip, gulping it down noisily. "I'm sure everything will return to normal between the two of you once we return to Whiteline."

Sho's words were said with all the warmth of a parent explaining a situation to a child. But the words did not inspire any comfort in me. No, quite the opposite. To have experienced an intimacy with Tesro the way I had, the thought of everything 'returning to normal' nauseated me, and made the fire I burned for her in my chest feel even hotter.

I gazed at Sho with all the hurt of a lovesick girl plain on my face, but she pretended not to notice, adding casually, "Well, in any case, we have our work cut out for us today. The men here, miners and fishermen," she chewed on those words for a moment, as if they annoyed her, "they don't trust us! Or, should I say, they don't trust *me*. We need one to agree to guide us to the location of their discovery. To the amulet. If we tried to find it ourselves, we would surely fall prey to the hazards this place offers and likely end up preserved in ice for all time within the day."

She spoke of dying so casually that the real danger of the situation didn't seem dangerous at all.

"I'll need one of you to find one of these humans willing to help us. I believe they will be more accommodating to those of their own kind. As much as it pains me to say, I need your help."

Coincidentally, I had already considered asking the other townsfolk of Sleetward to guide us. Possibly even for coin. Blindly searching through a frozen network of caves with no previous knowledge sounded like a recipe for failure.

And disaster.

"I think we can manage that," I replied, shifting uncomfortably. "But what will you do? Surely you don't want to just sit here all day?"

She laughed. "Of course not! I'll begin scouting ahead. I'm sure you know, but us deminean can survive much harsher conditions than you humans. The cold takes its toll, that is certain, but as long as I have reserves of magic to draw from, I can sustain it."

I listened to her words in a sort of awe. The deminean were hesitant to speak much about their magic, preferring to keep it shrouded in secrecy. Unlike humans, all deminean held the inward magic to varying degrees of potency. A ward of a Ri'sha, as Sho was, would likely have a considerable amount of power. I feared I had only seen the mere glimpses of it in our journey together thus far.

When I said nothing in reply, she took my silence for agreement. Standing up, she pushed the cup aside. "Best get some food to Tesro. We will rest for today, but guide or not, we will be pursuing our prize on the morrow."

As I reached the door of our modest-sized room, I wasn't quiet as I entered, letting the door swing and hit the edge of a small wooden table. "Wake up!" I shouted as I walked to Tesro, nudging her by the shoulder.

She moaned and swatted at me with the back of her hand, but I was insistent, dragging her warm blanket off the bed and throwing it to the unswept floor. Dust kicked up in the air, filling the room with dirt as the heavy cloth struck the ground.

Tesro sat upright, wrapping herself with both her arms. "Why'd you do that?"

"You know why," I replied in a mock-taunting voice. "Can't let you sleep until the sun reaches midday, can I?"

I could hear the low mumblings of defiance and annoyance that came from her throat, and I offered her a piece of lukewarm bread that I had already added butter to. She peered at me suspiciously for a moment before I heard her stomach growl. Then, as if she hadn't eaten in days, she snatched the bread out of my hand greedily—so quick a movement that I had not even seen it coming. Like a beast, she shoved the entire thing in her mouth, chomping loudly before her sense of propriety caught up with her and she forced it down her throat.

"Sorry," she muttered, almost to herself. Stretching, she asked, "What time is it?"

"Time for us to go."

Tesro looked at me with a raised eyebrow. "Go where?"

I explained our companion's request to her—explained that we needed to find a guide for the group, lest we make the trip alone. She nodded in approval at the plan, although her lip curled when I mentioned Sho by name.

While explaining, she had dressed. Sho had, luckily, taken the pack with our provisions after the fighting and we both welcomed the change of clean clothes, discarding our dirty rags. She tucked thick brown pants into her fur-lined boots and put on a coat that hung long. I helped tuck it into her short gloves. As for myself, I wore near identical clothing, except fitted to my height, and my studded leather gloves were near elbow length. Reluctantly, I left the gray wolf cloak behind to be cleaned and mended. Instead, I relied on the attached hood of my brown coat to keep me warm.

I hoped it would.

When Tesro finished, she quietly ate the rest of the food I had brought for her and drank a glass of water. She sighed out in satisfaction and leveled her eyes at me, appearing to be searching for words to say. When I turned my gaze from her, she asked, "What's the matter?"

I folded my arms and looked aside. "Nothing." A pathetic lie and I knew it. Tesro saw the truth and turned my head to face her with a gentle hand. I pressed my face against her palm and looked down into those green eyes, knowing I had to tell her. "It's just something that Sho said."

She scowled, and lines ran deep in her furrowed brow as she asked in a dark tone, "What did she say?"

"That this," I pointed between the two of us, "is just something that happened because of where we are—the situation we're in. That what we share is just something that happens when two people travel together. She doesn't believe it's real. I just—"

"Just what?" she interjected, stepping back from me as if I had slapped her. "Just believed her? Vi'eri, I've felt this way about you for some time. Remember, even Vrak knows. This isn't some whimsy fancy for me." Pausing, as if her next words would be particularly painful, she wrestled with herself before leveling a determined gaze back on me. "Is it for you?"

"No!" I heard myself say and was pleasantly surprised to find it was the truth. I reached for her, and she pushed me back. Gently, but the denial still stung. "Tesro, I don't feel that way at all. I want to believe it's real—I do believe!"

"Then why do you let the words of a deminean cloud what you know?"

I wanted to respond and found that I didn't have an answer. I stood there, stupidly, flailing to say something—anything that would mend the rift I had just caused between us.

Eventually, she scoffed. "I'll let you think about that." The dismissal hurt, but she turned and opened the door, adding, "We still need to find a guide, right? Let's go."

Tesro and I had gone our separate ways for a bit, and that suited me fine. Part of me felt shame for letting Sho's words create such a schism, and the other, anger. Anger that Tesro could not understand where my insecurities came from. I wanted to believe our feelings were genuine, but what if they were just a product of a dire situation? I thought, what if, when we returned, she found someone else? Someone without the baggage I carried.

I looked at my hands. *Someone without these scales?* An overwhelming need to place a wall between us battered against me. I longed desperately to push her back out of the fortress I had built around my heart.

To protect myself from future pain.

"As I was saying, miss." The voice of a miner I had been speaking to interrupted my thoughts. He was an elderly man, skinny, with a patchy head of hair that had mostly gone white, matching his beard.

"Apologies," I replied, shaking my head. "I seem to be distracted today."

The man scratched at his face. "I see. Oh, how it was to be so young. In my day, we—" the man paused suddenly, as if his mind had wandered away. His eyes fluttered as he caught the flight of a pack of white birds flying overhead.

"Seasqualls," I said, turning to face where they were heading. "Fleeing a storm, perhaps?"

It wasn't until they were out of sight that the elderly man returned his gaze to me. "What were we talking about again?"

Frowning, I shuffled my boots on the icy ground. "I was just wishing you a pleasant day, is all." I nodded my head at him and flashed a genuine smile. In my mind, I cursed myself for having chosen someone so clearly past his prime to be our guide.

Too much time wasted, I thought. *Perhaps tonight will yield better results.*

"Such a kindly young lass. You've got to come for supper tonight, I insist." The man reached forward and grabbed my arm, as if he would lead me home straight away.

I tenderly, but insistently, declined his offer, pulling my arm from him. I explained that I was here for business and if I had time, I would say goodbye to him before I left town.

He frowned, but we eventually said our goodbyes, and I held my head in my hand as I walked back toward the inn. A migraine unlike any other thrashed in my skull. Suddenly, someone seized my shoulder and as I turned, my fingers raised in the casting position; fragmented magic already glittering in and out in my eyes, waiting to be used.

A dark man in a thick tan coat stood before me. Startled, he stepped back, raising his hands in a silent submission.

"What do you want?" I said, not altering my stance. "Typically, someone announces themselves before touching another person."

The man lowered his hands, but kept his distance. "And typically, a destroyer wouldn't be visiting this far north in the company of a deminean," he replied with a smile, his voice higher pitched than I would've expected. It held a type of mischievous ring to it.

I lowered my hands as well, sensing the man didn't have violence in mind for me. *If he wanted to hurt me*, I thought. *He could have easily before I'd noticed him.*

"What do you want?" I asked. "I don't have time for idle chatter now."

This man, young like myself, likely around sixteen years in age, stared at the elderly man I had been speaking to before. "You don't? But you have time to speak to a senile old man?"

I shook my head. "That's awfully rude of you. If you must know, I had something to ask him. But, as for you, I can sense when someone wants something from me. Everyone who acts the way you do wants something. So, spit it out. What is it?"

The man averted his green eyes. "That easy to see, is it? Apologies, my name is Madrof, but everyone around here calls me Mad Madrof. Although, I would vastly prefer it if you just called me Madrof."

"Then why would you even tell me your nickname?" I asked, not hiding my amusement. He smiled and shrugged his shoulders. "And why do they call you that?"

"I think it's because of the jobs I take. Beasts killing your livestock? I'm your man. Have a dangerous tunnel you need excavated, I'll do it...if the price is right. You asked what I wanted before? It's a simple question, with a simple answer: I want off this icy purgatory. I don't know where you're from, but I know you're looking for a guide. Someone to take you to the frozen man."

"Frozen man?"

"Aye, frozen man. That's what we call 'em. You won't find many here who'll brave that trip, and even fewer in the presence of your deminean companion. Ever since we opened the cave up, revealing the resting place of the frozen man, there is a feeling of something wrong in the air. I've felt it myself! The best way I can describe it is like something tugging on your soul." He rolled his arm exaggeratingly, as if that's all he cared to say about it. From Madrof's mannerisms and tone, I sensed that we were now bartering.

"So let me get this straight," I said, standing to my full height, and matching his faux casual stare. "You're offering to guide us, and, in exchange, you want to leave with us?"

Madrid shook his head. "Not quite," he replied, stretching his arms with a showman's excess. "I want to leave with you, *and* to be paid in coin. Many coins."

"And you say you'll take us to see this 'frozen man?' You know where he is?"

He smiled. "Know where he is? I discovered him myself."

"This is grayhorn shit," Sho said, looking Madrof up and down exaggeratedly. "This human cannot be the one who discovered the 'frozen man,' as you call him. Vi'eri, he's just trying to use us to run from this life." She looked around at the prying eyes of the patrons in the inn's common room. "Not that I blame him."

"I am," Madrof replied, unphased. "Using you, I mean. But I am the one who discovered the frozen man—ask around. Also, I'm one of the few humans you'll find who will work with someone like you." He bent his head toward Sho.

She flashed her sharp teeth for a moment, looking like she would have choice words for our new roguish friend. But eventually, she forced calm back to her face. "Very well then, Madrof. Since I've yet to find any better offers, despite my best efforts, you will be our guide. I trust you'll bring your own provisions for the trek?"

He scoffed. "Of course. Remember, you're the outsiders here, not I. I've done this my entire life."

"Indeed..." she replied, letting the words drift off. "You best be telling us the truth, human Madrof, or you'll be leaving this place, but I suspect you would not enjoy the manner of such a departure."

Madrof, smartly, took Sho's words as a dismissal, making a quick bow of his head. But as he moved to exit, he turned, asking, "And how much coin were we talking about again?"

The glare Sho leveled at him was full of righteous indignation. He smiled nervously and left the inn without his answer.

"Humans can be so..." she said, but noticed Tesro's cold gaze and changed the subject. "What do you two have planned for the rest of the night? Don't worry about your provisions, I've already taken care of that part. I suspect the boy will be useless, but I've gathered some strong information on the location of the frozen man, as the locals have taken to calling him. Might I suggest a long night's rest—"

"Vi'eri!" Tesro said suddenly. Sho leaned back with a huff, but added nothing further. At her silence, Tesro added, "Let's go see the lake. I hear at sunset, it can be... Well, let's just go see it!"

She seemed to be back to her cheery old self, even more so than usual, and I was glad for it. The argument we'd had earlier in the day left me feeling empty, like a piece of myself was missing.

"Don't make me wake you in the morning," Sho said, like a parent warning a haphazard child. But her words fell on deaf ears as we both rushed toward the door. I heard her begrudgingly demand another mug of beer before the wooden doors shuddered shut.

Tesro pulled at my arm. "It's this way," she said, moving down the street with purpose. I stepped lively to match her pace.

The sun was near setting by the time we reached the lake. Like the townsfolk said, the ever-frozen lake, or the 'Lake of Broken Glass,' as they called it, had sections of frozen ice surrounded by water that was not. The sight of it was magical. Like the name suggested, it appeared like a gigantic broken mirror set into the land that reflected the sky.

We reached the edge of a rocky hill overlooking the lake as a flock of birds flew overhead. They reflected on the ice as if they both flew in the sky and swam in the water simultaneously. She audibly gasped at the scene.

There was a path that led down to the lake, but we opted to sit at the edge, with our legs dangling off its rocky peak. The chill wind made me want to regret the decision to leave the warm inn, but this sight made the cold worth it. And besides, anything to make amends with Tesro.

"I've been thinking—" I said, and to my surprise she held out a finger to silence me.

"I've been as well. I was being stupid this morning, and I'm sorry. You have a right to be skeptical about this. About us." I opened my mouth to speak, but she silenced me again, adding, "I meant what I said before, Vi'eri. I love you. Love you, and I'll keep saying it until even the shadows that linger in your heart cannot reject the light I share."

I laughed. "And where did you hear that?"

She grinned. "An old poem that Vrak shared with me. To purgatory, I wish I could remember the rest. But it's how I feel. Deny me all you want, Vi'eri, for I will not deny you."

I slid my body over to her and leaned my arm around the back of her neck. "'My heart already shines with your light.'"

"That's how it goes!" she replied, and we shared in each other's laughter and joy.

She leaned her head on my shoulder and I leaned mine on top of hers. We stayed that way for a long time, letting the warmth of each other drive away the bitter chill that crept from outside and from within.

We were complete.

I felt contentment like never before, and I wished with all my heart that the Well would freeze us in this moment for all time. If the entire realm fell to pieces, and everything had ended at that moment...

I would have been at peace.

CHAPTER THIRTY
CONTROL

The morning was finally upon us, and I struggled to steady my racing heart.

"I don't know about you, Vi'eri," Tesro said, yanking on her coat. "But next time, let's go somewhere with some sun. I'm so tired of this cold."

"Agreed."

We walked downstairs to find Sho and Madrof already waiting for us, sitting in the same corner booth at the end of the common room. Bowls of what looked to be mashed oats sat steaming on a table in front of them.

"Finally!" Sho said, sliding over the bowls to the two empty places at the table. "Hurry, hurry. Today will be pressing, best to get some food in you while you can."

I sat at the table and pulled the pearly white bowl to rest in front of me. The food smelled good, like cinnamon, but looked...unappetizing.

I spooned a small amount of the pulpy gray matter into my mouth and it tasted overwhelmingly of the spice. I expected it was to mask the blandness of the meal, but a hot meal was a hot meal and I shoveled the rest into my mouth like a pauper at the edge of starvation.

Tesro followed my lead and actually seemed to enjoy it a great deal.

When we were finished, Sho thrusted a small pack at both of us. "These are for you. Basic supplies, in case we need them." I opened mine to see a few salted pieces of meat, a rope, and a metal chisel of sorts. It also had a torch and some matches to go along.

Madrof scratched at his clean-shaven face, his eyes darting around the room. Eventually, he slapped the table with his palms. "Are we ready to go now? You led me to believe that time was of grave concern?"

"Yes, I did indeed," she replied, slinging her own pack over her shoulder. "But you will do as you're told when you're in my company, human." She pointed at Tesro and I. "After you two."

"Are you sure this'll hold?" Tesro asked, tapping her foot on a frozen chunk of the lake.

"It will if you're careful and follow my lead," Madrof replied testily, a scowl crossing his face. "If I'd known you were such a frightened little thing, perhaps I would have thought differently about this arrangement."

She turned bright red, despite the frigid wind that battered the exposed flesh on our faces. I sensed she wished to say more, but the thought of plunging into this cold, albeit beautiful, lake consumed all other concerns.

Sho hissed in frustration. "If the ice breaks, I'll fish you out. Now hurry."

Our deminean companion had been more ornery today than usual. Her typical understanding and calm candor had been replaced with an almost intolerance of the worries and doubts of us mere humans.

A dip into this lake for a deminean would be a minor inconvenience—their internal magic of self able to protect them from the onset of hypothermia. For a human, however, it would likely be a sentence of death. Either through drowning or the sickness that would likely come after.

Neither sounded particularly pleasant to me.

Madrof suddenly jumped across a slight break in the ice to a segmented piece on the other side. It did not budge as he landed flatly.

"See!" he said, turning to face us. "Now hurry."

Tesro looked annoyed as Madrof waved her on insistently. Yet, despite her fears, she jumped without hesitation, bumping into him, and almost sending the young human tumbling into the crack in the ice, likely to his death.

He gasped, but regained his balance, looking awkward in the process. "There ya go!" he said in delight, laughing at his own misfortune.

I leaped over the slight gap. Landing, my legs flew out from under me and I fell, my bottom hitting the hard ice.

Madrof turned his gaze to me and grinned, then they both laughed. I even found myself chuckling with them. All except Sho, who looked fed up with human antics.

She suddenly made the jump and cleared it easily. We found ourselves on a piece of ice separated from the land, and yet, this floating platform did not seem to float at all. It was far too solid to be completely disconnected from the mainland.

"How is this possible?" I asked, hopping up and down to see if the ice shifted under my weight. When I realized it did not sway as expected from a floating object in water, I stopped.

Madrof placed a hand on my shoulder. "You're wondering why the ice doesn't float away, right?" I nodded, and he added, "It's because of the destroyers who made it. As for how they did so, I expect you both would have a better idea?"

I raised a curious eyebrow at him, but concentrated and saw magic in the air. It was quite dense here, and when I looked under my feet, I saw something odd about it. Fragments of the magic buzzed with untapped power just below where we all stood, and there appeared to be a string of woven light tied around them.

Instinctually, I knew that if I were to cut that string, the magic would react violently—only the Well itself would know what type of backlash that would create. As I scanned across the Lake of Broken Glass, I found that this was not the only platform of ice created this way.

"Look, Tesro," I said, pointing down.

She followed my gaze. Her mouth was aghast. "Incredible..." she mouthed, the word drifting away as we both stared, awestruck. The beauty and control it must have taken to create it was unimaginable.

This wasn't magic, it was art.

"What is it?" Madrof asked, not hiding his excitement to hear about something he didn't already know.

I indulged our guide, replying, "Magic is unstable by nature. It floats without purpose until something with a will gives it one. Nevertheless, the magic is fickle, and that purpose fades with time, often rapidly. These platforms of ice," I took a knee and ran my hand across the surface of the platform, "the magic that holds them in place is unlike anything I've ever seen. The discipline it must have taken to bind the magic against its nature for this long is just...indescribable."

"Control..." I heard Tesro mutter under her breath.

Madrof nodded as if he understood, but I suspect my explanation confused him even further. It was difficult to explain magic to those who couldn't see it for themselves. To explain its volatile nature, to feel it; words were not a powerful enough tool to convey it properly.

"Enough!" Sho said, drawing our collective attention. "Enough distractions, and enough idle musings. We have a job to do, or have you forgotten? Human, lead us quickly or I'll start reducing your pay."

"You wound me," he replied with a merchant's smile. But at her cold gaze, he dropped the act. With a sigh, he shook his head and added, "This way."

We walked where we could and hopped from one magical ice platform to the next, crossing the lake. Eventually, we were met with the sight of a cliff and an ancient tower standing atop its peak. Holes, man-made, I suspected, littered the base of the cliff, and the tower itself looked to be in disarray, but it was hard to tell being so far from it.

I looked at our guide and asked, "Is this where the miners work?"

"It's one of many," he replied. "The mountains that surround the towns and lake are filled with all manner of rare materials. Silver is our primary export, it—"

"Let's move," Sho said, shoving past us.

Madrof shook his head in disappointment, but held his tongue as he silently pointed to one of the many breaks in the cliffside and began walking toward it.

The trip was faster now that we had truly solid ground beneath our feet again. I knew I shouldn't ask—Sho's temper being the way it was—but curiosity got the better of me. "Madrof, what's with that tower?" I pointed to a building high atop the mountain, barely visible from this vantage.

"Ah, I forget that you all are not from around here and know not the things we are taught as children." He said the words lightheartedly, but there was a certain condemnation in them as well. "I assumed Dem'i Sho here would have known. We call it the Tower of Flight, because flying would be necessary to reach it. It's one of the reason's mining even began in these mountains in the first place all those years ago. As such, I know of none who've made it to the tower. Stories say that an ancient being known as a dragon lived there—which is why I would have thought our deminean companion would have more knowledge about it."

Sho clicked her tongue. "Not all deminean believe we are descendants of this supposed race of ancient flying beasts. I, for one, have seen nothing to indicate these creatures of legend ever existed. The more likely scenario is some deminean scholar was bored one day and made fanciful stories about our origins."

Tesro turned to her. "I'm surprised to hear you say that. According to the Court of Dragons, those types of sentiments may lead to banishment...or death."

"I'm aware of the inner workings of our society. It doesn't mean that I agree with everything they say. You humans like to think we're united completely. I... Nevermind, I'm quite sure you wouldn't understand."

By the time she finished speaking, we had arrived at the cave entrance Madrof had pointed to earlier. Almost as if I passed an invisible force field, a wave of...something—some presence—washed over me.

I stumbled, falling to my knees.

Looking around, I found that all but Madrof had succumbed as well. Sho was on both knees and barely was able to keep herself upright, using both hands to prop herself. Her forehead just touched the snowy ground beneath her, leaving small holes where the horns of her head touched.

"What...is...that?" Tesro said breathlessly, clutching at her chest.

"I warned you," Madrof replied, sweat building up on his brow. I suspected he was not completely unaffected by the pressure. He dabbed at that sweat with the back of his hand, adding, "The frozen man—there is something about him that causes these symptoms. The townsfolk abandoned this mine when he was first discovered. Most are too scared to even come this near for fear of prolonged exposure. The effects will wear off in a short time, but that pull you feel? That remains."

At his words, I realized he was right. The pressure slowly subsided, but it felt almost as if a fishhook was dug into my chest and an imaginary fisherman slowly reeled the line, as if they patiently waited for the fish to wear itself out.

A fish out of water, I thought sullenly.

Suddenly, Madrof took an exaggerated step away from the mouth of the cave, turning his head away and walking back toward the lake. "And this is where I leave you," he said, over his shoulder.

"Wait!" Sho replied, pushing herself to stand. "What's this? You think you can guide us here and just leave? If you think this will earn you the coins, you—"

Madrof turned, his face a mask of horror. "I can't be here!" Fear oozed from the words like pus from a wound. "The path to the frozen man is clearly marked, there is no reason for me to go inside."

She opened her mouth to object, but I reached up and put a hand on her shoulder. "Look at him," I whispered. She took a moment to stop fuming and actually gaze upon our guide, who was trembling, and it was not because of the cold. "I wouldn't want to get stuck in close quarters with him if he panics. Would you?"

She chewed on my words for a time before relenting. "Alright, but I'm reducing your pay. At least wait out here in case we have further need of you."

Madrof looked as if he would object at first, but after a time, he bowed low toward us wordlessly. We made our way to the entrance.

Outside the mouth of the cave, we lit our torches from the provisions Sho had brought for us and stepped inside. The cave passages were narrow and little clear icicles dangled dangerously on the roof above us. I could almost reach out and touch them.

"Look here," Tesro said, pointing to an engraving on the wall. Upon inspection, there was a chiseled *X* on a wall where the path split into two.

I ran my hand across the marking. "I suppose it's this way, then."

Sho nodded and took the lead, holding the torch out in front of her, banishing the intruding darkness. We were now properly into the heart of the caves under the giant mountain that the abandoned tower sat upon. It was cold, and my breath misted in front of my face with each exhalation.

"Once we reach the frozen man," Sho said abruptly, pulling our attention toward her, "be careful. All we know of the amulet is rumor and speculation. We do not know the power it may hold."

Tesro nodded, but I don't think she noticed as we continued to silently and slowly creep through the web of splintering paths.

After a time, Sho called for a rest. I was starving, and the growls of Tesro's stomach told me she was as well. As we sat on the ground, each of us rummaged through our packs. I took out a single piece of salted meat, ripping it in half with my teeth, and swallowing it. It was harsh, but it instantly eased my knotted stomach.

Tesro stood and crossed her arms over her chest, leaning against a wall. "How much further do you think?"

I shrugged, and before I could answer, I heard a howl in the distance. I stood, and soon, the sound echoed from everywhere around me. It sounded half-man and half-beast. With a dreadful feeling in my gut, I knew that this was not the howl of a varg.

Suddenly, there was a rumbling. The cave shook and pieces of the sharp ice that littered the ceiling broke from the roof, falling like little daggers. I threw myself against Tesro and felt a piercing in my lower leg. Sho cried out as one took her in the shoulder. There was another shake, and I was thrown away from her.

She slid into Sho and they grasped at each other while the rumbling whisked me away into darkness, my torch hitting the ground and the fire snuffing out. I heard the faint sound of Tesro screaming my name as I slipped, falling into the unknown. I fell and then hit solid ground.

Everything went black.

CHAPTER THIRTY-ONE

PEACE IN ETERNITY

A sudden rumbling roused me from my sleep, and as I opened my eyes, my head throbbed in pain. I felt a wetness sliding down the left side of my scalp, casually sliding off my ear as it fell to the ground.

I reached up and wiped at the liquid, forcing my eyes open. Total blackness greeted me, but I could smell the metallic scent heavy in the air.

I was bleeding.

Suddenly, the world reeled and my stomach lurched, sending a jolt of pain through the back of my skull. Glittering spots lurked at the edge of my vision, but I forced myself to breathe calmly, search for clarity, and to refrain from being consumed by that encroaching dark.

Blind as I was in this lightless place, I rolled until my back met something solid. Using what little strength I had, I braced myself up on the wall. Searching around the area with my fingers, I found the ground to be odd, like smooth stone. Very different to what the ground of a cave should feel like.

I need light, I told myself as I concentrated, looking for fragments of magic.

My perception spun before me and I twisted, heaving up what little contents remained in my gut to the ground. Wiping the remnants of spit-up on my mouth away with the back of my hand, I chastised myself for being so foolish. One should not play with magic after sustaining an injury to the head.

With little options left, I used my hands and searched around the area blindly, trying, and failing, to avoid the area where I had just vomited. Wiping my hand on my pants leg, I eventually found what I was looking for. The torch I had been carrying had fallen with me and dropped a short distance away. The flame must have died when it struck the ground. As luck would have it, my pack of supplies lay next to it as well.

Carefully, I searched through the contents of the pack until I found the flint. Placing the torch in front of me, I struck the flint off the ground. Sparks splintered out like little fireflies in the night, briefly lighting the room. After a few more strikes, a small fire took hold, lighting the torch and driving the darkness away from me.

I gazed around and found myself in a sort of hallway. An elaborate one at that. Spinning pillars of intricately carved white stone held the vaulted ceiling high above me and the floor I sat upon was as smooth as I had ever felt. I had a feeling about the place, like the imaginings of a child having taken shape in reality. It made me appreciate its smaller details. I felt as if someone had carved this place specifically for me.

After a period, I breathed in and compelled myself to stand, propping myself against the wall as I held back the bile that burned its way up my throat. Once up, I slung the pack across my shoulder and gave myself a prodding, touching my head wound. It stung, but the damage felt minor from as far as I could tell. Then, I put one foot after another as I made the laborious journey down the hallway, holding one hand to the wall to steady myself, and the other to hold the torch in front of me.

The place was immaculate, and not a speck of dust marred its beauty. It was impossibly clean. Despite that, the feeling that none had been here in ages plagued my thoughts. Questions pestered me relentlessly, like bogflies in a humid heat. *Where are the ones who made such splendid works? Why would they have abandoned this beautiful place of pure white stone?*

I found no signs that answered any of my questions, but eventually, I found stairs. These stairs spiraled upward, similar to how the columns looked before in the previous corridor. I held hope that perhaps they could bring me back to where I could rejoin the others.

With each step up that winding path, I felt as if my strength returned, albeit slowly. It was a lengthy walk, and my legs burned by the time I reached the top. I kept my sluggish pace and followed a few more hallways that all looked indistinguishable from my perspective, trying, and failing, to keep my location. Eventually, through haphazard luck, I reached an open area and the sight of it near caused me to drop my torch.

It was vast, and two glass windows that looked to be made of crystals gleamed as the sun sent its light through it in splintering rays. That light illuminated two figures on those windows.

Paintings of winged creatures.

The beasts themselves looked not of flesh and bone, but appeared to be made of magic. Stone claws, spikes of fire, and wings of air. They appeared unreal in their depiction, and yet, I found myself inexplicably drawn to them.

A large stone chair, a throne I later realized, sat mere steps from those immaculate windows, positioned to overlook this grand hall. The rest of the room lay completely empty, as if it had been long plundered of any valuables, besides the occasional broken stone that had fallen from the ceiling, likely due to age and abandonment. I walked toward the throne and as I reached it, I pulled off my glove, my silver scales glittering, and ran my hand across the stone.

Suddenly, a soft pattering of footsteps drew my ear, and I pulled my glove back on. Soft at first, but growing ever louder as time seemed to stand still. Each additional step bounced off the stone and the echo it made sounded as if an entire army approached. I identified the hallway where the sound came from and fixed my stance, my right hand forward and my left at my side. Concentrating, I saw the fragmented magic that fluttered around me, waiting, pleading to be used. I smiled to myself, unafraid, knowing that whatever came, I at least had a chance to defend myself.

Closer and closer the unknown being came and my heart beat in my chest like a war drum, marching to every echo of every step. I saw the shadow of a figure. Human; it had to be human. They stepped out, and when they entered the hallway in the fullness of the light, I dropped my arms and fell to my knees.

"It can't be," I said breathlessly.

They stepped forward, slowly, and with each step, it gave me renewed hope that what I saw was real and not an apparition my mind created to torment me. Tears streamed down my face as the figure reached me, staring down with loving eyes.

"Hello, daughter," my mother said, kneeling down and embracing me in a tight hug. The warmness of her body banished the cold and the smell of her hair strangled the staleness in the air.

My mind went blank as my arms reactively encircled her. Everything I had hoped to say, all of the pent-up feelings of despair vanished in a moment as I squeezed her tight, sobbing like a child into her ragged skirt.

"How?" I asked, but the words I truly wished to say failed me. I clutched her ever tighter, as if to release her would wake me from the dream and leave me alone again.

We stayed that way for some time before she broke off from me and stepped back, wiping a tear from my eye with her finger as she did. I stared at her, taking in everything she was. A small piece of my mind still rejected this reality, but seeing her this close, I knew.

Yes, it was her.

The curly blond hair, the soft smile and warm glow of her brown eyes. She was exactly as I remembered her on that fateful day.

The day I had abandoned her to die.

"You're so lovely, Vi'eri," she said, stroking my hair with the back of her hand. "And so tall now. Look at you!" Gently, she helped me up, and to my surprise, I now stood taller than she. Looking up at me, pride flowed from her large eyes.

"You are too," I replied, unable to keep the sobs from my words. "Lovely, I mean. I'm just... I don't know." I laughed beside myself with joy.

"Come, sit. You must be tired from your journey." She led me to the stone throne, and as we approached, the creatures painted on the glass appeared to ripple and move, as if they lived.

I sat and looked at her plainly. It really was her. Even the small bruise under her left eye was still there from the final day I had seen her.

"How?" I asked again, my thoughts just beginning to return to me. "How can you be here? This is the Frostwyrm. We are looking for—"

"For the frozen man, I know," she replied, leaning against the arm of the throne. I craned my head to look at her, and she looked away from me, staring off at something I couldn't identify. "Vi'eri, it's a long story. Do you remember the day you left me?"

"I..." I wanted to respond, to defend myself and my actions, but I couldn't. She was right, I had left her. I had failed her.

"I remember," I replied in a mere whisper.

"Deminean soldiers surrounded me," she said, almost to herself. "Unlike you, I don't have the benefit of being a destroyer. Still, I fought them and pulled out a small knife, driving it into the nearest deminean that came for me. I wanted so badly to protect you, it was all I could think about. I was desperate—like an animal. And like a rabid animal, they rained their weapons down upon me and left me scarcely breathing. As surely as the sun rises and sets, blood loss would soon ferry my soul back to the Well." It horrified me to listen as my mother recanted how the deminean had all but killed her and left her suffering. Alone.

I had left her to this fate.

"But then," she added, her voice picking up in an excited tone, "Anduinna saved me!"

"Anduinna?" I couldn't believe the words I was hearing as I repeated them back to her. "The Life Incarnate?"

My mother nodded, a smile tugging at her lips. Turning her head back to look at me, she added, "Anduinna saved me, daughter. She wants to save everyone. To save this realm!"

"But..."

"It's okay, daughter. Shh," she replied, cradling my head in her arms. "I understand. Anduinna told me of your first encounter with each other. How your conversation got...out of hand. She apologizes for scaring you and sent me here to tell you that you should trust her. No, more than that. To join her!"

My thoughts were cloudy, and a nagging tug on my emotions sent a note of warning that was quickly shrouded against the contentment of having my mother returned to me.

"Anduinna. She wants me to join her? But why? What could I do for the Life Incarnate?"

"You're special, Vi'eri," she replied. "Do you not wonder about these powers you possess? Why it is that every time you need strength, you suddenly have it?"

"That's the voice," I said, placing my hand on top of my mothers. "Vulana! He helps me. He gives me his strength when I need it most. It's hard to explain."

"Vulana..." My mother chewed on the word, and a slight look of disgust crossed her face. Then, like it had never been there, her warm smile returned. "I assure you, the power, the strength, is yours, and yours alone. You're the hybrid!"

"Hybrid? Anduinna called me that before."

My mother grinned. "It's because it's the truth. A truth that I have never told you. You were far too young to understand. At least, that was my excuse. But Anduinna's wisdom has since convinced me otherwise. I was a fool to have kept it from you."

"And what could I do? For the Life Incarnate, I mean."

"The amulet," she replied, almost in a growl. "Retrieve the amulet, but instead of giving it back to your Ri'sha master, give it to Anduinna. With it, she will create peace in this realm. True peace. All shall return to her and she will resume control of the flow of Souls as it should be. As it has been before. As destiny wills it to be."

There was another push on my emotions. Fear. I suspected Vulana pressed me. But why? Why should I fear my mother's return? In anger, I shoved Vulana to the back of my mind and blocked him there, unable to contemplate how I had done it.

"And what will happen to the deminean?" I asked. "Will their souls be controlled by Anduinna also?"

"They will get what they deserve. Extinction." My mother's reply was casual, as if it were a simple conversation over tea and not the eradication of an entire species.

The fear in me grew stronger, despite my wishes, and I chewed on my lip, forcing myself to ask, "And humans?"

"Humans will live peacefully in Anduinna's grace, daughter." I heard the words, but something felt wrong about them. I could almost hear the lie in those silk-laden words. Almost, if I concentrated...

I sat up straighter, forcing myself to face her. "What did you just call me?" She raised a questioning eyebrow at me, and I amended, "When I was young, what did you call me? What was I to you?" Then question after question poured from my mouth like a flood. "How did you survive the deminean attack? How do you know about me being a destroyer? How do you know about the amulet and the frozen man? How did you find me?"

My mother listened through my rapid torrent of accusatorial questions, continuing to lean at the edge of the throne, as if she were made of the very same stone. She stared off into the distance, unblinking. Then, suddenly, her head snapped toward me inhumanly. Gone were her brown eyes and instead, I found red orbs of fury staring down at me.

I jumped from the throne and tripped on a step, hitting the cold ground hard. I turned back to look toward whatever manner of creature followed me. It stood, walking toward me with a menacing gait. The creature's steps were no longer held by the grace of a woman, but instead, each was accompanied by an unnatural twitch, as if their muscles spasmed from the effort; the visible muscles contorting.

"I don't know what she used to call you, human," the creature said, each step making them less and less human themselves. "But do you really want to know what will happen to you? To all of you?" I dragged myself away from the creature on the ground with one arm, my mouth hanging open in utter shock. Still, I dared not look away as the creature added, "Extinction. Same as the deminean scum. Extinction for all who exist outside the order Anduinna will create. Extinction for any who act against the perfection of this realm."

Then, without any warning, they attacked.

I shrieked as the creature, who now only bore a slight semblance of my mother, launched itself at me. Lightning quick, it wrapped its foul hands around my throat. The face looked wrong—distorted. Their grip tightened as I tried to breathe, but my strength was quickly fading. I grasped desperately at the hands clasped around my neck, but instead of soft hands, I felt long, boney fingers that dug into my skin, drawing blood. I feebly pried at those skeletal fingers and knew that I had lost the fight before it had even begun.

The last I saw was that of my mother's face, slowly changing and distorting into a wretched thing of muddled bone and flesh.

I breathed out one final time, and an unnatural darkness dragged me under.

I drifted, weightless, like I was stranded in a calm sea. I opened my eyes and saw nothingness. Black, inky nothingness that spread out before me, everlasting.

Eternal.

I opened my mouth to scream, but nothing came.

The silence was deafening.

Then, suddenly, I heard a sound that was not a sound. Almost like a distant chime of a bell that I more felt than heard. With each chime, I felt the darkness around me tremble in response. Rippling, almost as if it were in a state of liquid. Another chime, another ripple. This happened too many times for me to count, until one ripple quaked stronger than the rest, opening a small tear in the dark directly in front of me. Behind the tear was light; pure and so bright that it nearly blinded me. Indescribably intense, and brighter than the sun. Another ripple and the tear widened. Instinctually, I reached for it. I could almost grasp it in the palm of my hand. And then one more chime, one more ripple, and I saw it.

Life.

As the tear opened, I saw life in its infinite form. The light that spilled forth consumed my being—consumed my very soul. I saw the birth and death of civilizations and everything in-between. I saw a bird, from the moment of its glorious inception to the moment it took its final breath. Not a bird, a child. Not one child, many. Not one realm, countless—endless. I glimpsed all of existence across all of time in the time it takes to breathe a single breath.

It was too much—far too much for my feeble mind to grasp. So expansive, so great the lives of all. It threatened to consume me, to drag me down in the threads of their memories, leaving my own life scattered to the wind like the clouds of a dandelion. Like a drop of water in their grand river of wants. I turned from it, frightened and ready to drift back into the quiet and peaceful twilight. From all that I glimpsed, I learned one simple truth:

With life came great suffering.

Vi'eri! I heard Vulana cry out and knew that the sound came from the tear. *Come to my voice. Come back.*

"I won't!" I screamed in defiance, and this time, as if my words echoed through the tear, I heard them. I did not want to return. Why would anybody? There was peace in the dark. Peace for all eternity. That's what I craved most of all.

Vulana pushed on my emotions, trying to force the will to live into me. I resisted. I resisted with all my being. But, insistently, the mysterious voice in my head, my guardian, kept trying, sending wave upon wave of emotion at me. Attempting to break me. I felt pure happiness, pleasure, despair, hope, and grief all mingle simultaneously. Vulana sent me what it means to live—forcing me to experience it all again. Again and again.

Slowly, against my wishes, my will to live returned. It stung—my own weakness, and it would have driven me to my knees if I were on solid ground.

If I existed at all.

"Vulana!" I said, but this time, for absolution. Life continued to pour from the split in the dark, drowning out my own voice. *Lend me your strength.* I wordlessly willed my request as far as I could.

There was a pause. The constant, overpowering flood of life crashed into my mind like a wave. I was at my end, almost lost in the noise of their lives forever.

Then I heard his reply. *No...* My heart plummeted at the words, and I nearly gave up hope when he added, *You must draw upon your own strength now. You're in the in-between, the place where magic is born and where it returns. Use it! Free yourself from your chains. From your burdens. Live again!* Then I felt Vulana depart from me, leaving me with a gaping hole inside.

I floated, with the darkness to my back and the hole of pure light at my front. I knew to stay in the dark would bring me peace, but it would mean my death. What lay ahead—the light—that was life. Noisy and cruel, filled with disappointment and despair. Why would I return to it?

Why should I?

And then, as if she were with me in flesh, I saw her. Tesro. I saw her birth and her death. The children she would have, and the children who would never come to pass. A thousand times, a million times, I saw her entire life play out before me. I saw all that was and all that could be. I saw all the times we were together and all the times where we were not. So many possibilities. So many endings of death...and I rejected them all.

Why would I live? I asked myself.

I would live for her.

I breathed deeply as air flowed back into my lungs, power following in its wake. With all my strength, I shoved the creature off me, rolling to my side. I coughed; it was a harsh thing. A burning sensation filled my chest and lungs, and my throat felt raw and hot. I could still feel the nails of the creature on my skin.

Forcing myself to look, despite my fear, I took in all the creature was. No longer resembling my mother at all, it was a being of bone and sinew. The face was distinctly not human. Instead, it had a long white skull with great twisting horns that swung around it like a gnarled tree branch greeted me. The horns were so tall that they stood at least a full head above the skull in height.

I realized that no eyes stared at me, just red glowing orbs obscured in the shadow of the skull's eye sockets. Misting breath leaked out of the mouth in small tendrils of smoke as the creature hissed, "It is Anduinna's will that you yet live." The words came from the mouth of the skull as if vibrating, like an echo in a distant hallway. "You will free the frozen man, and if you refuse, then I shall use the one you name Tesro."

I stood, then raised my hands toward the creature in a casting stance, refusing to back down. "You'll need to kill me first."

The creature, to my surprise, suddenly collapsed to the floor. I gazed upon it curiously, but never dropped my stance. Loud cracks and pops began to pour from the creature's body as it wriggled on the ground like a dying beast.

Slowly, it began to change.

The creature grew, muscle and skin forming over the breaking and reforming of bones. Then, suddenly, pure white fur sprouted like new grass in spring. When the creature had completed its transformation, I found myself staring down the largest bear I'd ever seen. It roared, sending spittle sailing out from its maw and showering me with the rank smell of decay. I couldn't help but be drawn to the massive teeth in its mouth, surely able to rip my body in half in a single bite.

I concentrated and found the closest magic near me as the bear rushed to attack. They struck, and just before an enormous paw with dagger-like claws ripped me, I tapped magic and a gust of wind slammed into them, pushing the attack off its mark. Another tap, and the creature's foot fell into the stone floor of the throne room, closing around it. The bear swiped again, but I narrowly dodged backward, a single nail catching my clothes at the neckline and leaving a rip in the fabric.

The bear effortlessly ripped its leg from the floor, sending small chunks of white stone clattering around the grand hall and kicking dust into the air. It reared up on its hind legs and I knew that if it brought that weight down upon me, I would be crushed under it. I decided in a moment of desperation that the bear had far too much room to fight here, so I turned from my enemy, and rushed toward the nearest corridor.

I ran, as fast as my legs could carry me. The roar of my pursuer let me know they were still too close for comfort—and gaining quickly. The ground shook, and pieces of the stone ceiling fell as I dove further into the corridor, just dodging a pile of stone that broke from the roof. One stray rock grazed me off the side of my shoulder as I rolled, setting me off my target, and sending me stumbling to the side.

I held my arm and turned back to find the creature stuck, its body too big to fit in the hallway. Luck was on my side, and I smiled at my fortune. But, as I turned to leave, I heard that terrible popping sound again. When I turned back again, I looked on in horror as the bear shed its weight, its form becoming sleek, and in mere moments, some type of enormous white-furred cat emerged. Like the bear, its size was much greater than should be possible, but to make matters even stranger, this cat also had the horns of a ram attached to its skull. With a sickening realization, I knew this creature could transform into any form it desired.

And it would never stop chasing me.

The creature shrieked as it continued the pursuit, using the horns to shove rocks out of its way, clearing a path through the rubble straight to me. I turned and fled, soon finding myself at the stairway that brought me to the upper floors. I tapped magic as I ran downward, skipping three or four steps at a time and summoning earthen spikes that jettisoned out of the wall to block the creature's path.

I heard the creature reach the top of the stairs and follow me down, then a screech, followed by a howl of pain. The cry of both a man and a beast. Hearing the strangled but advancing steps of the beast pushed me to run even faster.

I ran until my lungs burned with the effort, and I put my hands to my knees, heaving breath in and out as fast as possible. I leaned against a wall and realized that I was completely lost, darkness completely surrounding me. The torch I had carried before was somewhere in the throne room above. I tapped a small spec of magic near me and a tiny orb of light attached to the tip of my finger. It was far dimmer than the torch, but it was at least something to keep myself from wandering blindly.

Despite my weariness, I forced myself to walk onward. Keeping my mind alert was all I could manage in my weakened state. Now, alone in the dark, with just my thoughts to keep me company, an unnatural fear grasped at me like little cobwebs in my mind. That creature was a thing out of a story told to scare children, only worse than anyone could have imagined. I could still hear the cracking and popping of its bones breaking and reforming in the back of my head.

My body shuddered at the thought.

Eventually, I found my way back to the hall I had fallen in from previously. I looked up and yelled as loudly as I could, my voice echoing ever further away as it traveled upward. There was no reply. I suddenly felt a chill, as if a gust of mountain wind blew against bare skin. Loneliness crept at the edge of my awareness, and the adrenaline still pumping in my veins beckoned me to keep moving. I couldn't give up, not yet. Tesro's life may very well depend on it.

I stood there, contemplating what I should do. *I could try to climb back up,* I thought, but quickly abandoned the idea as I saw the sharp stone of the walls that led back to the top. I quickly turned toward the other corridor I had ignored before; my only option. With little choice left, I made my way toward it.

Like a mirror of the opposite side, I trudged through the dark passages, ever listening, ever watching. Eventually, I came upon another set of stairs and I sighed heavily. I ascended those steps like a person walks toward the hangman's rope, unaware of when my unseen enemy would strike to tie the noose around my neck.

Halfway up the stairs, it unexpectedly ended, a rockfall obstructing the path. Instead, a hole that looked to lead back into the caves greeted me. I smiled. Maybe, just maybe, I could find her. Maybe I could save her.

I just had to save myself first.

CHAPTER THIRTY-TWO

A CHOICE

I quickly found the location of the cave collapse and spent some time combing through the debris of fallen rocks, praying silently to the Well that I wouldn't find anyone. I breathed a sigh of relief when I turned over the last rock to find not a soul. No bodies, no blood.

Nothing.

This respite was short-lived as I heard a distant sound farther down in the dark of the passageway, but as I approached, there was another cave-in barring the way. My mind raced as I pictured Tesro being attacked by that creature. I decided there was no time for subtlety.

I fixed my stance and concentrated on the rocks that blocked my path. I pushed my will forward as I tapped a fragmented piece of magic that floated to my right. It zipped off at my touch, and moments later, the rocks convulsed. I felt linked with the boulder, and using my left hand, I pulled back, the rocks shifting as I did. They fell toward me, creating an opening large enough for me to just barely wedge through.

Gingerly, I traversed over the loose stone, squeezing my body through the opening and out the other side. A rock cut a small red line across my arms, but I felt little pain; adrenaline pushed me forward. As I passed through, I nearly tripped into the hole in which I had fallen earlier.

A small ledge held fast at the very edge of that pit. Slowly, I shoved my back against the ice wall and shimmied across, keeping my steps light. Another sound I couldn't recognize echoed from further down the passageway. In my lapse of concentration, my foot slipped, and my hand reached instinctually toward a small break in the wall. My heart raced with anticipation as I pulled myself straight. I kept moving, and eventually, made it safely across the pit. I wiped sweat off my brow and pushed aside my caution.

I had to be quick.

Nothing stood in my way now as I paced down the narrow and splitting corridors of the ice cave. The small light on the tip of my finger guided my way, but only just. More than once, I found a dead-end and had to backtrack. Frustration and fear raced through my mind as I imagined Tesro being ripped to shreds by that creature's long claws. The light leaving her eyes. The blood and gruesomeness of the scene that would be.

That could be her future.

It forced me to push beyond my limits as I ran from each dead-end to the next.

My foot slipped on a small patch of ice, and I slammed into the rock wall, leaving a thin cut on my forearm and breaking a strap on my glove. I paid neither heed as I continued my journey through the dark.

Then I heard it; a sound like talking voices. Louder and louder these voices became as I followed their echoing trail. When I had all but given up, I found a small overhang, just wide enough where I could slip my body through. Carefully, I stepped up to it and propped myself up to see.

Inside, three figures stood at odds with each other, lit by a ghostly blue light. One was unmistakably Tesro and the other, Sho. The third I could not recognize.

Perhaps, I told myself, *it is Madrof, come to help after he heard the commotion of the cave-in?* Doubtful, as Tesro looked dismayed and Sho appeared hypnotized, standing straight and unmoving.

Unnatural.

Tesro and this unknown person, stood chatting around what appeared to be a large crystal that stood between them. I squinted, and like a distant star on a cloudy night, I could just make out a figure from within, clutching onto a small object that shone with an unnatural glow.

The voices became louder, as if there was an argument of sorts. Suddenly, Sho reached and grabbed her from behind, wrenching her arm behind her back as she dragged her close.

She screamed in fear, and I answered it in return, forcing my body through the narrow opening, heedless as to what rested below on the other side. As my body slid through, I fell a short way, hitting solid ice with my back and sliding down until I was on the same level as the other three.

Sharp pain shot through me, and I could feel the warmth of fresh blood, but I pushed it aside, standing. They all turned to stare at me, and I matched their gazes. Taking the casting stance toward Sho, I demanded in my most threatening tone, "Let. Her. Go!"

"Vi'eri!" Tesro said before Sho placed her hand in front of her mouth to gag her. She bit down on the deminean's woman's finger, but she didn't even budge at the meager attack as her teeth sunk in. She pulled back, and spit out blue blood which splashed to the ground, freezing almost instantaneously.

"Ah, the last piece is here," the unknown individual said. Their voice was distinctly male, but the gray hood blocked me from seeing their face.

I took an aggressive step forward, my right arm facing Sho and my left facing the unknown man. "I said, let her go. This will be the last time I warn you."

Sho said nothing, but the man answered, as if I had addressed him. "A child's warning," he mocked, adding, "You will find yourself quite powerless here, I'm afraid."

Anger overwhelmed rational thought, and I concentrated, finding small fragments of magic near me, but something was wrong. Instead of being drawn to my will, it seemed as if the magic drifted away from me. I reached and tapped at a small source nearby, willing the ground beneath the man's feet to open and have him consumed by a gaping maw.

I felt the magic accept my will, but when I tried to control its location, it zipped away uncontrollably. As it connected with the wall opposing the man, a small piece of the ceiling broke, falling to the ground and sending an ear-splitting clash echoing the entire cave.

The man snickered. "See! It's as I told you. Now, will you be quiet and listen for a moment? I would hate for any of us humans to be harmed here."

The man pushed back his hood to reveal the face of a young human male. Tan, with black curly hair and eyes of deep brown. There was something deeply familiar about him that I couldn't quite place at the time. In the end, I remembered nothing of usefulness.

I glanced at Tesro and she looked horrified, as if she had seen a phantom. Her face went pale, and I suspect it had nothing to do with Sho's constraint of her. Interestingly, Sho looked on as a statue—not a sliver of life showed in those glazed, dull eyes.

"Who are you?" I asked, keeping my stance despite the clear uselessness of my magic.

The man grinned, walking back and forth in front of the large chrysalis of ice. "I'm surprised you don't remember, Vi'eri Trueblade. We've met before. So long ago, it seems. Alas, it has been a lonely time traveling...without a mother. Something, I've come to understand, we both share."

Then it hit me like the first chill of winter.

Roese's son!

"You," I mumbled, more to myself than to him.

"There it is. Acknowledgement. You know, I can still feel the pain of having my skin melted to ash. Quite painful, I can assure you. It keeps me up at night. Keeps me begging for the bottle. It's not something that one easily gets over. And, of course, you killed my mother. That's what burns most of all."

"That wasn't us. Vrak—"

"Vrak executed the deed, but you were all there with a purpose. There for the tear of eternity. Still, despite what you may think, I don't begrudge what you did. My mother acted with purpose for her desires, and you answered in return. A battle of willpower in which she lost. Two giants, fighting with different ideals. And I, just the collateral damage. But no more. Her...methods never stood well with me. That is why I offer choices as opposed to enslavement, as my mother once relied upon."

He walked toward the ice and I followed my gaze with him, finally recognizing what the ice held. Inside, it held the silhouette of a man. His features were shrouded, but from what I could grasp, he had a serene look on his face. Whoever this was, he had been at peace with this end. In his hand, he held an amulet, which he pressed against his chest. It glowed warmly, periodically increasing in intensity, following no pattern I could discern.

"What's your name?" I asked.

"My name?" the unknown man replied, drawing my attention as he placed his hand upon the frozen man's prison, like he touched something of immeasurable value. "Is Ruvor Locke, son of Roese Dasca-Locke. And you two have killed me twice, without even knowing my name. Yet, here I stand, still willing to work together for the sake of all humans." He paused and looked at the frozen man. "This is Gruratas, family name unknown, and he betrayed humankind when he sealed himself in here like a coward. In his hands he holds soulrend. Humankind's hope. A weapon capable of wiping these pathetic deminean from this realm entirely." He cast his gaze toward Sho, who remained motionless, as if she couldn't hear his words at all.

"What do you mean, betrayed? What did Gruratas do?" I asked, stepping forward, but keeping my concentration ready to cast at a moment's notice. *Maybe if I can get closer, the aim of my magic will be better.*

Ruvor spat on the ground. "Pacifist," he said the word with such disgust that even his nose crinkled at its sound. "He ended the conflict between humans and deminean, stealing with him the humans' best chance at winning the war. He condemned us to slavery, torment and death. With this tool in my possession, I will reignite the flames of hope for the humans in the south and beyond. All those with the heart to fight will rally to the cause, and the deminean will know their time has ended. Even the Well chooses us over them. Human superiority is only a matter of time, and I will accelerate the process."

"I'll...kill...you," I heard Sho mutter through ragged breaths. I glanced at her, and the grip on Tesro became suffocating.

"Stop!" I demanded, but Ruvor held out a hand to still me. He lifted that hand and a small ring glinted for a moment, and Sho's eyes returned to that inactive, dead state.

Ruvor chuckled and scratched at his curly locks. "Seems the ring only works for a short time, and she appears to be keeping her memories now. A pity. No matter, once I retrieve soulrend, I'll end her permanently."

Tesro used the distraction to free herself from Sho's grasp, leaping away as her hand reached back for her. She narrowly evaded and stood still, as if she hadn't a care in the world. Tesro now stood across from me, the frozen man in the middle of us, and she assumed a casting position toward Ruvor.

"Now, now…" he said, holding his hands up. "We've already concluded that magic is useless here."

"Not mine," she replied, staring daggers of pure fury at him. "I've never had much control, but I assure you, I more than make up for it in raw power. I'm sure you remember."

Ruvor grimaced at her words, looking behind him as if he could see his own back. "I do," he replied honestly, "but I don't see why we need to be enemies? Tesro, a question, if you please. What have the deminean taken from you? A mother? A father? Both? Don't be coy with me; all humans have suffered, in some degree, to deminean cruelty."

I knew the moment he spoke those words that they'd struck a chord with her. Hesitation danced in her eyes and her stance wavered as she glanced back toward Sho.

"He's trying to manipulate you, Tesro," I said. "Don't let him—"

"But he's right!" she replied, her fury redirected to our once deminean companion. "We've all lost to them." Her voice broke as she pointed toward the motionless deminean woman.

"We have, but Isodros' plan—she wants humans and deminean to co-exist as equals! We won't need to fight anymore. That is true peace. Ruvor just seeks war for his own selfish gains."

She scoffed, and Ruvor grinned silently at her. She shook her head at me. "You only know what Isodros tells you. Who's saying she is any different?"

"She's not!" he replied.

I flashed my teeth at him, biting so hard I tasted blood. "Stay out of this. I should have killed you back in those caves all those years ago."

Ruvor cocked his head toward me. "Perhaps, but I can prove that Ri'sha Isodros only serves herself." His words struck me and I stood motionless, waiting. After a time, he coughed and added, "This is not the first time I've spoken to Dem'i Sho'ti here. The battle with the vargs on the path to Sleetward. I was there. I know nothing of Anduinna's plans, but after the battle, I used my ring to...capture her mind. She told me everything. How a disagreement with her ally Hask caused her to take his life. How she was to retrieve soulrend—not for Isodros, but for the Dragon's Court. And how she intended to dispatch Isodros' pet humans when they were no longer needed."

"That doesn't prove Isodros—"

Tesro screamed as she turned to face Sho, fingers dancing, and I felt the presence of her will in the surrounding magic.

"Wait!" I yelled, but too late as a bolt of lightning flew from her hands, narrowly missing the woman who did not react in the slightest to the attack. The bolt struck the wall and broke rock, causing the entire place to give one lurching shake.

"That won't do," Ruvor said, unperturbed by the rattling of the cave. "Deminean have a nasty habit of surviving magical attacks. With soulrend, however, we can take what is rightfully ours. Her soul! It will allow us to turn their precious magic of self against them. Let us burn through the remnants of her soul until naught remains—together!"

"What do I need to do?" she asked.

I looked at her, horrified. "Tesro, stop! I know you hate the deminean, but he and his mother wanted to start a war. They wanted to sacrifice Crux! Don't you remember?"

She twisted toward me with shame and uncertainty on her pale face. The frozen man, his look of pure satisfaction, seemed to mock our bickering.

"A mistake, I'll admit," he replied. "While I do seek a war with the deminean, I want soldiers who believe in the cause. I won't enslave as my mother once did. I only offer choice."

Tesro, her wits appearing to return to her, turned back to Ruvor. "How did you even find out about soulrend? We got the information straight from Isodros herself."

"I was looking for it," he replied, grinning. "Ever since I escaped our previous encounter, I've been searching. Most said that the amulet was just a story. But, from the stories, it is well established that if the item existed, then Gruratas, the coward, hid it in the Frostwyrm. Eventually, I was able to discern a familiar link. One that loosely fits a timeline. And what did I find? A descendant of Gruratas himself. He helped me find this place, but fate is cruel. When I first laid eyes upon it, I found that I could do nothing to possess my prize. Gruratas' tomb uses destroyer magic that I cannot break, no matter how many of Anduinna's creatures' blood I enchanted and drank to increase my own strength."

She chewed on her lower lip, trying to piece the puzzle together. "And how did Isodros learn of it?"

Ruvor leaned on the frozen man's ice prison, cracking his knuckles and moving his neck from side to side. "That was me as well. I needed the help of destroyers, and with the deminean capturing them to use for their own ends, there were but three I knew to be close. Having contacts with those who've sought employment from the True Blade mercenaries did wonders. All I had to do was wait. Wait until the destroyer Vrak was out on other errands and..." he waved his hands out in front of him, a look of self-assured victory plain on his expression.

"And what makes you think we'll help you? That I'll help you?"

"A wager. A chance."

"You wagered wrong," I replied. "If the choice is to leave without our prize or help you, then I am content to leave the frozen man and soulrend as is."

"You will do no such thing," I heard a voice that sounded human-like, but spoken with the deep growl of a beast.

Red eyes glowed from the dark of a tunnel, and then an amalgamation of different animals appeared in the passage. The creature had a long reptilian head attached to a catlike body, with sharp, spiky scales flowing the entire length of the body to a muscular tail with a spiked tip.

I had met this creature before.

Tesro looked upon it in stark terror and promptly shifted her stance to face them, sensing the threat it possessed. I found myself doing the same.

"Ah, Anduinna's servant. We meet at last," Ruvor said proudly. "I am Ruvor, and I have a proposition for Anduinna, The Life Incarnate."

CHAPTER THIRTY-THREE

BATTLE AT THE FROZEN PRISON

The creature stared at Ruvor, and what could only be described as a smile crossed their scaled face.

"A proposition, you say?" the creature said, stepping forward into the frozen man's last resting place. "And what can a human offer the Life Incarnate?"

Ruvor gave the creature a knowing grin, and I noticed a missing tooth among his otherwise perfect smile.

"Simple," he said, "I offer what Anduinna has not yet acquired, but longs so desperately to have." His words were laden with silk, as if he sought to charm this beast of nightmares.

They stomped the ground. "You try my patience, human. Make plain what it is you offer."

"As you wish," he replied sullenly, letting his fake smile slip into a scowl. "I offer this: a war against all deminean."

I saw the creature's face shift, as if they considered his proposal in earnest. Eventually, they turned their sharp cat-like eyes back toward him. "And what of other humans? Surely you do not expect Anduinna to be fulfilled dividing the souls of the Well with such inferiors as yourselves."

Ruvor looked to take offense at the remark, stepping forward as if he could challenge the creature head-on. "Your master may not think much of us humans, but surely they can recognize the benefit of an alliance—even if temporary in nature. The deminean are a scourge upon this realm, but they do control it, for only those who possess the Well for themselves can make such a claim. It is time that changed. I offer the Life Incarnate this: a truce between humans and those of her dominion—"

"What is this?" the creature said suddenly, its muscles visibly contorting as its head hit the floor, its front paws failing to hold the weight. When the creature looked back up, its eyes blazed the purest green, and I could see the lushness of an entire forest in them.

Ruvor crossed his arms. "Anduinna, I presume?" he said, going as far as to give a light bow. "It's an honor to meet one as great as you."

"Rosey words will only get you so far," Anduinna growled. "This body...it displeases me. Such a perversion of my creations can never do." She stood, lifting each paw methodically, as if testing the limbs. Evidently content, she focused back on Ruvor, who waited patiently. "Now then, human, I've heard the offer. On one hand, you offer truce, but one as old as I remembers. I remember the pain of mine as you robbed them of life to use in your wicked ways. Even now, I smell the blood on you—drunk with its power. Strength that does not belong to you."

He looked taken aback, and he slashed his arm in front of his face as if he swatted at a pest. "This power...it is to fight a common enemy. Surely you cannot begrudge me—"

"It is for yourself!" she replied harshly, causing him to visibly flinch, taking one large step backward. Apparently used to her new body, she prowled close to the ground, circling him. "Humans are all the same—they care for naught but themselves. Not even their collective wellbeing is of any consequence. They seek power, wherever it is found, paying no mind to the natural order of the realm. And yet, you would presume that I would disgrace myself by allying with yours? And as equals, no less?" She seemed to give out a small laugh, but it was wrong and sounded more akin to a tortured animal. "No! One such as yourself is only fit to serve with the tightest of leashes. When all the deminean of the realm are long forgotten, their bones ground to dust, and their souls returned to the Well, I have no doubt that your kind would come for mine. And with this amulet..." Anduinna let the words drift away, turning to the frozen man and staring in awe.

Ruvor shook his head sadly. "Then humans must truly do this task alone." He said the words so quietly that I could scarcely make them out. Suddenly, he looked up and resignation flared in his brown eyes. "I beseech you, fellow humans, make your choice. The deminean will never let us live free and Anduinna will never suffer us to live at all. We must fight to preserve ourselves above all others. Anything less will be the death of us all."

"Ijiraq," Anduinna said in a growl. "Kill them, but save the hybrid. She will free the amulet from its prison." And with that, the creature's eyes returned to their normal cat-like slits, glowing deep red. Ijiraq scanned the room before fixing their attention on Ruvor. He looked unafraid as he took a weaponless brawler's stance.

Then the creature attacked.

Ijiraq's initial strike hit Ruvor dead-center, driving his body into the frozen man's icy prison, but the creature didn't stop, snapping at him with its serpent-like maw.

Ruvor, unphased, caught one of the creature's fangs with his bare hands. He screamed as he twisted, breaking the creature's tooth. Shifting against Ijiraq's claws, he turned and rammed the tooth into the creature's shoulder.

Ijiraq shrieked in pain, stumbling back from him; suffering in those cat-like eyes.

Something drew my attention away from the fight and toward Sho. The deminean woman appeared recovered from whatever spell or enchantment Ruvor had bound her with, and she glared at Tesro with pure hatred plain on her face. Her intention was obvious—she intended to kill. And Tesro, so immersed in the battle taking place, did not even notice the danger she was in.

"Look out!" I said, tapping frantically at the fragments of magic near my fingers. The magic obeyed me and cascaded toward Sho, but when it fluttered too close to the frozen man, it spiraled out of control, the spell hitting the roof and provoking a mass of rocks to fall from the ceiling.

Tesro heard my shout and the noise of falling rocks as she turned to face Sho. The deminean woman laughed, and, as if driven by madness, lunged at her. Quickly, she tapped a small fragment of magic, and just as Sho was within arm's reach, a gust of wind blew her back away.

Too close!

An unhindered step further, and Sho would have caught her. With the deminean's strength, Sho would have broken her body like a dried twig left out in the sun.

Meanwhile, the battle between Ruvor and Ijiraq raged. The creature had landed a few more blows on Ruvor, ripping his clothing to pieces and leaving trails of blood on the floor, but Ijiraq looked to be losing a fair amount of blood themself.

Ruvor, during the fight, had ripped the creature's tooth from their shoulder and now wielded it as a sort of makeshift dagger. I ignored him. Whatever fate awaited Ruvor, it was of his own making.

"Hold on!" I said, dropping my stance and sprinting toward Tesro.

Suddenly, a small boulder, meant for Ruvor, came flying toward me. I narrowly dodged to the right, falling to the ground and scraping my shoulder against a sharp rock. It collided with the wall, shooting small shards of stone that battered against my back. I forced myself up, driven by fear and rage. Sho, recovered from Tesro's previous attack, charged at her.

At that moment, I saw Tesro tap a sliver of magic, and as she did, the magic pulled toward the frozen man. On its course, it connected with other fragments of magic that she couldn't have foreseen. The frozen prison made magic unwieldy, and for someone who already had problems with control, this place was a tinderbox.

Her eyes went wide as this mass of magic smashed again into another larger mass, causing a chain reaction. She opened her mouth to yell something, but as she did, an immense ball of fire engulfed the area near the frozen man.

The force of the explosion flung me back to the ground, the heat of it immense against my skin, despite my distance. Sho was not as lucky. She and the frozen man were completely engulfed in flame. While the fire couldn't harm Tesro, unless she willed it to do so, the dispersion of air around the explosion could. It flung rocks in every direction, one bouncing off her head, leaving a deep, bleeding cut and knocking her to the ground.

The brightness of the explosion blinded me, and I turned my head from it to shield my eyes. I heard Ruvor scream a curse before the boom deafened me as well. When the explosion finally died, rocks tumbled from the roof, yet the frozen man's icy prison remained completely unharmed. Not even a single icy flake broke from it.

"Tesro," I said, pushing myself back up with some effort. I squinted as I tried to focus my eyes, black dots dancing at the edge of my vision. My ears rang, but I could still hear the desperate fighting between Ijiraq and Ruvor somewhere else in the cave. At this point, all I cared about was getting to her—to purgatory with all the rest of this madness.

I stumbled, noticing the wetness on my arm and the red drops falling to the floor. I clutched the bleeding wound and walked around the frozen man to where the explosion had been. A blackened hole in the floor greeted me and I silently hoped that would be the end of our deminean companion.

I searched through the dust, coughing wildly as I did so, until I eventually found her.

Tesro!

Sho, somehow alive, held her limply with one arm, suspended in the air. The deminean woman looked haggard, her features covered in burns, and her hair all but gone; only small wispy tendrils of it remained. Even her scales appeared blackened. I suspected it was only due to the deminean's magic of self that she could have even survived such an explosion. Her fortitude to continue the fight told me of her determination to live, but she was not as determined as I was to save Tesro.

Her eyes were closed, and as suspected, she was out cold. She looked almost peaceful in that state, as if she hadn't the will left to resist.

"Sho, wait!" I said, wincing as I forced myself to assume the casting stance, lifting my bloody arm. "Don't hurt her."

She turned toward me with fury in her eyes. Her face was scarred horribly, small strands of flesh clung to the right side of her face revealing the muscle underneath. I gasped at the gruesomeness of it.

"I only need one of you alive," Sho replied, squeezing tighter.

"Please wait! If you want the amulet, it's yours. But if you kill her…"

"Then you'll what? Refuse to give me what's mine? I have ways of making you."

"No, you don't," I said flatly, holding my head down before I gathered the courage to do what I must. "Because I'll do this." I tapped a fragment of magic, sending it to the floor near me. It was slightly off target, but close enough that I controlled the small spear of earth that grew from the ground. I held it, the point a mere breath from my throat.

"Ah," she said, lowering Tesro. As soon as her feet touched, she let go and Tesro fell, her head striking the ground. Blood leaked from a gash on her forehead.

I forced myself to maintain my position—to not react. This was the only ultimatum I could think of.

Sho smiled, sensing I had called her bluff. "Well then, at least one of you can remain composed."

"Die, bitch!" I heard Ruvor scream as he appeared from the settling dust. He still held Ijiraq's tooth, and he came down on Sho with an overhead strike, the point aimed straight for her heart.

The deminean woman grinned as she sidestepped, kicking him in the ribs, stopping his downward descent. I saw his eyes widen and could have sworn I heard his ribs crack from the impact.

He landed roughly on the ground, kneeled with his head to the floor. He clutched his right side, and the creature's tooth spun away as Sho delivered a quick kick to it. She casually lifted him off the ground, and with a speed that defied reason, punched a hole into his midsection.

Ruvor screamed—an animalistic wail. Sho ripped her hand out, soaked red. Blood now poured from his open wound as she held him still in the air, and his constant screams eventually became frustrated grunts of agony. He stared at her with a hatred that I had never seen before.

If only a glare could kill.

"Such strength," she said, pulling Ruvor close, so she could say it directly into his ear. "Pity it's in the hands of a human." She muttered the last as a taunt—an insult to the very last. Then, like a child throwing away an old plaything, she thrust his body away from her. I lost sight of him as his body entered the dust and smoke that now filled the room. I heard him strike ground some ways away as Sho turned back toward me. "Now, where were we?"

"If you leave us alone, I'll give you what you want," I said, forcing my voice to remain steady.

"Still such defiance. Can you not see that you've lost? Isodros' pet...her human experiment." Sho walked closer to me and I held out my right hand to her. "I—" Her casual face took on a look of utter horror in an instant, her golden eyes going wide with shock. She took a step back. "What... What are you?"

Her question confused me, at first, but when I looked at my arm, I realized in horror:

My glove was missing!

Out in the open, for all to see, my silver scales glistened from the small traces of light that the torches set on the wall provided.

I pulled my hand back, but it was too late. Sho took a curious step closer. "You're... You're the hybrid! By the Well! Here...now?" She looked beside herself as her emotions danced between curiosity, panic, exultation and everything in between. Eventually, she calmed herself and took one step more to stand directly in front of me, looming. "This changes everything. Not only will I bring back soulrend, but the hybrid as well! Do you know how many prophecies of your coming there are? No matter, my name will be told by the deminean kind for all eternity. They will honor my soul in song, told by all manner of bards and puppeteers! I will be a Ri'sha... No, I'll be Sovereign!"

I looked over my shoulder at the frozen man, still encapsulated in his own peaceful prison. I muttered something of an apology to the man whom I did not know. All he wanted was peace in the afterlife.

It looked like it was not to be.

Concentrating, I picked out the fragments of magic that held the ice of the prison together, and I followed the strings that weaved between each segment. It was like multiple separate pieces that had been spun together with such a fine web that none could see it—like the finest of silk. Using the rest of my strength, I cut through the line that held the largest of the fragments. Such a simple thing, but so disastrous.

The magic that held the prison suddenly cascaded out of control, pulling other fragments of magic closer and closer until a ball of light, so bright it resembled a small sun, formed for my eyes alone.

I heard the ice encasing the frozen man crack, and I ran past Sho, who turned in surprise to look at what was happening, too fixated on the breaking of the ice to pay me any mind. The cracks became louder and louder as the entire cave shook.

I threw myself over Tesro's lifeless body, pulling her into a corner, and placing my body between the icy prison and her.

There was a large crack, a jolt, and then the prison of ice erupted.

Chapter Thirty-Four

LOVE AND LOSS

I screamed as a blanket of ice shards exploded from the frozen man's prison. Tucking myself as thoroughly as I could into the small crevice of rock for protection, I felt Tesro's warm breath against the side of my face as the shards buffeted all around me.

"We will live," I promised softly into her ear. "We. Will. Live."

An eternity passed before the pummeling of ice ceased, leaving me shivering and wet. With one loud shift, the rock ceiling overhead groaned. I looked up frantically and noticed large cracks splintering out on the roof like a spider's web.

Turning back to Tesro, I shook her, but there was no response. I looked at my hand, my scales glittering brilliant silver, and cursed them. I needed to find my glove, and fast. I couldn't let her see me like this.

I scanned the room and saw nothing with all the smoke that filled it. Well, nothing besides the large hole where the frozen man's prison had once stood. It greeted me as the sleet of ice settled to the ground, and I reluctantly walked toward it, my nerves sending a shuddering jolt up my spine the closer I came.

As I reached the chasm, I peered over, my heart racing at what I might see. There, alone, at the bottom of the hole, was the frozen man. No longer encapsulated in his shell, his features remained frozen in place, but that illusion of peace the man once had looked more like torment now.

In his hand was the item. Isodros' prize and the cause of all of this chaos and pain.

The amulet, soulrend.

Perhaps this man, Gruratas, had been correct all those years ago to lock himself here. To make that ultimate sacrifice to save the realm from this evil.

I shook my head. Now was not the time to waver. I would focus on my duty and save Tesro and me both, or so I thought. But when I considered it, now that the amulet's location was known, there would be no keeping it safe here. Others would come. If I had to trust someone with this power, let it be Isodros who had never given me any reason to doubt her.

Carefully, I slid down into the hole, using the least sheer of the edges to do so. As I struck the bottom, my legs failed me, and I went to my knees, hard.

When I looked up, I found myself staring directly into the frozen man's face. The paleness of it was sickening, and the thinness of his frozen hair made him appear ghoulish. I paid him little mind as I pried the glowing amulet from his icy, dead grip. I heard a snap and a pop before the amulet was finally free of its tomb.

"Thank you," I said to the dead man, not knowing how else to honor his sacrifice. I decided that protecting what he gave his life for would have to be enough. "You can rest now. Truly rest."

I stood and wiped the snow off the amulet to reveal its gleaming silver making. Like metal made of liquid, the glow of the amulet seemed to ripple light off of it, like waves in the ocean. I had only held it for a moment before I felt it—a barb, piercing—but more than that. The amulet fixed itself into my very soul, and I could swear I heard a maniacal laughter coming from within it.

I turned the item around and around in my hand, undaunted by the new sensations that plagued me. Besides the glow and the shining silver, it had a small loop where a chain could be strung through. Another glance revealed small words carved into the face. The words read, 'I give my life for the people, so that we may see the light of a day where we are free.'

Ominous, I thought.

Get rid of it! I heard Vulana scream, nearly splitting my head with the headache he caused. *Now! It'll consume you!* And then, just as abruptly as he had come, he was gone; our connection completely cut off.

A sudden pain drove me to my knees, and I held my head against it, my vision spinning in circles. Suddenly, the knowledge that Vulana had been taking my suffering and pain for himself flooded into me.

"Vulana?" I whispered to the dark, forcing my thoughts as wide as they would go.

Nothing.

Not even the slightest of presences awaited me in that void. Just vast, empty nothingness.

It's only for a short time, I told myself. *Just until I can find something to wrap the amulet in. He'll be back...*

He has to.

As I reached the top of the fissure, I slipped, narrowly catching a slit in the ground using my ungloved hand. With some effort, I swung my leg up and rolled onto solid earth. Breathing heavily, I prayed to the Well that this nightmare was finally over.

After a modest rest, I searched and found my torn leather glove. The latches and buckles were ruined, but I pulled the glove on anyway, tying the broken leather strap around my wrist to hold it. It felt loose around my hand.

"Give...it...to...me," a voice said in the dark. It sounded pained, and like an extra sense, I felt someone approaching from behind. I turned to see Sho barely standing, her torso pierced by multiple reddened ice shards that still stuck out of her and reflected the pain and fury on her face.

"How are you alive?" I asked, my words coming and going as lightly as a misted breath on a frosty morning.

She hacked and blood fell from her lips. "I...won't be...killed...by a human!" She moved forward, as if to rush toward me, but after two steps the deminean woman fell to her knees, blood pouring from her wounds. "Purgatory!"

Slowly, she raised her head, leveling her golden eyes at me with a smirk on her mangled face. "Who knows about you, hybrid? Isodros? Crux?" she glanced over at Tesro who still laid unconscious on the floor. "Her?"

"You shut your mouth, traitor!" I replied, rage fueling my words. "Do you think to judge me? After you murdered your own kind and threatened to kill us? You're pathetic. A miserable wretch, not even worthy of the words I speak to you now." Anger overwhelmed me as I felt the pull of the amulet. Looking down, it glowed crimson. "Not worthy of the life you still have."

Sho's gaze went wide as she noticed the trinket I carried, its reddish glow illuminating in those fearful eyes.

"No...don't," she begged, her words dying in her throat as she coughed up more blood. She fell back and dragged herself away from me as if to flee. Frantically, she added, "You wouldn't use that on me. Please, no. Just kill me... Please!"

I felt hatred—the same I felt the day the deminean killed my mother.

So long ago.

Now, I grinned as I stepped up to Sho, who stared at me, sweat pouring down her face. Now I had the power to fight back.

I leaned down and whispered into her ear, "You don't deserve another life. Traitors' souls are forfeit." I ripped my glove off as I reached toward her. As my hand pressed against the skin of her chest, I felt our souls connect. She screamed, not with breath, but in her mind as I delved into her, latching my soul onto hers. Using the amulet as a vessel, I pulled her very soul from her body. It flowed easily into the amulet, which burst alight, sending a cascading red across the entirety of the cave.

Her body collapsed, utterly drained of its source, and her once brilliant scales dulled and then faded completely to dark gray. Small pressure cracks formed in them, as if they were made of thin clay.

A fitting end.

I felt her energy well up inside me, the power of her soul trapped in the amulet. I knew that I could bend it to my will, and I basked in my newfound strength.

"Vi'eri…" I heard another voice say.

I spun and had to put my hand to my mouth to stop from weeping. There, in front of me, Tesro stood aghast. She was scraped up, bruised, and dried blood covered her face.

"Tesro!" I said, but as I walked toward her, she took a step back, placing both of her hands to her mouth. "What's wrong?"

"You're…" Tesro said, pointing at me. "You're deminean?"

A pit in my stomach opened as I realized the truth: I had removed my glove when I had taken Sho's soul. Looking down, I still held the leather glove in my uncovered hand. Instead of silver, my scales glowed red, mirroring the amulet's crimson light.

I tried to think of a lie, something she would accept. But, like a naive girl, I was suddenly sick of it. The lies. The deception. I loved her with all my heart. I would give my life for hers. So, for this love, I resolved to do the hardest thing of all: to tell her the truth. And more so, admit that truth to myself.

I am the hybrid.

"No," I said in my most calming voice. "I am not a deminean. Well, not exactly. I'm a hybrid, or so I've been called. A cross between deminean and human. It's why I had to keep my arms hidden. Look." I lifted my arms for her to see my scales fully. "I've known for some time now, even though I was hesitant to admit it. But now…now I've shared everything with you! Finally, you know my secret. Nothing needs to change between us."

I forced a smile and walked toward her, but she hastily stepped away from me, muttering, "Liar…" Hurt filled her reddened eyes as she added, "You were one of them. Always one of them! Did you secretly bask at my pain? Did you… Did you laugh when I told you how much I cared for you? When I said that I loved you?"

"I'm not one of them!" I protested. "And I never mocked your love. By the Well, I love you too. So much so that my heart feels like it'll burst. So please, just listen…" My voice hastened and my heart pounded in dread. "I consider myself human above all else. Tesro, please." I walked toward her with purpose, reaching out to embrace her—to feel her warm touch.

"Get away from me!" she screamed, tapping a fragment of magic as she did. A powerful gust of wind sent me hurdling backward. I tripped and rolled before I found purchase on the ground, letting the air cross over me.

"Tesro!" I yelled, projecting my voice over the sound of the wind. "I'm still me!"

"You're not, you never were. Freak. Halfling... Monster!"

Monster. Those words wounded me like none ever had before. Like nothing physical can. The cut was to my heart and my soul, and I knew in that moment that I had lost her forever. Worse, she scorned me for who I was. Who I am.

Who I had no choice but to be.

I stood, my head hanging down, when I heard another voice. "By the Well..." Ruvor appeared in the corner of the room, holding his hand against the gaping hole in his chest. Blood leaked through his fingers, flowing freely to the ground in little pools. "The hybrid. Just like the stories."

I didn't bother to even look at him, but kept my attention focused on Tesro. "I'm human. You need to believe me. You can hate me for lying, but I will always love you. Just give this time—"

"Stop!" she interrupted me, cradling her head in her hands. "Just stop. Stop, stop, stop!"

"Hey..." Ruvor said, drawing her attention to him. "It's alright, come with me. I'll protect you from this traitor who dares use our human gifts to help the deminean kind."

Fury gripped me. "To purgatory you will!"

"And what?" he asked. "You'll protect her, half-breed? I've read all about you." He suddenly coughed, catching blood in his hand. Casually, he wiped it on his pant leg. "While there are many interpretations, the seers all seem to agree on one point. The hybrid will bring salvation or ruin for the deminean. For humans, you'll bring nothing but pain and suffering. It is you who'll be the end of us. Mark my words."

My anger boiled as I countered, "Then come, then. Show me what the great Ruvor Locke can do. Kill me, if you can." I assumed a casting position, my right hand extended out toward him.

He spat blood on the floor, as if he considered fighting. Casually, he glanced at soulrend, which I clutched tightly. But then he turned away from me, walking toward Tesro instead. "I offer choices, hybrid," he said, sparing me a glance as he stepped in front of her. He turned to her and offered his hand. "Come with me to the south, away from this dreaded cold. To be with your own people. I protect my own."

I gasped. "Tesro," I pleaded, "please don't leave." My words were pathetic, even to my own ears.

She turned and spared one final glance toward me, tears flowing freely from those beautiful eyes. I have that image of her; the mix of hurt, rage, fear...and love. It is forever scorched into my soul.

She took Ruvor's hand and turned from me.

I wailed as I drew all the power of Sho's soul into me, tapping fragments of magic as furiously as my fingers could move with no real aim or goal. In an instant, explosions of earth, fire, wind, lightning and ice flashed across the cave in a brilliant cascade of colors and destruction. It was a deadly display.

And beautiful.

I was lost in madness, and I didn't care if I were to live or die. No, I wanted to die.

The fracture in the roof grew larger and larger until one final shift collapsed it. Sheets of rock fell dangerously to the ground, and I burned through the rest of Sho's soul in that instance of fury, just in time to come to my senses and see the ruin I had wrought.

The entire cave shook steadily now, and boulders fell that were larger than me by at least three times. I heard Ruvor shout and then crash after crash of rocks slammed near him as he and Tesro were entombed behind the falling debris.

I ran toward them, but a boulder fell directly in front of me, driving me back. Fear seized hold of my legs and, like a coward, I fled, following the path back toward the entrance. I didn't even spare a glance back at them as some primordial will to live overtook me. Despite wishing for death mere moments before, this force would not let me have such an end.

Narrowly, I dodged rock after falling rock as the tunnel collapsed all around me. As the last boulder fell, I threw myself out of the cave entrance, rolling in the snow as the wind from the rapidly closing cave buffeted my eyes with sleet, temporarily blinding me.

I laid in the snow breathing heavily, and inhaling small bits of it as I did so. Pushing myself up, I pulled the glove that I still grasped onto my arm. Strangely, I could still feel the hold the amulet had on me, even through the thickness of the leather gloves. The amulet and I were still connected.

I forced myself to look at the damage I had caused, tears rolling down my cheeks. My outburst completely shut the cave in, a mess of rocks blocking the entrance. I had killed them.

I killed Tesro.

"By the Well," Madrof said, rushing toward me. "Vi'eri, are you alright?"

"Oh…" I replied in a daze, holding my swaying head with one hand. "Yes, I'm alright, Madrof—" Then, suddenly, I remembered. My vision focused, and I turned to look directly into his eyes. "You!"

"I?" he replied as he stared back at me with a mix of curiosity and fear.

"You gave us to Ruvor. You knew he was there waiting to take the amulet."

"Now wait a moment, Vi'eri, that's not—"

It was too late. In my fury, I had tapped a fragment of magic and tendrils of air enveloped Madrof, lifting him off the ground. The amulet, still in my hand, burned with anticipation for its next meal. I nearly fed Madrof to it then and there, but I wanted answers first.

I needed answers.

"Tell me," I said, forcing myself to stay his death—to reject what I so desperately wanted to do. "Why should I not execute you?"

"Because I had no choice!" he replied. His natural, calm demeanor broke as he struggled against my magic. To my surprise, he began to sob. "My parents, my grandparents—gone. I have nobody, and yet, I have not the means to leave. Ruvor promised he acted for the benefit of all humans. He said no harm would come to either you or Tesro. He told me not to trust the deminean woman who traveled with you, not that he needed to tell me that. If Ruvor hurt you—if he hurt Tesro—then that was not what I agreed to."

I still wanted to do it. Wanted to kill him. Badly. But there was already so much pain and death for one day. To the displeasure of the amulet, I relented.

"Fine," I said, releasing the magic. His body gently floated down to touch the ground. "But I won't honor our original deal." I reached out and grabbed his jacket, pulling him close. "Know this. Your trust killed my love."

I spoke the lie, trying to shift the blame that I knew lay solely with me. I knew not why I wanted to spread my pain, only that I desired all around me to know what I had lost. I shoved him back.

To Madrof's credit, he looked hurt by my words. Truly, he cared that his actions pained another.

"By your will, Vi'eri," he said. "And for what little it's worth, I am truly sorry."

Without another word, he turned and walked back toward Sleetward. I waited until he was out of sight, and then made my own way back.

Alone.

Chapter Thirty-Five

THE END OF ALL THINGS

I arrived in Sleetward to see a familiar sight. A grayhorn, one of the staples of the White-Raven Caravan, grazed just outside of the town on the small scraps of greens it could find under the patches of snow that the sun had revealed during the day.

"Vi'eri!" I heard a familiar voice call to me, and as I turned, I found Rhas jogging my way, her red scales catching faint hints of the afternoon light. When she caught up to me, she bent over and exhaled. "I've been searching for you all day."

"Rhas? Why are you here?" I asked, turning my head from her as she appraised me with a curious eye.

She scowled, likely noticing my cuts and bruises. "I spoke to Boltulk, and told him how worried I was. As a favor, he tasked me with delivering the next shipment of ore from Sleetward to Whiteline. 'Can't lose our favorite girls,' he said. I know you both can handle yourselves, but I figured, since I was in the area, that we could travel together again. The Well knows I've always enjoyed your company. Even Tesro's, as ornery as she can be. Speaking of..." She let her words trail off as she scanned around. "Where is she? Sleeping back at the inn if I know her, and I dare say I do."

"She's..." I replied, my words withdrawing into me, as if speaking them would make it real.

Would make her death a reality.

Rhas' face went from casual amusement to utter shock in a moment. "Oh, Vi'eri…" she said, reaching out with both arms to embrace me.

I startled backward and shrieked, "No! Don't!"

Rhas withdrew, her hands placed out defensively. She murmured reassurance as she stepped back. I felt something in my hand and, looking down, realized I held the amulet in my palm. Hesitantly, I forced myself to pocket it, being as discreet as I could.

I looked back toward Rhas and forced myself to meet her eyes. "I'm sorry, it's been a trying day. Tesro… She—"

"It's alright, Vi'eri. It's alright." Her words were full of understanding and pity. I saw her want—her *need* to embrace me, but she respected my wishes and kept her distance. "I understand. There is no need to speak of such foulness. It's as Boltulk always says, 'Never discuss bad news before a job. Speak of good things, for you never know when this job will be your last.'"

"Rhas, he never says that. You do."

"Do I?" she replied. "I never noticed before. Either way, it rings true, eh?"

I wanted to return her kindness, but I couldn't bring myself to it. The woman's scales, her horns, her eyes… Everything about her reminded me of Sho and other deminean who had harmed me in the past.

My enemies.

Rhas' smile eventually diminished and concern filled the void. I turned toward town and said, "I'll travel with you if we leave today. Now, preferably."

"But…" she objected, but one look at my face told her the truth: I could not bear to stay in this town another moment, let alone another night. Rhas straightened her white cloak. "It is as you say then, Vi'eri. We leave today, just after I load wagons and gather some provisions for the trip."

I nodded at her, and she took that as her cue to leave. She reached out, even against the warning glare I leveled at her, and placed one hand on my shoulder. I trembled at the touch, but resolved not to back away from it. Returning my nod, she squeezed my shoulder firmly before releasing it, and walked into town. I waited for a moment and followed shortly after her.

"Are we ready to go?" I asked, frustration tainting my words. "I want to leave this place as soon as possible."

"We are," Rhas replied. She stared at me with those golden eyes, and the look she gave me said that she was just about done with my persistence. Then, as if she remembered something dire, she relented, adding in a gentle tone, "Just need to load one last thing. Well, and speak to the new hire." She casually threw her pack into the riding seat atop the grayhorn with one arm.

"New hire?"

"Yes." She turned to look out toward the town. "Ah, I think I see him now. There!" she waved her arms emphatically, as if the large pack beast we traveled with would be difficult for anyone to spot.

I peeked from around the grayhorn's head, scratching absently behind his ear, and saw Madrof sauntering toward us, clearly dressed for travel with a modest pack slung across his shoulder. He wore a thick off-white coat that contrasted his dark skin.

"No!" I exclaimed, not meaning to mutter the word out loud. I looked up, hastily addressing Rhas. "What's he doing here?"

She looked down at me from atop the grayhorn with a confused look and shrugged her shoulders. "Madrof asked me about leaving this frozen waste just a few moments before I met with you earlier. You know we're always looking for those with the determination and grit to work for the Caravan, and he seems to have a solid enough head on his shoulders. Well, better than most of the lot who try to work for us. Why? Did he do something wrong?"

"No," I admitted. "Well, not exactly. But Rhas, I don't want to travel with Madrof. He—" Again, my words failed me, dying in my throat.

"I see," she replied, sparing me a piteous look. "Well, what's done is done, Vi'eri. I understand you're in pain, but I already gave him my word. And honestly, the Caravan could use the fresh blood. If he disturbs you so much, just ignore him. I won't make you interact with him. Like I could make you do anything at all."

I ground my teeth in irritation, glancing over one more time at Madrof, who saw me and turned his head away from my judging glare. But, despite the bad blood between us, he continued to walk in our direction.

"Fine," I muttered. "I hope we can leave now?"

She finished fastening the load on the grayhorn's back. "We can. Let's not delay any further."

I trudged next to the grayhorn in complete silence for what felt like an eternity.

On the route back toward the crossroads, I had halted to see an odd sight. Next to the road was a mound with a single stick protruding from it. Glancing at it, I immediately knew what it was.

Turning to Rhas, who rode topside the grayhorn, I asked, "Did you bury him? Hask, I mean?"

She leaned over with a scowl. "Yes, I did. I saw a marking on the tree. Your work, I assume. Anyway, I stopped to check it out. To be truthful, I feared I would find you or Tesro, injured or worse." Her words stung with the mention of Tesro and she grimaced, adding, "But I found Hask instead. Poor bastard. He was long dead, and, as you know, quite frozen. The fatal wound he suffered was clear to me. Pieced straight through the heart. It pained me to see one of my own, no matter how disjoined I am from my own kind, to be left out like that. It still does. So I took it upon myself to bury the man. I didn't like him, but he deserved better than to be left like that—not that I blame you. From the pile of dead vargs, I presume you were forced to make a quick retreat? Either way, it was decent of you to leave the markings. You've truly had a rough time, haven't you?"

"Yeah," I whispered my reply, frowning. She offered no additional comment as she kicked the grayhorn, signaling it to move on.

We had not even traveled for very long when Rhas called for another halt. The crossroads was still a ways away, and it was midday, but she dropped off the grayhorn, landing in the snow and kicking white powder into the air. Her white cloak whipped behind her, nearly hitting me as it followed her down.

"Wait a moment," she said, taking a few steps off the path and into the trees. She ran her hand across the base of one, and nodded to herself, turning to face me. "Follow me." I took a few steps off the path and heard Madrof step up from behind me. She faced him, adding, "Madrof, stay and watch the caravan. I'll be back in just a moment."

I turned and saw him nod wordlessly, turning back and leaning on the side of the grayhorn, who'd found a small piece of grass to gnaw on. He looked almost happy that he was not to join us. Not that I blamed him for that.

We walked deeper into the forest and I followed silently, dodging the various branches and shrubbery. No discernible path marked our way. Small white rabbits scampered away and birds scattered as we intruded upon their homes.

"Where are we going?" I asked, stepping into a hole hidden in the snow. I sunk deep and cursed as I struggled to pull my foot out. Snow began to melt, soaking my wool stockings, leaving my foot freezing.

Great, I thought. *Just perfect.*

"Here we are," she said, halting with a quickness. As I stepped to her side, what greeted me was a majestic view of a valley of snow-covered trees that extended all the way out to the horizon. "Vi'eri," she went on, staring out over the brilliance of nature, "I've never shared this location with anyone else. Truth is, I'm an outcast from my kind, something I don't expect you to fully understand."

I forced myself to remain quiet and hid a scowl from her.

She placed her arm around my shoulder. "I found this place soon after I began working for the White-Ravens. It has a certain...tranquility about it. A stillness that soothed my scarred soul. I suspect it may do so for you as well. Take the time you need and I'll set up the camp for the night back on the road."

She withdrew, but I turned to her, drawing her attention. "Rhas, thank you for this. I'll... I'll be back soon." She nodded and continued toward camp.

I turned and stared out for a time, observing the sun lazily ease down on the opposing mountainside, casting a red tint across the valley of peaked white.

Desperately, I wanted to feel at peace, but I just couldn't.

Why do I deserve to live when Tesro isn't?

Why did she reject me?

Why did I kill her?

These reflections spiraled in my mind as anger conquered rational thought.

Fragments of magic suddenly danced around me, and I thrusted my hands in the air, striking the magic and willing all of it around me as I screamed my rage to the realm. The fragments spun out of control, colliding with each other and growing beyond my meager sway.

Floating away from me, they met in a cacophony of power as the air above the valley exploded. Fire of every color flared alight, twisting winds formed into giant strands, lightning flashed in arcs of blue, and ice fragments soared all around. It was a beautiful sight to behold.

And terrifying.

I breathed heavily as the display of power quelled my frustrations. I let my head droop as I looked out upon the land, undisturbed by my wonton use of magic. It served as a reminder that my life had no meaning. It never had.

I fell to my knees and held my head in my hands, weeping. I wept for what I had lost, and I wept for the losses I knew were yet to come. I yelled my sorrow out to the realm for in that moment, I knew.

Death, pain and loneliness were all that awaited a creature like me.

After a time, I started the trek back through the woods toward the main road, following the still visible footsteps we had left. On the way, I heard a strange sound, as if something followed me through the snow, hiding in the shadows of the trees.

"Rhas?" I asked toward the shadows, creeping around an adjacent tree myself and pressing my back against it. I felt a pull from the amulet that told me that another soul was around, and the pull of its soul was massive.

Instinctually, I ducked and rolled as an enormous claw struck the tree where my head had been a moment before. Fear hastened my steps, and I didn't bother looking at my attacker as I ran through the snow, shoving through brush as I went.

I heard the breaking and snapping of wood behind me as the thing chased wildly. I, sluggish from my previous childish outburst, was being gained on quickly.

Again, I had to dodge as the creature burst through the base of a tree, uprooting it and flinging dirt into the air. This stunned the creature as I heard it fall to the ground, kicking sleet all around.

I turned to find Ijiraq, the creature from the caves, staring pure hatred at me from glowing red eyes. It once again wore the form of a gigantic white-furred bear, and the claws on its paws were long and sharp, with black pointed tips. Its back had large scales with spikes of bone protruding from it.

A monstrosity beyond imagination.

"Hybrid," they addressed me in a surprisingly human tone. "The amulet belongs to Anduinna, the true ruler of this realm. Drop it and go. You will no longer be required in the fate that Anduinna spins."

"Go?" I asked, standing straight and lifting my arms in a casting position. It was a bluff, of course, I felt completely drained from before, but this creature couldn't know that.

I forced a fake smile onto my face, and said in a taunting voice, "And why would Anduinna suffer me to live? The Life Incarnate has asked me to join her before—practically begged me. I doubt she would allow someone or something like me to exist."

The creature took a noticeable step forward and, in doing so, swayed as if the effort of rising took all the strength they had. Blood seeped from various cuts in the creature's flesh. The fight in the cave with Ruvor had left them wounded and tired—to my advantage.

Ijiraq took another step forward, leaving a large, bloody footprint painted in the snow; a crimson sigil that spoke of our oncoming conflict. Both of us just stared at each other, waiting for the other to attack.

I looked down and realized with a pit in my stomach that I had pulled the amulet out of my pocket without realizing it. The amulet's silver plating rippled in my hand as if it were made of liquid metal, and as Ijiraq saw it, they opened their maw wide, as if they intended to swallow me whole.

"If Anduinna wants it," I declared, "then come and take it from me!"

Ijiraq roared their fury at me, and with one thump of their hind legs, charged. I just had to touch them one time. If I was able to do so, I could rip the soul from their very body. I longed for that power—the power of soulrend. Almost like an ache in my chest, I longed for it like nothing else I had ever sought before.

Ijiraq was upon me and they swung their bear-like claws with killing intent. I dodged a swipe to the left, ducking my head as long nails grazed my skin. Then a strike from the right, dodging again, just as nimbly. Ijiraq slowly forced me back as I narrowly kept my feet moving away from each blow as they came. I knew that one strike from this massive being would end my life in an instant.

Ijiraq abruptly spun, and a long lizard-like tail whipped me in the ribs, throwing me face first in the snow. The amulet flew from my hands, rolling away from me as the air was driven from my lungs.

"No!" I screamed harshly.

I tried to stand, but fell instantaneously, my lungs unable to draw the breath I so desperately needed. Ijiraq leaped past me, galloping toward soulrend.

I grabbed the scaly tail as it whipped past me, but I was no match in strength to the bulk of the beast as they dragged me along with them toward the amulet, and what I suspected was the end of both humans and deminean.

Ijiraq screeched as an arrow struck their right shoulder. It sounded so human—so pained. Then another arrow, and another. Ijiraq turned to face the attacker, and in that hesitation, I slipped by them, and forced air into me, focusing my entire being on recovering soulrend.

The amulet was there, just within my grasp. I reached for it and felt a force bear down on me. Ijiraq's giant paw collided with my back, slamming and pinning me to the ground. I yelled in frustration as they put the entirety of their weight on me.

Unbearable. I felt as if my bones would snap from the pressure.

I heard more whistling of arrows as they plummeted into Ijiraq. The creature's weight shifted as they attempted to dodge the onslaught. Taking this as my chance, I clawed my way forward. So close, I was so close! The very edge of my finger lightly grazed the amulet, but I could not grasp it.

"Vi'eri!" I heard Madrof yell. He seemed so close as he bellowed out a roar, like some warrior in a fairy tale. I turned to look, and he pulled a knife from his belt, charging Ijiraq like a madman.

"Idiot!" I yelled back at him, but it was too late as the creature raised its free paw in the air to swipe him away, but in the moment of doing so, the weight on me lessened, and I used all my remaining strength to reach for soulrend.

I gasped when I felt the amulet in my hand. The link rekindled in full, and I reached behind me to touch Ijiraq's paw with my left hand.

Massive. The soul I felt from Ijiraq was utterly and completely overwhelming. Despite its immensity, I latched onto and pulled on the soul—so large it felt as if it were made from the collective of tens of thousands of them.

Perhaps more.

Ijiraq looked down at me with what I assumed to be shock. As I ripped the soul from the creature, their weight lessened, and I didn't know if it was they who weakened or I who gained in strength. Slowly, I pulled my way out from under Ijiraq's grasp, keeping my hand pressed firmly against them as I did so.

The soul flowed into the amulet, but I speculated, the vast emptiness of the trinket could never truly be filled. Soulrend had a mind of its own, and it would invariably crave for more. Hungrily, as if gorging itself in some sort of blood frenzy, I felt my own soul begin to enter the amulet as well, and my mind fluttered into blackness.

When I opened my eyes, I found myself once again standing in the grove of the Life Incarnate. However, looking around, I couldn't help but notice the subtle differences from when I was here before. Ominously, at the edges of this place, little wisps of light floated off in a vast emptiness just beyond its borders, as if the very sky itself rotted away into nothingness.

"Do you see it, hybrid?" Anduinna said from behind me.

I spun to confront her, standing but a few steps away, towering over me with her half-human, half-deer body. Anduinna did not bother to hide her right side, the side of death, from me this time. I felt as if it were an act of honesty between us.

Honesty...at the end of all things.

Surprisingly, Anduinna lowered her head into her hands sadly. "So, you would bring me ruin after all? Pity. All I've ever done was for the safety of this realm. For its continued existence."

"Safety?" I replied, doing my best to stand tall against her overwhelming height. "You seek the complete destruction of human and deminean alike. Genocide. How is that safe?"

"It's for the good of the realm. I will do anything for its survival," she said, as if explaining to an unruly child. "I've seen over countless genocides and with each, new life emerges. You speak of your species as if you belong here, as if you were always meant to be. Not as the infection you are. A blight. Bah, you humans and deminean are all alike. Despite your constant wars with each other, both seek to change the realm to fit your own perceptions, neither considering the natural order. The fate that awaited this realm before the first arrived."

The darkness at the edges of the realm continued to close, the wisps of light floating off to be consumed forever in the void. It filled me with an inexplicable sadness as I asked, "The first?"

"Before your time, hybrid. Before either human or deminean existed as you do now. Your species' are parasites—feeding off the energies of the realm. You both take and give nothing back. Your transgressions against the balance are the reason I cannot suffer either of you to exist. You bring war, pain and suffering. You bring drought and ruin. And yes, while you have also brought beauty, at times, it does not absolve the harm caused. It all started with the first; now those were truly a blight upon reality."

"You didn't explain anything," I muttered to myself, but before I could ask further questions, my eyes were drawn to the destruction laid before me as the grove slowly disappeared from sight. Instinctually, I knew that Anduinna's fate and mine were bound to whatever was happening here.

I swallowed hard, asking, "What's happening?"

"You!" Anduinna replied, a hint of grief in her voice. "The creation of humans—soulrend, you call it. It is as I said, humans transgress the natural balance, and that amulet is of human design."

"Then why do you want it?"

She laughed and spared me a sad smile. "Even a tool of great wickedness may be used for the good of all, if it finds itself in fit hands. Do you doubt my words, hybrid? What you do now, you think it is good for the realm, but it is not. At least, not in the future I seek. For when I ultimately fade, something worse will take my place. Something will always invariably fill the void."

"And what if I stop?" I asked, clinging to a desperate hope. "What if I let you go? What if I destroy the amulet?"

"It cannot be destroyed!" she seethed. "It is made of a material that is unknown, foreign...even to me. Soulrend is not of this realm, and nothing I know of could destroy it."

"Not destroyed then," I countered. "Locked away, hidden. Never to be used again."

Anduinna appeared to ponder my words. Studying the decay of her world, she grimaced. "And what would you wish in return for this abdication of power?"

I lowered my arms to my side, not sure if the threat was over, but all will to fight drained out of me. "For you to leave me in peace. Allow me to fulfill my task; to bring soulrend to Ri'sha Isodros."

"And you trust this Isodros? What makes you think she will not use this trinket to her own ends?"

"Trust," I replied, "and a leap of faith."

"Such childishness," she replied, laughing as she stepped ever closer. "But I somehow do not doubt your words. Or your intentions." Anduinna now stood over me, well within arm's reach. Her green glowing eyes studied me quizzically and I would have been lost in those eyes if the subtle, pungent smell of decay had not kept me grounded.

Finally, she made her decision as she said, "Very well, I accept. But this is only temporary. I will allow you to keep possession of the amulet for now. Take it to your master. Hide it away so that none may use it again. In this, I will leave you unhindered."

"And after?"

"After?" she asked, puzzled. "I already told you, I cannot permit humans or deminean the power of rebirth through the Soulwell. I will bring about your end."

"So you will still try to kill us all?"

"Kill is such a human word. I want to restore balance to the realm, to return what once was. I seek to return your bodies to the ground, and your souls to the Soulwell under my control, so that I might maintain said balance."

I sighed. "So truly, we will always be enemies?" I asked the words and knew the answer.

"If you seek life, then yes. But perhaps I will grant you a gift. You're something special, and I know the crushing weight of being one of a kind."

I stared at her, trying to uncover the lie. She faced me steadily as I asked, "What gift?"

"Linked as we are, I feel it. Your pain. Your anguish. I would have your soul whole and strong when it returns to me, not flayed and broken as it is now. I would give you peace...by taking something from you."

"And what is it you would take?"

She just stared at me wordlessly until her left hand slowly reached out toward me. I stared at it as if she offered a vial of poison, but seeing no other options, I reached out and shook the Life Incarnate's hand. Anduinna pulled me close, pressing her right hand to my chest.

The hand of death.

The broken, decaying hand revolted me as I felt it press through my clothes, touching my bare skin.

The smell of decay consumed my senses as I tried to scream, but it was as soundless as the realm that shifted around me. Suddenly, the darkness ceased its ever-moving consumption of the grove's light. Slowly, I separated from her, floating away from this realm and into the void while she remained firm in what remained of the grove.

"Live in peace, hybrid, and seek not what I have taken. What is yours can always be reclaimed, but you must relive the pain." Anduinna's voice rang out in my ears as the realm's light slowly disappeared from my eyes.

"Anduinna!" I bellowed, forcing my voice through the narrow light remaining. "What did you take?"

At the very edge of Anduinna's grove, I heard her final words to me, so small it was as if she whispered them in my ear.

"Your love, hybrid. I took from you your love."

I gasped, yanking my hand away from Ijiraq, and falling to the ground as I did so.

Soulrend screamed inside my head, and it sounded as if the final moments of a thousand lives cried out in fury and then were suddenly silenced. I clutched the amulet to me, but I secretly craved to throw it as far away from me as I could.

"Where is she?" Ijiraq said as I turned to find the creature down on their forepaws.

Gasping, I replied, "What do you mean? We made a deal. I—"

"Deal!" Ijiraq interrupted. "Anduinna makes no deal with your kind. I cannot hear her—I cannot feel her! It's so lonely. I'm all alone. What did you do to me? What did you do?"

Ijiraq spared me a last glance as they reared on both hind legs, ready to come down on me with their full weight. I shifted to move, but my body wouldn't obey, as tired as it was. I looked up helplessly at my incoming death.

Madrof roared as he appeared, thrusting his knife straight into Ijiraq's chest. The blade sunk deep, and he released the knife as he grabbed me, throwing me out of the way. Ijiraq's claws came down, striking a blow off the side of his head.

Blood poured out from Ijiraq's wound as they fell to their side, soaking the snow in red. I saw the creature's chest rise and drop. Then, after a brief moment, it stopped completely, the creature letting out a final sigh.

I could almost sense Ijiraq's relief in death, the final clarity of a ravenous animal. Crimson blood flowed and made a little river in the snow that trailed toward us.

Madrof, a bit dazed from the attack he received, lay next to me. I noticed a wound on his scalp where Ijiraq's nail had nicked him, small drops of blood leaking from it. As for myself, I was ragged and tired. My bones hurt from being crushed, and I felt vulnerable to my very core. Still, there was a subtle pulling of the amulet tugging gently, but insistently, on my soul.

It disgusted me.

Forcing myself to stand, I looked at Madrof. "Let's head back." Surprisingly, my body felt lighter than before, as if a substantial load had been lifted from my shoulders. I reached out a hand to him. "And thank you!"

He stared back at me for a moment, his eyes glazing over, but then a sudden realization overtook him, and he reached out, grabbing my arm as I pulled him to his feet. He brushed snow off his cloak.

"No, thank you," he said, turning to face Ijiraq. "What is that thing?"

"Ijiraq," I replied.

"And what's an 'Ijiraq?'"

I shrugged my shoulders. "I don't know, it's what Anduinna called it. Whatever *it* is, it's an intelligent being. It spoke to me before the end."

"Anduinna?" he replied incredulously, his mouth aghast. "The Life Incarnate?"

I smiled. "One and the same. Anduinna and I have...history. But we should be safe, for now." Soulrend drew my eye to itself, pulsating in my hand. The connection to my soul was still there, but the desire to use the amulet had abated. "Well, we will be safe when I deliver this to Isodros."

"Isodros? Ri'sha Isodros?" he replied. I nodded, and Madrof put his hand to his chin. "History with Anduinna, the Life Incarnate and assisting a deminean Ri'sha. Vi'eri, just who in purgatory are you really?"

I smiled at him as I walked in the direction back toward the path. Leaving his question unanswered, I said, "Come on, or Rhas will begin to worry."

"One day," he replied, matching my casual gait as he walked lockstep with me, "you'll need to tell me of your adventures. I'm sure they will be interesting, to say the least."

I laughed. "Maybe after a drink or two. Your treat, of course."

CHAPTER THIRTY-SIX

A GIFT

Madrof and I led Rhas to the corpse of Ijiraq—the shapeshifter, as we had begun to call it. The deminean woman turned her golden eyes from the creature, muttering a curse and said a silent prayer to the Well.

She looked unwell.

Afterward, she forced us to pack up and push on long past the time the guiding light of the sun had faded. She tasked me with using my magic to usher the way, and I summoned an orange flame high above the caravan, mimicking the tie around the magic I had witnessed in the frozen man's prison. It took a massive burst of strength to make the magic hold, but afterward, I let my will slip and the flame remained. We used its light to traverse the perilous journey to put as much distance between us and that cursed place as possible.

It was a few days until we reached Whiteline, and not a moment too soon. Strangely, a deminean guard dressed for battle blocked our path, and the outskirts of the town, usually packed with merchants, was empty of hawkers while guards roamed where their carts had once been.

The guard stepped forward, hailing us. "State your business," he said, eyeing us as if we were assassins.

"Deliveries from the White-Raven Caravan," Rhas replied, adding, "Where is everyone? Why are you blocking the path? Did something happen?"

"You been under a rock?" The guard sneered, and I couldn't decide if it was for the questions or the general dislike all deminean seemed to show toward Rhas. "If you must know, fanatics in that cursed Dragon's Court cult attacked Ri'sha Isodros."

"They attacked Isodros?" I replied, and the guard leveled a sidelong glance at me, one that warned that I was overstepping my station. "Ri'sha Isodros, I mean, of course. No disrespect meant. The news shocked me, that's all."

"I don't have time for this," the guard said as he turned his golden eyes to one of his compatriots, who held a large pike at the ready, giving him a quick wave of his hand. The other guard lifted the pike in the air and waved us forward. Rhas, lost in thought for a moment, swished the reins, but before the guard stepped to the side, he added, "Ri'sha Isodros was attacked, but that rebellion was put down swiftly. You citizens don't need to worry, it's all taken care of. Now go about your day and don't cause any trouble. Peddle your wares and leave." Finally, he stepped aside, and the grayhorn moved, pulling Madrof and me along in the cart behind it.

When there was a safe distance between us and the guards, Madrof, keeping his green eyes trained on the guards, asked, "What was that about?" Eventually, the guards disappeared from sight and he turned back to me, adding, "I'm still not used to seeing so many deminean in one place. In Sleetward, seeing the occasional patrol every few months was enough to set tongues gossiping for weeks."

"You should see the Soulwell then," Rhas replied. "I hope being around my kind isn't a problem for you?" She turned to give him a questioning glare.

He smiled, showing his neatly-rowed teeth. "Not at all, my esteemed companion. It's just a change. When you spend your whole life living in one place, well, it'll take time for me to adjust to this new environment."

Rhas, seemingly pleased with his answer, nodded, and turned back around to guide the grayhorn as it entered the town proper.

"And what about you Vi'eri?" he asked. "What will you do now?"

"I'll head back to the High Tide and report to Crux. He'll want to be with me when I present Ri'sha Isodros with her prize."

He shook his head. "It's still a wonder to me you speak of a Ri'sha in such a casual way. In Sleetward, the very mention of one would get you a stern talking to from the town elders—as if merely speaking their name would bring about ill will." He spat off the side of the cart. "Superstitious nonsense."

"I wouldn't be too sure about that," I replied. "Isodros may be sympathetic to the human plight, but from what I've heard, she is one of the few who are. Supposedly, the further south you travel, the worse it becomes. The war has the deminean on edge, or so I've been told."

He ran his hand through his black hair. "I'll keep that in mind."

I said my goodbyes to them both, and, to my surprise, Rhas embraced me, holding me as if to let me go would sentence me to death. Reluctantly, after some persuasion, she did, ushering me to haste with returning to High Tide. Madrof gave me a nonchalant wave as he carried on with his duties of helping her unload the grayhorn for their merchant buyer.

It didn't take me long to get back to High Tide. The streets, normally filled to the brim with people, were all but empty. I put on a lighthearted face as I opened the door and proclaimed jovially, "I'm back!"

There was an immediate stench of defeat that clung to the air like a rotten corpse left to bake in the summer sun. It assaulted my senses, and I longed to step back outside into the warm and welcoming sun.

I held firm.

Searching around, I saw Crux sitting alone at a small table. Jezza, now just noticing me, brought her eyes up to look at me. I could smell the smoke that Vrak enjoyed, but his absence was noticeable.

Crux, realization dawning on him, turned to stare at me, and looked to have aged ten years in the small time I was away.

"Oh, Vi'eri," he said, the color slightly returning to his gaunt face. "Thank the Well you're safe." He stood and practically ran toward me, picking me up in an embrace. "Thank the Well. Thank the Well," he muttered over and over.

"What happened, Crux?" I asked, forcing him to put me down. "There are guards outside the city asking questions. Something about an attack on Ri'sha Isodros."

"Cursed Dragon's Court is what happened," he replied, clenching his jaw so tight the veins of his neck bulged. "Not long after you and Tesro left on your task, there was an attack, just as Isodros had predicted. Still, we were woefully unprepared. We rallied a few fighters to defend Isodros—with the help of her personal guards. It was sheer luck that Vrak had made his way back here or the High Tide and Jezza... Well, let's not speak of that. Let's just say that we've made some enemies with our close dealings involving our Ri'sha friend. Those deminean of the Dragon's Court are a menace and were killing humans by the dozen in the street. Unarmed humans. Women and children."

I sat listening to Crux's explanation with utter horror plastered on my face. "And Isodros?" I asked. "Was she hurt?"

"She was." He turned away from me, his face red with shame. "But that woman is pure death when angered. She did not even hesitate to slay her own kind when threatened, but..." He let his words trail off.

"But, what? Is she alright? Is she dead?"

"She's not," Vrak replied, his footsteps signaling his arrival. A thick layer of dust covered the clothes he wore, but before I could ask why he was so dirty, he added, "She kept her life, but lost something very dear to her. Something that means more to her than her own soul. However, we can speak of that later. I am glad to see you returned safely, Vi'eri, but I don't see Tesro is with you. Is she in the town on some sort of errand? Likely trying to find somewhere to eat, I presume."

I heard the name Tesro and knew that it should be important. Should, but at the same time, it seemed a distant thing to me, as if I was on the cusp of remembering something very important.

Unable to recall, I shrugged my shoulders. "Oh Tesro, the redheaded girl? Sho, one of Isodros' companions, betrayed us at the tomb of the frozen man and she died in the battle's aftermath from a cave-in." I spoke the words calmly and without emotion. I felt nothing, but tears welled from the edges of my eyes.

Time seemed to stand still as both Crux and Vrak stared at me. Then, almost as if he didn't wish to know the answer, Vrak asked, "What do you mean she died? Tesro... My Tesro...is dead?"

I looked at him and did not hide my annoyed smirk. "Yes, she's dead. Why does it matter? During the battle, she betrayed us, went with Roese's son Ruvor—"

"Doesn't matter?" Vrak replied, his scowl matching the dark tone of his words. "Who are you? Because you're certainly not the Vi'eri I know. Tesro was your friend, you've known her for years. How can you speak of her this way?" He put his head in his hands, muttering her name over and over, and his knees looked about to buckle from the weight of his grief.

"Vi'eri..." Crux said, placing his hand on my shoulder.

"Did you two not hear? She was a traitor. Traitor!"

"Shut your mouth, girl!" Vrak shouted, his grief gone, replaced by pure rage. He assumed the casting position, right hand faced directly toward me and the look in his eyes said he meant to kill.

Crux stepped in front to defend me, and I saw the glint of his blade as it rose into the air from a nearby table. Hovering, ready to strike with a simple thought.

Jezza stepped from behind the bar. "Now wait a moment—"

"Walk away, Jezza," Crux said, waving her away with his hand. "This is between him and me." She huffed, but did what she was told, stepping back behind the bar and waiting patiently for what was to come.

Crux turned his attention back to his new enemy. "Vrak, I consider you a friend, but Vi'eri, she's my daughter—"

"And Tesro is mine," he replied with venom-laced words, taking a step forward, refusing to back down.

"I know, I know. There is something wrong here. Something we don't yet understand—surely you can see that. Vi'eri's been through so much."

"And why is that?" Vrak replied, realization dancing in his eyes. "It's because Ri'sha Isodros' used them as pawns in her games. She sent them to die. Sent my Tesro to die...and *you* let them go." He turned his hand toward Crux, but the knife slid in the air even closer as he spared it a nervous glance, sweat pouring down his face.

"You are mistaken. Tesro chose this for herself, fully aware of the consequences."

"So you're saying she deserved this? These deminean hold our futures and lives, pretending their hands aren't soaked red with our blood. We are nothing to them. Nothing!"

Reluctantly, Vrak let his hands slide to his side, where they quivered with untapped sorrow and anger. "I never should have had her become involved. I never should have abandoned the war." He breathed a long sigh out, as one does who has a lifetime of regret. "This is all my fault."

The dagger fell to the floor, and Crux moved forward to place a hand on his friend's shoulder, but Vrak slapped his hand away as it neared him. He stared into Crux's eyes, unnerved. "Consider this my resignation from the True Blades." He stealthily pulled a pipe from his coat pocket, lighting it with a small flame at the tip of his finger, and his eyes fell back on me. "Tell me, where did she die? Did she receive a proper burial?"

"It was in a cave to the north," I replied. "In a town called Sleetward. Ask the townsfolk to bring you to the frozen man, you'll find her beneath the rubble."

"You really don't care, do you?" Vrak asked, staring at me for a long time, clearly expecting an answer.

While I didn't care, I felt it was prudent at the time to remain quiet. Eventually, his head lulled to the side, and he added, "She loved you, you know? Told me all the time." He took a long drag from his pipe, and the intoxicating smoke left his nose in tendrils, quickly filling the room with its smog.

As if he made some monumental decision, his eyes came to rest on me, devoid of emotion. "You'll live to regret your callousness today. Stay in the north, child. If I ever see you out on the battlefield, I won't forget what happened here."

Vrak shoved past Crux, and I stepped to the side, narrowly avoiding his contact. He left, and slammed the wooden doors closed behind him, not saying another word. I turned back toward Crux, who looked even older now than he had been when I had first entered.

Jezza, stealthy as ever, approached me from behind and wrapped me in a big hug. "Thank the Well you're okay, Vi'eri."

"Same to you," I replied, pulling back from her and giving her a genuine smile.

"Vi'eri," Crux said as he took a seat in his usual booth, "it's time to report. Jezza, four mugs."

"Four?"

"Yes, four. We will honor one of our own, one last time."

Jezza looked undisturbed as she replied, "Four it is then."

"Vi'eri," he placed both his hands out flat on the table, "you're going to tell me everything that happened from the moment you last saw me to the moment you walked through that door. Every. Single. Detail."

And there we sat, talking about my journey through the tundra of the Frostwyrm. From the battle with the vargs, to Sho's betrayal, I told him...but I kept some information to myself. Not from a willingness to protect myself from scrutiny, but there was something wrong—like a fog that kept me from remembering the finer details of the journey.

That kept me from remembering about Tesro.

In the end, Crux was satisfied with my explanation, saying, "You've had quite the journey. Still, I cannot believe that Tesro would go with this Ruvor. You mentioned a ring that could control Sho, at least for a time. Do you think he used it on Tesro?"

I shrugged my shoulders. "Honestly, I don't know."

"That's another thing," he said, his blue eyes drilling into me. "Don't take this poorly, but there is something wrong with you. Something happened, and I think it damaged your memory."

Anger flooded into me. "And who are you to say that to me?" I stood, slamming my fist into the table, the wood groaning as my closed fist struck it. "I risked my life out there to protect this peace we have with Isodros and—"

"Easy, Eri. Easy. I meant no offense. What I meant is that I think you need rest. Rest to put things straight." He put on a faux smile as a way to ease the tension.

It didn't work.

Eventually, he coughed, adding, "I'm also concerned about Isodros' companions' betrayal. She gave us her word that she trusted them with her life." He sprang from his seat, downing his liquor and setting the cup on the table. "I need to discuss this with her. Immediately."

"Then I'll come—"

"No, you'll get some rest," he said, in a tone that said his decision was final.

I pushed my chair against the table. "I'm coming with you. We should just go and not argue over it."

Crux met my eyes with defiance, and I matched his glare. Then, like a man who knew he was beat, he turned from me.

"Fine," he muttered, "but if things go badly, let me handle it. Isodros may not be the woman you remember from before."

We once again stood outside the blackened doors of Isodros' dwelling, with its intricate artwork that told of great battles past. Except, unlike last time, the door was now broken in various places, small splinters of wood littering the entrance.

"Step away, humans," a deminean guard said as he moved to block us. Skillfully, he slid his sword from its sheath with an accompanying clang, leveling it at us with a deft hand.

"That won't be necessary," another deminean replied. Lightly clad in a thin veil and a plain, soft fabric robe, this man placed his hand on the guard's shoulder. "Ri'sha Isodros' champions are always welcome here without an appointment."

"Thank you, Trelku," Crux said, sparing the guard a sidelong stare, "but we're here on business. Where can we find Ri'sha Isodros?"

"In her sitting room. Rumors of young Vi'eri's return have already reached her ears, and she knew you would be along shortly. Come then."

The guard gave a huff of contempt, but sheathed his weapon, stepping aside. Trelku glared at him but remained silent, signaling for us to follow.

He led the way to the sitting room, even though I had been there enough times that I could have easily found it for myself. Still, he opened the door and beckoned us inside. Curious, I'd never seen a deminean act that way toward a human before. As Crux and I once changed the course of the realm here before, I felt as if it had changed again while I was away, and I felt a small bit of guilt that I wasn't a part of it.

When we entered, the room was filled to the brim with white smoke, the same type of smoke that Vrak would find pleasant. I felt its mind-altering effects almost immediately play against my mind, as if falling into a deep thicket laden with fog. Lost, even in my own thoughts.

A small push on my back brought me to my senses, and I stared across the room to find Isodros sitting, head in her hands, with a large decanter of dark liquid sitting nearby. Noticeably, there was no other adjoining silverware.

"Finally," Isodros said testily, "I've been waiting here for the better part of the afternoon. You should know better than to keep me in suspense."

I noticed something was wrong about her attitude and poise. The once proud and straight-backed Isodros looked barely able to keep herself up, and I suspected by the slight slurring of her words that she'd had a bit too much to drink. Her face, and the parts of her body uncovered by scales, were flushed red.

"Are you okay?" I asked, forgetting to guard my tongue. It was a surprise when Crux didn't chastise me for my break in protocol.

"No, I'm not," she answered flatly. "But we'll get to that soon enough. Sit."

We did as commanded, sliding the wooden chairs out and sitting across the table from our patron.

Suddenly, there was a sliding sound as the decanter slid across the table as Isodros pushed the container toward us. "This is for you two. Forgive me, there aren't any glasses. So much was lost or destroyed in the attack."

"Not a problem," Crux replied, popping the glass lid from the decanter and taking a long swig straight from the top. He sighed out and offered it to me. I waved him off with my hand and he shrugged.

Slowly, he twirled the liquid around in the glass before setting it back down, fixing his gaze upon the scaled woman. "Isodros, we need to talk."

"That we do," she replied. "Vi'eri, did you retrieve it?"

I needed no explanation about what she meant. "I did."

"Good. That's good." Isodros breathed out as if she had just set down a load of weight that she had carried for years. A burden heavier than a building. "Bring it to me."

I rose wordlessly from my seat, sparing Crux a glance. He nodded, and I took that as permission. Carefully, I pulled the amulet, wrapped in a soft white cloth, from my pocket. Isodros' golden eyes lit up with anticipation as I brought it to her, placing it down on the stained black table to rest. She reached for it and, instinctually, I grasped her wrist before she could touch the amulet. The glare she hurled at me almost caused me to wet myself from fright, but, in a moment, she relented, pulling her hand back.

"I'm sorry," I said, releasing her wrist. "It's dangerous to even be this close to it, let alone touch it. Believe me, I know."

"Is that so?" she replied, and I couldn't tell if she was shocked by my words, or displeased. Carefully, she reached out and hovered her hand above soulrend. "I can feel it. Feel it tugging on me. Like little claws in my chest. It's...unnerving."

"That feeling will pass, but not the danger of touching it. From my time with it, it seems to have a will of its own. A goal. We need to keep this hidden. It's better if we destroy it. If that isn't possible, then throw soulrend to the bottom of the ocean and be done with it. You were right when you said it was dangerous, but I don't think you know how right you were."

Isodros examined me, searching for hidden meaning in my words. I realized then that she didn't trust me. Suspected me of hiding information. It struck me as odd; she had never shown signs of distrust before.

Casting a wary look across soulrend, she added, "As you say, Vi'eri. Once again, you've done this realm a great service."

I smiled at her and returned to sit next to Crux. When I sat, he folded his arms across his chest as if he meant to say something to Isodros, but didn't know how to proceed. Eventually, he put both hands on the table and met her eyes. "Ri'sha Isodros, I would have word."

She, unsurprised by this sudden request, sat up straighter. "You would? I think I have an idea of what this concerns, but I would hear it anyway. Speak."

"May I speak plainly?" he asked. She nodded, and he added, "You almost killed Vi'eri, and you've killed Tesro—"

Isodros slammed the table with her fist, and I heard a crack deep within the wood. "That wasn't me!"

"It was!" Crux answered back, matching her anger. "It was your people who killed her! You gave me your word."

"I—"

"Crux," I said, setting my hand to his shoulder. "It's alright."

He shrugged my hand off his shoulder, never meeting my eye. He muttered, "It isn't."

"I know." Isodros said, placing her head once again in her hands. "I've failed you both, just as I've failed my people. My head was so high in the clouds that I couldn't see the rot beneath my own feet. Vi'eri," she turned to look at me, "I am truly sorry to you and for your loss. I know you and Tesro were close."

"I wouldn't say that—"

"She is grateful for your kind words, Ri'sha," Crux replied, cutting off my words. "However, kind words will not restore the people I've lost. It will not stop the distrust that now festers in the minds of both deminean and humans. Has our dream of peaceful coexistence been for naught?"

"No," she replied. "I've seen the realm change many times in my long days. There will always be those who will fight with steel and claw to keep matters the same. They are blind to progress. They wander, and tell others stories of color when they see naught but gray. For those of us who see a brighter future, we owe it to those who cannot, to see it fulfilled."

"Well said," he replied.

"Simple words are all I can afford at this time, Trueblade. However, if you wouldn't mind, I would have words with Vi'eri. Alone."

"Anything she needs to hear I can—"

"Please!" There was desperation in her words, and sweat pooled on her face. Here was a woman whom I could not believe was capable of being vulnerable, and she looked now to be on the edge of tears.

"It's okay, Crux," I said. "I'll meet you back at High Tide after we are through."

He shifted in his seat, but, after some time, rose and turned toward the door. "Don't stay too long. As I said before, you need rest." The man turned his back and exited the room, muttering a curse on his way out.

I smiled and turned back to Isodros, where she tapped the table with her long nail. "Come here," she commanded, gesturing to the seat on her right.

I rose wordlessly, carefully moving toward the seat indicated as a man walks toward the gallows; not knowing what to expect. I felt the weight of her world, and it threatened to crush me with its vastness. I pulled the chair and sat, turning it so that I could face her directly.

She turned her golden stare on me, and it felt like she pierced my soul, delving into my every secret. "First, I wish to offer you congratulations...and my sympathy. I will not forget the loss of Tesro, I assure you." I simply nodded to her words, and she went on, adding, "I would have you tell me exactly what happened during your journey, so that I might fully understand the turmoil I put you through."

I went through an account of what had happened. Hask's death at Sho's hand. The frozen man. Everything that bore relevance. However, I left out the parts that made me feel vulnerable, not wishing to dredge my memory for things that did not concern her. The past was the past, and I was content to move forward.

When I finished, she began a nervous tapping on the table, shaking her head with frustration plain on her face. "Betrayed by some of my closest companions," she muttered.

"Hask didn't betray you, it was just Sho."

"Of little consequence. I was told by my deminean companions that trusting humans would lead to my downfall. Little did I know that it was to be attempted by my own people."

Isodros appeared lost in thought as her words mingled in my head. To be betrayed by your own... I prayed to the Well that someone I trusted so intently would never turn on me.

"If our business is concluded," I said, "I would like to return to High Tide. Crux seems particularly worried right now, and Vrak departing the True Blades has left him feeling down."

"Vrak quit the True Blades?" she replied. Then, after thinking about it for a moment, she nodded. "Actually, that makes sense. Tesro was as his daughter, if I'm not mistaken. And the manner in which he left?"

"True Blade business. Sorry."

She waved an exacerbated hand. "No matter, but before you depart, there is one more topic I would like to discuss with you. One that I am reluctant to utter. Something very painful."

I was halfway out of my seat when her words stilled me. Turning back to face her, I sat back down in the chair, my hands folded in my lap.

"What is it?" I asked.

Isodros reached under the table and brought out a deep red wooden box. It looked magnificently carved, but what caught my eye was a picture of what looked to be a satyr carved eloquently at the top.

"What's this?" My words felt distant as the item drew my attention.

"A gift, but not one meant for you. It is to be a gift for my unborn child." She paused, taking a deep breath before adding, "*Was* a gift. That future is now lost."

Her words shocked me, my mouth hanging open. The dryness of my mouth stilled my tongue, but I managed a quick, "No..."

"I'm afraid so," she replied. "My enemies were perilously close to completing their mission of ending my life. So close, in fact, that I lost the child." Isodros suddenly stood straighter, and I knew what it took to force calmness on her face. "Since you assisted me with the tear of eternity all those years ago, I wanted to tell you the news directly. And to give you this." She slid the box over, prompting me to open it.

As I did, a familiar sight met me. The light hit the item just right, showing the pure white of the mother's horn in all its glory. I held my hand against my mouth to keep from gasping, tears of awe and shame streaming down my face.

"It is my understanding that you recognize this?" It took a moment, but I eventually lowered my hand and nodded, not trusting my words. "Good," she added, "because I gift this to you, my subject. My champion. My friend."

If I hadn't been so overwhelmed with emotion at the time, I would have recognized the importance of her words. As it was, I reached down and ran my gloved fingertips across the horn's surface. I could almost hear Pipar's sad song in the back of my mind, and it caused me to take a shuddering breath as my chest tightened.

"Are you sure?" I asked, hoping that she was.

"I am," she replied. "It was to be my child's gift, and I can think of no other who deserves it more."

In one swift movement, I rose from my seat and wrapped my arms around her. "Thank you," I said, my tears wetting the scales on the edge of Isodros' face.

At first, she pulled away from my grasp. Then, like a dam giving way to the inevitable flow of the river, she released her guard and returned my embrace.

We both wept for what we had lost.

Wept for a lifetime of pain.

And wept for what we had still yet to lose.

Chapter Thirty-Seven

Epilouge

Vi'eri twisted and turned in her sleep.

The nightmare had come again.

She found herself back in her old room at the High Tide, lying awake, staring at the empty bed across from her own.

A feeling of loss burned in her chest, matching the small candle light that flickered across from her, casting dancing shadows off the walls. A hairbrush sat on a wooden desk nearby, curly red strands twisted around it like a rat's nest.

A remnant from a specter.

She could almost see a recognizable figure in the dark. A shadow from her past, or a new enemy stalking in the night?

Vi'eri contemplated the fight with Crux she'd had earlier in the day. The gift from Isodros, the mother's horn, had become somewhat of a rift between the two of them, and she heard his words playing back in her mind.

"That damnable Ri'sha," he said. "She doesn't know the pain we went through for that horn. How did she even get it?"

"I don't know," she replied for the third time, shooting him an exacerbated glance. "Isodros just gave it to me suddenly. I think I want to give it back to Pipar. Could we—"

"No," Crux replied flatly, scratching at the old scar on his lip. "You heard what the satyr said. He'll kill us if we return to the forest, and I, for one, believe him. We're in the mercenary business. We fight for profit, and there is no profit in that."

"But if we come with the horn—"

"I said no! We can't risk it. I can't risk you!"

The words were desperate, and his feelings were written plainly on his face. When she didn't acknowledge those deep insecurities, Crux let out a huff and turned away, refusing to speak more on the matter.

Later that night, he sent a few men to remove Tesro's possessions. In a fit of anger, Vi'eri sent them away.

If he wanted to be unreasonable, then she could as well.

When she had returned to bed, sleeplessness plagued her. Feelings of a loss that she couldn't quite place kept her from rest, but trying to remember a shadow from her past was proving difficult.

"I could help you," a voice called from the shadows. Deep and smooth, she focused her eyes to the corner of the room where an unnatural dark seemed to eat light like a void. Soon, the silhouette of a figure appeared there, like a morning mist made of pure darkness. It seemed to flow from the figure as they stepped out.

As they came, their visage seemed to scare the light away until all Vi'eri could see was the faint outline of her own hand. She sat up as fear gripped her.

"Who are you?" she asked.

"A friend," they replied in a male voice. "Just a friend."

Vi'eri turned, placing her feet off the edge of the bed, and the feeling of the wooden floor assured her that something had not magically pulled her back into the in-between.

"I don't need any more friends."

"Very well," the shrouded man replied. "But regardless, I have a job to do here. I've been summoned, so to speak, to help this realm. Since then, I've traveled for days, looking for the cause of the disturbance, and I finally found it. You!"

Vi'eri reached for the magic in the air, but as she did, she felt the magic pull away from her and toward the shrouded man's void.

"I wouldn't do that," he said. "I've no wish to fight you, and even less to be slain by you."

"Then maybe you shouldn't sneak into a woman's room at night unannounced."

The figure was silent for a time, as if thinking. Finally, he said, "It's a fair point. Fine, let us start over. My name, for all intents and purposes, is Shadowalker."

"Shadowalker?" she replied. "What kind of name is that?"

"A name that you do not choose for yourself, but one that comes from the legacy of past deeds."

"Cryptic. My name is Vi'eri."

"It is as you say. I need to be cautious about how much I speak, otherwise I risk upsetting the Balance," Shadowalker said. "However, it is the name I am best known for in the vastness of the Dragonrend."

"The Dragonrend?"

Shadowalker sighed. "See what I mean? That topic will have to wait for another time. I am here with a singular purpose. One that, if I do not perform, will lead to this realm's untimely end. Tell me, my spark of change, what has happened to you?"

Vi'eri stood silent for a time. *What has happened to me?* she thought. *Could this man be any more vague?* Not knowing what he meant, she answered the best she could. "I almost lost my soul to an amulet named soulrend."

"Lost your soul," Shadowalker replied, his words full of unasked questions. "A near-death experience is as likely an event to cause change as an actual death. If you would permit me, I would delve into your memories."

A cold shiver ran up her spine, and she scooted away from the figure.

"Stay away from me," she muttered.

"I need you to trust me, for too much is at stake if you are to reject my offer."

Shadowalker's words somehow eased her worries, and she turned her eyes toward him to try glance at the features of this mysterious man.

"And what is it you offer?" she asked.

"Truth," he replied. "Nothing more, nothing less. I can remove the shroud that lingers over your memories and reveal to you the truth."

Vi'eri was stunned. Too convenient; it was all just too convenient. As she herself tried desperately to remember, a mysterious figure appeared and offered to her exactly what she desired.

"And what would this 'gift' cost me?" she asked.

"More than you can possibly understand," Shadowalker replied flatly. "This memory of yours—one strong enough to change the course of an entire realm—will be painful. It will hurt. But, before you deny my offer, I say this: I know what it's like to forget, and to seek blindly for the truth. To be ignorant of the hurt. Numb to its pain. It can seem like such a blessing. But not when it is at the expense of others. So, I ask you once more, will you allow me to remove the shadows from your mind?"

"Yes!"

The candle exploded in light, revealing the face of a middle-aged man for a brief moment. His bright-green eyes focused on her, and he seemed to be grinning. Then, as fast as he appeared, he was gone, and in his wake...

Pain.

Vi'eri screamed as the pain of Tesro's loss flooded back into her. No, it was always there, just hidden. Now that the wall that protected her was gone, she remembered every little detail of their time together.

Every fight they'd had from a misunderstanding.

Every secret they had told each other in the dead of night.

Every laugh they had shared.

Tesro's final scream rang so loudly in her mind that she thought she would go deaf. She prayed to the Well she would, so she wouldn't need to hear it any longer.

Her body struck the floor, and she held her head with both her hands, banging her forehead against the wood. She wanted to claw her own eyes out. Anything to stop the wild torrent of memories.

"It'll get better with time," Shadowalker said, although his corporeal form was nowhere to be found. "I leave the rest up to you. Pray to the Balance that we never meet again."

"Stop this. Please! Don't leave me alone. Don't leave me..."

Then there was a rush, like cold water being thrown over a blistering burn, soothing the hurt.

You're not alone, a voice called out.

The pain lessened in an instant, as if someone or something took the brunt of it for themselves.

Vulana! Vi'eri called out in her mind. *Is that you? Are you back?*

I am, Vulana replied, sending a wave of comfort. *And we will get through this together. I will never leave you again.*

END of Book 1
The Realm of the Soulwell

AFTERWORD

Just wanted to take the time to thank each and every one of you who have taken the time to read my book. I am currently busy writing book 2, but if you don't want to wait for more content, I have a bridge book that happens between 1 & 2 available for those who signup for my newsletter.

Best part, it's free!
Website: https://marcwyattauthor.com
Also, preorders are available for Book 2 on Amazon.

Thank you again, and a special thanks to those who Beta Read and ARC'd for *Reflection: Realm of the Soulwell* and I hope to see you all for Book 2